SUSPICION OF DECEIT

*Also by Barbara Parker
in Large Print:*

Suspicion of Innocence

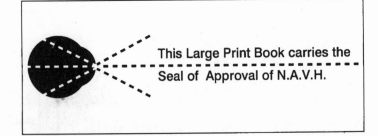

This Large Print Book carries the
Seal of Approval of N.A.V.H.

SUSPICION
OF DECEIT

BARBARA PARKER

Thorndike Press • Thorndike, Maine

Published in 1998 by arrangement with Dutton, an imprint of Dutton Plume, a member of Penguin Putnam Inc.

Thorndike Large Print ® Cloak & Dagger Series.

The tree indicium is a trademark of Thorndike Press.

The text of this Large Print edition is unabridged.
Other aspects of the book may vary from the original edition.

Set in 16 pt. Plantin by Minnie B. Raven.

Printed in the United States on permanent paper.

Library of Congress Card Number: 98-90192
ISBN: 0-7862-1460-0 (lg. print : hc : alk. paper)

Acknowledgments

As a writer, I weave together the ideas that other people so generously share. For taking me into the Cuban exile experience, I am indebted to Nina Casal, Max J. Castro, John L. DeLeon, Esperanza B. DeVarona, Raul Diaz, Carolina Garcia-Aguilera, Bertha Herrera, Martha Marich, Joe Sanchez, and especially to *la familia Pérez:* Juan, Magali, Dinorah, and Chino. My gratitude also goes to singers Kelly Anderson, Ara Berberian, and Joy Davidson; Nancy Woolcott, New World School of the Arts; and Robert M. Heuer, General Director, Florida Grand Opera. On matters legal and otherwise, thanks to investigator Felix Delgado, attorneys Sidney A. Goldberg and Milton Hirsch, bomb expert John Murray, and U.S. Customs agent Mike Spitzer. For their encouragement and clear-sighted criticism, I could not have done without Laura Parker and Andrea Lane.

Karen sends a special hello to her friends Amanda Johnson and Dana Southerland.

Author's Note

A few of the events established in two prior books, Suspicion of Innocence *and* Suspicion of Guilt, *have been changed. Certain small liberties have also been taken with DaPonte's libretto of* Don Giovanni, *herein.*

After all, what is a lie
'Tis but the truth in masquerade.

— Lord Byron, *Don Juan*

ONE

Seen from the Atlantic, the lights of Miami are a chain of jewels balanced on a narrow rim of land between swamp and sea. Overhead, on clear cool winter nights, the stars are brilliant, pulsing.

Gail Connor waited until her fiancé's Cadillac bumped onto the Fisher Island ferry, then asked him to open the sun roof so they could see the sky. She took off her high heels and climbed onto the seat.

"And where are you going, *bonboncita?*"

"It's beautiful out here!" A gust of wind ruffled her hair. She pulled her lacy cashmere shawl tighter around her shoulders. The ferry turned in the ship channel and headed southeast past the Coast Guard station. Water splashed steadily on the hull. A few leftover Christmas trees blinked in windows of the condominiums on South Beach, and farther out the Atlantic vanished into darkness.

Tonight the Miami Opera was holding a fundraising party on Fisher Island. Gail had recently been hired as general counsel. Her mother was a board member — that had helped — but Gail had the qualifications: eight years in a top law firm on Flagler Street before opening her own office. As a final inducement, she had offered to donate fifty hours of legal services a year. The opera was loaded with potential contacts. She had been given two tickets for the event tonight — one for herself, one for a guest. The guest was, of course, Anthony Quintana, who had learned by now not to be surprised when the thirty-four-year-old woman he was engaged to kicked off her shoes and stood up to sightsee through his sun roof.

The small terminal was located on the causeway that ran from the city to the southern tip of Miami Beach. Passengers were required to remain inside their vehicles, but there were so few on board — a dozen or so — that from her vantage point Gail could watch the approach to Fisher Island. She liked to see the familiar view from a different angle.

A hand went around her knee. "Having a good time?" Anthony was leaning over to look through the opening in the roof. She could see the white vee of his shirt and his black silk bow tie.

"The best. It's Friday. Karen won't be back till Sunday. I have no cases to spoil my weekend." She stroked his thigh with

10

her toes. "Are you busy later?"

He smiled wickedly. "*Que chévere*. People are staring at you."

"Do you care?"

"No. I think they're jealous."

Maneuvering back inside, Gail lost her balance and fell halfway across his lap, tangled in her shawl, laughing, her dress riding up her legs. He held her where she was and turned her face toward his. The air outside had chilled her, and his mouth felt steamy. Finally he pulled back, giving her a little shake. "You're a crazy woman, you know that?"

"You love it. Without me you'd sit alone in the dark and brood."

"Oh, you think so? I'd be out having fun. Dancing, parties —"

"Don't I take you to parties? Tonight you get to hear Thomas Nolan."

"Who is he?"

"*Who?* The singer. Tonight's entertainment?"

"Ah. Yes, I remember."

"Liar." Gail smoothed the lapels of his tuxedo. "Don't worry. We'll sneak in, mingle for a bit, then leave."

"Why go at all?"

"Because, sweetheart, how would it look if their new lawyer didn't show up? The president of the board called to make sure I was coming. Rebecca Dixon. You met her in the lobby before Hvorostovky's recital, remember? The brunette with all the diamonds?"

"Yes, I remember. What does she want?"

"I don't know. We don't socialize, so it must be related to opera business." Gail slid over to the passenger seat and flipped down the visor mirror. Her dark blond hair fell around her face, a style that was easily repaired.

"Rebecca Dixon." Anthony tapped a rhythm on the gearshift. "She used to be Rebecca Sanders. I met her when I was at the University of Miami. She was dating a friend of mine."

Gail put on her lipstick. "You know Rebecca Dixon? Why didn't you say so when I introduced you?"

"No, no. Sometimes people don't like to be reminded. Maybe she doesn't remember me."

"I can't imagine." Gail snapped her purse shut. "Well, your former acquaintance and her husband have made a donation to the opera of two hundred and fifty thousand dollars."

"*¡Alaba'o!* Who is he? Or is the money hers?"

"No, it's his. Lloyd Dixon. He owns a cargo airline, I think. A quarter of a million. It certainly puts my paltry five hundred bucks into perspective." Raising herself off the seat, she pulled her narrow skirt farther down her thighs. "I promise we won't stay long, but I really need to be here tonight, maybe cultivate some paying clients. Lucky you, to be so well established."

"Ah, but my clients — I usually find them at the jail, not at opera parties."

When the ferry bumped against the dock, Anthony slid down his window and told the guard where they were going. On the south side of the island was a clubhouse that used to be a winter home for one of the Vanderbilts. Flowering vines and a marble fountain marked the entrance. Anthony gave the keys to the valet, and they went inside. From the paneled lobby they could hear a piano, a torrent of notes, and a deep voice singing in Italian. They followed the sound.

At the door to the ballroom Gail whispered, "Let's wait till this one is over."

Anthony discreetly squeezed her backside. "We're not staying late. I have plans for you."

She smiled, told him to hush, then eased open the door when applause began. The attendees were mostly middle-aged and up, attired in tuxes, gowns, and fancy cocktail dresses. Most people sat at tables with drinks and small plates of hors d'oeuvres. The lights were low, except for those illuminating the singer and his accompanist.

Gail and Anthony edged against the wall and found chairs in the back.

There were some opening chords for the next aria, then Thomas Nolan's vibrant bass-baritone filled the room. Nolan was in his mid-thirties, dressed in a black silk jacket and white turtleneck. His thick blond hair was pulled back in a ponytail, making the angular structure of his face seem even more so. He had a tall, lean physique. Onstage, in makeup and costume, he would be gorgeous. Most of the women — and a few of the men — seemed on the point of swooning.

"O mio sospir soave, per sempre io ti perdei!"
Someone had left a program on the table. Gail picked it up and found the translation. Oh, my gentle breath of life, forever are you lost to me. . . . He was good . . . no, he was wonderful. Gail was sorry now that they had taken their time getting here.

"Ah, per sempre io ti perdei, fior d'amore, mia speranza . . ." Forever lost, flower of love, my hope . . .

She whispered into Anthony's ear, "Do you like it?"

"Very much." He put an arm around the back of her chair, and she curled his left hand around hers. There was a ring on his fourth finger, but the third was bare. Until recently he had worn a heavy platinum ring with an emerald too perfect to seem excessive. The night he asked her to marry him, he had dropped it carelessly into his pocket, and said he wanted only a plain gold band. She had found it odd, this sudden switch from overt display to the simplest of adornment. And then she considered where he had come from.

At forty-two, he had seen his life swerve from one extreme to the other, rarely resting in between. His mother's family, sophisticated and wealthy, had lived in Havana; his father's people were dirt-poor *guajiros* from rural Cuba. Just after the revolution his mother had fled with her parents and two of her four children. Through some terrible mistake of timing Anthony and one sister were not at home the day the others had to leave. Anthony spent most of his childhood in Camagüey province, a hot flat land of endless sugar cane. He got out at thirteen, his mother's family paying dearly in bribes. Since then, flouting U.S. law, he'd gone back many times to visit his father and sister, but promised Gail he would never go back to stay, even when things changed. His life was here.

She leaned against his shoulder and felt his breath in her hair, then his lips briefly on her temple. When the last song was over everyone applauded, many of them rising to their feet. Thomas Nolan made his bows. Gradually the applause faded away, and people moved forward to speak to him.

Before Gail could turn to pick up her purse and shawl, a delicate hand touched her arm.

"Gail? Yes, I thought it was you." Rebecca Dixon stood smiling at her side, a thin woman in a flowing gold silk dress. Her dark hair was wound into an elaborate knot, and earrings glittered against her long neck.

"And Mr. Quintana. It's good to see you again. I'm Rebecca Dixon."

"Of course." He took her extended hand. "This singer is excellent. I'm happy that Gail invited me to come with her."

Gail looked from one to the other, wondering who knew what about whom.

Anthony put his arm around her waist. "We're engaged to be married. Gail, did you tell her?"

"I tell *everyone*."

Rebecca gave a silvery laugh. "Yes, she does, and I don't blame her a bit. Congratulations to both of you. Now, may I be selfish and take Gail away for a few minutes? Let me introduce you to some friends of mine first, so you won't feel abandoned."

He demurred politely. "Thank you, but it isn't necessary. There are people here I know." He lightly kissed Gail's cheek and told her to take her time.

The two women walked away through the crowd, Rebecca smiling, saying hello, no name forgotten. But all the time they were moving toward an exit door.

Gail had first seen Rebecca Dixon a few years earlier between acts of *The Marriage of Figaro*, the only opera Gail had seen that season, practicing law downtown sixty hours a week. She had asked her mother who she was. Irene Connor knew everybody. Oh, that's Rebecca Dixon, a perfectly lovely woman. You should meet her. But Gail had declined. At the time, after another raging argument with her husband, she felt intimidated by perfectly lovely women.

With a billow of silk and the click of heels on parquet, Rebecca led Gail along the corridor, then turned into a foyer. Past the sloping lawn and row of royal palm trees, the ocean was visible through uncurtained glass. Moonlight lay down a path of silver across the water.

Rebecca let out a breath. "I was afraid you hadn't come."

"Is there a problem?"

"I hope not, but quite possibly — What did you think of Tom Nolan?"

"He's superb."

"Isn't he. We've hired him to sing the lead in *Don Giovanni*, which opens at the end of the month. One of our board members called me this morning. She said that two years ago last November, Thomas Nolan sang at a music festival . . . in Havana." With a lift of carefully drawn brows, Rebecca Dixon waited for a response.

"Ah. Havana . . . Cuba."

"She heard it from one of her friends — a Cuban woman, in fact — at a benefit for the Heart Fund. Who knows where *she* got it. I asked Tom if it was true. He said, 'So what?' " Rebecca lifted one golden-clad shoulder, imitating his reaction.

Gail had to smile. "But *two years* ago —"

Rebecca looked at her. "Gail, you live here. Can you seriously tell me we have *nothing* to worry about?"

"Well . . . no, I can't."

The previous spring a Brazilian jazz combo had been booked into a theater downtown. Nobody paid much attention, until a Little Havana radio host announced that the band had just appeared in New York with a group straight from Havana called Los Van Van — a gross insult to the exile community. The theater manager received death threats. The scene outside the concert turned ugly — shouting, pushing, the police trying to keep the crowds behind barricades. The second performance was canceled, and the story wound up on *Night-line*.

"What would you like me to do?" Gail didn't know what could be done, except to roll down the hurricane shutters and bring in the plants.

Rebecca twisted her gold necklace around her finger, then slid the diamond pendant back and forth, metal clicking. "The general director is in New York looking at talent. He doesn't know about this yet, and I'll have to give him a recommendation. We have two choices — find someone else to do *Don Giovanni* or keep Tom Nolan. It's not that easy. We don't want a controversy in the middle of a fundraising drive. On the other hand, do we fire him and look like cowards? My husband says we have to hold our ground, no matter how much it hurts. Lloyd isn't on the executive committee, but he can be such a horse's behind."

A quarter of a million dollars gave him that privilege, Gail thought. "What do you want to do, Rebecca?"

The pendant clicked on the necklace. "I . . . haven't decided yet."

"Well, here's your lawyer's position," Gail said. "Keep the singer. If you cancel his contract without cause, you still have to pay him. How much does he get, by the way?"

"Six thousand five hundred dollars per performance. Seven performances."

"Yikes."

Rebecca took Gail's arm. "A few of us on the executive committee are getting together at my house tonight. I'd like you to be there. Bring Anthony Quintana. We need his input. I wanted to consult you first, of course, in view of your relationship with him."

"Tonight?" Gail groaned. "Oh, Rebecca. Don't say that."

"Gail, I've got to have someone who can tell us how the Cuban community is likely to react once the news gets out — and it will. I can't just go into that meeting and say well, I think this might happen, or that —"

"Look, you have Cubans on the board, don't you? Ask them."

"I would, but they have no connection with the — I don't want to say extremists. Let's say certain groups who take a different point of view."

"What? Anthony doesn't —"

"It's his *family* I was referring to. His grandfather is a member of every hard-line exile group in Miami. His brother-in-law, Octavio Reyes, has a radio talk show. Anthony would have an opinion on what might happen. Maybe he'd even help us with PR if we decide to keep Tom Nolan. Please, Gail. I'd ask him myself, but it would be better if you did."

"In view of our relationship," Gail repeated. A man in love wasn't likely to turn his fiancée down. "All right. I'll ask, but what he wants to do is up to him."

"Fair enough." Rebecca squeezed her hand. "You're a dear."

"Just curious. How did you find out so much about Anthony's family?"

"Well . . . we knew each other in college."

"Oh, yes. The University of Miami," Gail said. "Anthony mentioned that."

"He was very political in those days," Rebecca said. "That's why I believe he'll help us now."

"Political? No . . . I don't think he was ever . . . like his grandfather."

A laugh danced off the tiles in the foyer. "Good lord, no. The other end of the spectrum. Anthony had a poster of Che Guevara in his bedroom."

Gail managed to smile. "Really. Che Guevara." The bearded poster boy of campus radicals. Hero of the Cuban Revolution. In Anthony's bedroom. Which Rebecca Dixon had somehow seen.

"Oh, don't tell him I brought that up, after all this time. It would embarrass him."

What an odd sensation, Gail thought. Almost physical. A slight turn on the axis. A shift in the angle of light. Edges in what had seemed smooth.

Rebecca gestured toward the corridor. "I suppose we should go back. They'll be wondering where we are."

TWO

Without a word Anthony jerked his keys out of the ignition and opened his door. He slammed it and came around. Gail was already out her side. She grabbed her shawl off the seat. "I said you didn't have to be at this meeting."

"What am I supposed to do? Sit in the car until you finish?" He aimed his key ring at the Cadillac, and the locks clicked shut. "Let's do this and get out of here." He was several steps along the tiled walkway before he realized she wasn't with him. He said sharply, "Gail, come on."

"Don't you *ever* walk away from me like that!"

"*Coño*, what's the matter with you?"

For a long moment they looked at each other, Anthony more stunned than angry. The parking lot was illuminated only by moonlight and a line of small lamps that led along the walkway, then to a six-floor building of Mediterranean design, where the Dixons owned an apartment.

He let out a breath and looked toward the ocean, which gurgled and splashed gently against the seawall. "Okay." He came back. "I'm sorry. It's not because of anything you did."

"I know that."

"Gail —" She shifted her eyes away. He kissed the spot between her eyebrows. *"Niña, no me hagas sufrir."*

"You should suffer, you jerk."

"Ah. Your Spanish is improving."

She looked straight at him. At five-nine, in high heels she was nearly as tall as he. "Get engaged, you think you're entitled to treat me like that?"

"Of course not." He made a smile she didn't really believe. "Let's go upstairs. I'll speak to these *comemierdas,* and then we'll leave. All right?" He took her arm and turned her toward the building.

"Hold it. Why are you so pissed off? Slamming the door, calling people names —"

A shrug. "I wanted to be with you tonight."

"No, it's something else."

"Let's just go —"

"Not until you talk to me."

He looked past her at the building. A breeze shifted the fronds of a palm tree, and shadows moved on his face. "I don't like to be a spokesman, an example — whatever the hell they expect."

"What they expect? I think they'd like to have your opinion. Maybe your help. Rebecca would, anyway. She'd like to avoid any controversy over Thomas Nolan, but some people on the board don't get it. Nobody's going to push us around, by God, this is the U.S.A. You know."

"Oh, I know very well."

"Will it cause you problems with your family? Your brother-in-law —"

"To hell with Octavio. I don't care about him. What he says on his radio show, I don't care. If he mentions my name, to hell with that too."

"Your grandfather —"

"Gail, I have always been independent. You know that." Anthony laughed and threw his hands up. "Why do you think the old man and I don't get along? Because I refuse to take sides. I won't do it. You watch. Those people up there don't want my opinion. They want me to tell them what those crazy *cubanos* have against an opera singer, an artist without a political agenda. So he sang in Havana! What's the big deal?"

"You feel disloyal."

He laid a hand flat on his chest. "Disloyal? Why should I feel disloyal? I'm not one of them. I'm the good guy, the one they

25

can reason with. Explain to us, Mr. Quintana, why they make so much trouble. Why can't they forget about it? It's been almost forty years. This is their home now. Why can't they be good Americans?"

"Anthony —"

"Explain to us why they still care about the place that gave them life, a place as close as their blood, where a man can be put in jail for taking a lobster from the sea to feed his children — Gail, I love this country. I chose to be a citizen, I didn't have to. And Cuba — I don't talk about that. I don't try to explain it to people who can't understand, because every time I do, I feel sick."

"Oh, Anthony. They won't be like that to you."

"No, they're too polite."

Nearby headlights went off, then someone opened and closed a car door. An alarm system chirped.

Gail took his arm. "I should never have asked you to do this."

"It doesn't matter."

"It does. I think it matters a lot."

He let out a long breath and played with his keys. "Well, some things you just have to leave alone."

After the concierge called upstairs, they

stepped into the elevator just ahead of the man Gail had glimpsed in the parking lot, a stocky figure in jeans and a pullover sweater. Anthony pressed a button, then glanced around as if to inquire what floor he wanted.

They stared at each other, a mildly curious gaze that worked into puzzlement, then recognition. But there was no hearty greeting, only steady appraisal. The other passenger was in his late forties, a few inches shorter than Anthony and twenty pounds heavier, with curly gray hair and gold-rimmed glasses. A smile slowly lifted the corners of his mouth.

"Tony? I'll be damned."

Anthony remembered she was there. "Gail Connor, Seth Greer."

Gail glanced from one to the other. "How nice to meet you, Mr. Greer. It seems we're all going to the Dixons'. You're the treasurer for the Miami Opera, aren't you?"

"Right, but call me Seth. And you're the new lawyer. Welcome aboard." He shook her hand. "A distress call from Madame President induced me to trek all the way over here. Something about a problem with the Cubans." He grinned at Anthony. "Speaking of *el diablo*. She didn't mention you."

"We ran into each other tonight at the party."

"Imagine that." Seth Greer looked at Anthony for a moment longer, then at Gail. "I sense a relationship here."

"Definitely," Gail said.

"You poor kid. I could tell you stories about this guy."

Anthony said, "Seth and I used to be neighbors in Coconut Grove."

"Ah, the Grove. Just not the same anymore. Planet Hollywood on one corner, multiplex cinema on another. The steady march of progress."

"You still live there?"

"I do, in my own little tropical wonderland. Stop by sometime, we'll reminisce about the days of old. You're looking good, *amigo*. I see your name in the paper, defending the downtrodden and no doubt falsely accused." The remark had a touch of sarcasm. Anthony's clients were some of the richest defendants in Miami.

"And what are you doing now, Seth?"

"I have an accounting firm downtown."

Anthony made a slight smile. "What happened to your law practice?"

Seth Greer spread his arms. "I've moved up in the world."

The bell dinged softly on the top floor.

The men let Gail out first. She glanced at Anthony, but he wore a blank expression. Seth Greer led the way, a bouncy stride across an open terrace where plants spilled from clay pots along a carved limestone railing. In daylight, the view to the sea would be breathtaking. They walked around the corner, the wind lifting Gail's hair.

Greer leaned on the buzzer. "Dis mus' be da place." A young Hispanic woman in a maid's uniform opened one side of the double doors. "*Juanita, ¿qué tal?*"

"*Bien, señor. Le esperan en la sala.*" She smiled and nodded at Gail and Anthony. They followed her through the marble foyer to a living room with uncurtained floor-to-ceiling windows. Everything was the white of bleached sea shells, except for a huge abstract canvas spattered with the colors of the ocean. Long white sofas and a thick handwoven rug marked the living room. The five people sitting there looked around when Seth called out a loud hello.

Aside from the Dixons, Gail recognized only one of the others, an elderly man named Wallace something, who had been general director of the opera a few years ago. Rebecca Dixon's gold tunic swirled as she crossed the room, arms extended. She told them to come in, have a seat. Juanita would bring coffee and dessert. Or would they prefer a drink?

Introductions were made. Eleanor, a woman about sixty in a black beaded dress, whose face-lift had tilted her eyes. Martin, a bald man with a neatly clipped beard. The elderly gentleman, Wallace, toddled from the other end of the long sofa to shake their hands.

Lloyd Dixon walked behind the bar at the opposite end of the room. Lights in the high ceiling shone on his white hair and white shirt. His black silk bow tie hung from his open collar. "What can I get for you folks?"

Seth Greer passed. Gail took red wine, Anthony asked for scotch.

"Red wine. Jesus, we've got about ten different — Pinot noir, how's that? Pinot noir and a single malt scotch. Glenfiddich okay?"

Dixon was a big man with a barrel chest, a heavy jaw, pale blue eyes, and a smile that started on one side of his mouth and didn't quite get to the other. Suspenders made an X on his shirt when he turned to drop ice into Anthony's glass.

For a while there was the usual chitchat about the recital. The selections Thomas Nolan had chosen. How many people had shown up. The quality of the hors d'oeuvres.

Seth Greer sat at the baby grand picking out the melodies of old standards. Rebecca walked past him on her way to the bar, and his eyes stayed with her across the room. She asked her husband for another martini on the rocks. Seth watched her come back.

The maid came in with a tray, which she put on the low glass table between the two sofas. She set it down slowly, carefully, not to let the silver pot tip over onto the plate of tiny frosted cakes.

Rebecca called to Seth Greer, "Seth, could you stop, please?" He dropped his hands into his lap. Rebecca settled into a high-backed armchair with a cup of coffee. The president, presiding. "Everyone is aware of the facts, so I thought rather than a formal meeting, we'd simply discuss our options and see if we can arrive at a consensus." There were nods all around.

Lloyd Dixon was rotating the ice cubes in a rocks glass with a forefinger. "We were talking about you, Quintana. My wife thinks you've got some pull with the Cubans."

As everyone looked at Anthony, Gail saw his mouth twitch into a smile that quickly vanished. He said, "No. I have no such influence with anyone. For personal and business reasons, I stay out of politics."

The bald man — Martin — said, "Oh, this is useful."

"Martin, please." Rebecca frowned at him, then said to Anthony, "What do you think might happen? How will the exile community react? That's what we need to know."

"The exile community — if there is such a thing anymore — does not speak with one voice. Some people will care, some won't. You could have problems, but I can't tell you how serious they would be. It depends on the circumstances. I'm sorry I can't be of more help."

Rebecca apparently hadn't expected this. The man she had hoped would hand her an easy decision was sitting there watching her struggle.

Gail decided to chime in on the legal questions, which would at least get the focus off Anthony. "You're all aware, I assume, that you can't just fire Thomas Nolan without paying him. What you've got here is a policy decision, not a legal one. If you do decide to replace him, we could possibly negotiate a settlement with his manager." She added, "Honestly, though, they don't have to settle for a dime less than what you agreed to pay."

The old man turned to the woman in the

beaded dress. "I didn't think the Spanish cared much about opera. Well, Carreras and Domingo, of course, but I don't think I can name any others. Luis Lima?" He stared into his brandy snifter. "Juan Pons."

The woman held a cigarette between red-tipped fingers. "Wally, Havana is in *Cuba*."

"I know that!" he snapped back. "I was simply making the observation that, in general, opera is not a notably Spanish art form."

She exhaled smoke, then smiled at Anthony. "We have some Cubans on the board of directors, lovely people."

Anthony smiled back. "I am so happy to hear it."

Lloyd Dixon gave a low laugh. "Jesus, Eleanor."

Rebecca still had her eyes on Anthony. "What do you think we ought to do?"

"To avoid trouble completely? Tell Thomas Nolan to get out of Miami."

Martin snorted, then looked down at Anthony as if he had personally dragged this situation through the door like roadkill. "What kind of trouble? Death threats? Bombs?"

Anthony's dark eyes turned slowly upward. He propped his ankle on his knee and leaned back, arms spread, jacket open. The casual position was subtly insolent. "Call a press conference. Nolan can make up some story. He wanted to see how miserable the conditions are, he didn't sing for anyone important, he made no money, and so on."

"Lie. Grovel a bit. There's a thought."

From the piano came a schmaltzy lounge tune. Seth Greer, gamely playing through some wrong notes, said, "Don't forget, Rebecca. Tom Nolan is giving master classes at the New World School of the Arts. The vocal director won't like it if we fire him. They've already started the semester."

Martin pointed at Seth. "What if some hothead threatens a student? What do you do about *that?*"

Eleanor rolled her eyes. "Martin, you are paranoid."

The old man glared around the room. "Who hired Thomas Nolan? Who failed to check him out?"

"Wally, it doesn't *matter.* There haven't been any bombs in years. They don't do that anymore." Tapping her ashes, Eleanor looked over at Anthony. "Or am I wrong?"

"How would I know?"

"You *are* wrong, Eleanor." Lamplight shone on Wallace's pink scalp, visible through thin white hair. "Just last year there was a fire at a restaurant where a singer from

Cuba was going to appear, and they had to close down."

"It was arson," Anthony said. "The owners set the fire to collect the insurance." No one was listening, and Anthony leaned back on the sofa with his drink and muttered something in Spanish. Gail laid a hand on his knee.

"Well, the *opera* never had any trouble," Eleanor insisted.

"Of course we have." Wallace snapped his fingers, trying to remember the particulars. "We invited some singers from Moscow on a friendship tour, performing in the county auditorium, and the exiles brought mice in their purses and pockets and let them go. You could hear them scurrying around in the rafters for *months*."

"That was twenty-five years ago!"

Martin said, "One lunatic with a can of gasoline is all it takes."

"Jesus H. Christ!" With his crooked half-smile, Dixon surveyed the people sitting around the room. "We're lucky to get this guy. He invited Rebecca and me to hear the opera in Dortmund when we went through Germany. His performance in *Lucia* blew me away. Tom wanted to come to Miami, so I said sure, I'll work it out. Now look where he is. His career is taking off, and he's going to debut at the Met next year. I'm the one who brought him here, and I am not going to see him flushed because we're scared of the Cubans." He stood belly forward, feet planted squarely on the marble floor. "Quintana, you said there's a *possibility* of problems, but it depends on the circumstances. What did you mean by that?"

Anthony rotated the heavy glass slowly in his hands, taking his time. "Well, it depends on how you handle it. I would advise you to be as nonconfrontational as possible. Try to show that you understand the exiles' position. What happens also depends on why Thomas Nolan went to Cuba and what he did there. That is the most important factor. What was his purpose? To make a statement against the embargo? Was he paid? Who did he sing for? The party elite or ordinary people on the street? What else has he said or done with regard to Cuba?"

Seth Greer called out from behind the piano, "Maybe he french-kissed the Beard."

Anthony finally laughed. "Oh, yes. If they have that on videotape, you're finished."

"I hate this sort of thing," Wallace said. "Just hate it. I say let's all go home and the general director can handle it when he gets back from New York. What do we pay him for, anyway?"

"Oh, Wally! What a spineless response." Eleanor leaned forward over crossed legs to crush out her cigarette in a crystal ashtray, and her bracelets jingled.

"Then let's get rid of Thomas Nolan, like this fellow says. Send him packing. That's my vote."

"You know, Wally, there is such a thing as freedom of artistic expression in this country."

A lively melody came from the piano — Seth Greer playing the first few bars of "God Bless America." Everyone looked at him. "We at the Miami Opera support a man's right to sing anywhere he wants — even Miami." His hands came down on the keys.

Rebecca turned around and said sharply, "Seth, please!"

"Another vote for Nolan," Eleanor said. "Wally's pooping out on us. What about you, Martin? Come on." She raised a fist, and bracelets clattered down her arm. "Don't let them push us around."

"Two to one," said Seth. "What'll it be, Martin? You gonna let the right-wing wackos call the shots for us?"

Martin yelled at him, "This isn't a game! The Cubans are going to come after Tom Nolan. They have to, or people will think they've gone soft. They don't compromise, and they're proud of it! What if somebody shoots at him? Blows up his car? We should ask Ms. Connor here about a liability lawsuit. She might have to defend us in court. I say we replace him."

Eleanor groaned, "Oh, Martin!"

Rebecca said, "Stop! I didn't want this to be a *vote*. I wanted us to agree. We have to, or it's going to be so divisive. We haven't even considered the effect on the community. Dissension is the last thing we want."

"Absolutely right!" Martin pointed at her. "What would this do to our fundraising efforts?"

Dixon growled, "Not a damn thing, Martin. Where are your *cojones?*"

Seth said, "Come on, Becky, do the right thing."

Rebecca Dixon was sitting forward on the edge of her chair.

Gail stood up. "Okay. Time out." She held up both hands. Everyone looked at her. "One question. Has anybody asked Thomas Nolan what he did in Cuba?"

Silence. A melting ice cube clinked in someone's glass.

Rebecca slowly sat back in her chair. She laughed, then bit her lip. "Yes. That would seem rather important. And . . . as you are the only one not interested in the outcome — Would you mind?"

In the semidarkness of his bedroom, Anthony was rubbing Gail's back, hands moving between her shoulder blades, sliding to her waist, then rising over her bare buttocks, then down her thighs.

Gail said, "I just can't picture Seth and Rebecca together."

"They had more in common then."

"Why were you surprised when he said he was a CPA?"

"He used to be so dedicated to the law. He wanted to be an advocate for the poor. If you had said to him, 'Seth, one day you'll be an accountant,' he would have laughed at you. Or shot himself."

"A lawyer. Why did he quit?"

"I don't know. I went to New York and we lost touch."

"So. You were neighbors in the Grove, back in the funky days. How old were you then?"

"Twenty when my grandfather kicked me out. I had already met Seth. He let me stay with him and Rebecca till I found a place."

"Wait a minute. You said you left home, but you never told me your grandfather kicked you out. What happened?"

"According to him, I was a communist." Anthony laughed. "I had long hair and a beard, and I read leftist books and dared to disagree. Seth let me sleep on his sofa for a while, then I rented an apartment in the same building. It was on Elizabeth Street, not a great neighborhood. There was a drug dealer across the street and a Pentecostal preacher behind us. So on the weekends —" Anthony leaned over to kiss her back. "— we heard gunfire and sometimes —" His mouth moved lower. "— speaking in tongues."

Gail's skin tingled. "How did you survive?"

"My mother gave me money, and I found a job. Several jobs."

"What was Rebecca studying?"

"She wanted to go to medical school. I guess she never did." Anthony stretched out beside her. "That's enough talking."

Propped on an elbow, Gail pulled a strand of his hair through her fingers. It curled when she let it go. "Long hair and a beard. Did you look like Che Guevara?"

"What?"

"Rebecca told me you had a poster of Che Guevara."

"*Ay, Diós mio.*"

"I wondered how it was that Rebecca

. . . had seen the inside of your apart-

. . . d now you know. What else did she . . . ?"

"Nothing — except she seemed familiar with your family history."

"It was a long time ago."

"Let's see. Twenty years ago I was fourteen, in ninth grade. Very skinny, with long straight hair. I wore knee socks and clogs. Jimmy Carter was president. What else was going on in the world? Disco? The first *Star Wars* movie?" Gail traced a line down Anthony's long nose, then around his full lips. "I was wondering about something."

"You always are."

"You spent three years at the University of Miami majoring in philosophy, correct? And then you went to New York and graduated in business. With only a year to go?"

"I wanted to get out of Miami and see the world."

"Come on. You're too sensible."

"Now, yes. Then —" He smiled. "I was young. My grandfather and I had argued again, and I wanted to get away for a while. So I went to NYU, then law school at Columbia. Married, had two kids, moved back to Miami, divorced. Then I met you. The story of my life. And here we are." He rolled

41

toward her. "Guess what I want now."

She moved her hands lightly over th[e] muscles in his back. His skin was like satin. "There's a lot about you I don't know."

"Nothing important."

"Would you tell me if I asked?"

"Not tonight." He kissed each corner of her mouth. "Tonight we're going to do something else."

"Anthony —"

"Shh. No more talking."

THREE

In winter Miami International Airport became a chaos of cars, tour buses and taxis, exhaust fumes and police whistles. Long lines formed at ticket counters. Aviateca, Aeroflot, Lacsa, Taca, Lufthansa, Halisa, Varig — humanity flowing in all directions.

Gail and her mother maneuvered toward Concourse E, where the 3:15 P.M. American Airlines flight would arrive from Puerto Rico, bringing Karen from her winter break as a ten-year-old first mate on her father's sailboat charter cruises. She had called a few times to say what a great time she was having. *How selfish of me,* Gail had thought, hanging up the phone, *to have hoped that Karen hadn't sounded quite so happy.* What if she decided to stay with her father? What if he wooed her with sailboats and snorkeling and going to school barefoot on an island? Dave was not happy about the prospect of Karen's having a stepfather, particularly this one. *Oh, Gail. A Cuban? Are you nuts?*

On their way to the airport Gail had told her mother about the scene at the Dixons' apartment two nights ago, and her assignment to speak to Thomas Nolan. Who was he? What was the right way to approach him?

Irene Strickland Connor was the best source of information about anyone connected to the Miami Opera. A debutante in her day, and a member of Young Patronesses of the Opera (now defunct), Irene had been on the board for years. Comfortable but by no means wealthy, she worked like a bee collecting her required $10,000 a year from willing donors. This put her in the office frequently, where she would hear all sorts of tales. Her small stature, curly red hair, and innocent blue eyes made people want to talk to her. And she never revealed anything said in confidence — except to her dearest trusted friends, and of course her daughter.

"Let's see what I can tell you. Tom Nolan is thirty-five. Never married. As far as I can tell, he's unattached. He was born in Miami, did you know that? He left as a boy, though, and grew up in Virginia."

Irene stepped back to avoid a businessman running full tilt with his suit bag. She was quick on her feet today in a pair of bright yellow sneakers.

"He's spending the winter season with us.

Most of the lead singers we hire fly in, stay for a few weeks during rehearsals and performance, then leave, but Tom is here for the semester, teaching classes at New World. That means he's approachable," Irene concluded.

"That's something," Gail said. "What's he like?"

"It's hard to say. He's very quiet. He can be charming, but there's a . . . distance. I've met quite a few famous people, and they seem so aware of being observed. Tom gave me that impression — he's always onstage playing the role of opera singer. Oh, they're like anybody else once you get to know them, but it must be hard, traveling so much, trying to please total strangers."

Irene checked her watch, then offered to buy Gail a soda at the cafeteria, lit up with neon and bustling with travelers.

"Listen, I've been meaning to ask you," Irene said, putting away the change. "In addition to a birthday gift for Mr. Pedrosa, I'd like to take his wife something, too. But maybe they don't do hostess gifts. I was thinking about some flowers from my backyard. What's the etiquette?"

Digna Maria Betancourt de Pedrosa, Anthony's elegant, platinum-haired grandmother, had invited Gail's family to join them for her husband's, Ernesto's, eighty-fourth birthday. Bring everyone, she had said. Irene had taken *Señora* de Pedrosa at her word. She had phoned relatives all over the state. Six of them had promised to fly or drive down for the event, which Irene was starting to refer to as an engagement party.

"Flowers," Gail said. "That would be good, but put them in a nice vase. A *very* nice vase. Maybe Baccarat crystal."

"What? Oh, my. No, that's too extravagant. They'd think we were showing off."

"This is upper-crust Cuban society, Mom. They'll love it."

"If you say so."

"They will. Take a look at the clothes and the jewelry at the party."

Irene swept her eyes over what Gail was wearing: sneakers and jeans and a Miami Hurricanes sweatshirt.

"I know, I know," Gail said. "Anthony's the peacock, not me."

They continued toward the arrival gates with their drinks. "You know, darling, you and Anthony shouldn't leave things to the last minute."

"Things?"

"Wedding plans. You don't even have an engagement ring."

"We haven't had time to look."

"No time to look for a house, either?"

"We've seen a few, but nothing we liked. Mom, it's six months away."

"How do you know, if you haven't set a date?" Irene poked her straw farther down in the cup and took another sip. "Is everything all right?"

"Of course."

"You'd tell me, wouldn't you?"

"It's wonderful. We're crazy about each other. Anthony refuses to move into a house that I once lived in with a former husband, and I agree." Gail added, "We're giving Karen time to adjust. She doesn't like change. It could be a disaster if we got married right away, moved into a new house in a strange neighborhood, and expected Karen to go along quietly. We'll wait till her school is out for the summer."

Irene nodded. "She seems to like him well enough."

"She does. And he likes her."

Gail stopped to study the monitors for Concourse E. "I don't see the flight from San Juan — Oh, wait. There it is. Expected on time." She gazed down the long corridor, which was blocked by X-ray machines and security personnel. Departing passengers were lined up at the metal detectors, and arrivals hurried toward baggage claim.

"Don't worry," Irene said. "She'll be with an escort. We won't miss her. Look what I found — a new Beanie Baby." She held up a green and orange lizard with splayed toes and shiny black eyes. "Isn't he cute?"

"Perfect. God know what she's going to try to sneak home in her suitcase. A boa constrictor. I can't wait to see her."

"I miss her, too." Irene tucked the toy into her pocket. "What do we do if somebody mentions Tom Nolan at the party next weekend?"

"They won't. The Pedrosas are too well-mannered to bring it up. Besides, Anthony and his grandfather have learned to avoid hot topics. That may be the only Cuban house in Miami where politics is *not* discussed — at least when Anthony walks through the door." Gail finished her soda. "Speaking of Tom Nolan, what do you think Rebecca wants to do about him? She says one thing, then another. She's president of the board. She'll have to make up her mind."

"What she wants," Irene said, "is to survive. She'll do whatever is best for the opera, but there are so many egos to stroke. Not everyone is happy with her. Try to help her if you can."

Gail hesitated before asking the next one. "Is she having an affair with Seth Greer?" There was no immediate gasp of shock from her mother, only the wide blue eyes quietly demanding to know where that information had come from. Gail shrugged. "I saw the way he looked at her at the meeting."

"I've heard talk," Irene said in a low voice, "but it seems so unlikely. If her husband knew — !"

"How did Lloyd and Rebecca meet?"

"At the Biscayne Bay Yacht Club, I think. Lloyd is quite a sailor. There was a party after the Columbus Day Regatta ten years ago, and Lloyd took one look at Rebecca and told her, you're the one I want. He wasn't rich then, not like now. Rebecca was already married to an older man named Arthur Halliwell. Arthur's dad was a business partner of my father, in fact, and he shot himself over some scandal with a secretary, but that's another story."

As if someone might be listening, Irene came closer and put a hand on Gail's arm. "Anyway, Lloyd wanted Rebecca, and he went after her. He called her on the phone, sent her flowers — Well, Arthur threatened to cause a big stink. The story is, Lloyd went by Arthur's office to talk about it. No fights, no shouting. Lloyd came out, and within a week Arthur resigned from the bank, signed the divorce papers, and retired to Palm Springs. Rebecca never heard from him again."

"My God."

"You're not to breathe a word of this," Irene said.

When she was a girl Gail had overheard the women of her mother's bridge club talking while they played cards. They met at Irene Strickland Connor's house one Saturday, then the next week somewhere else, and so on. They would sit at three or four tables on the back terrace if the weather was good, and Gail could hear them from her bedroom window. They would have sandwiches and salad and get up from time to time to freshen their drinks, and the cards — and the stories — would go around and around.

One diamond. Why doesn't she throw him out, is what I want to know . . . One heart. She can't. She's expecting again. . . . Oh, my God. One spade. . . . She must have done it on purpose. . . . Two clubs . . . Two spades. And why should she just let him go, after what he's put her through? . . . Pass . . . What do you mean, pass? . . . Oops, I mean three spades. . . . He'll leave her, you watch. A man like that never changes —

50

Even as young as she was then, Gail could see the conflicts in the stories, how one version often contradicted another. There never seemed to be a resolution, only another chapter, another interpretation. Gail had propped her chin on the windowsill, listening, trying to make sense of it. She had finally come to the conclusion that these women just liked to talk. They were like the birds that fluttered out past the screen, twittering because it was their nature.

She might have continued to hold that view if she had not seen more twittering in the courtroom. Lawyers, witnesses, judges, all sure they had the real story. All going at it, *wham wham wham*. Power takes the prize. Gail had to hand it to the women of the Saturday bridge club — they were more willing to have their stories shaped, modified, or even discarded. Add to it, subtract, turn it over, look at it a new way. Around and around. The truth somewhere in the middle, spinning a foot or two above the table, only glimpsed, rarely fixed.

Irene denied that this was gossip. No, these were actual events happening to people she knew and cared for. They told stories not to gloat but to understand, and Irene had always said you never know a person until you know his past.

"Tell me more about Rebecca. Where is she from?"

"Her people are from Atlanta. You can hear it sometimes in her voice. Her father was in construction, but he died young. Betty Ott — you know Betty — was friends with Rebecca's mother through the Theater Guild, before she passed away. This is going back several years, now. Betty told me that Rebecca was one of those girls who knew everything, and she caused her mother no end of trouble. But she had brains. Rebecca was admitted to medical school, and she started classes, but all of a sudden she dropped out. Rebecca's mother told everyone, Oh, she changed her mind. But Betty remembers Rebecca sitting on the back porch alone. Just sitting there. If she had a book, it would be closed on her lap. This went on for weeks and weeks. It had to have been some kind of breakdown. Something terrible happened. A tragic love affair. Maybe she had to end a pregnancy. That's what Betty thinks. Of course Rebecca won't talk about it, and Betty would never pry. So after this thing happened, whatever it was, and she left medical school, and had her breakdown, she married Arthur, who was much too old. And then Lloyd Dixon came along. He made a pile of money with his cargo company, and Rebecca could have anything she wanted — except children. She was never able to conceive. Lloyd's not very nice to her. He must be difficult to live with. I don't think she has a happy life."

Rebecca's story — with so much left out. Which parts had really happened? Could the truth ever be fixed, or only guessed at?

At the meeting at the Dixons' apartment Gail had seen Seth Greer, half-hidden behind the open top of the baby grand, watching Lloyd Dixon's wife. But did that mean love? They had lived together when they were young, and had loved each other then, Gail supposed.

Chunky, gray-haired Seth Greer, wise-cracking and stumbling over melodies on the piano. A world away from representing the indigent. And Rebecca had never become what she wanted, either. What turn had their story taken? What tragedy? But he still loved her. Gail wanted that to be the ending.

She jumped slightly when her mother grabbed her arm and pointed toward the stream of passengers emerging from the concourse — some speaking Spanish, others with tourist tans, some wearing T-shirts from Puerto Rico.

They moved forward. With her height,

Gail could see better than Irene, who stood on her toes. The people streamed past. Gail looked, and looked. "What if she missed the flight?"

"She couldn't have."

"I should have called Dave."

"No, he'd have called you if she wasn't on it."

"Well, where is she?"

There, walking alongside one of the flight attendants. Karen. She seemed taller and browner, a gawky girl in shorts and big sneakers, ten years old, her sunstreaked hair hanging down from a baseball cap. Bright blue eyes swept over the crowd.

"Karen! Sweetie, over here!"

The bill of the baseball cap turned quickly. "Mom! Gramma!" Karen ran across the lobby, dropped her bag, and launched herself into Gail's arms.

FOUR

It was almost ten in the morning when Gail pulled into her space in the parking garage. The upside of having your own business, she told herself, was being able to take your kid out to breakfast on a Monday morning. Drive her to school instead of sending her off on the bus. Then linger at the curb to watch her run to catch up with her friends. Still be there when she turned around to wave goodbye. And after that, make a bank deposit, drop off some dry cleaning, and go by the computer store. At Hartwell Black & Robineau, Gail would have been at her desk for two hours already.

There was a downside, of course. Hartwell Black had been in business since the twenties. Gail A. Connor, Attorney at Law, P.A., had opened for business only three weeks ago. Gail had time to run errands today only because there were no trials, no depositions, and nothing that she couldn't put off until Tuesday. Except for speaking to Thomas Nolan. She would do that after lunch.

Sometimes Gail would imagine the clicking of pulleys and gears, and the laughter of crowds down on the midway, and seeing only sky with her back pressed against the seat like that, and her sweaty hands on the bar, hoping to God that the old leather belt they'd strapped her in with would hold. At Hartwell Black she had specialized in complex commercial litigation, and still had some leftover cases to finish, but they would soon be over. She did pro bono work for charities to make a good name for herself, and friends sent things her way. Even so, it would be some time before she would turn a profit. Anthony had said that if she ever needed help — No, no, I'll be fine.

When she came in, her secretary, Miriam Ruiz, was kneeling on the floor putting files into the bottom drawer of a cabinet. She scrambled up to take the bags out of Gail's hands. "Hi. What's this? Oh, good, you got the accounting software. How is Karen? Is she glad to be home?"

"Very glad. She brought you something — from Dominica, I believe." Gail found it in her purse, a tiny box wrapped in pink paper, tied with a bow.

"Ohhhh —" Miriam unwrapped the package and withdrew earrings made of shells on gold wires. "That is so sweet. I'm going to put them on right now." She took a mirror out of a drawer. At five feet and a hundred pounds, with long curly brown hair, Miriam looked more like a high school girl than a young woman of twenty-two.

She held back her hair and made the earrings swing and rattle. "I love them!"

"*Que* cute," Gail agreed. "Karen brought me a necklace with a shark's tooth. I should wear it to court." She picked her messages out of the giant plastic paper clip on Miriam's desk and shuffled through them. Nothing. Nothing. Do tomorrow. Return this call. Then one from Anthony. He would pick her up at home at 5:45 to look at a house. Gail showed it to Miriam. "Is this all he said? To look at a house? Where?"

"I don't know. He had to go right back into court. He said he'd try to call later."

Gail flipped through the messages again. "Nothing from Thomas Nolan?"

The New World School of the Arts had informed her that Mr. Nolan was holding a master class for vocal students at two o'clock, and could usually be found in the building before that. Gail had left word that she would come by.

"There were some calls, but nobody with that name. Who is he?"

"An opera singer." Gail pulled up the extra chair. "Let me get your thoughts on something. Thomas Nolan has been hired to do the lead in *Don Giovanni* for the Miami Opera. Two years ago he sang in Havana. Do you think that's going to be a problem?"

Miriam looked at her blankly, then said, "What do you mean?"

"Do you think anybody's going to care that he went to Cuba?"

"I don't care."

"What about your parents?"

Miriam's expression said this was a strange thing to be asking. She herself had been born here, and so had her husband, Danny, and most of their friends. Finally she said, "Gail, look. Papi's working two jobs to make some extra money because my sister just started college. My mom has the house to take care of, and she watches Berto for me. They're busy. If something major happened — like if Fidel dropped dead? — they would probably take a week off and party with everybody else. But this? Because an opera singer went to Cuba? Please. They've got better things to do."

Gail thought about that, then got up to pour herself a cup of coffee. The coffeemaker was on a shelf near the copy machine. Miriam made a fresh pot twice a day. First thing in the morning she put the *Miami Her-*

ald and *New York Times* in the waiting room, turned on the lamp between the two love seats, and dusted or watered the plants in the window, as needed. The window gave a nice view of sky and clouds, or Dadeland Mall, if one really wanted to see it.

She blew into the mug, then took a sip. "Miriam, does your mother listen to those Spanish talk stations at home?"

"Not really. She watches TV. She likes the soaps." Miriam was flipping through the computer manual for the accounting program, and Gail visualized gigabytes of information flowing over a high-speed data line. "You want to know if people are talking about this guy, right? Thomas Nolan?"

"I was wondering," Gail said.

"I'll call my grandmother," Miriam said. "She lives with my uncle, and she listens to the radio all the time."

"Ask her —" Gail hesitated, feeling almost traitorous. "Ask her if she's heard of Octavio Reyes. He's a radio host, but I don't know what station." She added, "He also owns a chain of furniture stores, King Furniture. There's a billboard on the Palmetto Expressway. *El Rey de los Muebles.* The furniture king."

"Oh, sure. Danny and I bought our living room suite there."

"He's also Anthony's brother-in-law."

Miriam's mouth opened. Then she said, "Oh."

Leaving Miriam with the computer, Gail picked up her messages and went down the corridor past the spare office, where she hoped to put an associate one day, and the conference room, still empty, but the furniture had been promised this week. Her office was at the end, a bright room with plenty of plants at the window.

One of the calls this morning had come from a Silvia Sanchez of Century 21 Realty, having to do, no doubt, with the house in Cocoplum that Anthony had wanted Gail to see.

"Cocoplum," she said aloud, dialing the number. A million dollars might get them into the neighborhood.

Silvia Sanchez answered, and the noise told Gail that the woman was in her car, probably a Lincoln or Lexus or one of those cushy machines that made prospective home buyers feel loved. The house would be available for viewing this afternoon. Six bedrooms, gourmet kitchen, a pool, beautiful landscaping. It wouldn't last long —

"How much are they asking?" Gail asked.

"You really should see it first."

"We will, but how much?"

"They're asking three-seven-fifty, but we'll make an offer."

"Three . . . seven-fifty." Gail squeezed her eyes shut, then opened them. "I think Mr. Quintana is in court today, a trial that's probably going to last all week —"

But the efficient Silvia Sanchez had already contacted Mr. Quintana's secretary. He was indeed in trial, but he had left word that he would pick up Ms. Connor at home at five-forty-five, then they would all meet at the property at six o'clock.

"Sure, why not?" she said, after the silence had extended for several seconds. They said their goodbyes and hung up. Gail leaned back in her chair with her face in her hands.

The first house he had taken her to, on Biltmore Way in Coral Gables, was a 1920s coral-rock monstrosity with buckling wood floors. Then a French country house in South Miami for two million dollars. Finally the ranch style out in the Redlands with a horse stable in back.

He hadn't liked what she had picked out — normal houses, one story, three or four bedrooms, maybe a pool. The houses he had chosen were older, their big yards shaded with trees. Similar in location or design to the house where he had grown up, in fact.

His grandparents' house, where he had lived from age thirteen to twenty. The Pedrosa mansion — and it was one — had seven bedrooms and a guest house. The floors were tile, the kitchen immense, and in Ernesto Pedrosa's study, where one sniffed the aroma of old leather and expensive cigars, there were maps and historical photographs, a jar of dirt from the country estate, and a bullet-torn flag of Cuba over his desk.

This was the house that Anthony had been thrown out of, so he had said, after an argument with his grandfather. Gail had met the old man several times now, and despite his advanced age, the shuffling gait left by a stroke, and his poetic manner of speech, he still made her nervous. Ernesto José Pedrosa Masvidal. Over six feet tall, with piercing blue eyes. Descendant of Spanish aristocrats. She thought that he probably did not like Americans, but he tolerated them.

For love of his youngest daughter, grieving the loss of two children, Pedrosa had recovered one of them. He had reached into Cuba and pulled Anthony out, resentful and angry, demanding to be sent back. He got into fights at school and for a long time refused to speak English. His younger cousin Carlos, who despised him, mentioned at the dinner table that his own father, Pedrosa's only son, had died at the Bay of Pigs fighting for the liberation of Cuba, while Anthony's father had fought for the enemy. Anthony waited until after dinner to take Carlos into the backyard and grind his face into the dirt.

As the years passed he settled down, but Pedrosa never broke him. Anthony asked nothing from his grandfather, neither money nor approval. He made his own way through law school, earned his own living, married, and divorced. And yet — Gail had seen this clearly — these two men respected each other, even if neither would admit it. Anthony flew his children down from New Jersey as often as he could, and on each visit took them to see their great-grandparents. He knelt each month at his mother's grave, remembered birthdays and saints' days, and attended every family event as if his presence were expected, which of course it was. His grandmother adored him. He would rise when his grandfather entered a room, speak to him formally, and receive a nod in reply. Gail had seen how the old man watched him. How he listened. And how they often ended up sitting near each other, apparently without conscious thought.

At her desk Gail kicked off her shoes and

sat down, curling her feet under her. What a scene it must have been, when Pedrosa told his grandson to get out.

Late afternoon. A room upstairs. Through the open window one can see the heavy foliage of a banyan tree. Stretched out on the bed, reading, is a tall, slender young man with a beard, age twenty or so. His skin is honey gold, his hair rich brown, curling to his shoulders. He has thick lashes and eyes so dark they seem black. When he is angry they glitter.

No, wait. Ernesto Pedrosa would not have permitted long hair and a beard in his house. Anthony is clean-shaven. He is not lying down, he is sitting at his desk reading a textbook on philosophy. A brilliant student. He arrived in this country just seven years ago, speaking no English. It was to be only a visit, but of course his mother, who had fled with her parents, never intended to let him go back once she got him here. Does he still dream of home? The green fields, the river where his father taught him to fish?

On the back of the door, hidden under a coat on a hanger, or even a flag of Cuba hung vertically, there is a poster of Che Guevara. Black, white, and red. Che with his wispy mustache, his beret, and his burning eyes. And through the door, very softly, comes music. His grandmother is playing her radio. Beny Moré or Celia Cruz. Old music from Cuba, preserved on the stations in Little Havana. So many things from el Cuba de ayer *are preserved in this town.*

The young man turns a page. He has an exam or report the next day. He doesn't know that he will become a lawyer. What does he think he will be? Who knows?

Suddenly heavy footsteps are pounding up the stairs. They come closer. They stop. The doorknob rattles. Then a fist on wood. His grandfather yells for him to open up. (No one locks doors in this house.) Open it, I tell you! Open this door!

He is afraid, but of course he won't show it. He swings out of his chair and calmly turns the lock. His grandfather shoves him aside, and he stumbles backward. His mother runs into the room. Papi, no, please! He's a boy! He doesn't know what he's doing!

Too late. The coat or the flag on the back of the door is swept aside, and there is the face of Che Guevara, glaring back at Ernesto Pedrosa. Maybe the maid saw it and told. More likely his cousin Carlos.

Pedrosa slaps Anthony across the face with a huge, hard-knuckled hand. Get out of my house! I should have left you in Camagüey with your communist pig of a father. Ingrate! Traitor! Get out! He tears the poster into pieces.

But no. Even at twenty, Anthony would not have been foolish enough to have a poster like that in his grandfather's house. The poster came later. Say there were books on communist theory. Or a copy of Juventud Rebelde, *or the newspaper,* Granma, *straight from Cuba. Whatever. Pedrosa rips them apart. Get out of my house!*

When Anthony leaves that very night with his clothes and his books crammed into a duffel bag and his mother's tears on his face, he calls his friend. Sure, come on over, man, no problem. Becky won't care. You can sleep on the couch.

It was some time before Gail realized her intercom was buzzing. She picked up the telephone. "Yes?"

"Come out here, quick! Hurry!"

Gail ran, not pausing to put her shoes back on. As she neared Miriam's desk, she heard a male voice speaking Spanish.

Miriam waved at her. "Shhh-shhh!"

There was a radio on a shelf over her desk.

It was a slow, deep voice — the kind that might narrate a state funeral after the assassination of a president. Gail picked out words, tried to translate them in her head, then lost the next sequence. The Rs were drawn out in long trills.

". . . *apoyarrrr la comunidad, no la dictadura . . . Tenemos el deberrrr — la rrrresponsibilidad de —*" Gail missed it. "*Gracias por su atención. Soy Octavio Rrrreyes, el rey del comentario, WRCL, Rrrradio Cuba Libre, 870 en su dial.*"

Thank you for your attention. Octavio Reyes. King of the commentary. Radio Free Cuba.

Miriam smacked the desk with an open palm. "My grandmother said that he has a commentary at 10:55, and I looked at my watch and said I have to hang up! We missed most of it."

"What did he say?"

"I don't know exactly. He was talking about the arts in Miami. How they have a responsibility to support the community, not the dictatorship. He didn't mention the opera." Miriam added, "I mean, not by name."

"Not yet," Gail said.

FIVE

"Gail Connor! Gail, wait!"

She stepped back onto the curb. A man with curly gray hair was hurrying toward her, jacket flapping open, tie askew. When he got closer he put a hand on his chest and pretended to gasp.

"My God, you walk fast." He smiled broadly. "I hope you remember me — Seth Greer? I'm not some nut accosting beautiful blondes on the street."

"Of course I remember. Hello, Seth."

He touched his fingertips to his forehead. "I'm getting a reading. It's coming . . . hold on. I think the lady is going . . . that way." He pointed to the flat-roofed building across the street, four stories with a grid of sunshade on the upper windows.

"Amazing," Gail said.

"Your secretary said you went downtown. Didn't say why — you obviously trained her well — but I put two and two together and got Thomas Nolan." Seth smoothed his tie down over his slight paunch. His blue suit was of good quality, if a little rumpled. "Would you mind if I go along? I've met him. I could introduce you."

"Thanks, but —" Gail smiled. "You're not exactly nonpartisan."

"At least let me buy you some coffee." There was a McDonald's just across the street, students going in and out. "Come on. Five minutes."

She hesitated, then said they could walk to the end of the block. They turned west past the community college, a modern concrete structure with a broad plaza in front. A cool breeze moved through the bright green fronds of palm trees.

"What are you going to say to Nolan?"

"Don't start lobbying, Seth. All I plan to do is ask how he happened to travel to Cuba, what he did there, and so forth."

"A completely neutral fact-finding mission."

"Completely."

"Not influenced by anybody, not even Anthony Quintana."

She looked at him. "Excuse me?"

"Well, it would be better for Quintana — hence, better for you — if Tom Nolan packed up his music and got the hell out of Dodge City."

"Why do you say that?"

"Why?" His gray eyebrows shot upward as if testing whether she were serious. When

Gail continued to smile politely at him, he said, "Because this little brouhaha puts Tony right in the middle, between you and his grandfather. Who is Tony's grandfather? A right-wing exile, a very rich one. Tony doesn't want to alienate him. If granddad thinks we've got communists in the opera, and Tony's engaged to the opera's attorney —"

"Oh, Seth. No way. Anthony hasn't put any pressure on me, and I wouldn't respond if he did."

"Good. I was hoping you'd say that." Seth put a hand on her shoulder. "Want to hear a prediction? Tom Nolan will not be replaced. I've had phone calls all weekend. People are outraged we're even considering it."

"They can be outraged all they like," said Gail, "but the general director may decide it's too risky."

"No! Jesus. A fight would be glorious. Think of the publicity! Free, and lots of it. As treasurer of the Miami Opera, as Lord High Fiduciary Factotum, I guarantee that if the right-wingers came after us, donations would pour in so fast our adding machines would melt down. Pledges would double. We'd get checks from every opera company in the U.S. and half of those in Europe."

"Why didn't you say so at the meeting?"

"I didn't think of it till I was in the shower the next morning." He laughed, then grew serious again. "Listen, I wanted to talk to you about what the city might do if we stand up for Nolan. That shouldn't influence our decision, but we've got to consider it."

"What do you mean?"

"Who runs the city of Miami? To what ethnic group do most of our councilmen, clerks, and miscellaneous department heads and officials belong? They could claim they're afraid of violence at the performance and sock us for thousands of dollars for extra off-duty police protection."

"Seth, for heaven's sake — they can't do that."

"Wanna bet they'll try? Of course it's illegal. Violation of due process, free speech and assembly, *et cetera*. But do they know this? Do they care? When you applied for the position as the opera's general counsel, we all got a look at your resume. Top ten percent, law review at the U of Florida. For eight years you specialized in complex commercial litigation at one of Miami's best law firms. Impressive. But it's not the same. You'll need some help. I'm offering myself. I'm a lawyer as well as a CPA, and there's nothing I'd like better than to kick some bureaucratic ass."

They paused to let four students cross the sidewalk — Haitian, from the sound of their Creole.

"Yes, Anthony told me you used to be a lawyer. Do you still practice?"

"Not as such, but I still have my license, oiled and ready."

A license did not make a lawyer. Gail knew this, even if Seth Greer preferred to ignore it. "Where did you go to school?"

"Georgetown, 1973." Seth said this with some pride. "I clerked at the Justice Department on civil rights cases, then did some field work in Texas and New Mexico. I came to Miami in 'seventy-six and got a job with Legal Aid. Even after switching careers, I've maintained my interest in constitutional issues. I've talked to some people at the ACLU about Tom Nolan. They'd love to get involved."

Gail glanced sideways at him. "Why did you become a CPA?"

"You find that strange? Me too. I've always had an orderly mind — despite what you see on the outside, right? Figures you can always trust, that's the thing. I go into my office, shut the door, it's like . . . a monastery. I even have a collection of plainsong and Gregorian chants. Around tax time, pop those suckers in the CD player — not a care in the world."

They had reached the end of the block. Two lanes of one-way traffic flowed north. A city bus took off in a gray cloud of exhaust.

Gail decided to prod just a little. "Anthony said you and Rebecca used to live together." When Seth stared back at her, she said, "Sorry. I shouldn't have mentioned it."

"No, it's okay. Just keep it to yourself. I don't want people talking."

"Of course. I understand."

Seth turned around, and they headed back the way they had come. He kept his eyes on the sidewalk. "We're not involved currently. I mean, in case you were wondering. But damn, she's one hell of a classy woman, isn't she?"

She smiled at him. "You obviously care about her."

He continued walking, hands in his pockets. "Damned if I know what happened. Nicaragua was a bad scene. After that, I went my way, she went hers. Ten years later, when I moved back to Miami again, she was married to Lloyd."

"Nicaragua? I'm sorry, I must have missed something," Gail said.

Seth looked around. "Oops. Tony said he

was going to tell you about that. He called me over the weekend and said he would. I guess he forgot."

"Well. This is mysterious." They reached the corner where they had met. Gail said, "I'm dying for an explanation."

"No biggie. We were in Nicaragua doing some volunteer work in the summer of 1978. Sandinista activity was picking up, and we had a hard time getting out. It was pretty grim, off and on. It's not the sort of experience you keep snapshots of in the photo album, if you know what I mean."

"No, I don't, actually." The wind blew her hair across her face, and she tossed it back.

"Well, you should talk to Tony." Seth looked at his watch. "I screwed you up on the time, didn't I?"

"No, it's all right, but I should go."

"What about my helping you out with Tom Nolan?"

"Oh." Gail had to remember what they had been discussing earlier. "I'll keep it in mind."

"Will you? I'd like to help."

"Yes. If the city makes any noise, I'll speak to you about it. But let's be clear about one thing. I'm the opera's attorney. I call the shots. Okay?"

"Yes, ma'am. Whatever you say."

In the lobby of the New World School of the Arts, Gail paused to look back through the glass doors. Seth Greer was gone. If she had seen him, just a glimpse through the crowd, she might have gone after him. Bought him that cup of coffee. Made sure she had heard him correctly.

They had been in Nicaragua. What had happened there? Not three months of summer studies at Managua U, but something so *grim* that Seth wouldn't talk about it. Whatever it was, Anthony had never mentioned it. Why?

"Dammit."

Gail wanted an answer to those questions, but it would have to wait. She asked the receptionist where to find Thomas Nolan.

He was on the second floor. Gail shifted to the back of the elevator to allow a dozen or more students to get on, some carrying instrument cases. She exited into a square lobby with gray carpet and metal lockers. One wall had been painted electric blue. From down the hall to her left, a chorus was singing. From another direction, two pianos played entirely different pieces.

She found the right office and looked through the glass panel beside the door. A man in a white oxford shirt with the cuffs rolled up sat at an upright piano. This had to be Nolan. She had seen him only briefly at the fundraiser, and that from a dozen yards away, but recalled blond hair, wide shoulders, and big hands — which now were dancing lightly over the keys. For a while he hummed wordlessly, then stopped and with a pencil marked something in the book of music he was playing from. His lips moved. He tapped the pencil in rhythm, then dropped it onto the piano and resumed. He sang softly in Italian.

Standing on the other side of the glass, Gail felt an odd sense of familiarity stir in the far corners of her memory. Not the man, surely. The music? She reached and came up with nothing. The piano stopped. He turned a page.

Gail knocked. Nolan's hair, tied at his neck, shifted as he glanced around. He said to come in, and she turned the knob. The room was crammed with books, papers, and magazines. The lid of the piano was stacked with them. It was also draped with a lace mantilla. When he stood up, the room seemed even smaller.

"I'm Gail Connor. I left a message that I'd be here at one o'clock. I'm a little late."

"Yes, of course," he murmured absently,

looking around for a place for her to sit. He finally moved a box of music off the desk chair and set it on the floor beside the piano, shoving a gold-painted Roman breastplate aside to make space.

As she put her purse down on the desk, Gail noticed the walls. They were covered with posters, black-and-white photographs, framed reviews of performances, signed programs. So many costumes and singers. With her eyes sweeping across them, she could almost hear music. Distant but distinct, a jumble of instruments and arias.

Nolan picked up a Spanish fan. Snapped it open, then shut it with long pale fingers. "This isn't my office," he said. "It belongs to the head of the department. They say she was an excellent Carmen."

Gail had expected a deep, booming voice, not this slow and quiet speech, pronounced so carefully it seemed scripted.

"What were you playing?"

"Oh. Puccini. 'Vissi d'arte' from *Tosca.* It's a part for a dramatic soprano — not me, obviously. One of my students will sing it today. I have twenty students, and we do five at each class. I have the piano scores so I can go over their selections beforehand."

"You're not teaching just basses and baritones?"

"No, anyone. Sopranos, tenors, it doesn't matter. They choose an aria and we work on it. These kids are quite good."

"High school?"

"A voice that young isn't ready for opera. These are upper-division college, and a couple of grad students. Singers ripen around thirty. The next fifteen, even twenty years, are golden. We hang onto it as long as we can." Thomas Nolan sat on the piano bench, leaning forward, elbows on the thighs of faded jeans.

"I heard you sing last weekend on Fisher Island. You have such talent."

"Thank you." His face was all ridges and hollows, with a prominent nose and clearly defined jaw. Blue eyes, set deeply under straight brows, fixed on her with complete self-possession.

"You must be used to hearing compliments."

He continued to gaze back at her until Gail wondered if her mascara had run. Then he smiled, just a slight upturn of his lips. "When I was young, I wanted to be a concert pianist. Miss Wells — my teacher — finally said no, you don't have the talent for that. You should sing. Who wants to hear that at fifteen? But I took her advice, and here I am. What if I hadn't listened?"

He laughed softly. "I owe everything to her. I would have made a lousy piano player."

"We can all be grateful to Miss Wells." Gail smiled, then said, "I should explain why I'm here."

"I think I know. When I saw your message I was curious. The attorney for the Miami Opera. I called my manager. He had heard nothing. The opera's general director is out of town, but the grapevine says I might be fired for having been to Cuba. I said no, that's insane. There must be some mistake. Do you have bad news for me?" His brows lifted.

Gail said she did not, but spent a few minutes telling him what the opera had to worry about. She went over various choices, not stressing any of them more than the next.

"Incredible. Only in Miami. Are they going to shoot at me? I'll be famous."

"You're famous already."

"Hardly. Tenors are famous. Basses are usually ignored. Well, I can't leave the cast, that's out of the question. This is my debut in the title role in *Don Giovanni*. Did you know that Luciano Pavarotti had his American debut in Miami? It's one of the top companies in the U.S., and continued good reviews mean a lot to my career." He propped his chin on knitted fingers. "Could I be prosecuted?"

"That's highly unlikely. Thousands of Americans travel to Cuba every year, and unless someone is provocative about it, the federal authorities don't press the point. For the opera, however, it's not quite so easy. I need to know about your trip — at whose invitation you went, what you did there, and so on. Do you mind?"

He assented with a slight lifting of shoulders. "It wasn't sponsored by the Cuban government. I was in Dortmund, Germany. The weather had been cold and wet for weeks, and I had just done . . . *Lucia di Lammermoor*? Yes. Some of my friends in the cast said let's go to Cuba. That sounded like fun. I had to start rehearsals in Houston within a month, so it made a nice detour. I came back through Mexico."

"Were they Americans, your friends?"

"Three Germans and one Englishwoman. We stayed . . . where was it? The Tropicoco on Varadero Beach. There were loads of Canadians and Brits — and Americans, too. I wasn't the only one. There were a lot of international musicians around that week for a music festival — mostly jazz, as you would guess. One of the guys told me he'd gotten us on the program. I can't remember what I sang. We didn't get paid. It was to have something to do, that's all. They took us into Havana, to an old theater downtown. Such a heartbreaking city. You can see how beautiful it must have been years ago."

"Who did you sing for?"

"Just . . . people. I believe there was a large group of students from the university. I doubt they had ever heard music from opera performed live. I was glad to show them a small part of the outside world. All the events were listed in the newspaper, but this wasn't a major event. I didn't see any cameras."

"I don't suppose you noticed a tall, gray-bearded gentleman in the audience."

That brought a smile. "No."

"Who paid for your hotel room?"

"My English friend."

"Who was she?"

"A soprano in the cast."

"Does she have a name?"

"Lucia." With a smile he shook his head. "I'd rather not say. She was married."

Gail glanced again at the photographs crowding the walls. Silent, all of them. Carmen, Salome, Lady Macbeth. Bearded men in cloaks, their arms spread. Everyone in makeup and costume. High drama.

"So you went to Cuba at no cost to yourself, the government didn't pay you, and you sang on the spur of the moment for ordinary people, including a group of students. Is that about it?"

"Yes."

As she looked at him, there was another flicker of something familiar, but again it swerved out of reach.

"May I call you Gail?"

"Please."

"And I'm Tom. What do you think, Gail? What will they do with me?"

"At this point, I don't know. It's not my decision."

"Convey this to the board: If they ask me to leave, I will take legal action."

"I'm certain you would," she said.

He made his slow smile. "Nothing against you."

"I know."

Nolan glanced at his watch. "Follow me upstairs. We can continue our conversation on the way." He stood at the piano and picked up a stack of scores. "This is so ridiculous."

"Yes, I agree."

"Would you like to sit in on the class? They're used to singing in front of visitors." Nolan shuffled through the books as if looking for one in particular. "You'd be impressed by how good they are."

"Today? I don't think I —"

"Ah!" He pulled one out of the stack. "This is for a senior I'm working with. I love this part. Leporello, the servant to Don Giovanni. I've done this aria scads of times. It's great for a bass. Great fun."

He put the scores on top of the piano and opened *Don Giovanni*. "Here Leporello shows Donna Elvira, one of the Don's victims, a catalog of women his master has loved. He invites her to read along with him. There are over two thousand names!"

Leaning over the keys, Nolan pounded out a few bars of introduction. Then his voice burst from his throat with such startling force that Gail took a step backward.

Madamina, il catalogo è questo
delle belle che amò il padron mio,
un catalogo egli è che ho fatt' io.
Osservate, leggete con me —

He stopped as suddenly as he had begun and removed the music from the piano. "Do you know the story?" he asked. "Don Giovanni, the lover, the deceiver of innocent women. He seduces them all, every rank and age, simply for the pure pleasure of adding them to the list. A man who lives only to satisfy his own unquenchable appetite. He remains unrepentant even as he is dragged into the flames of hell."

Gail found herself unable to look away.

Thomas Nolan picked up the scores. "Come upstairs. I'll sing the entire aria for you."

"No, I — Thanks, but I need to get back to my office just now. Will the invitation stay open?"

"Of course." He turned off the light and closed the door, checking to make sure it was locked. "I take the stairs. The elevators are impossible this time of day. Come on. You can get to the lobby from here."

He pushed open a metal door leading to a stairwell that echoed with footsteps and voices. Students with backpacks and instrument cases rounded the landing and clattered downward. Others went up. Hard surfaces of concrete and metal magnified each sound.

A young man yelled, "Hey, Mr. Nolan!" Others were standing with him on the landing below, waiting with grins on their faces.

Thomas Nolan looked over the painted pipe railing. He scowled darkly. Pointing at the young man, he sang out, *"Pentiti! Cangia vita, è l'ultimo momento!"*

Gail caught her breath. It was frighteningly loud.

Nolan glanced at her. "I'm telling Giovanni to repent. It's his last hour. Let's see if he remembers the next part."

There was whispering from below, then the young man's deep voice boomed upward from the landing. *"No, no ch'io non mi pento. Vanne lontan da me!"*

"The cad. He will not repent. He says to go away." Once more Nolan's expression became fierce, and his voice thundered. *"Pentiti!"*

"No!"

"Sì."

"No!"

"Ah! Tempo più non v'è!"

The student gave an agonized scream that rattled the light fixtures, and the others in the stairwell laughed as he writhed on the floor of the landing.

"Too late." Thomas Nolan smiled, then said to Gail, "I'll hear from you about this other matter?"

"Yes."

He nodded, then turned and went up the stairs, surrounded by students. Once more he sang, and they joined in. They moved upward, bodies, then legs and feet disappearing. Gail listened until the steel door on the third floor clanged shut.

SIX

"A superb property, no? Six bedrooms, seven baths, plus maid's quarters."

With these words, the realtor swung open the mahogany and etched-glass doors to the house in Cocoplum. "The living area has elegant marble floors, as you see, and there is carpeting in the bedrooms. We'll go up in a minute. Look how impressive the stairs are. Twenty-foot ceiling in the living room. Look, the wall there, all mirrors. Ms. Connor, you will love this kitchen — European cabinets, stainless steel appliances. Okay, follow this way, please. Formal dining room, the chandeliers go with the property. All the windows are double-insulated glass, very secure. Saves you money on the air-conditioning bill, too. Look through here, Mr. Quintana. Such a lovely terrace, all Mexican tile. Ceiling fans, bar, hot tub. Up there — you see? — a security camera for keeping an eye on the children in the pool. You have just the one girl, Ms. Connor? Someday maybe you'll have more, you never know. She's so cute. What's your name, honey? Karen? Look at that backyard, Karen. Look. Incredible. The boat goes there, you see? The davits I think need to be fixed, but it's only a motor, no problem. Can you believe the landscaping? The owners are in Venezuela, very motivated. I believe you should offer them three."

Silvia Sanchez had been waiting on the porch. Not a porch but a portico, a two-story extension over the circular drive and broad curving steps to the entrance. She was around fifty, superbly coiffed and made up, and her brilliant pink suit was a moving spot of color against white walls.

White walls that still had holes where paintings had been taken down. There were two black leather couches shoved into a corner. Beside them sat a zebra whose stripes were made of shards of silver and black glass. Gail pulled Anthony closer and whispered, "That zebra. I must have it."

It had been Anthony who suggested that Karen come along, although Gail had planned to leave her with the sitter. Clever man. Get the kid to like the house, Mom would put up less of a fight. Karen herself was walking along with her mouth open. The bill of her baseball cap would turn this way or that.

In a low voice Gail said, "Why did the owners clear out so fast? Were they one step ahead of the DEA?"

"That could be," Anthony replied.

Their reflections moved in the long mirrored wall. Woman in a tailored brown dress, man in a suit, girl in jeans and a sweatshirt from Biscayne Academy. These people, she concluded, would not fit in here no matter what the kid happened to like.

"Mom, this is the most awesome house. It's huge."

"You could skate in here," Gail said.

"I could?"

"Karen, your mother is kidding."

"Believe me, I *know*." Her sneakers squealed as she took off for the wall of glass doors leading out to the terrace. "Can we go outside?"

Silvia Sanchez turned to her prospective customers. "We can see the backyard now, if you wish."

Gail smiled. "In a few minutes. Mr. Quintana and I need to discuss a couple of things. Would that be all right? Karen, you can go outside, but stay in the yard."

With a small shrug, then a smile of acquiescence, Silvia Sanchez said she would be on the terrace. Gail took Anthony's hand, and they curved up the carpeted staircase to a balcony on the second floor.

He asked, "What do you think so far? It's

more modern. You said you didn't want an old house."

"Six bedrooms plus maid's quarters? We couldn't live in a place like this, I don't care if it was only one million. Ha. *Only*. Anthony —" She tugged on his hand. "Come on. I have to talk to you."

"Oh? I thought you wanted to find the master bedroom."

"We'll do that, too."

They opened a door and peered into a room with a swirly plaster ceiling and built-in laminated cabinets and shelves. The carpet was so thick it snagged her heels. Anthony said how easy it would be to redecorate. He pointed out how secure this house was — the windows were all wired with burglar alarms. There were security cameras, an electric gate —

"I saw Thomas Nolan today."

"That's right, you did. What happened?"

"It was perfect. Nothing anyone could object to. He went with some friends and paid nothing for his hotel room. College kids attended his performance. Fidel didn't show up. I was moved, hearing him talk about Havana in ruins. And he didn't earn a peso."

Anthony shrugged. "I suppose it's possible."

"Oh, really? Isn't this suspiciously like what you said at the party at the Dixons' on Friday? If somebody coached him, and it's all a lie, we might have trouble later."

"You'll have trouble either way," he said.

"Well, what should I do?"

"There's nothing you *can* do."

"I had sort of hoped for some help here," she said.

"Gail, it isn't your decision. Tell the board and let them decide."

"Fine."

He opened the door to a walk-in closet, and his voice was muffled. "Look how big this is." The shelves and drawers and rods went on and on. Someone had left a few padded pink satin hangers.

Gail leaned against the door frame with her arms crossed. "On my way to see Tom Nolan, I ran into Seth Greer. He wanted to talk about Nolan, which we did, and then he said something odd. He said that in 1978 you and he and Rebecca went to Nicaragua together."

Anthony looked around at her, then closed a drawer and came out. "What did he tell you?"

"That you were there one summer as volunteers. He gave me the impression it must have been a pretty bad experience for all of you. You never mentioned it to me. Why not?"

"Are you angry? It was so long ago, I don't think about it anymore."

"I'm not angry, I'm just wondering what's going on. You pretended not to know Rebecca Dixon. And then Seth said you called him over the weekend, as if you had to get your stories straight."

"Honey —" Anthony was shaking his head. He slid a hand down her arm, then held onto her wrist. "I called Seth to say hello, to catch up on the last twenty years. Then I said, 'You know, I never told Gail about our time in Nicaragua. I should do that.' All right. Seth and I went there to help build a school in a town in a rural area of Jinotega province. Rebecca worked in the clinic. It wasn't a safe place to be. Sandinistas were in the area, and government troops came through looking for them. We saw dead people in the fields. I think for the first time in our lives, we were afraid. It was a complicated experience. I wasn't consciously trying to keep it from you."

She put her arms around him. "Okay. I just wanted to know. You can tell me about it someday. I'd like to hear what happened."

"When we have time."

"Time? I wish. That's in awfully short supply lately."

He hugged her and whispered, "After the party on Saturday, I'm going to kidnap you to my house and carry you upstairs."

"I'll be screaming all the way."

"Come on." He took her hand. "Let's see the master suite before we go downstairs."

They found it at the end of the hall. Light leaked through heavy curtains drawn over a wall of windows that would otherwise look out to the bay. Indentations in the plush cream-colored carpet marked the position of furniture. A chandelier in the shape of a fireworks explosion hung over a raised platform designed to hold a king-size water bed. The wall behind the bed was painted black, and the wall opposite was mirrored.

Gail stared into it, watching Anthony's reaction to all this. He stepped onto the platform where the bed used to be, looked through a crack in the curtains, then came down again.

She said, "Why do I have a sudden urge to tell you to take off your clothes?"

His image was behind her, hardly more than a silhouette. His face disappearing to a curve of forehead and nose when he lowered his mouth to her neck. Hands and the edge of white shirt cuffs moving over her dress. His voice at her ear. "Come into the bathroom with me."

"You're crazy."

"Now. Hurry up."

Their footsteps echoed on the tile floor. He pushed the door shut. There was a huge bathtub with water jets and gold fixtures. A separate shower room, a long marble vanity with two basins.

Anthony set her on the edge of it. They were both laughing. He told her to be quiet. She clung to his neck. Her purse fell off the counter and spilled open. Things clattered and rolled.

Going down the staircase, they could see Karen by the seawall examining the lines that would lift a small boat out of the water. They crossed the cavernous living room and slid open one of the glass doors. Mrs. Sanchez, who had been sitting by the pool conducting other business on her portable phone, concluded her call, then escorted them along the paved walkways.

She pointed out the security fence. The sprinkler system. The flowers, the fruit trees, the tropical plants that grew in lush green profusion, even now, in winter. The property was on a canal, much better than being right on the bay, in case of storm surges. Anthony agreed. He wanted security more than the view.

The sun had moved behind the poinciana tree, leaving the thick grass dappled with patches of light. He told Gail that by late spring the tree would be heavy with red-orange flowers. He used the Spanish word. *Framboyán.*

Karen was walking along the seawall, and Anthony went over to make sure she didn't fall in. No chance of that. She was as sure-footed as a cat. The wind played with his tie and flipped the edge of his jacket.

Already he owned this place in his mind. Not the house. It was ridiculous, and he knew it. If only they could bring in a huge helicopter crane, hook the house to cables, and drop it into the bay for an artificial reef. He wanted the *framboyán* tree, the electric gate, and the burglar alarm. No one could come in and by force or trickery take him away.

Several months ago they had been taking a walk after dinner, and he had told her about his childhood in Camagüey. How idyllic he had made it sound. An Eden — but it had not been his own sin that expelled him, but a mother's desire for her child. And a grandfather's power.

He had lived in a small house outside

Cascorro with his father and sister. There had been a garden and chickens to tend. He made his own toys out of wood. His first girlfriend had lived down the road. Yolanda. He had not mentioned much more than her name. No reason. The rudderless conversation had simply drifted to a story about working one summer in the orange groves with the other boys. A young blond Russian with a permanent sunburn forced them to sing songs as they rode back to camp in carts pulled behind tractors. They made up obscene verses, falling over themselves with laughter while the Russian screamed at them to shut up. A happy childhood.

Now Gail found herself thinking about the girl. Yolanda. She would have been pretty. He might have walked her to school on the road alongside the fields, then over the wooden bridge that crossed the river where his father had taught him to fish — before his father lost his sight in an exile raid and retired from the army. Endless green fields of sugarcane that turned brown before harvest. Palm trees, banana, *framboyán* . . .

Armásico, aguacate, ciruela, guayaba, mango, mamey. Ceiba, with its thick shin-

ing roots that snake over the ground.

Yolanda has laughing brown eyes. An-thony is tall for his age, and so thin his ribs show, but his face is still rounded and smooth. What do they wear? She's in a yellow cotton dress. No. Coming from school, they would be in uniforms. Gray shorts or skirt, white shirts, red scarves at their necks. Pioneers. Seremos como el Che. *We will be like Che. They sit under the tree. He tells her not to worry, no one will see them. The tree catches the sun, red and flaming, with the bluest of skies be-tween the blossoms. Her skin is soft. She smells of earth and perspiration, and un-derneath is a sweet fragrance, and he presses his nose to her hair. A wind moves the branches, and a few red flowers drift down.*

There are birds. Sinsonte, totí, paloma —

He says her name, Yolanda, the sounds sliding one into the next, his lips forming a kiss on the first syllable.

They are late getting to her house, and her father comes through the door with a stick. Get inside, you disgraceful girl! An-thony grabs the stick before her father can hit her. It's my fault, he yells. But I didn't touch her. She's going to be my wife.

Go on, get out of here before I break your head. The boy does not budge. My name is Anthony Luis Quintana, son of Luis Quintana, a hero of the revolution. I am first in my class at school, and I will go to the university and graduate, then Yolanda and I can get married.

This outburst is so unexpected that the father can only stare, then look around at Yolanda's mother, who stands in the doorway hiding a smile behind her hand. Anthony asks permission to see their daughter at home. The father consents, but only one day a week, and right here, under supervision. And no more walking home by themselves. Understood? Yolanda is blushing with pleasure. Anthony nods. Thank you, sir.

A month or two later he tells her that he is going to visit his mother in Miami. She cries. You'll never come back. Of course I will, he scoffs. I have to come back to take care of my father. He's blind. They can't keep me if I don't want to stay. I promise you, I'll be back. And you must promise to wait for me.

Gail leaned her cheek on Anthony's shoulder. "I like the backyard."

"You're right. This house won't do."

"We'll find one that will."

They walked across the lawn. Karen had disappeared inside, and Mrs. Sanchez waited on the terrace, giving them privacy while they made their decision.

"Do you want me to check out Thomas Nolan's story?" Anthony asked.

Gail smiled at him. "Thank you. What are you going to do, go down there yourself?"

"No. I have an investigator with contacts in Havana."

"I keep seeing us at your grandfather's birthday party next weekend, and somebody turns on the news, and there's a video of Thomas Nolan shaking hands with Fidel Castro. Then your grandfather points to the door. Out, out."

Anthony waved the idea way. "No. He'd let you eat first, before he told you to leave. My grandmother doesn't allow anything to interfere with a family dinner."

"Please say you're making a joke."

"Yes, Gail."

"Oh, by the way, I heard Octavio Reyes this morning on the radio at my office."

Anthony's smile vanished.

" 'The arts have no right to support a dictatorship.' I didn't hear all of it." They reached the edge of the patio. "Have you considered, sweetheart, that your brother-in-law could use this issue to stab you in the back?"

"Yes, I have considered that."

"Then perhaps you should tell the investigator to hurry."

SEVEN

They stopped at a Chinese takeout on the way to Gail's house. Anthony told her to go in and order, he would be right there. And take Karen with her. With some grumbling, Karen got out of the car.

Gail told the cashier what they wanted, then went over to the window and looked past the printed menu taped to the glass. Anthony had a new black Eldorado, so shiny that the lights from inside seemed to float on its hood. She could see him talking on his cellular telephone. She and Karen were carrying bags and cartons out of the restaurant when Anthony finally hung up. He hurried to help put the food in beside Karen.

"I'm sorry, sweetheart. I was talking to the investigator. He says to come to his house tonight, but I have time to eat with you and Karen first." He started the car, glanced over his shoulder, and backed up. "Tell me everything you know about the singer, including what he said in your meeting today. Felix wants to know."

"You plan to go alone?"

"Yes. You don't need to be there." Anthony added, "It's too late for Karen to be out. She probably has homework."

A voice came from the backseat. "I already did my homework."

"It's still too late for you to be out."

Gail looked at him for another moment, then turned in her seat. "Sweetie?"

Karen rolled her eyes. "I know. You want Gramma to come over and babysit."

"*Ay, Diós.* Gail, you don't have to go."

"This is my case, remember?" When Anthony finally agreed that it was, Gail said, "Tell me about the investigator."

The streetlights moved over Anthony's face. "Felix Castillo. You might not like him, but you can trust him. He's absolutely reliable. Don't bother asking him questions, because he doesn't like to talk about himself. He came to the U.S. in 1980, the Mariel boatlift. He's forty-nine, I believe. Two fingers of his left hand are missing. He lives with his girlfriend. I tell you this so you won't ask if she's his daughter." Anthony paused, his eyes going to the rearview mirror. "Karen. What are you doing?"

"Nothing."

Gail looked around. Paper crackled as Karen slid an egg roll back into the bag.

Her lips were shiny with grease. "No eating in the car. We'll be home in a minute."

"I'll tell you more on the way to Felix's," Anthony said.

Karen asked, "What happened to his fingers?"

There was a hesitation just long enough to tell Gail not to believe whatever came next. "An accident at work."

Felix Castillo lived east of Coral Gables just south of Eighth Street, an area of small stucco houses and three- or four-story apartment buildings. A car went by booming Spanish rap music. Gail assumed the neighborhood was safe because Anthony left his pistol in the glove compartment instead of putting it on the seat.

He told her that Castillo had lost his fingers to a machete. He'd been making love to his mistress when her old boyfriend came out of nowhere. Castillo had gotten to his gun in time to prevent the next blow. He always carried a gun. In Cuba he had been in state security. When Anthony told her what branch, Gail asked, "What is that? Haydo?"

He pronounced it in English. "G-two. In Spanish it's *hay-dos*. It's the equivalent of the CIA. Don't bring it up tonight." Anthony looked at the street signs and turned at the next corner.

"He was a Cuban spy?"

"More or less. He quit, and they threw him in jail, then about a year later, the port of Mariel opened, and they put him on a boat. He came here with the hundred and twenty-five thousand others who got out. He told immigration he used to be a mechanic. He started his life over again, and he wants to forget anything that happened before 1980."

"Does he ever talk about it?"

"Not with strangers."

"I didn't even think to ask you what he charges," Gail said.

"No, no. Consider it my gift — my anonymous donation — to the opera." Anthony turned another corner, slowed his car, then pulled off the street under the thick canopy of a banyan tree, letting the engine idle and leaving the parking lights on.

The house to Gail's right was completely dark. "Is this where he lives?"

"No, it's just ahead, but I think you should know something else about Felix. When I went to Nicaragua, Felix was there as an advisor. That's where I met him." The dashboard lights barely illuminated Anthony's face.

Gail said, "An advisor. Could you be a little more specific?"

"He was . . . helping the local Sandinistas with tactics and weapons."

"Anthony, my God, what were you *doing?*"

"Nothing. It was a small town, and people get to know each other. I met Felix, found out he was from Cuba, and we became friends. He had a cover — fixing engines in farm equipment — but in that area, they didn't have many tractors. After leaving Nicaragua, I never expected to see him again. Then two years later I was in New York, and my mother called asking if I knew a Felix Castillo, who claimed to be a friend of mine from Camagüey. She was skeptical because I'd left at thirteen. Felix had called my grandfather's house from a camp in Miami where Immigration put everybody till they had sponsors. So I said yes, I remember Felix, ask my grandfather to find him a job. I think he worked in the car dealership for a while. What he did after that, I don't know. When I moved back to Miami, he was working as a private investigator. He's very good. I chose him for this job because nobody could do it better than Felix. But Seth and Rebecca — I don't think they know he's here. I'll call them in the morning."

Gail said nothing for a while, assimilating all this. "Do you catch the irony here? A former Cuban spy helping find out the truth about Thomas Nolan's trip to Havana."

"Tricky more than ironic. If anyone became aware of his background, it might look bad for the opera. Be discreet, okay?"

"And I'm not supposed to bring this up with Felix," she said.

"Don't even think of it." Anthony turned the headlights back on and drove the remaining half block to Felix Castillo's house.

Like most other houses in this neighborhood, this one had decorative ironwork on the windows. A chain-link fence ran along the cracked sidewalk. Someone had pushed back the gate to the driveway. Anthony pulled in behind a battered gray van, the kind a handyman might drive. There were the usual bumper stickers one saw in Cuban neighborhoods. HERMANOS AL RESCATE. WQBA. NO CREO EN EL MIAMI HERALD. Gail wondered if this was sincerity or camouflage.

The front door, set back into an alcove, opened before Anthony could rap on the barred security door. A man came out with a key ring. A pair of rubber thongs slapped on the tiles. Felix Castillo was laughing. "Look who's here." He unlocked the deadbolt. "Come in, come in." He and Anthony embraced. There were some slaps on the back. Castillo was shorter, but muscular and quick.

"*Viejo, ¿qué tal?*"

"*Bien, bien. Hace tiempo, mano.*"

"Gail, this is Felix Castillo."

He was bald, except for a close-cropped fringe of gray hair. His mustache drooped below the corners of his mouth, and when he smiled, heavy lines fanned out from his eyes. "Ahh, Tony, she's beautiful. I am honored, Gail." He kissed her hand.

Anthony took two metal cigar tubes from his breast pocket. "Felix, I've been saving these for you."

"Oh, my God, look at this. Cohiba *corona gorda*. You're too much, man. Come sit down." After locking the door he led them through an archway into a living room with white tile on the floor and puffy brown furniture with bases of laminated plastic. In a four-foot high cage, a dozen lovebirds squawked and fluttered. The television was on, and a young black woman who might have been twenty unfolded herself from the sofa. Her breasts wobbled under a fuzzy purple sweater, which had fallen off one shoulder. She gazed at the new arrivals with the sullen expression of someone whose evening had been rudely cut short.

Castillo introduced her as Daisy, then asked what they wanted to drink. "*Café,* rum, vodka, scotch, beer?" Gail agreed to a beer. Anthony asked for rum. Castillo told the girl, "*Una cerveza, dos ron añejo. Y apague la TV.*"

The television went silent. The birds continued to chirp. Daisy clopped from the room in backless shoes with shiny gold heels. Her legs were slim, her butt like two melons.

Gail sat down on the sofa, feeling decidedly out of place. Castillo and Anthony remained standing, Spanish flowing so fast she could pick out only a word here and there. They were sniffing the cigars, Castillo telling Anthony to have one, Anthony saying no, no, *son para tí,* they're for you. Finally giving in. Switching to English, Anthony asked if Gail minded. She shook her head. Castillo raised the miniblinds and cranked open the window. Cool night air drifted into the room. Gail had changed into slacks and a turtleneck, but she felt chilled. She put her tweed jacket on.

Castillo went over to a bookcase near the front entrance and moved a box of ammunition, looking for something. The cigar clipper. He found it under an ankle holster with Velcro straps. There was a small black pistol inside.

He held the cigar in his left hand, took a small snip off one end, then lit the other one with a green plastic disposable lighter. His last two fingers were completely gone, and part of his hand was missing. A gold bracelet glittered on his wrist, as if daring anyone to comment. He passed the lighter to Anthony, who turned the cigar slowly, his lean cheeks going hollow. A circle of orange appeared. He let out the smoke in small puffs.

Gail studied them, trying not to be obvious. She had never seen Anthony in the company of this kind of man, in a house like this one, yet he seemed perfectly at ease. He had fit in equally well on Fisher Island last weekend, listening to Thomas Nolan sing *bel canto* arias.

The girl came back in with the drinks — one beer and two shot glasses each half-full of amber liquid. She set them on folded paper towels, then glanced at Castillo. He made a slight motion of his head toward the hall. Her footsteps diminished. A door closed. Music started playing, the quick pace of a salsa tune, muffled by the walls.

Castillo picked up his glass, saluted them, then took a sip.

"*Que rico,*" Anthony said. "What is this, Bucanero?"

"The best for you, man." Castillo dropped into the armchair and put his ankle on his knee. The rubber sandle hung crookedly from his toes. The sole was white with callus. He looked at Gail over the end of his cigar. Let out some smoke.

Anthony sat beside her and pulled an ashtray closer.

Gail took a sip of beer. "I understand you were a mechanic in Cuba."

Smiling a little, he glanced at Anthony. "That's right."

"How did you become a private investigator?"

"Well, a mechanic is hard work and not much money. I said what the hell, you know? Might as well try this. Be my own boss. Tell me about this person, the opera singer."

In as much detail as she could recall, Gail related her conversation with Thomas Nolan. Supplied as much of his biography as she knew. Described what he looked like. "I can get you a photograph, along with whatever written information the opera has on him."

"That would help."

"What do you think about his story?"

"It's bullshit."

109

"How long will it take to find out what really happened?"

"Maybe a few days, maybe a week or two. Maybe never. We'll see." He glanced at the lovebirds, which had begun fluttering in their cage.

Gail said, "I can find the woman who went to Havana with Nolan."

"Lucia," Castillo said. "Or whatever her name is. How are you going to do that?" It was not a challenge. He wanted to acquire the method and file it away.

"A phone call to the opera house in Dortmund. Someone there must remember. Once I have her name, it won't be hard to find her manager. All singers have managers. He can tell me where she's performing now."

"That's a good idea. You speak German?"

"No, but I'll think of something."

Castillo laughed. "She's pretty smart."

"Yes, she is." Anthony was leaning back on the sofa, arms spread. He had left his tie in the car, and his jacket was open, revealing a shirt that had cost him two hundred dollars. From time to time his fingers stroked through her hair. The other hand, on which he wore a black jade ring, held the cigar, and the rich smoke, sweet with an undertone of coffee, spun and curled toward the open window.

Gail asked, "Have you heard anything on the street about Thomas Nolan?"

"On the street?" Castillo seemed to smile. "No."

"What do you think might happen, if they want to make trouble?"

"Who are you talking about?" He looked back at her with patient brown eyes. "Who do you mean?"

After a moment, she said, "I see. 'They' don't exist."

"Nobody wants to make trouble. That's not the reason. See, Gail, these are people whose relatives were executed or tortured or maybe died in prison. People who lost everything they had, not that most of them had so much. You know? I'm not saying it's right or it's wrong, but I can understand where they're coming from. What do I think will happen? A lot of noise. The radio hosts go on the air, then people with nothing better to do will make nasty phone calls to the opera. You don't worry about that. You worry about the ones who use this for their own purposes."

Gail repeated a word she had heard Anthony use. *"Oportunismo."*

"Yes. The opportunists."

"What do they gain by stirring it up?"

"They feel big. Important. Maybe they want to get elected. Or they've got a business and they want publicity. Or there could be personal reasons."

Referring, possibly, to Octavio Reyes. Anthony could have told Castillo about his brother-in-law during that long phone conversation. There were currents flowing in this room that she couldn't tap into. She felt impatient with the oblique conversation.

"Do you expect violence?"

Castillo sipped his rum, then with a knuckle dabbed at his droopy gray mustache. "No, I don't think you'll see much of that. If you do, it's probably coming from the other side."

"Other side?"

"Cuba."

She looked at him steadily. He did not elaborate. "What do you mean?"

"They have people up here."

"Who does? The Cuban government?" There was no reply. "You're telling me the Cubans would send spies or terrorists to Miami to . . . what? Set off a bomb at the opera, then blame it on the exiles?"

Anthony tapped some loose ashes into the ashtray, then turned toward Gail to say, "No. They don't set bombs. They keep an eye on what's going on. If the opportunity presents itself, they might push others to violence. The exiles are aware of this. They know they can be used, so they're careful."

"What if there's someone out there who doesn't get it?"

His hand rested on his knee, and smoke drifted from the cigar. "That's an unfortunate possibility."

For no reason Gail could see, the birds began chirping again, flying wildly in the confined space, their wings beating on the cage. She had the odd impression of having wandered into a flick from the forties. Film noir. And nobody had given her a script.

Castillo picked a flake of tobacco off his tongue. "A lot easier if this singer decided to go away, you know?"

This at least was real: She had no doubt at all that if Anthony asked him to, Felix Castillo would take care of the problem. One neat chop to the larynx would do it.

EIGHT

On Wednesday, the soonest she could make it downtown, Gail went by the opera building on Biscayne Boulevard. Rebecca Dixon was expected in at two o'clock.

Gail arrived early to speak to her mother first. Irene Connor was one of the volunteers, and Gail found her in the anteroom of the general director's office talking on the phone. She looked unusually businesslike in a bright green dress and her size-five *faux* alligator pumps. Gail came closer. Her earrings were tiny frogs on lily pads, just visible beneath her auburn curls.

Irene finished the call, which had to do with a tour for high school students, then retrieved a lit cigarette from a potted philodendron on the window sill. The window was open, drawing out the smoke. "Hello, darling." She took a last puff and crushed it out in the pot. "When the cat's away —" She dropped the butt into a piece of paper, which she wadded and threw into the trash. "Don't worry. Next week I'll have to be a good girl. Jeffrey Hopkins will be back. How nice to see you. What's up?"

Gail closed the door and told her about Felix Castillo — everything except how and where Anthony had met him.

Irene pressed fingers to her heart. "Sometimes — not too often, but sometimes — I think I ought to move to Tampa and live with my sister."

"But how boring," Gail said, "and then who would I rely on for gossip?"

"I don't *gossip.*"

"No, you're my . . . snitch." Gail laughed. "My counterspy, my mole in the organization." Then she grew serious. "And you never heard any of this."

Irene fixed her with a sharp blue gaze. "They could tear out my nails. All right. What are you after?"

"Just a couple of small favors. I need a photo and resume of Tom Nolan from the files, if you have it." Irene said that they did. Gail continued, "I also need to find the English soprano he sang with in *Lucia di Lammermoor* before they went to Cuba together. This was a performance in Dortmund, Germany. Rebecca and Lloyd Dixon were there, but I don't want to ask them because somebody — probably Lloyd — told Tom Nolan to lie to me about his trip. It wouldn't be too hard to find the soprano, would it?"

"I shouldn't think so. Lloyd told him to

lie to you? Well, no wonder it sounded so innocent. All right, I'll call the Stadts Theater in Dortmund," Irene said after a moment. "No problem. Now for the rest of it." Opening a filing cabinet, she walked her fingers over the tops of folders, then pulled out one of them.

A black-and-white publicity photograph showed Nolan looking straight into the camera. No smile, just hollow cheeks and deep-set eyes. His performance credits covered four pages. There were copies of reviews from major newspapers. His appearance in Havana was not mentioned.

Gail returned the photo and papers to the folder. "When Rebecca gets here, tell her I need to talk to her. Meanwhile, I'm going to find Tom Nolan. Could you make me two copies of these? I'll be back in a few minutes."

Irene curled one small hand around Gail's elbow. "Darling, what about Mr. Pedrosa's birthday party on Saturday? Should we go? Maybe you should discuss it with Anthony. It might be too awkward for everyone."

"I refuse to allow Octavio Reyes to spoil it," Gail said. "Of course we'll go. Don't worry. It's going to be fine."

The main rehearsal hall was generally

used by the orchestra. Today the chairs and music stands were in a far corner, and the wood floor was marked with different colors of tape, indicating the various stage sets for *Don Giovanni*, still under construction elsewhere in the building.

There were two dozen people in the room, dressed casually in jeans and sneakers and faded T-shirts. Some were singers, others not. It was hard to tell the difference. Gail assumed that some of the younger ones were students. One man walked backward unreeling a measuring tape. A woman on her hands and knees was sticking blue tape on the floor. The director and conductor stood by the piano. The pianist played a few bars, then stopped for some discussion.

Gail had come through the corridor that linked the offices to the other parts of the building — rehearsal rooms, dressing rooms, carpentry and costume shops, finally the theater itself. The receptionist had told her that the principal singers would be in the orchestra room working on blocking. Through the partially open door Gail could see most of the room, but she did not see Thomas Nolan.

She came a step farther inside, then stopped.

Lloyd Dixon was walking in her direction.

Having been spotted, Gail had no choice but to go in. She let the door click shut behind her.

It had taken her a few seconds to recognize him in loose khaki pants and a brown leather bomber jacket. Long use had left scratches and nicks, wearing the leather to suede around the zipper. There was a plaid shirt underneath. Dixon looked her up and down, a quick male appraisal. "Well, it's our lawyer. Tom says you spoke to him Monday. Back for a follow-up?"

She noticed Thomas Nolan a few yards behind Dixon. Apparently they had been talking. Nolan glanced back at her, then went to join a group of his friends. "No, I dropped by on some other matter and thought I'd take a look at the rehearsal."

"They don't like visitors," Dixon said.

"You're here."

"I'm taking off."

Gail gestured toward Dixon's jacket. "I didn't see a biplane in the parking lot."

"Uh-uh. A Cessna Citation Five jet out at Tamiami Airport. My new toy. I'm taking her out for a spin. You ought to come along sometime."

There was something sexy about this man, Gail decided, surprising herself. He was up in his fifties, with a thick neck and heavy shoulders. His white hair was clipped short. But such a *guy*. She had heard that Dixon had been a helicopter pilot in Vietnam. Gail imagined him in a scene from *Apocalypse Now*. Flight helmet and sunglasses. Rockets streaking into the jungle. The rattle of a machine gun in the open doorway. He had stolen Rebecca away from her first husband, the banker. The poor man had fled rather than fight for her, so the story went.

Gail turned her back on the room and spoke quietly. "Lloyd, let me ask you something. Did you speak with Tom before I went to see him? Maybe offer him some ideas on how to respond to my questions?"

His smile lifted one side of his mouth. "No, Gail, I didn't. Why are you making a big deal out of this? Let me clue you in. The Cubans I know think it's a joke. The others — the so-called hard-liners — they don't really give a shit. It's a pose they have to take, or they can't belong to the club. They got here all pissed off because they didn't have the power anymore. Now they do. They're older, they'd rather go about their business. My advice is, don't push it. What happens, happens."

"Maybe you should tell that to Octavio Reyes."

He continued to look at her. "Who is Octavio Reyes?"

Gail said, "The Cuban radio commentator on WRCL."

"A member of the club. Don't worry about it." From his back pocket Dixon took a billed cap, dropped it on his head, and smoothed it down. The words DIXON AIR TRANSPORT made a circle around a small jet.

"You might worry," Gail said, "when the receptionist out there starts getting death threats. I'm going to recommend that the opera hire a full-time security guard."

"Tell the receptionist to hang up the goddamn phone."

"If anything happened to one of the employees or musicians and we had not taken precautions, the opera could be held liable."

"Lawyers." Dixon shook his head. "Hell, I don't care. If a security guard makes you sleep at night, hire one." He grabbed the door's metal push bar in a meaty hand. The smile reappeared. Then he winked. "Some fun, huh?"

Not wanting to follow him through the corridor, Gail crossed the rehearsal room and looked out the window. The vertical blinds were open, giving a view of the parking lot.

Who, he had asked, *is Octavio Reyes?*

There had been at Gail's former law firm a partner so elderly he had clerked at the Supreme Court during the Depression. He would often drop a quote from Cicero or Virgil into his oral arguments — in Latin, making Miami juries squint in confusion. He was finally exiled to a tiny office, where he wrote convoluted, increasingly philosophical legal briefs, which clerks in their twenties would rewrite, then laugh about over lunch. Gail had been among them. She rode down in an elevator with him one night and talked about the trial she would do the next day — her first. How do you tell, she asked, if a witness is lying? Easy. If he's lying, he either looks at you or he doesn't.

It had taken a long time, but the meaning had finally clicked. Sometimes the eyes drift away. Sometimes they stay right on you, not a blink.

A blue Ford pickup truck was parked among the cars and vans out there. Not a new one, but the kind a man could toss engine parts into and not worry about scratching the paint. The windows were tinted. There was a trailer hitch. A CB antenna. A bumper sticker with an American flag. Dixon appeared, keys in his hand.

Just as he opened his door, a silver Jaguar

121

turned into the parking lot, sunlight glinting on the windshield. Rebecca's car. She parked in the general director's spot near the entrance. Dixon stood watching her. The wind opened her long white sweater — probably cashmere. From a distance of ten yards she looked coolly at her husband, but neither of them spoke.

Dixon took off his leather jacket, tossed it into the front seat, and got in. His truck tires squealed going around the corner. Rebecca disappeared under the walkway alongside the building.

"I think that must be the reason I never married."

The soft voice had come from behind her. Thomas Nolan. He made a slight shrug. "One can't help noticing. You would notice even more if you were around them. Did you come to speak to Lloyd Dixon or to me?"

"To you." Embarrassed to have been caught spying, Gail walked away from the window, Nolan following. "I don't suppose you listen to the local Spanish talk stations. Over the last few days a commentator on WRCL has been stirring up trouble."

"Yes, we've been talking about that. Everyone's sure it will blow over."

"No. Today my secretary heard him say

that the opera had invited a man of communist sympathies to take the lead role in its next production."

That produced a little laugh from Thomas Nolan. "A man of . . . communist sympathies? Oh, my God. They can't mean *me*."

"It's a loose translation," Gail said. "If they mention your name, you might have some problems. Don't take any phone calls from people you don't know, and make sure nobody's in the parking lot before you walk out to your car alone."

Alarmed, Nolan said, "Is it that serious?"

"Just be careful, that's all."

"I've never sung in a bulletproof vest."

"Tom, could I ask you why Lloyd Dixon was here?"

"Sure. He wanted to tell me not to worry about being replaced. Maybe I shouldn't have been so happy to hear it."

"Is it official? No one told me."

"It's his opinion, but he seemed certain. What I have found, Gail, is that people who donate wads of money to the opera usually get their way." Tom pushed some blond hair behind his ear. "Lloyd Dixon also invited me and a couple of the others to sing at his house the weekend after next. He's having a dinner party for some business associates. They like opera, and I think he wants to make a good impression."

"Do you get paid for this?"

"Oh, no. Opera singers often do such favors for big donors like the Dixons." Nolan glanced toward the director. "I should go."

"One other thing. Lloyd said that you invited him to *Lucia di Lammermoor* in Germany. Did you know him already? I was just wondering."

After a moment in which he may have been deciding if this was any of Gail's business, he replied, "No. I knew the Miami Opera wanted to do *Don Giovanni*. My manager was trying to get me the job. I heard that the Dixons were taking an opera tour of Europe that fall, so I sent them tickets to *Lucia*. They came, we talked, and I got the part."

"And how did you happen to choose the Dixons to send tickets to?" Gail asked.

The smile reappeared. "Well . . . it helps to research who's who before you start lobbying."

Someone yelled across the room, "Tom! We're about to start."

Again the steady gaze from deeply set, placid blue eyes. "You could stay, but the director is funny about visitors."

Gail nodded.

At the door, letting it close very slowly, she looked back. Thomas Nolan was crossing the room, and once again she sensed something familiar about him. Born in Miami. He was only a year older than she. She wondered when he had moved away. They might have met, but she could remember no tall blond boys with a talent for singing.

Gail found Rebecca in the lobby checking brochures that the young woman behind the reception desk was preparing to label and mail. The Opera Guild was sponsoring a program of lectures designed to pull in more donors.

Rebecca noticed Gail, smiled quickly at her, then told the girl to take messages, she would be in conference with Ms. Connor. Rebecca herself disappeared for a moment, then came back putting on her long white sweater. She pulled her shoulder-length hair free of the collar.

"Come with me, Gail. I need some fresh air." She unfolded a pair of tortoiseshell sunglasses.

Once past the double glass doors at the entrance, Gail said, "I'm going to recommend that you hire a security guard to patrol the building." She explained the latest from WRCL. "If it means anything," she added, "I spoke to your husband in the rehearsal room. He said he had no objection."

Rebecca frowned. "Why didn't you just ask me? Lloyd doesn't have anything to do with running the opera."

"Well, I'm sorry," Gail said. "But what about the security guard?"

"I don't know. I don't think I have the authority to hire people."

"Of course you do," Gail said. "The executive committee has the power to take emergency action. You're the president."

"I could call Jeffrey Hopkins," Rebecca finally said. "I'll see what he thinks, but Jeffrey is so tight with money."

They walked to the corner to cross four lanes of Biscayne Boulevard, then took one of the smaller streets that led toward the bay. The sky was blue and cloudless. A front had come through last night, leaving temperatures close to fifty. In the wool suit she had worn to court this morning, with a scarf at her neck, Gail was warm enough. The wind sailed a scrap of newspaper along the sidewalk. She was on the point of mentioning the investigation of Thomas Nolan when Rebecca spoke.

"Gail, I need some advice. Legal advice. Please don't tell anyone. Not even Anthony."

"As long as it doesn't involve him —"

"It's about Lloyd. Do you . . . handle divorces?"

"Oh, Rebecca. I'm so sorry. Are you sure?"

"I've been thinking about it for a while." The wind whirled Rebecca's hair across her face.

Gail said, "I do primarily commercial litigation. I could handle a divorce, but for this marriage, I'd recommend an expert. Isn't there any way you and Lloyd could work it out?"

The bright sunlight accented her sharp features — the thin nose and small pointed chin. "We aren't suited. We never were."

"You must have loved him at one time," Gail said.

A weary laugh came from Rebecca Dixon. "I'm going to say some things that I hope you will keep private. Do you know why I married him, Gail? Because I couldn't take care of myself. That's the truth. My first marriage failed because . . . well, I got into a little problem with pills. Nobody knew, because I managed to keep up appearances, but I felt like I was getting hollow, and that any minute I'd cave in. I cared but I didn't. It's hard to explain. Anyway, Lloyd came along. And Arthur? Well, he pretended to be shattered, and then he was gone. I really can't blame him. Lloyd took me to a clinic in England."

Gail remembered the story her mother had told her. It had been more than slightly inaccurate. "If you divorced Lloyd, what would you do?"

"Get out of Florida. Live in a small house. Read books and tend a garden."

Acorn caps crunched underfoot. They walked along a sidewalk that curved north, Miami Beach lying to the east, a causeway ahead of them. Small apartment buildings lined the inland side of the street.

"Rebecca, that sounds peaceful, but it isn't much of a life. You'd be bored in a week."

"I'd find something. I'm certainly not part of Lloyd's life. Except for music, we have nothing in common. We went to the opera in Moscow, and he left me in the hotel for three days. When he got back he had a cracked rib and a huge lump on his head. Lloyd just laughed about it and told me not to worry. He's out there having himself a grand old time. I can't deal with it anymore."

Gail let out a breath. "I see. Well, I'm going to give you the name of a friend who's an expert in marital law —"

"No, not yet. Let me think what I want to do. I'm not sure." She suddenly put a hand to her forehead, laughing at herself.

"Listen to me. I can't make up my mind about anything. Seth keeps telling me, Becky, leave him. You're in a swamp, get out. It's like someone shouting to you in a dream. It's impossible to move." The dark glasses turned toward Gail. "Seth and I have been friends for a long time. You know that, don't you? He said he talked to you."

"Yes." Gail let it go at that. Seth Greer had denied they were romantically involved, but she preferred not to ask. "Let me know what you decide to do. I'll help if I can."

They walked for a while, then Gail said, "I wanted to bring you up to date on Tom Nolan." She repeated what Nolan had told her about his trip to Cuba, and said that she didn't really believe it. The issue was beginning to hit the talk stations, and the opera had to know the truth.

"You can expect that soon the *Miami Herald* and the TV stations are going to come around asking for an interview. It would be embarrassing if our facts were wrong. That's why I'd like to hire an investigator. We should make Jeffrey Hopkins aware, so I'll be calling him in New York, with your approval."

"An investigator? I doubt Jeffrey would pay for it."

"No, Anthony's paying. He says it's his

gift to the opera."

"Well, hurrah," said Rebecca. "I thought he was deserting us entirely. Go ahead, then. Is Anthony finding somebody, or do we have to?"

Gail looked at her. "Didn't you talk to him? He said he would call you."

"I got a message yesterday and called back, but we've been missing each other. If he wanted to ask about the investigator, it's all right. Go ahead."

For a moment Gail hung on the edge of letting Anthony explain, but decided it didn't matter. "He told me about the trip to Nicaragua in 1978." Into the pause, Rebecca nodded. "The investigator is Felix Castillo. You met him there. He went back to Cuba, then came to Miami in 1980 in the Mariel boatlift. Anthony has used him on many criminal investigations. He's supposed to be quite good, and he still has contacts in Havana, so I have no doubt —"

She noticed that Rebecca had drifted to a stop.

"No doubt he can do the job, Rebecca?"

White-faced, Rebecca took hold of Gail's arm.

"Rebecca, are you all right?"

"Yes." She took several deep breaths. "I'm fine."

"I don't think so," Gail said.

"Really, I am. Let's go."

The street would curve around and come back out on the boulevard, so they kept walking. A gust of wind sent leaves and dust flying along the street. The debris whirled into a vortex, then vanished. Rebecca had recovered her firm, steady stride. Gail said, "Before I call the general director, I need to ask if you approve of Castillo. He'll want your opinion."

"Approve?" There was a hesitation. "I don't want to see Felix Castillo or hear from him. Otherwise . . . all right. Call Jeffrey. Tell him it's necessary."

"Look, if there's some problem with Castillo, what is it? If I'm going to be working with him, give me a clue."

Rebecca made a dismissive wave of her hand. "Felix is all right. I just don't like being reminded."

"Of what?"

That brought a smile. The wind blew from behind them, and her hair danced around her face. "Oh, this is priceless. He hasn't told you a damn thing, has he? Felix was in Nicaragua with us."

"I know."

"Oh, you do. Have you ever seen a bloated body lying in the open? I have. It was horrible. We got out of there as soon as we could. It was hard because we had no transportation. Try hitchhiking in a situation like that. You just don't know who's going to pick you up. You should have seen us. We looked like guerrillas! Picture me — right? — in men's cutoff army pants and a filthy T-shirt with my hair cut short. Anthony spoke Spanish fluently, so he managed to steal or beg food. We slept anywhere we could. On the ground if we had to. And God, the rain! I was so exhausted. We all were, and sick of each other, but Anthony said he would leave us if we stopped. And he would have, too.

"Seth and I don't talk about it anymore, but in a strange way, it holds us together. When I was in that clinic in England, I told Lloyd about it. I wish I hadn't. I would like to forget it ever happened. Anyway. There we all were again last Friday, Seth and Anthony and me in the same room — I didn't sleep at all that night. The bones were rising from the earth." She tossed her hair back from her face and laughed again. "In a manner of speaking."

Stopped in the middle of the sidewalk, they looked at each other.

"Gail, your eyes are as big as saucers." Before Gail could respond, Rebecca spun around and headed up the sidewalk. "Come on. Let's go back. I have things to do."

As they pushed open the glass door, Gail heard the excited babble of voices. The receptionist was bent over her knees on the sofa, red-faced and crying. Irene was trying to calm her down, and two other women argued back and forth about whether or not to call the police. The girl said this was too much, she was scared, she wanted to go home.

"What happened?" Gail said to Irene.

"Another phone call. The third one in the last fifteen minutes."

Rushing to the sofa, Rebecca sat down in a whirl of white cashmere and took the girl's hands. "What did they say? Tell me."

"It was in Spanish. He's going to kill me, kill all of us. We should die!" From the reception desk the phone started ringing, and the girl jumped. "*No quiero contestarlo.* Somebody else answer it. I can't."

"Bastards," Gail muttered. "Bastards!" On the next ring she grabbed for it, her heart thudding. "Miami Opera . . . Just a moment, please." She released a breath, then held the receiver out to her mother. "It's for you, returning your call about the tour for the high school."

Irene said she would take it in the other room. Her blue eyes snapped with anger, and she marched off, business as usual, her little pumps pounding on the tile floor.

Gail took Rebecca aside. "We were discussing a security guard. You might consider changing your mind."

Wearily Rebecca nodded, then asked the other women to answer the phones while she got some estimates from security companies. She said to the receptionist, "We'll have someone here from now on, just in case. You can come back tomorrow if you want, and I'll make sure you get paid for today."

The young woman said she was all right now. She returned to her chair and began stamping envelopes where she had left off.

NINE

After dinner on Friday, Karen said she would teach Anthony to play Spit while Gail took a shower. Wearing jeans and a long T-shirt, Gail came back through the kitchen to make some coffee. She heard the sound of cards snapping onto a table in the family room.

Karen's voice said, "If I had my own stereo, then I wouldn't have to be in here making noise when you and Mom want to talk."

Anthony replied, "You aren't a bother."

"Well, she tells me all the time to turn it down. If I had a stereo in my room, then I could listen to music in there, and you guys could be out here."

Gail peered around the corner. Anthony sat forward on the edge of the sofa, and Karen was cross-legged on a floor pillow, the coffee table between them. Karen's sun-streaked hair hung down her back. Her thin arm flashed back and forth, dropping cards, picking them up.

"The problem is, Mom won't get me one. She says I have to pay for it myself."

"I see." Anthony shuffled through the

cards in his hand. "You have an allowance, no?"

"Ten dollars a week. It would take *forever*."

"What about your chores in the house?"

"She won't give me any money at all unless *everything* is done. I want to start a corporation and do odd jobs for people."

"Like what?"

"I could wash car windows. I could wash the windows in your car."

"Well, I'm very particular." Anthony snapped down a card. So did Karen, then another. "It has to be a good job. How much do you charge?"

"Those are pretty big windows. Plus the sunroof."

"What about . . . five dollars. Two extra for the chrome."

"Okay. Next time you're here, I'll do it." Karen suddenly shrieked and bounced on the pillow. "Spit! Spit!"

Anthony tossed his cards and moved a quarter across the table.

Gail leaned over to kiss Karen on top of the head. "Time to get ready for bed, sweetie."

"Mom! It's Friday!"

"And we're having an early breakfast at Gramma's house. Go on, brush your teeth,

I'll be right there."

"I have no life," she muttered. She dropped the playing cards into their box and scraped some quarters and dimes into her palm.

Anthony reached across the table to pat her cheek. "Good night, Karen."

"Night." Then an angelic smile appeared. She came around the table and kissed him on the cheek. *"Buenas noches."* She bounced off the sofa and skipped toward the hall.

Watching her go, Gail said quietly, "I heard that little conversation about your car windows. Be careful. She wants her own phone, too."

"Karen says she's going out with a boy at school. I didn't want to say anything to her. Did you know this?"

"His name is Bobby."

"She's only ten years old."

"Listen, 'going out' means sitting together at lunch and calling each other on the phone. You hear these long silences, but neither one wants to be the first to hang up. It's perfectly innocent."

"I guess so."

"I'll be back in a minute."

He stopped her with a slow smile and a tug on the hem of her Miami Hurricanes T-shirt. "Put something else on."

"What's the matter, you're not a 'Canes fan?"

Of course she knew what he meant. After tucking Karen in, Gail changed into a soft cotton dress that buttoned up the front. She put a touch of perfume at the low neckline.

When she came back, Anthony was listening to the radio so intently he didn't notice she was behind him. It wasn't music but a talk show in Spanish, the volume turned so low Gail had not heard it until she came into the room. The thin voice of an older man said, *"Repugnante . . . un insulto a la comunidad cubana."*

Then the host replied. Gail recognized the voice immediately: Octavio Reyes. His convoluted sentences made translation difficult. Yes, an insult to permit a man to sing who has performed for the dictatorship. *Arrogancia.* The arrogance of the Miami opera not to — not to —

"Anthony, what is he saying?" He looked quickly around. "No, don't turn it off. What's he saying?"

"He says the opera and its supporters arrogantly refuse to acknowledge the suffering of our people — meaning the people in Cuba."

The two of them looked at the blue digital display as if Reyes's face might appear. Gail had seen him at Ernesto Pedrosa's house, once at a family dinner and more recently on Christmas Eve. Gail remembered an expensive suit, silver-rimmed glasses, and steel-gray hair combed back from his forehead.

Another call. *"Buenas noches, está en el aire."*

"Octavio?"

"Sí, señora, está en el WRCL. Adelante."

"Que barbaridad, que la opera invitó a una persona comunista a nuestra ciudad."

"Estoy de acuerdo, señora —"

Anthony hit a button and the room went silent. He continued to stare at the radio.

Gail murmured, "Such a barbarity, the opera inviting a communist to our city. Does he truly believe Tom Nolan is a *communist?*"

"Well, their definition of communist is fairly broad. It can mean anyone who supports the regime of Fidel Castro in any way." Anthony glanced at Gail. "Does Octavio believe Nolan fits that definition? I don't know. But he is patriotic, so he will use it."

"Strange definition of patriotism," Gail said.

"In a war," Anthony said, "to yield one inch is to lose everything. It's what we call 'noble intransigence.' The struggle to liberate Cuba comes before anything."

"Like your grandfather," she said.

"Precisely."

"I'm not sure," Gail said, "whether Octavio is principled or just ambitious. I suspect that if I weren't involved with the opera, and you weren't engaged to me, he would find some other issue to hammer on. I do regret that."

"Don't let it bother you," Anthony said.

"It's hard not to. He's putting a knife between your ribs. I know you don't care about inheriting your grandfather's businesses, but he could alienate you from your family. That's what concerns me. I know how much they mean to you." She put her arms around his waist. "I love you. They'll be my family, too."

He kissed her forehead. "Don't worry. Ernesto is too smart to fall for Octavio's bullshit."

"He's almost eighty-four years old," she reminded him.

"So hard to believe. I never thought of my grandfather growing old, and now he has. I don't want to think about it."

"Then I guess we'll just have to find something else to do."

Gail turned off the torchiere, leaving the soft light of a smaller lamp across the room.

When she came back to him, Anthony finally noticed what she was wearing. His eyes moved slowly over her body, then up to her face. *"Ay, tú estás pa' comer."*

Holding his face, she stroked her thumb across his mouth. *"Te quiero."*

He bit the end of her thumb before she could pull it out of the way. *"Yo te quiero más."* I love you more.

She wanted to go for his buckle, but settled for a kiss deep enough to make her dizzy. He would spend the night, but until Karen was soundly asleep, he would not go near Gail's bedroom.

They brought their coffee to the sofa. With a long exhalation, Anthony slumped into a pillow and closed his eyes. He had delivered final arguments in a manslaughter trial this morning, but the jury had not come back with a verdict. They would resume deliberations on Monday.

Her head on his shoulder, Gail said, "Tell the truth. How will your grandparents feel about my being at the party tomorrow night? Not just me. Karen, my mother, my aunt, my cousins —"

"They're looking forward to it. The opera or Thomas Nolan will not be mentioned. I promise." He picked up his mug from the end table.

"I've wanted to talk to you all week," she said.

"If you would make up your mind about a house," he said, "we could get married, and then we could talk every night."

"Me? Make up *my* mind?" Gail smoothed her hand down the front of his collarless black pullover, tucked into pleated gray wool slacks, which were belted with snakeskin. "Anthony, tell me about Nicaragua."

"Why?"

"You said you would."

"Did I say when?"

"Stop acting like a defense attorney," she said. "I talked to Rebecca Dixon Wednesday. She said it was horrible. She saw bodies. Bones rising from the earth. That's awfully grim."

Anthony sipped his coffee. "Yes, it was. I don't want to ruin our evening with it."

"What was Rebecca talking about?"

"We saw dead people. I told you that. It's a long story."

"Just give me the short version. Ten minutes."

"Gail, please. Not tonight."

"How long do you plan to avoid it?"

The sharpness in his tone startled her. "I am tired. I did not come here to get into a discussion about events that occurred twenty years ago, that do not matter to me, to you, or to anyone. I am not in the mood."

Slowly she sat up straight. "Fine. Then leave if you're in such a pissy mood."

They stared at each other. Color flooded into his cheeks, and his lips were pressed together so hard they turned white. Then he gave a shrug and stretched his arm toward the end table.

"If you put that coffee cup down, I swear to God I will break it over your head."

The mug hug suspended. He said, "Okay. I'm not leaving." It clunked softly onto the table.

"Dave and I —" Gail took a shaky breath. "Dave and I stopped talking to each other. It didn't happen immediately, and at first we hardly noticed, but then it became a habit, and one day our marriage was over. I don't want that to happen to us. I refuse to allow it." Anthony was frowning at the mug, positioning it just so. "It isn't Nicaragua I care about. It's you. Whatever you saw there had an effect. It's part of you, and I want to know what happened."

After a long silence, Anthony began to speak.

"Seth Greer knew a priest from Nicaragua who had come to the U.S. to do fund-raising and recruit volunteers to help build schools and clinics. He passed through Miami and we spoke with him. He was a sincere and charismatic man, and we decided immediately to join his movement. Seth wanted to bring social justice to Central America. I wanted to strike a blow against Yankee capitalist oppression." He laughed softly. "That was the view I'd grown up with in Cuba — what my father taught me. I breathed it in the air.

"After the semester was over, we took a flight the next day for Managua. The city was still in ruins from the earthquake in 1972 — a very poor city surrounded by slums. Whoever was to meet us at the airport never showed up, so we had to find our own way to Los Pozos, about a hundred miles north into Jinotega province."

As she listened, Gail remembered things Anthony had already told her about himself. His decision to work in Nicaragua could not be understood otherwise.

Anthony had told her that he had grown up believing that he was part of a great change in human history.

Luis Quintana, a decorated hero of the revolution, had told his son that there would be no more inequality between the races and the sexes. No discrimination, no poverty. Teachers poured into the countryside, educating the peasants. Clinics were built. People referred to each other as compañero — comrade. There were ration coupons, but no one minded. For the first time, Cuba would be free. But always on the horizon were the exiles, backed by the Americans, preparing to invade. "I remember the missile crisis in 1962. Everyone was terrified that we might die in a nuclear explosion. My sister Marta watched the sea with binoculars. The entire country was mobilized."

In the Young Pioneers Anthony learned to take a rifle apart and put it back together. He marched. With the other boys, he jeered at the non-communist teachers expelled from the school. At twelve he went willingly to the countryside to do agricultural work, slept in barracks on jute mattresses, rose at dawn, and ate bread and sugared water before going off to the fields. He missed his father and sister, but was too much of a man to complain. He heard some of the others crying at night.

His mother had taken the two youngest children, leaving Anthony and Marta behind. His father said, She abandoned you. Caridad was a gusana, una traidora — a worm, a traitor — and her father Ernesto Pedrosa was a monster.

At fourteen Anthony would have been admitted to the Young Communist League — if he had not been attending junior high school in Miami. If he had not been tricked — or rescued — out of Cuba. Which was correct? The boy soldier kidnapped and imprisoned far from home, or the young prince saved by the king? They could not both be true. Or perhaps they were — depending on who told the tale.

Why had he boarded that DC-6 to Miami? Because he wanted to ask his mother why she had left. This had never been explained, since Luis had destroyed all her letters. Perhaps Pedrosa had forced her to go. In that case, Anthony would persuade her to come home. If she refused, then he would confront her with her selfishness. Luis, hospitalized for old wounds, knew nothing about it. Anthony had been told he would be on a return flight within a week.

He knew, walking out of customs at the Miami airport, seeing his mother run toward him, weeping, that his father had lied: She had never stopped loving him. In the next moment he saw the other lie: They had never intended to let him go home.

Anthony said, "When I was young, I

thought my father was a hero, but he was only a man. Not a hero. Patriotic, yes, but he turned in his own brother for selling food on the black market. He cheated without remorse on my mother. He said to me, a man isn't a man unless he has women. My grandfather was not that way. When I was fifteen he took me into his study and lectured me about women. His ideas sounded so old-fashioned. You must never betray your God, your country, or your wife. I might have laughed if he hadn't spoken with such sincerity. He was — is — a man of great strength. Unfortunately, like my father, he can see only one side of things."

This was the same study where late one night, passing by with a sandwich, Anthony had heard men's voices through the heavy door. He listened. They were jubilant about having blown up a radio transmitter in Pinar del Rio.

Expulsion from this house sent him not back to Cuba but into limbo — an outcast among the exiles. He found shelter with two friends, Seth and Rebecca.

"We took a bus to La Vigia, then hitch-hiked the rest of the way. Los Pozos is a small village in the hills, very remote. The tops of the hills are covered in mist and rain, and the earth is red. Tremors are common, but after a while you get used to them. The weather is similar to ours in the summer. The sky is very blue, then it fills up with heavy gray clouds. The foliage is tropical and green, except where the farmers have cleared the land."

Gail could see the countryside as if looking at a series of snapshots. Dirt paths winding up the hills to tin-roofed shacks. Men in straw cowboy hats tending thin cattle. Women with long black hair. A little girl in a ruffled dress, no shoes. In the town, dusty streets and decaying red tile roofs. Banana leaves drooping in the rain.

"The organizer of the volunteer effort showed us what to do, then pretty much left us on our own. Seth and I were expecting to build a school, but there wasn't much to work with. We paid for lumber ourselves, expecting to be reimbursed. Rebecca worked in the clinic, which had no doctor, only a nurse. It was one room with six iron beds in it, no screens on the windows, and hardly any supplies or drugs."

For a while Anthony was silent, the empty mug in his hands. He leaned over to put it on the coffee table, then sat with his elbows on his knees.

"There were four of us, not three. A girl

named Emily Davis came with us. I had met her at the university. We were dating."

"You took your girlfriend along?"

He nodded. "She was twenty years old, a music student. Not exactly what you need on a trip to rural Central America, but she wanted to go with me. Seth was taking Rebecca, but at least she had a skill to offer. I told Emily she could teach English. You see how unrealistic we were. Teach English in two or three months to people who couldn't even read or write in Spanish.

"We lived about a mile outside Los Pozos in a house that belonged to the church. It had a tin roof and concrete block walls painted turquoise, but the paint was faded and mildewed. The beds were folding army cots. On the wall was a framed print of Mary and one of Jesus with his heart in flames. Roosters would crow every morning outside the window. We had no plumbing, but there was a well. *'Pozos'* means 'wells,' so at least we had plenty of fresh water. Anyway, it was not what we had expected, but we did the best we could, and for a while we were happy with our efforts. The people appreciated it. That helped.

"But I didn't go there to pick up a hammer. As soon as we had settled in and knew who was who, I sought out the rebels. I was twenty-two years old, bigger than most of the men there, in excellent physical condition, and very sure of myself. In Miami I kept a rifle and a revolver in my room, and I knew how to use them. I had studied Che, Fidel, Fanon, Marx, Lenin, the American and European leftists. Freedom would only come about by force — so I believed at the time — and I was ready to join in the fight.

"There weren't many Sandinistas in that area — maybe fifty. The leader's name was Pablo. He was a few years older than I. He'd been in Cuba — there was a Sandinista training camp there, as well as one in Honduras. He was clever and educated — to some extent. He had a small library with books I'd studied, and we talked late into the night on many occasions. Most of his men were young and very poor. As uniforms they wore whatever they could find — usually surplus U.S. Army camouflage. Some of them carried bandoliers of mortar shells or rifle cartridges over their chests, and they put heavy weapons on burros or horses. To be a Sandinista, you took an oath of allegiance to Augusto Sandino and Che Guevara with your hand on the black-and-red banner. *Patria libre o muerte.* You don't even think of dying. Or you don't say so."

Gail looked wonderingly at Anthony, who

still sat with his elbows on his knees, hands loosely clasped. "You joined the Sandinistas?"

He laughed. "No. Pablo wouldn't have trusted me that far, but I felt like one of them. I even looked like a guerrilla." He stood up and spread his arms. "You should have seen me. Twenty-two years old, long hair and a beard, a sleeveless T-shirt and camouflage pants, and black boots. In the forest I carried an AK-47 that Felix Castillo lent me. And I smoked. What a tough guy."

She smiled up at him. "All you need is a sheen of sweat and a bandanna around your head, like Rambo."

"Oh, we sweated a lot in that weather." Anthony's arms fell to his sides. "The rebels let me near them only because Felix vouched for me. I was a *'norteamericano.'* It was funny being thought of like that. I felt Cuban with Felix. We talked about home. I expected him to say it was still the paradise I remembered, but he said that if he had the chance, he would be in my shoes, living in Miami. We were both drunk when we had this conversation, otherwise he wouldn't have been so open. He told me about the prisons and what he had seen inside them. He didn't know anymore if it was right. The revolution was right, he was sure of that, but something had changed. Anyway, he wanted to get out of the country for a while, so he came to Nicaragua. I ignored most of what he said about Cuba because he was getting old and tired — he was almost thirty.

"Meanwhile our group from Miami was having problems. There were things going on among us — jealousy and resentment. Seth complained because I wouldn't take him along with me and Felix. He was older and he thought of himself as our group leader. He and Rebecca were constantly in fights. She was a feminist, and in Los Pozos a man didn't take shit from a woman. Rebecca and Emily hated each other. Emily complained about everything — the heat, the food, the people. She wanted to go home, but we didn't have the money for a flight back to Miami, and no way to get her to Managua. We expected any day to be repaid for the lumber we had bought, and I told Emily she had to wait."

He took some time putting his thoughts together. He glanced at the doorway through which Karen might come, if she were awake, but no one was there. The house was quiet. Down the street a dog barked. Then nothing.

"About six weeks after we arrived, government troops started searching the area for rebels, questioning the farmers. We found bodies of people who had disappeared. People we knew. Some had been covered over with a thin layer of dirt, others were dumped in the weeds along the road. But then things were quiet for a while, and we got on with building the school as best we could with some of the local men helping us on the project. One day we heard that the National Guard had hit the camp where the Sandinistas stored their weapons. Eleven rebels were killed, and half a dozen were captured. A few days later their bodies were dumped in the road to La Vigia. They had been tortured and castrated before being shot."

Gail closed her eyes. When she opened them, Anthony was looking at her. "Do you want me to finish now? Or later."

"No. I want to hear everything now."

He said, "La Vigia was about ten miles away. Not large, maybe two thousand people. Emily and Rebecca would go there once a week to shop, catching a ride with a farmer. Rebecca said that she had seen Emily talking to a known CIA operative in the market. These people were usually peasants who were paid to inform, and they would have informed on their own brothers, but in this case, the man was an American. It seemed clear that she had obtained information from one of us or one of Pablo's men she had talked to, then passed it to the CIA. We confronted her, and she denied talking to anyone in La Vigia. Rebecca was furious and hit her. Then Emily said she didn't know the man was CIA. By then we didn't believe anything she told us.

"I don't remember how Pablo heard about it. I don't know, but late the next day he came to the house with some of his men. It was raining, and we were inside waiting for it to stop. Emily saw them and went into the bedroom to hide. Pablo asked me what she had done. I was going to tell some lie, but Seth was afraid of what Pablo would do to us. For a few minutes there was total chaos. Rebecca was cursing at Seth, and I was telling them both to shut up. Pablo sent one of his men into the bedroom to bring Emily out, then he sat her in a chair and he asked her what had happened. She was crying, but he was very calm. He just asked, like a father would ask a child. She told him that she had wanted to get back to Miami, and that the man had promised that the next time she went to La Vigia, there would be a ticket waiting for her at the hotel.

"It was still raining. I remember the noise

on the tin roof, and how it came off the edge of the porch in streams. The yard was muddy with red dirt. Pablo took her out there and made her kneel. Then he shot her in the back of the head."

Anthony had his forehead in his palms. Staring at the floor between his feet. Gail leaned on his shoulder.

"Oh, no," she whispered. Her lips barely moved. "Oh my God."

"They gave us some shovels, and Pablo told us to bury her in the woods behind the house. Deep, so the rain wouldn't wash the dirt away. There was one man guarding us with an M-14. The sides kept caving in because of the rain, but we managed to get it about four feet deep. Rebecca wiped off Emily's face and closed her eyes. Then we lifted her in. It was beginning to get dark. We worked slowly filling in the grave, and somehow Seth sensed what I wanted to do. He pretended to fall, drawing the man's attention, and then . . . I used my shovel.

"We ran into the woods, going north because they would expect us to head in the other direction. We had nothing with us, no money, not even our passports. We went as far as we could, then rested for a while and ran again until it was too dark to see. At first light we crossed a river, and I submerged to get the dirt and blood out of my clothes and my hair. I think that was the only time I cried, and I remember thinking, *Stop it. Don't do this or we won't make it out of here.* It took a week to reach Managua. Sometimes we found a ride. Usually we walked, and we begged food where we could. At a small hotel on the outskirts of the city I found a telephone and called Miami collect. This was the strangest thing. My grandfather himself answered it in his study. I told him where I was. He told me to wait there. Within an hour — one hour — we were picked up in a Cadillac and driven to a house in a wealthy district of Managua. We were given rooms and baths and food and fresh clothing. Three days later we were in Miami on new passports. One of my grandfather's employees met us at the airport. He dropped off Seth and Rebecca where they wanted to go and he took me home."

Looking around at Gail, Anthony said, "You know, that was the first time Miami felt like home. It did. Like you see in the movies, I wanted to fall on my knees and kiss the ground."

Gail put her arms around him. "Are you all right?"

He laughed softly. "After twenty years, I think so."

"I mean . . . talking about it. I didn't know it was so bad," she said. "I wouldn't have asked if I'd known."

"No, you would have asked. You're like Pandora."

"How did you explain Emily's death?"

"Another question. You see?"

She leaned on his arm. "I just wondered."

"It's okay. Emily had lived with her aunt. Her mother was dead, and she hadn't seen her father for many years, so that made it easier. I couldn't do it immediately because I was in the hospital for two weeks with pneumonia, but when I recovered I went to see Emily's aunt. And you know, she accepted it completely, the story I gave her. We had decided what to say before we left Managua. Emily had fallen in love with one of the men in Los Pozos. We pleaded with her to come with us, but she refused. And that was the last we saw of her.

"Her aunt said she wasn't surprised. After all, Emily had fallen for me, a Cuban, and she had been warned. It was funny, in a way. This woman's prejudice saved me. Of course we should have told the truth, but a lie was easier. It was all we had the strength for."

"Did you ever tell your grandfather what really happened?"

"There was no reason to. I caught enough hell from him just being there, and having to be rescued from the Sandinistas." Anthony smiled. "He said I was an idiot, a fool, that I had caused pain to my mother, to the entire Pedrosa family to the end of time, et cetera and so on, and he hoped I had learned my lesson. Of course I didn't humiliate myself further by agreeing with him. That was the last time we talked about it. Or about much of anything."

After a while he said, "You can ask Seth and Rebecca about Los Pozos if you want."

"I won't ask them," Gail said. "I've heard what I needed to know."

He closed his eyes and rested his forehead on hers. "I think we should go to bed now."

TEN

The out-of-town relatives stayed the weekend with Gail's mother, who found room for all of them — Irene's sister and brother-in-law from Tampa; their daughter, in her twenties; Gail's cousin from Atlanta and her husband; and an elderly aunt from Ohio who said she had always wanted to meet some Cubans in person. At breakfast on Saturday morning she produced a Berlitz phrase book for travelers. *Me llamo Doris. ¿Cómo está usted?*

Gail's cousins hid their smiles behind coffee cups while Irene told her aunt not to worry: Anthony's family could speak English — except for a few older people who found the language impossible. Aunt Doris could try out her Spanish on them. Gail sent Karen to get the C volume of the encyclopedia from the study, then showed everyone the map. Here is Havana. There is Camagüey, where Anthony spent most of his childhood. But don't bring that up. Gail told them about the situation at the opera, and told them not to bring that up either. Don't talk about politics. Don't mention

Castro or the embargo. Talk about music or food. The weather in Miami. Sports.

Gail and Karen went home to get dressed. Wrapped in a towel from her shower, Gail took her black dress out of the closet. Was it too short? What else could she wear? Nothing red, nothing sparkly or tight. But nothing dowdy or plain. Anthony had to like it. She finished her hair and makeup, then went to check on Karen. She found her sitting on the edge of the bed in panties and camisole, watching TV. Her hair, which Gail had put into a French braid, now hung in her eyes. What have you *done?* Gail turned off the TV while Karen explained that her scalp had felt funny, and why couldn't she just wear her hair like always — straight? Fine. The dress was laid out on the bed — blue velvet with short sleeves and a silk rose at the neck. Do I have to wear that? I hate velvet. That flower is stupid. And the shoes hurt my feet. They're size seven already! I'm going to be huge! Gail took several deep breaths. All right, then. Wear what you want. No jeans. No sneakers.

She went to the kitchen and poured herself a glass of wine. Back in her bedroom, she pushed hangers back and forth for ten minutes, then came out with the same slim black dress she had already chosen. She put on black hose and pumps, simple gold earrings and a necklace, a touch of perfume, and that was that. She knocked lightly at Karen's door. Karen was putting on her new dress. I still hate it, she said. Gail brushed her hair until it turned to silk, then tied it back with a ribbon.

The relatives arrived at her house at six-thirty, and Anthony arrived shortly thereafter, his car purring into the driveway. Gail felt a little rush of pleasure opening the front door, seeing his eyes sweep over her. His kiss on her lips said more than hello. She brought him inside. There were handshakes. Smiles all around. Gail's female cousins blushed when he spoke to them. He noticed Karen's dress — *¡Que linda!* Karen rolled her eyes, then flipped her hair back over her shoulders and sat primly with her ankles crossed. There was silence, then Bill, the relative from Atlanta, asked, So, how about the Miami Heat this year? They finished a bottle of wine and a tray of hors d'oeuvres. Gail had told them earlier, Eat something before you go, because dinner will be served late.

When their three cars arrived at the Pedrosa house in Coral Gables, the circular drive was already full, so they parked along the wall and walked through the old iron-work gates. Irene's sister Patsy noticed the arches and twisted Moorish columns along the front porch. Coming nearer the entrance, they could hear laughter and conversation from within. Anthony opened the door.

Through the foyer with its polished tile floor, then into the living room. People everywhere. Children running around, no one telling them to hush. Anthony's grand-mother came forward with her arms out. The new arrivals were pulled inside, coats were taken. A blur of introductions. Alejandro, Xiomara, Betty, Marielena, José, Humberto — Handshakes and kisses on the cheek. The right cheek, Gail had explained beforehand. And don't be surprised if the children kiss you, too.

Then taken to meet Ernesto Pedrosa. He sat in a big leather chair at the opposite end of the room, dressed formally in suit and tie, thin silk socks and shiny black shoes. He broke off his conversation with the two men who had pulled up chairs beside him. As he looked around, the lights flickered in his glasses. His gaze fixed on Anthony.

Anthony leaned down to kiss his grand-father, but there was no hearty *abrazo*. Pedrosa steadied himself on his cane.

Anthony's hand automatically went out, but the old man got up on his own. He smiled at Gail and lifted her hand to his lips. Held an arm out to Irene, then patted Karen's cheek.

The relatives were introduced to him. Doris, Patsy, Kyle, Dawn, Ashley, Bill — Happy Birthday, *Señor* Pedrosa. What a lovely home. Pleased to meet you, sir. Aunt Doris said, *Feliz cumpleaños.* They set their gifts on a table already covered with them. Irene gave Digna perfect pink roses in a Baccarat vase and Digna placed them on the mantel over the fireplace.

Pedrosa beamed at the faces gathered around him. "*Bienvenidos, todos.* My wife wanted this to be a surprise party. It is. I am surprised to be here at all. I feel so good tonight, maybe one of these ladies will dance with me."

Earlier at Irene's house, Gail had told the story of this man, who longed to return to a home that was no longer there. The youngest daughter, Caridad, falling in love with the son of peasants. Luis joining the rebels in the Sierra Maestra. The war, the exile, a family torn apart. Pedrosa's only son killed at the Bay of Pigs. Caridad's early death. Of her four children, one refused to leave Havana. The others were here: Anthony, Alicia, and the youngest, Eduardo, brain-damaged at birth.

Gail had omitted the part about Pedrosa having been investigated by the FBI. His ties to the CIA that supposedly saved him from indictment. His membership in exile groups alleged to have run raids into Cuba, set bombs in Miami, and targeted traitors who wanted dialogue with Castro. This had been many years ago. Nor had Gail told her relatives about the estrangement between Pedrosa and his oldest grandson.

Karen was twirling on the heel of her shoe. Her dress belled out. She stopped suddenly, caught herself, then at a break in the conversation stood directly in front of Pedrosa. He looked down at her.

"I have a joke for you," she said.

"A joke?" He straightened his glasses.

"I told you a joke when I was here at Christmas, and you said you wanted me to tell you another one when I came back."

"All right. Tell me the joke." Pedrosa leaned on his cane, tilting his head to favor his good ear.

Karen laughed behind her hands, then cleared her throat and spoke seriously. "If you're an American when you go into the bathroom, and an American when you come out of the bathroom, what are you when you're in the bathroom?"

Gail cringed. Anthony smiled and shook his head. There were giggles from the children.

Pedrosa took a breath. "Hmm. American when I go in . . . and when I come out." Finally a sigh. "I don't know. What am I, when I'm in the bathroom?"

"European!" Karen laughed in her high voice. "Get it?"

From Pedrosa came a soft chuckle. "Yes, I get it." He wagged his finger at her. "A good joke. You have another one for me next time. All right?"

"Okay. Mom, can I go play video games?"

"Please do," Gail said softly. "Be good."

"Bye!" She sped off with the other girls, her new shoes skidding when she took the corner.

Pedrosa was still chuckling. "I heard that one fifty years ago."

Alicia asked if Gail's family would like to see the house. Anthony said for Gail to go with them, if she wished. He would sit with his brother awhile. Eduardo recognized him, smiled, and leaned on his shoulder.

Carrying glasses of champagne, Gail and her relatives followed Alicia into the formal dining room, then the long hallway. She showed them the works of exile artists that her grandfather collected. Then his study, the desk facing toward Havana, and over it, an old Cuban flag torn by bullets. Down a corridor to the kitchen, where the caterers were finishing dinner. Something sizzled on the stove, sending up a cloud of steam. The enclosed terrace had been turned into a party room, decorated with candles and flowers. Balloons soared from a chair at the head table. Outside on the patio, Alicia pointed out the old coral rock fish pond. Over there, the guest house. The gardener had worked for the family in Havana, Alicia explained. Past that wall is the golf course.

In a low voice, Dawn's husband Bill asked if this house would be Anthony's someday. Dawn whispered, How romantic. Pleasantly embarrassed, Gail shook her head.

They came back in, and Alicia took them up the broad staircase to the second floor. A look at the upstairs gallery, then into Digna's sitting room. Other doors opened off the hall. Gail knew which room had been Anthony's. When they had come here for *nochebuena,* he had showed her. A small room, simply furnished. He had trailed his hand over the desk. Then had stood at the window, looking out.

Downstairs after the tour Gail saw two men in tuxedos tuning their classical guitars in the dining room. Their music would be Anthony's gift to his grandfather. Gail went to find him. Passing the foyer, she felt cold air on her legs. The front door was open, perhaps to let out some of the heat. From outside came the low murmur of male voices. She walked onto the porch, lit dimly by a row of small lamps affixed to the columns.

Her eyes adjusted. Some of the men had come out here to smoke. One had his back to her. The voices were low, and in Cuban Spanish besides, with the consonants blurred and the endings of words lopped off. She couldn't pick up enough of it to make sense, and didn't recognize Anthony's voice.

One of them noticed her and said something. The man with his back to the door turned around. Octavio Reyes. Gail had wondered where he'd been lurking. He had the dark complexion and broad body of a man who might have once worked with his hands, but now ate a little too well. He watched her as she walked closer.

"Hi. I was looking for Anthony. He's not here, is he?" She crossed her bare arms, shivering a little.

"No, he isn't." Octavio Reyes said to the others, "This is Gail Connor, the attorney for Thomas Nolan." Throwing down the gauntlet already, she thought. The other four said nothing.

"I am not Thomas Nolan's attorney," she said slowly. "I am the attorney for the Miami Opera. Look, Octavio, I came over here to say hello, not to get into a debate. We have different opinions. I'd love to discuss them with you, but not tonight. This is Ernesto Pedrosa's birthday, and the announcement of my engagement — which you are aware of — to Anthony, who is . . . somewhere inside." She let out a breath and backed up a few steps. "Great to meet you guys."

"No, don't leave." Reyes put down his drink. "I have a suggestion, Gail. Be a guest on my radio show. Let's discuss our opinions on the air. If I am wrong about Thomas Nolan, then tell me."

"Sorry, I don't speak Spanish."

"I have translators. You could say whatever you want. I'm not trying to keep Nolan from singing here in Miami. Not at all. This is a free country. I agree with the Bill of Rights. I believe in freedom of speech. I want the people to know who he is and what he did, and then they can make up their own minds."

Gail retorted, "And meanwhile we've had to hire a security guard. We're getting death threats. That's not my understanding of free speech."

"Do you listen to my show? If you did, you would hear me say to my audience, You have a right to protest, but not to use violence." Octavio Reyes looked around at his friends, laughing as if he couldn't believe this woman could be so dense. "If Thomas Nolan were a Nazi, the Jews in Miami would have the right to speak out. Wouldn't they? If he were in the Ku Klux Klan, you would allow the blacks to complain about it. They have this right. Why don't I get the same freedom to say what I believe?"

She laughed. "That is the most self-serving, tortured piece of logic —"

The men stared at her. One flicked his cigarette ashes off the edge of the porch.

Gail took a breath. "Let's drop it. Forgive me for interrupting your conversation." Walking away, she heard a few low chuckles behind her. "Screw you," she muttered under her breath. She leaned on the foyer wall until her heartbeat was back to normal, reminding herself that Reyes was only a furniture salesman, for God's sake. He sold cheap furniture at discount shopping malls.

Then she heard a laugh. A comment, not

from Reyes. They were talking about her. She didn't know what it meant, but *la chica* could only be one person. Silently Gail moved past the door but stopped short of the column where the wall turned right. One of the men asking another what he thought.

Reyes laughed. *"Tortillera. Que Anthony se entere antes de la boda."*

More laughter. Hoping that Anthony found out before the wedding. Found out what?

Gail heard the tinkle of ice cubes, as if Reyes were taking a sip of his drink. Then a string of words, barely audible. Then he became indignant. *"Es una ñángara de basura."*

Another voice. *"No lo creo. Que va."* The man didn't believe it, whatever it was.

Reyes again. *"Increíble que ella venga aquí, a esta casa. Que insulto."* An insult that she comes here, to this house.

You son of a bitch, Gail thought. Cowardly bastard.

She heard the light, quick tap of shoes on the tile floor behind her. "Mom!"

Whirling around, Gail clamped a hand over Karen's mouth. She pulled her away from the door. "Shhhh." Karen's eyes were wide. Gail let her go.

"What did you do that for?" Karen whispered.

"Never mind."

"Who's outside?"

"I said never mind." They walked into the living room, Gail smiling at people whose names she had totally forgotten. To Karen she said, "What did you want, sweetie?"

"Anthony sent me to find you. The guitarists are here."

She led Gail to the party room, where Ernesto Pedrosa was being given a chair in front. The guitarists sat by the windows, the curve of the guitars resting on their knees. Gail saw her relatives among the crowd and waved back when they smiled at her. She found Anthony standing to one side and stood on tiptoe to kiss the back of his neck. He looked around. "Ah, there you are. I thought you had run away."

Gail whispered, "Your grandfather seems so happy. It's a perfect gift for him."

"He loves the guitar. Here. Sit down." Anthony pulled a chair closer. He stood behind her, a hand on her shoulder.

One of the guitarists asked Pedrosa to make the first request. Without hesitation the old man said, *"Siboney!"* As the music filled the room, he closed his eyes. The older people seemed enraptured, and Gail guessed that they must have heard this piece when they were young. After the applause, more requests came. *Como Fué. Perfidia.* After a little while the guitarists stood up and began to move through the crowd, playing and singing as they went.

Anthony leaned down to speak into Gail's ear, "Let's go outside for a few minutes. Bring your wrap, it's chilly." Gail looked at him curiously, but he only held out his hand.

They went out a side entrance, then walked through the back gate onto the golf course. In the middle of the fairway, the moon floated almost straight overhead. From behind them came the sound of guitars, an intricate melody that could have been written hundreds of years ago. Gail held her arms out and twirled around. "This is perfect."

Anthony walked slowly along, watching her. "I'm glad you approve."

"Don't try to soften me up to move in, if that's what you're thinking."

He laughed. "Are you kidding? Not in this place, but . . . maybe something smaller — if you could stand an old house. You said no."

"I could reconsider." She pulled him to

a stop. "Kiss me. A good one."

He did, till she felt the ground under them fall away. His breath came faster. A long inhalation, then his hands moving under her shawl. Undoing her zipper to touch bare skin. She pressed herself against him, wishing they weren't out here in the open. Last night they had done no more than hold each other.

After a while he must have realized how visible they were to anyone walking by. Laughing softly, he backed away. "Let me cool off."

"*Atrasa'o,*" she teased. He had taught her that one in bed. Horny.

"Gail! How do you learn such things?" He made a noise with his tongue, then turned her around, kissed her neck, and zipped up her dress.

"I have another word. What is a *tortillera?*"

"It means a lesbian. Where did you hear that?"

"Oh, that's nice. Never mind where. One more." She said it slowly, trying to pronounce it correctly. "*Ñángara de basura.* What's that?"

His expression changed, and the moonlight cast shadows that made his face seem strange to her. "Dirty commie would be a fair translation. Did someone call you that tonight?" Her hesitation was enough to give him the answer. "Who was it?"

"Whoa." She had never seen this mood before. "What would you do? Make a scene and embarrass me?"

He lightly touched his chest with his fingertips. "Would I do that? At my grandfather's birthday party? Come on." The mood, whatever it was, had vanished. He stood directly in front of her and took her shoulders. "Gail. You don't lie very well, honey. I'm going to ask you names until I hit the right one, so you'd better tell me now. I won't make a scene, but I should know who it was. When we're married, are you going to keep secrets?" He looked straight into her eyes. "Who was it?"

"Since you've promised to be nice — Okay, it was your wonderful brother-in-law. He was on the front porch with some of his friends. He said it was an insult that I showed up. He didn't say it to my face. In fact, I was eavesdropping."

"Ahhh. You overheard Octavio talking about you. What else did he say?"

"Nothing. Don't make problems for your sister. Let it go. One of the others said he didn't believe it anyway. Who are those men? They were serious as death. Did you happen to see them?"

He nodded. "They came to pay their respects to my grandfather."

The casual way he said it sent a chill along the back of her neck, even with the woollen shawl wrapped tightly over her shoulders. "Are these the guys who take their automatic weapons out to the Everglades on weekends to conduct practice maneuvers?"

"Some do, yes." Anthony shrugged. "My grandfather likes to listen to them talk. They wouldn't get a hundred yards offshore before a U.S. Customs cruiser pulled alongside. Every organization like that has been so thoroughly infiltrated, it's a joke."

"Infiltrated by whom?"

"FBI, Customs, the local anti-terrorist task force, agents from Cuba. And we've infiltrated Cuban intelligence. Everyone knows everything, and no one trusts anybody. They're all crazy." He looked away from the house. Smiling at her, he came closer. "Why are we talking about this?"

"Pretty dull topic — spies, counterrevolution. What have you got in mind?"

He put his arms around her, started to kiss her, then said, "I almost forgot." He took something out of his pocket and slowly opened his hand. Moonlight seemed to sparkle blue-white in his palm. Gail could only stare at it. He kissed the third finger of her left hand, then slid the ring on — a pear-shaped diamond the size of her thumbnail.

"What do you think?" When she didn't reply, he raised his brows. "Well?"

"I — It's beautiful, but I —"

"You don't like it? It's a perfect stone."

Her fingers were splayed wide apart. "Of course I *like* it, but —"

"But *what?*"

"How much did it cost?" She dragged her eyes away from the diamond to look at him. "How much?"

"What a question! All right, I traded in some pieces I don't wear anymore. That covered most of it."

"Oh, my God."

"How can you be engaged without a ring? I want you to show everyone. Wear it, you'll get used to it."

Gail continued to stare at the ring.

"You don't like it at all, do you?"

"It's so . . . big. I'd be afraid to wear it."

"Here. Give it to me." He put it back into his pocket.

"You're angry."

"No. I'm not angry. I don't know what you want."

She took his hand. "You. That's what I want."

By ten-thirty, Gail's relatives were drooping with fatigue. Aunt Doris dozed in her chair. They revived with the promise of food. The caterers heaped a long buffet table with tenderloin steak and paella with shellfish. Salads, side dishes, and breads. Gail's cousins went back for seconds and thirds.

More wine was poured. There were ornate toasts to Ernesto Pedrosa in Spanish and English. There were toasts to his lovely wife. Then Anthony stood up and reached for Gail's hand. He held his wine glass in the other. *"Estoy feliz de anunciarles —"* In both languages he announced his engagement to the most beautiful woman in Miami, the woman whom he would love for the rest of his life. Pedrosa raised his glass, wishing them as many years of happiness as Digna had given to him. Anthony smiled, raised his own glass, then leaned down to kiss Gail on the lips as everyone applauded. She whispered, "I love you."

It had already been arranged for Karen to stay over with Irene, so after many embraces and kisses, Gail's relatives made their way out the door. It was past one o'clock in the morning. Gail and Anthony walked them to their cars and promised to come to Irene's for Sunday brunch. Not too early, Aunt Doris whispered.

Going back inside, Anthony said he wanted to stay long enough to have a cigar with his cousin Bernardo, would Gail mind?

In the living room half a dozen of his female relatives chatted quietly in Spanish. Alicia was on the sofa and Digna Pedrosa was in her rocking chair. A great-grandson, Alicia's youngest child, lay across her lap, eyes half-closed, sucking his thumb. Anthony ruffled his nephew's hair, then asked, "Nena, is Grandfather asleep?"

"Oh, yes. Ernesto had a wonderful time. Gail, he said to tell you good night, and to all your family. They are so nice. Your mother and I talked about the opera. In Cuba I saw Renata Tibaldi. I don't remember the name of the opera, but she was brilliant. We had operas, concerts, ballet. Miami was only a little tiny resort town. The women used to come to Havana to shop."

"Everything was better in Havana." Anthony winked at Gail. "Right, Nena?"

Alicia added, "It hardly ever rained. There were more flowers, and no bugs. We didn't need air conditioning because we had the breeze from the ocean."

Digna playfully stuck out her tongue. "They tease me." She rocked in her chair and stroked the child's head. Her own eyes were closing, and her wrinkled face sagged.

Anthony took a cigar out of his breast pocket. "Gail, why don't you help Alicia take Nena and the baby upstairs? I'll be out back for a few minutes. Wait for me here." He walked out of the living room and disappeared into the hall.

"Maybe I should learn to smoke cigars," Gail said, half to herself.

She heard Alicia's low laughter. "I know what you mean. At least they don't do it in the house anymore. Nena won't allow it." She stood up and lifted her son off his great-grandmother's lap, legs dangling.

Digna blinked, then pushed herself out of the rocking chair. She said good night to the others, and Gail walked with her to the stairs. The old woman mounted them slowly, one hand on the baluster. She smiled at Gail, kissed her on the cheek, and told her again what a lovely evening. And how lucky her grandson was, to have found such a charming girl. They parted at the door to the master suite.

Alicia came out of another room, closing

the door softly. The Reyes family did not live here, but apparently they would stay the night. Alicia whispered, "Gail? Could I speak to you for a minute?"

They went into Digna's sitting room. Gail said, "Thank you again for showing everyone the house."

"It was my pleasure." Alicia Quintana Reyes had wavy brown hair, like her brother, but her eyes were deep blue. He still had a slight accent; she did not. At forty, after three children, she had put on just enough weight to soften her features. It was Alicia who deserved to have this house, Gail thought. If only she weren't married to Octavio Reyes.

Alicia took both her hands. "Gail, I have to tell you, I'm so sorry about this awful situation with the opera singer. We're going to be sisters soon, by marriage. I want us to be friends. I love my brother very much, and it would be terrible to have a division between us. What Octavio says on the radio — He doesn't mean it personally, against you. It isn't his intention to hurt anybody. He has to keep people aware, so they don't forget. Can you understand?" Alicia's eyes had filled with tears.

In that instant Gail knew that she had kept her distance from this woman tonight for the sole reason that she was married to Reyes. She had felt that Alicia disapproved of her. But that had been her own interpretation, not the reality of it. Alicia loved her husband, and she loved her brother. She would close the gap if she could. Gail impulsively hugged Alicia, who was shorter and bosomy.

"Thank you. I think we're going to make great sisters."

"Oh! Come here, I want to show you a picture of Anthony when he was a little boy. I bet you haven't seen it." She turned a light on over her grandmother's desk and opened an envelope. Inside were black-and-white snapshots with ruffled edges. "Nena was showing these to me the other day."

She shuffled through them quickly. Family photos taken many years ago. A much younger Ernesto Pedrosa riding a horse in the country, royal palm trees in the background. Digna waving from the stands at a race track. Caridad, slender and pretty, holding a baby. Many shots of people Gail didn't recognize. "Okay, here's Anthony. Isn't he cute? He was about two years old."

A courtyard — an atrium. Terra cotta planters with areca palms. Tiles in geometric patterns on the shiny floor. A laughing, dark-eyed boy with glossy hair stood on the seat of a wicker sofa. He wore shorts and a striped pullover and laced leather shoes. There was a toy truck at his feet. To his right, nearly out of the frame, the shoulder and arm of a man in a white linen suit.

"Where was this taken?" Gail asked.

"That's the house in Vedado. It's been torn down." Alicia put the photo into the envelope. "Here. You can have it."

Exhausted from so little sleep the previous night, Gail decided to get her purse and her shawl, then try to hurry Anthony along. Avoiding the party room, where she had last seen Octavio, she went out the side door and took the walkway that led to the rear patio.

She didn't get that far. Nearing the guest house, she saw a movement ahead of her. Two figures. Anthony and another man, walking slowly, chatting. Gail heard bits of conversation in Spanish. She could understand none of it.

Then she heard her own name.

A glowing ember rose toward the other man's face. A glint of light on a pair of silver-rimmed glasses told her who it was. Quickly she glanced toward the back of the main house. There was no one on the patio. She started forward, then froze, undecided whether to call out to Anthony or to leave them alone.

Suddenly a quick movement. A brief arc of orange as the cigar flew to one side. A split second later, a thud. Octavio was gagging. Anthony pulled him upright and slammed him into the wall of the guest house. Then he did it again.

Gail stared open-mouthed.

Anthony spoke slowly, each word clear, his voice raspy with rage. *"¡Hijo' puta! Escúchame bien —"* You son of a bitch, listen to me.

"¡Ay, por Diós!"

Anthony jerked Octavio forward, then back. The air went out of Octavio's lungs. There was a moan. *"Te juro, si hablas de ella otra vez así —"* If you talk about her again like that — Their faces were inches apart. *"— te voy a matar."* I will kill you. Gail held her breath, horrified. *"¿Me comprendes? ¡Respóndeme!"*

Still gasping, Octavio nodded.

Gail slowly backed away, moving farther into the shadows toward the side door. She knew Anthony would not want her to see this. Nor did she want him to know that she had seen it, until she could decide what she felt. At the moment, she only felt ashamed and confused.

183

ELEVEN

The concrete block, twenty pounds of cement and gravel, lay among shards of plate glass in the foyer of the opera offices. The parquet floor was gouged. A gloved workman was gingerly picking up pieces of glass, and another pushed a broom. Office staff stood around watching.

The general director, back from New York, had called Gail asking her to come downtown. When she arrived, two City of Miami police cruisers were pulling out of the parking lot. They had just written up the report. Around five o'clock in the morning, someone had waited until the security guard had gone around back, then tossed the block through the door. A message had been left on the machine: *Get rid of the communist singer or we'll blow up the building.*

"Maybe I should keep it," Jeffrey Hopkins mused as one of the men picked up the ugly lump of concrete. "A reminder that the arts is a dangerous business. We could mount it on a pedestal in the lobby with a color enlargement of the broken door. What do you think?"

Hopkins was a slim, youthful-looking man with a fringe of white hair. Little red dragons patterned his bow tie of rich yellow silk. He had run opera companies for years, and had perfected the smooth voice and quick smile necessary for dealing with egos of major donors, prima donna singers, and, less often but no less important, public relations emergencies.

"I think you should hire an extra guard," Gail said.

"I may have to consider it. Come into my office, Ms. Connor. Let's chat." He whirled on one heel and beckoned her to follow. He led her in and closed the door.

Gail asked whether the media had showed up yet.

"Channel Seven was just here, and I expect the rest of them to descend on us any moment. I've already called the head of the Community Relations Board, whom I know — and who happens to be Cuban, which is irrelevant but interesting. He was furious. Couldn't believe anyone could — Well, he could believe it, of course. Loonies abound."

Hopkins had perfect white teeth, no doubt the handiwork of a very fine dentist. He flashed them at her as he offered her a seat before his desk. "I called you because

I've also heard from one of the pinheads in the city of Miami permit department. They want to know what additional security arrangements we have planned for the run of *Don Giovanni.*"

"You hire off-duty officers, don't you?"

"Three for each performance," Hopkins replied, "but the city is concerned about demonstrations in the street. They're thinking about requiring us to erect barricades and hire enough policemen to keep us separated from the thousands — yes, he said thousands — of people in the Cuban community who might come to protest."

"Jeffrey. Tell me you're making this up."

"Oh, no. The permit department suggests, oh, a hundred or so extra officers to line the streets." Hopkins counted off some figures on his fingers. "Let's see. Sixty dollars per officer, a hundred officers . . . six thousand dollars. That's for each show. Plus the barricades. *And* — how could I have forgotten? — they want us to pay to clean up the trash, eggshells, and broken glass, and to have paramedics on call, just in case it really gets out of hand." A tinge of red had crept into Hopkins's cheeks. "This doesn't count the money we lose on ticket sales because people are too afraid to show up."

Gail laughed. "Has the police department been abolished?"

"We live here. We pay taxes," Hopkins huffed. "We're a recognized cultural organization. It's *their* responsibility to protect the citizens. That's what I told the person who called me. He said he'd discuss it with staff — his phraseology was priceless — then get back to me. I have no desire to deal with these morons. Do you mind taking care of it?"

"Of course not," Gail said. "I'll call the city manager. I wouldn't worry too much. He knows they can't do this."

"Bare your teeth for us," Hopkins said. "We need to get this settled. Opening night is less than three weeks away. My God. Look at me. I never sweat, and my forehead is perspiring."

"Tell you what," Gail said. "I'll call the city manager before I leave and make an appointment to see him, all right? I'll say, The opera gonna kick yo butt." She grinned. "How's that, Jeffrey?"

"Perfect — or some variation thereof." Waggling his fingers like a broom, he shooed her toward the door. "I've got to get busy. See that stack of messages? They're from nervous nellie board members wondering if their lives are in danger."

187

Holding onto the doorknob, Gail leaned back in. "Jeffrey, have you heard of an English soprano named Jane Fyfield?"

He focussed on the ceiling, "Fyfield. Yes, I think so. Why do you ask?"

"She flew to Havana with Tom Nolan. He didn't tell me her name, only that he'd traveled with the woman who sang *Lucia* with him in Dortmund. I let my mother do some detective work for us. She tracked down Ms. Fyfield's manager, and he gave us the number where we can reach her. She's in her flat in London now, but she'll be leaving for Scotland in the next day or so to sing in Glasgow." Gail tilted her head toward his anteroom, where an extra telephone waited. "We should call her before speaking to the city manager."

"And why should we do that?" Hopkins was frowning.

"Wouldn't it help to have all the facts?"

"Aha. This is the investigation that Rebecca Dixon authorized in my absence, isn't it? Do we really need to pursue that?"

"We should know if he lied to us," Gail said.

"Well . . . wouldn't *you*? If you came to Miami to debut in the title role in an opera, and suddenly you were told that a petty incident two years ago might get you kicked

188

off the cast? Forget whether the opera has a *right* to do it — which we don't."

"Okay." Gail stepped back inside his office and closed the door. "I understand his reasons, but it doesn't change our position. What if you assure the press that he did nothing but sing for some college students, then we see a videotape on the nightly news — Nolan getting a big hug from Fidel Castro? I couldn't care less, and neither could you, but not everybody feels that way. Lawyers are paid to worry. I worry about what Nolan was doing in Cuba."

"I agree," Hopkins said, "but Tom does a great Don Giovanni, and I'm going to support him. Let it not be said that we would fire a singer for political reasons. Oh, all right. Look into it if you want, but be discreet."

Gail crossed her arms and tapped her fingers on the sleeves of her jacket. "I'm going to make a recommendation I hope you take seriously. Hire a bodyguard for him."

"What?"

"Not around the clock, just someone to escort him to and from home or wherever he has to go, if he's not with friends. Here's the thing, Jeffrey. If the next concrete block is aimed at his head, you'll have more damage than one broken door. Try explaining that to the press. Or worse, to our liability company. At least it would make Tom feel safe. If I were in his place right now, I'd be concerned. I might even say forget it, use the understudy, I'm out of here. And wouldn't that make certain radio commentators happy."

Jeffrey Hopkins chewed on a cuticle, then frowned at it and dropped his hand in his lap. "You've got a point, but we should see what Tom thinks. Would you like to talk to him? It's your idea."

"I'd be glad to."

"Who do we hire for this?" Hopkins asked. "A hulking ex-cop in a fedora?"

"I have someone in mind," Gail said.

The lobby had been cleaned up when Gail came back through, and two men were lifting a new sheet of smoky bronze plate glass off a carpeted dolly. A third man was unscrewing the door frame. Their truck was parked just down the walkway in the employee lot. Gail skirted around them through the open, and intact, twin door, then saw a Channel Four news van with a satellite dish on it turn in from the street. Two men got out — one in a suit, the other carrying a video camera.

"They're all yours, Jeffrey."

She was halfway to her car when a silver Jaguar came into the lot from the other direction. Rebecca Dixon. The Jaguar slowed, then the wheels cut toward Gail. The car parked next to Gail's Buick, and the door opened. Rebecca swiveled, hem up her thighs, one suede Prada pump hitting the pavement, then the other. Her chic little suit said she might be on her way to a charity luncheon, but had been detoured by the unpleasantness at the opera.

For a moment her tortoiseshell sunglasses pointed toward the broken door, then the news van. "What a mess." She looked back at Gail. "You've already talked to Jeffrey."

"Yes, a little while ago."

"Damn." Rebecca's perfectly lipsticked mouth tightened. "I told him to wait."

"If you want to know what we discussed, I'll tell you."

"He isn't happy with me," Rebecca said.

Gail said, "We didn't talk about you."

"I don't know what else I could've done." She put a hand on her forehead, mussing the neatly trimmed line of her brunette bangs. "We had a security guard."

"Rebecca, take it easy. I have an appointment with the city manager tomorrow morning. Meanwhile, Jeffrey is going to make a generic statement to the media, the opera will look heroic, and you'll have standing room only for the rest of the season." Gail walked her toward the rear of her car, closer to the trees at the edge of the parking lot. It seemed more private.

"He wants the investigation to stop, but we agreed to hire a bodyguard for Tom Nolan. What do you think?"

"Oh, God. Whatever." Rebecca exhaled heavily, apparently willing to let somebody else put shoulder to wheel.

"I'd like to use Felix Castillo. He's already familiar with what's going on here, and I trust him. But if you have any objections, please tell me. I'll find someone else." For a few seconds Gail stared into the little dots of sunlight on Rebecca's sunglasses.

Rebecca laughed, a single peal more of disbelief than humor.

"You won't have to talk to him," Gail said. "He can deal directly with me."

"Oh, my God," she said softly, smiling a little. "This is unbelievable."

"If you'd rather he didn't —"

"Do what you want. I don't care." Rebecca shook her heavy hair back from her face. She studied the progress of repairs on the door. The glass had been set into the frame, and now it was being caulked. "For two cents I'd resign. This job was Lloyd's idea. People say he bought it for me, and they're right. Mrs. Lloyd Dixon, society princess, doyenne of the arts. Oh, God. Wait'll he gets a load of this. I could laugh. He was so sure nothing would happen. Oh, baby, come on." Rebecca's voice grew deep, a mock imitation of Lloyd Dixon's growl. "The exiles don't give a shit. It's an act they gotta put on, prove they got balls. It's all talk."

Gail recalled standing in the rehearsal room talking to Lloyd Dixon. Dixon in his leather bomber jacket, so certain of everything. "Rebecca? Can I ask a dumb question? Do you know Octavio Reyes?" When Rebecca looked around at her, Gail added, "He's that pain-in-the-ass commentator on WRCL. Anthony's brother-in-law. You mentioned Reyes by name after Tom's recital, when you asked me for help, and it just occurred to me — How do you know him? Not from Anthony in college. Not that far back."

"I don't know him. He's a customer of Lloyd's." Rebecca leaned against the mirror-finish rear fender of her Jaguar. "Dixon Air handles all of King Furniture's air shipments to Latin America. Lloyd said he'd speak to Reyes if he got to be a problem, but he was so sure nothing would happen."

"They know each other."

As if finally focusing on what Gail was saying, Rebecca said, "They don't *know* each other. It's a business acquaintance. Dixon Air has a lot of customers." Then she smiled. "Maybe one less when I tell Lloyd about the door."

Gail kicked at some gravel with the toe of her shoe. "What do you mean? Lloyd will tell Octavio he won't ship his furniture unless he shuts up? It doesn't seem like much leverage to me. Dixon Air isn't the only freight airline in Miami."

Rebecca raised her hands in a gesture of surrender, then went back to get her purse out of her car, a sleek Fendi bag with a dangling gold clasp. She slammed her door, took a few steps toward the building, then stood there with her hands clenched at her sides. "This is pointless." She aimed her security key at her car, which chirped at her. The locks popped up. She jerked the door open and threw her purse across the seat. The gold clasp clattered against the window on the other side. "You and Jeffrey deal with it. I am obviously superfluous."

At a stoplight on Biscayne Boulevard, heading back to her office, Gail flipped open her phone and hit a speed dial button.

"Miriam, it's me. Any messages?"

Felix Castillo had called, and Gail should beep him when she had time to talk.

"Oh, my God. The man must be psychic. No clue what he wanted? . . . Okay, we live in suspense. Do me a favor and call Thomas Nolan. Try his apartment and the School of the Arts, and leave a message if he's not in. Tell him I need to talk to him, and to give me a time when he's available. Did that noon appointment call to confirm?"

Miriam assured her that he had. At noon a new client would come to the office. The man had shipped 5,000 ladies shirts and dresses from his factory in Hialeah to a chain department store based in Georgia. They had stiffed him for the payment. This was more Gail's kind of case than arranging bodyguards for opera singers.

She turned the corner, heading for the ramp to the expressway. "Are you up for some research? . . . See what you can find — articles, studies, books, whatever — on Cuban exiles in Miami. Also, get me information on terrorism going back, oh, to the mid-sixties. Try the *Miami Herald* archives as well as the library. If you need to buy any books, I'll reimburse you. . . . It was only one concrete block and lots of glass on the floor. . . . No, I'm not worried, I just want to know if I should be. Hang on a second."

She maneuvered up the ramp, then said, "Let me have Seth Greer's number." Keeping one eye on the road, she jotted it down on a notepad she kept in the console between the seats. "Thanks, *chica*. See you in fifteen minutes." After the disconnect she steered with her wrist while punching the buttons with the other hand. "It is people like you," she said to herself, "who drive up insurance rates."

She asked for Seth Greer and said who she was. As she waited, the expressway ended, dumping traffic onto South Dixie Highway.

When he came on the line, Gail said, "Your prediction came true. The city is thinking of sticking us with about a hundred extra off-duty police for security during the run of the opera. . . . Yes, Seth, you told me so. Are you busy? . . . What I'd like are some cases to show the city manager when I go yell at him tomorrow morning. . . . I don't *need* to have legal research with me, but it would be nice to keep in my holster. You know. Show them we're willing to take this to federal court if they try to push us around."

Profanity came over the line. Joyous profanity, the call to arms. Then Seth was asking to go with her to the meeting.

"Well . . . I'd better go alone this time. Thanks a million." Gail made a smooch into the phone. "You're terrific."

And then Seth said he had to go. It was almost 10:55, time for Octavio Reyes's commentary, more gasoline on the flames. And by the way, the other Cuban stations were picking up on the issue. So tune in whichever she wanted, WQBA, WWFE, WRHC —

Gail tossed the phone to the passenger seat and turned on the radio, finding AM 870. She kept an eye on the road, slowing when brake lights came on ahead of her.

Octavio Reyes's recorded commentary had already started. She turned up the volume to drown out the road noise. Something about people suffering. *Ni pan ni leche para darle comida a sus niños.* Gail translated slowly. Neither bread nor milk to feed their children. Nolan had been there. He must have seen the hunger, *la miseria, el terror, la destrucción,* how thousands and thousands of our countrymen live on *nuestra bella isla* — our beautiful island.

A horn blasted behind her. The light had turned green. Reyes was still talking. Nolan had performed for *el regimen del tirano* — the regime of the tyrant — and in singing for Ricardo Alarcón —

"Who?" Gail asked aloud.

— his art had been converted into a political act. Blah blah blah no different from artists who worked *en el servicio de Hitler y Stalin*. A hypocrisy for Thomas Nolan to perform here, *en la capital del exilio* — the capital of the exiles — hiding behind claims of artistic freedom.

"Oh, bullshit."

Then Reyes announced that he would like to invite any spokesman from the opera to appear on his nightly interview program to explain —

"Oh, yes. We'll be right there. You bet."

He closed with a thank you for listening. *"Soy Octavio Reyes, el rrrrrey del comentario, Rrrradio Cuba Libre."*

"You're full of *mierda.*" Gail hit another button on the radio, flipping it to one of the English-language talk stations, hearing an airline commercial, and she wondered about leaving town until this was over.

She had hoped — obviously in vain — that Octavio Reyes might have given it a rest, after Saturday night. But in shoving him into the wall of the Pedrosas' guest house, Anthony had not said, *Stop the editorials about the opera,* but *Stop calling Gail names.*

After witnessing this display of temper, she had come back inside. Not to sit obediently on the sofa — she'd been far too wound up for that — but to pace in the front hall. When Anthony appeared — his eyes dilated to black pools and his cheeks blazing — they stared at each other. And he realized she had seen him. And she knew that he knew.

In the car on the way to her house: "I'm not going to discuss it, Gail."

On arrival as she got out and slammed the door: "And you can go play with yourself, because I'm going to sleep." His tires had screeched going out of her driveway. In the half an hour it usually took him to drive home, Gail stood under a blasting shower crying, then pulled herself together, drank a glass of warm milk with two aspirin, and called him. He wasn't there. Nor was he there an hour later. Or he wasn't answering the phone. She left a message: "I still love you and don't forget brunch at my mother's tomorrow morning. She expects us at ten-thirty."

His good manners, if not his mood, had gotten him there. The circles under his eyes were worse than hers. The relatives had probably assumed other reasons for their yawns. With Karen waiting in her car, Gail had hugged him goodbye. For a minute he held her tightly. Said he was sorry. Not sorry for smacking Octavio around. But sorry anyway. His kiss said he meant it.

Dodging and weaving through traffic, hurrying back to her office, Gail wished she could be in the Pedrosas' back garden again, her hands cupped at her mouth. *Anthony! Make him promise to shut up about Thomas Nolan!*

After a while she heard someone yelling on the English station and stared at the speaker. The radio announcer was irate. "Hey, folks. Where are you? Can you repeat after me? I'm in the U.S.A. now. Yeah, that's right. The country that took you in, that fed and clothed you, and you have the *gall* to tell us that we can't go hear any opera singer we want to hear? Okay, I hate opera as much as the next guy. So what? Have you ever heard of the Bill of Rights? We have freedom of speech in this country. Surprise! If you can't grasp the concept, then go home, you ungrateful bunch of whiners. That's right. Go home! Take a raft right back to Uncle Fidel if you don't like it here! If you'd had the guts to fight instead of run away —"

Gail turned it off.

Noticing the sign for Twenty-seventh

Avenue, Gail checked the rearview mirror and put on her right turn signal. At a break in traffic she whipped the car across two lanes, barely making the turn. Her right rear tire clipped the curb. She glanced around for a police car. "Sorry, sorry."

There was just enough time for a detour by Felix Castillo's house.

TWELVE

If Felix Castillo had an office — which she doubted — Gail didn't know where it was. She found the street Anthony had taken into Castillo's neighborhood, got lost for a few minutes, then saw a familiar chain-link fence. She paused at a stop sign. The old gray van was in the driveway.

"Lucky me," she said, parking outside the gate.

The house looked smaller in the daytime, an ordinary little stucco box with a ficus tree for shade and security bars over the windows. The gate across the driveway was the only way in. There was a lock on it. Pondering whether the mailman usually vaulted the fence, she heard a steady noise from around the corner of the house. *Thwock thwock thwock thwock.* A slight ringing, as of a bell, accompanied this. She walked along the sidewalk.

Castillo was trimming a hedge of overgrown crotons with a machete. The metal flashed, and the branches with their multicolored leaves slid to the ground, reduced from the height of a man to waist level. A gold chain gleamed on Castillo's dark, muscled chest. A cigarette jutted from between his teeth.

He saw her, made no sign of recognition, but with a flick of his wrist imbedded the point of the machete in the dirt. The wooden handle shook, then went still. He picked up a faded plaid sport shirt from the grass and put it on as he walked toward the fence. His rubber thongs slapped at the soles of his feet. Gail had an image of toes rolling off if he even miscalculated where the machete would land.

"I got your message," Gail said.

Castillo buttoned his shirt up halfway. He wore brown polyester pants, and Gail wondered if his pistol was strapped to his ankle. He unlocked the gate, then flipped the cigarette butt into the street. "Come inside."

As the front door closed, the lovebird cage on the other side of the white-tiled living room became a blur of fluttering gray wings. The birds chirped and twittered and gradually settled down.

"I don't like to do business in my house," Castillo said. "The neighbors see people in and out, they wonder what's going on. The other night was social, you know?" He waved away Gail's apology. "You want some coffee?"

She thought he might snap his fingers and his young girlfriend would appear to fetch it, but Castillo led Gail into the kitchen, a small room cluttered with evidence of his domestic life — a plastic dish drainer loaded with dishes rinsed and reused, limp dime-store curtains drawn back with matching loops of cloth, a rice cooker with starch clouding the glass lid. By the door, empty beer bottles were stacked in their cardboard carriers. And on the countertop between the door and the window — both secured with bars — was a long-barreled, chrome-plated revolver. Twenty years ago he had lent Anthony Quintana an AK-47 to carry in the forests of Nicaragua. Gail wondered what she would find if she went through his closets.

She sat at the chrome-legged table while Castillo unscrewed the top off a burned and stained *cafetera,* ran some tap water into the bottom, and put in fresh grounds, patting them level with the spoon. During this, Gail told him about the vandalism at the opera, then about the message left on the answering machine. Did he have any ideas who might have done it?

"Anybody. There's no way to tell." Castillo poked among the dishes in the drainer for two espresso cups.

Not wanting to, Gail noticed the old wound. The blade must have gone in between the middle fingers and exited near the wrist, slicing off half his hand. She could not imagine how he could ever have touched a machete after that. She concentrated on finding a place on the table for her purse, moving aside a cellophane package of round white crackers. "On the way here I heard Octavio Reyes's commentary. I suppose you were outside trimming the bushes."

"No, I heard it." Castillo sat down across the table, not getting comfortable yet because the little coffee pot was starting to tick on the burner. The hair left on Castillo's head was clipped short, and his gray mustache reached below the corners of his mouth. Heavy-lidded eyes gave him a sleepy look.

"I heard from my friend in Havana. He can't tell if Thomas Nolan stayed at the Tropicoco on Varadero Beach. That's too long ago. His name was in the newspaper, though, in the schedule for the music festival. Three times. The National Theater in downtown Havana on Tuesday, November 12, then on Friday at the Hotel Las Americas, which is new, and I think built with money from Spain. The next Monday he was at the beach amphitheater. Nolan didn't tell you about those other two, did he? No? The one at the Las Americas, my friend is going to look at again. There was a business conference at the hotel that week, not part of the festival. The story was in the newspaper, and it said that some opera stars from Europe came to do the entertainment. Six of them. Nolan's name was on the list."

"What about Jane Fyfield? Was she listed?"

"Yes. Who's she? I know. The lady that sang in that opera."

"Looks like you saved me the trouble of calling her," Gail said. "The general director hates the idea of an investigation. He says it doesn't matter what Nolan did in Cuba."

Castillo's heavy gray brows rose. "You don't want to hear anymore?"

"Please. I have no intention of dropping it. We'll just have to be discreet."

"Yeah." He gave a soft, husky laugh. "Tony said you were like that. Okay. The meeting at the Las Americas. That's the one that bothers me. The story in the newspaper said that Ricardo Alarcón gave a speech at the conference. That's a problem."

Gail said, "Octavio Reyes mentioned that name in his commentary today."

"That's correct. Reyes thinks Alarcón was in the audience when Tom Nolan sang. Maybe so, maybe he's guessing. Two years ago is not yesterday."

"Who's Ricardo Alarcón?"

Castillo's mustache lifted, showing crooked, smoke-tinted teeth. "Who? Ricardo Alarcón is the president of the Cuban National Assembly. He's very big. It's like singing for Fidel, almost."

"Sorry, I don't know Cuban politics."

The water in the coffeemaker bubbled, the last of it drawn upward through the grounds. Castillo got up and turned off the stove. The glass jalousies were cranked open. Across the small backyard, past clothesline and hedge, someone had a radio tuned to a comedy show in Spanish — a comedian whose diction was garbled past comprehension. Jokes and a laugh track.

Gail said, "That's surprising. A business conference in Cuba. I thought the economy was shot to hell."

"They're trying to fix it. Bring in people with money, make a partnership with the government." Castillo measured several teaspoons of sugar into a glass, then poured in a thin stream of espresso. "It's like the old days, when the Americans owned half the country, but now it's the Mexicans, Canadians, and Israelis — everybody but the Americans. Even the Russians, do you believe that? If a Cuban, a person off the street, wants to go to one of those hotels — forget it. They save them for the tourists. They give away vacations to these businesspeople, and hotel rooms and food, and usually they have Cuban jazz and salsa, but this time — maybe for something different, who knows? — they had opera singers."

The spoon clacked in the glass until a frothy, caramel-colored syrup appeared. Castillo poured some into each small cup, then filled the cups with espresso. He pushed one of the cups to Gail's side of the table. Gail had become used to the taste — both intensely sweet and biting, a juxtaposition of opposites. "Thanks. This is delicious."

He sat across from her. "If you lived in Cuba you would drink coffee stretched with roasted chickpeas. How about that? No good Cuban coffee left in Cuba."

Gail took another sip. "Are you licensed to work as a bodyguard?"

The hooded brown eyes moved to look at her. "Yes, and to carry a gun."

"I was thinking of Thomas Nolan."

"Has he been threatened? Anybody following him?"

"People leave messages at the opera and at the school where he teaches."

"They do that. When you were here before with Tony, I said don't expect violence. Okay, maybe a concrete block through the door, but to attack this man — No. It would be a very stupid thing."

"I agree, but Tom Nolan has been mentioned by name on the radio. Today, Reyes said he was like the artists who worked for Hitler and Stalin."

Castillo laughed. "He invited somebody from the opera to be on his show. Are you going to do it?"

"No, thanks. Listen, Felix. This is for Tom's peace of mind. You wouldn't be with him around the clock, only as needed." She wondered how Nolan would feel about this man. Either horrified or completely safe, nothing in between. "I'm going to discuss it with him first, of course."

Castillo got up to pour more coffee. He lifted the little pot in Gail's direction. She shook her head. "I charge fifty dollars an hour, five hundred in advance."

"Is that the usual rate? I've never hired a bodyguard."

"For you, it's a discount."

"Wonderful." Gail pinched the handle on the little cup and finished the coffee in it.

"Felix, this may not be relevant, but as you were talking about investment in Cuba, it came to mind. One of our biggest donors is a man named Lloyd Dixon. He's married to Rebecca Dixon, the president of the board of directors."

Making no indication that he recognized either name, Castillo scraped more syrup into his cup.

She continued, "Dixon owns an air cargo company based in Miami, Dixon Air Transport. Rebecca told me today that Dixon Air does business with Octavio Reyes's company, King Furniture. She said that her husband doesn't know Octavio Reyes personally, but when I mentioned his name to Dixon, I got the impression that he does."

The little spoon clicked softly on the porcelain.

"I'm not saying it means anything."

"But it bothers you." Castillo sat down with his coffee.

"Yes. Lloyd Dixon pretended not to know who Reyes was, but there was no reason for him to lie. All he had to say was, Yeah, sure, he's a customer, and I'm going to tell him to back off."

"Maybe he needs the business," Castillo suggested.

"No. I'll tell you who Lloyd Dixon is —

a big, tough, and very rich ex-army helicopter pilot with an American flag bumper sticker on his pickup truck. He likes opera for the blood and guts, not the pretty tunes. He doesn't need Octavio Reyes. He would stomp him on principle. So why isn't he doing it?" Arms on the table, Gail leaned toward Castillo. "I don't know why he lied, and I can't tell you it makes a difference, but Octavio Reyes was in the lie, and I keep thinking . . . it might make a difference to Anthony."

Castillo pulled absently on his mustache. "Did you talk to him?"

"I plan to. Come on, Felix. See what you can find out. I'll pay you myself."

He shook his head. "For this I don't charge."

THIRTEEN

Thomas Nolan held his Monday master class in the choral room at the School of the Arts. Back from a break, the students thudded up the risers to their seats, laughing and talking as they went. The accompanist, who couldn't have been over eighteen, shifted scores on the piano until he found the one he wanted and opened it on the music rack.

Nolan waited until the conversations had quieted. "We have a visitor with us for the remainder of the class — Gail Connor, the lawyer for the Miami Opera. I hope you aren't shy about singing in front of a lawyer."

Two dozen pairs of eyes looked at Gail where she sat at the far edge of the risers. She lifted a hand from her lap, and there were some smiles in response. She had planned to wait outside, but Nolan had spotted her and brought her in.

"Today, a duet from *Don Giovanni*. Like much of Mozart's music, this piece appears simple but isn't. To sing it well requires both lightness and power." He lifted his arm toward two students waiting by the piano. "Aaron and Kathy are our singers. Aaron, let me do Giovanni first, then you take over. Come here, Kathy. This is our Zerlina."

The petite, dark-haired young woman pushed up the sleeves of her pullover, then stood with her hands clasped, waiting for instructions. The top of her head barely cleared Nolan's shoulders.

"For our guest, I'll set the scene. We are in Spain. Don Giovanni wanders into a country festival. A pretty young girl, Zerlina, is engaged to Masetto, a peasant lad. Giovanni proposes a party for everyone and tells Masetto and the others to go ahead. He will bring Zerlina. Masetto is reluctant, but Zerlina says there's nothing to worry about, Don Giovanni is a gentleman. Masetto leaves. The seduction begins."

Nolan walked slowly around the singer, who followed him with her eyes. "Giovanni wants to add this lovely young thing to his list of conquests. He is clever. He knows what to say to a girl like this. My dear Zerlina, a noble cavalier such as I cannot allow your sweet beauty to be stolen by that clumsy oaf. You weren't meant to be a peasant! Do you see that little villa there? It's mine, and there we will be married." He pointed at the piano. "Begin."

The accompanist played and Nolan's rich voice filled the room. *"Là ci darem la mano, là mi dirai di sì —"* As he sang, one arm moved behind the girl, not quite touching, and he slowly opened his hand, waiting for her to take it. Gail could visualize Zerlina being drawn into a velvet cloak. The effect was breathtakingly sensual. The girl suddenly laughed and hid her face.

"What is this?" Nolan drew back. "Blushing? Good. This is a sweet, ignorant child. She has never seen a man like this, none as sophisticated and sexy as I. No snickering from the audience, please. Accompanist, begin a few bars before she comes in." He turned back to the girl. "Now, Zerlina. Will you go with me?"

Her clear soprano replied, *"Vorrei, e non vorrei, mi trema un poco il cor . . ."*

"Yes. Her little heart is trembling. Not quite so eager, though." He lifted her chin with an extended forefinger. "Think of the words. Come with me, my beloved. And what does Zerlina say to that? Tell me in English."

"I feel sorry for Masetto!"

"But it's not funny. That's not the response we want here. He's a clumsy peasant, but don't be unkind to him. Music, please." The piano came in, and Nolan sang, *"Vieni, mi bel diletto!"*

"Mi fa pietà Masetto." This time she sighed with worry.

"Yes, poor clod, what can he offer? Don Giovanni will change your life." Nolan lightly caressed her cheek. *"Io cangierò tua sorte."*

The girl looked timidly up into his eyes. *"Presto non son più forte. . . ."*

"Ah. She's weakening. She can't resist much longer. So I close in. This time when I ask her to come with me, she agrees. *Andiam!"* Nolan beckoned to the other student. "Aaron, come here. You do it. You are sexy, hot." The class laughed. "The word is seduction, Aaron. Think of a mouse and a cobra."

The young man was pudgy, with straight black hair hanging over his forehead. "In our interpretation, Zerlina secretly wants Giovanni. She plays hard to get, so later she can say he tricked her."

"Oh?" Nolan considered that. "Then what is the point of the story? If she is guilty and he is innocent, why does he go to hell at the end? No, I see him as a rapacious seducer, and Zerlina as his young victim." Nolan spread his arms wide. "But it wouldn't be art, would it, if there were only one meaning. I'm willing to be persuaded."

A student in the back said, "Mr. Nolan, we want to see you play Zerlina."

Over the laughter he said, "I think not." He sat on a tall chair, one sneaker on the floor, the other on the cross brace.

The young man's voice was strong and supple, but his movements were stiff. Nolan told him to have fun with it, relax. He left his chair several times to correct pronunciation or phrasing. As she watched, Gail could see the changes. From a static duo, the singers turned it into a scene. She found herself smiling and humming along. After they had finally run through it without stopping, the other students applauded.

"Bravi!" said Thomas Nolan.

After a short lecture on vocal technique, the class was over and feet thundered down the risers. Some of the students stayed to speak to Nolan for a few minutes. Gail found Zerlina and Giovanni and complimented them both. Gradually the room cleared.

Gail said, "I enjoyed it. You're right, they're very talented."

Nolan closed the door and came back. He stopped directly in front of Gail and smiled slightly as he crossed his arms. "Let me guess. You're here to tell me I need a bodyguard." The animation he had shown in class was gone, pulled back inside as if a switch had been flipped.

"You must have been talking to Jeffrey Hopkins," she said.

"No. Rebecca Dixon called me at home. She's not happy with the guy you picked out — assuming I want a bodyguard, and I don't."

Gail tapped the flat of her hand on the back of the molded plastic chair she had just vacated. "Well. Did Rebecca give any reasons? I'd be interested to hear them."

"He's Cuban — not that it bothers me, you understand, but Rebecca Dixon thinks it's a disqualifier, given the political implications. Reason two — which does bother me. This Felix, whatever, is a former member of Castro's secret police. Is this the kind of person I want lurking around me? No, thanks. Were you aware of this?"

"Yes. I can't discuss it in detail, but you've got the wrong impression. It's true that Castillo worked for the Cuban government, but he quit and they threw him in prison. He came to the U.S. through Mariel, and he's been here almost twenty years."

What in hell, Gail wondered, was Rebecca doing? Had she related the entire story about Nicaragua? It was more than Gail could bear to think about, but she had to know. "Did she say anything else?"

"Basically that we can't be sure who he's working for." Nolan went to collect his notes and scores from the small table next to his chair.

"I don't know what she means. This has got to be a misunderstanding. I'll talk to her." Gail followed Nolan across the room. "I've met Castillo, and he's thoroughly trustworthy. My fiancé is a criminal defense attorney here in Miami, and he uses Castillo on many of his cases." She took a business card from her jacket pocket. "Here. Talk to him. If you don't like him, we'll find someone else."

"I don't need a bodyguard, Gail."

"How many death threats have you gotten?"

He flipped shut a spiral notebook and tossed it on the stack. "Anonymous assholes who scream in Spanish, then hang up. Sure, it gets on my nerves, but a bodyguard won't stop them. The other guys in the production said they'd look out for me. But thanks. I appreciate your concern."

He started to pick up the stack of music, but Gail dropped her hand on it. "There are a couple of other things we need to discuss. You lied to me about what you did in Cuba. You did more than sing for the folks at a rundown theater in Havana. There were two other performances, one at an amphitheater on Varadero Beach and another at a business conference at the Hotel Las Americas attended by at least one of the highest officials in the Cuban government. The local radio stations knew about it before I did. What if we had made a statement to the press denying it?"

Nolan's only response was to purse his thin lips. The blue eyes stared back at her as if she were a window.

"Just play straight with me, Tom. Nobody's going to fire you at this point."

"I told you," he said quietly, "this role is important. I wanted to do it in Miami."

"If I remember right," Gail said, "Lloyd Dixon helped you get here. Did he also suggest what your Cuban story should be? Between you and me, Tom."

He hesitated for a second, then nodded.

"In Cuba, were you paid for your performances?"

"No. We only got our hotel and food."

"I see. The government took care of it."

"Well, they didn't give me any money." He paced away a few steps, hands on his hips. "Who'd you get to check up on me? Felix Castillo?"

"Yes."

"He's wrong. I only did two performances. I didn't do the amphitheater concert."

"Your name was on the schedule."

"I don't care if it was or wasn't. I didn't
perform there."

"But you were at the Hotel Las Americas."

Nolan stared up at the ceiling. "This is
insane."

"Who was in the audience? Do you recall?"

"I don't know. There were about a thousand people, mostly foreigners. Cubans
were there, too. There was a lot of security,
so there were probably some VIPs. I didn't
pay attention. I went there to sing. It's these
Miami extremists who are making it into a
big deal. You ought to hear what my friends
in other parts of the country are saying
about this. They can't believe it."

Gail said, "Have you been asked for an
interview?"

"A reporter from the *Miami Herald* called,
but I was on my way to class."

"Refer everything to Jeffrey Hopkins. He's
handling all statements to the media. Don't
go on TV and don't go on radio. There is a
commentator on a Cuban station who wants
a spokesman from the opera to appear. Don't

do it. If someone does stick a microphone in your face, smile and look bewildered and say that you went to Cuba hoping to study the situation first-hand. You wanted to rise above political barriers, something like that. And you sympathize with the exiles and sincerely regret any unintentional offense that you may have given."

Nolan's lips curled into a little smile. "Should I get on my knees?"

"Why don't you try telling the exiles they're a bunch of reactionary bullies? Maybe that would work."

He arched his hand across his forehead and squeezed. "Okay. Point taken. Let me have Castillo's card. I'll call him from the office." Nolan read the card quickly, then slid it into his shirt pocket. "I never expected singing to be a life-threatening occupation."

As he picked up his music, Gail said, "Tom, wait."

He glanced at his watch. "I've got to go. I have a staff meeting."

"Just a quick question. When did you leave Miami? You were born here, but when did you leave?"

Frowning slightly, he gazed at the far wall. "I don't know. I was sixteen. I guess that's . . . 1979."

"Where did you go to high school?"

"Ransom-Everglades."

She laughed. "My God, so did I. I thought you looked familiar."

His eyes moved over her face. "I don't remember you."

"I graduated in 1981. You weren't in that class, were you?"

"No. It would've been 1980, but I'd already moved to Virginia."

"I should find my old yearbook and have you sign it," Gail said. "No one else I knew ever became famous."

He gave a small laugh and shook his head as he went out the door. "Please don't do that. I was a skinny recluse. Those weren't my best years. I would not like to be reminded."

Gail stood in the lobby of the music school with her portable phone and called Rebecca Dixon. The housekeeper answered. Mrs. Dixon was not in. She had a social engagement this evening and was not expected back until late. Gail left her number and a message to please call Ms. Connor, reference Tom Nolan.

She called for her own messages. Miriam gave her three, but they could wait until tomorrow. She said there was good news from

Anthony. The jury in his manslaughter trial had come back with a not-guilty verdict. How about dinner to celebrate? Karen too, of course.

Gail hadn't had a chance to speak to Anthony since his grandfather's birthday party. Sunday brunch at her mother's house didn't count. She still wanted to find out what he'd been thinking of, going after Octavio Reyes, but had decided not to push him to talk about it. Anthony's defenses went up when pushed. She hit speed-dial for his office. He was on another call, but his secretary said he wanted to be interrupted if Ms. Connor called. When he picked up, Gail said, "Congratulations on the verdict. I never doubted victory for a minute."

"You wouldn't say that if you were a criminal lawyer. Listen, I just heard from Felix. He says you want him to investigate Octavio?" Anthony's tone was a mixture of incredulity and annoyance. "Gail, what are you doing? You don't ask Felix — you don't ask anybody — to conduct an investigation into a member of my family without speaking to me first. I didn't know you were going to do this. I hear about it from Felix —"

"Hold it!" Gail walked farther away from the people going in and out of the lobby. "Of course I was going to tell you, but I was there, and the subject just came up —"

"Just came *up?* You have a telephone. Why didn't you call me and say, Anthony, this is what I found out about Octavio, and I think you ought to ask Felix to look into it. You couldn't have done that?"

Gail pressed her fingertips to her forehead and held back an urge to yell at him. "Okay," she said softly. "Stop raving, Anthony."

"I'm not raving. I'm making a point."

"Which — in retrospect — I could possibly agree with." She gritted her teeth, then said evenly, "Doesn't it ever occur to you — darling — that what affects you affects me? That I happened to care about you?"

"I don't question your motivation — sweetheart — but your judgment. You're too impulsive. You don't think anything through first, you just do it."

"Never think *anything* through. Well, thank you very much, Mr. Perfect. Who was that man I saw behind your grandfather's house having that nice little chat with Octavio last Saturday night —"

"Gail —"

"Couldn't have been you."

"Don't change the subject, Gail."

"I didn't ask a *stranger* to do this," she said. "Felix is a friend. Isn't he?"

"*Coño*. Okay, okay." Anthony added, "But you should have talked to me."

Gail said, "All right. I didn't. I'm sorry."

There was a pause. "Okay." Then an exhalation of breath. "Did you get my other message about dinner? I was thinking we could look at some engagement rings first. Mayor's in Coral Gables is open until nine o'clock. Karen can come. Two of us against one, I might have a chance."

"Oh, we can't. Karen has a soccer game." Gail turned her back on the lobby and leaned a shoulder against the wall. "Come to my house after. We can forage in my refrigerator. I have a cold bottle of champagne."

"You do?" She heard the squeaking of chair springs. He would be leaning back, looking at the ferny, sun-dappled atrium through the big window in his office. "I don't know. It would be dangerous to drive after having champagne."

"Well . . . I could make up the bed in the guest room," she said.

"No. That one's too small for what I'm going to do to you." His low chuckle sent a flutter through her stomach down into her legs. Then he asked what time she would be home, and they agreed he would arrive at eight-thirty.

Gail was about to drop the telephone into her purse when she remembered the other call she had to make. "Damn." She looked at her watch. Already close to five-thirty.

She found Seth Greer's number in her address book.

He had left an hour earlier. Gail explained who she was, the attorney for the Miami Opera, and that she was supposed to pick up some papers. "Perhaps he left them for me. Could you look?" Past the windows, long shadows extended eastward, but the sky was still that clear, saturated blue found only on late afternoons in winter, a trick of light or variation in humidity.

The secretary came back to say she couldn't find anything with Ms. Connor's name on it. "He must have taken them with him." When Gail made a small groan, the woman said, "He went home. You could go by and get them."

"If he's there."

"He should be. He said he had somebody coming over for dinner."

"Really." The glass door swung open as two young men went out with a huge black box, possibly a tympani case. "I'll just drop by, then. Could I trouble you for the address?"

FOURTEEN

The streets in Coconut Grove were narrow and shady, with expensive walled condo communities gradually pushing out the small wood-frame houses where the original inhabitants had lived. Gail had gone to school in the Grove when real artists and crazies had studios there, before it became too aware of itself, too commercial, with some of the worst crime statistics in Miami. Gail made sure her doors were locked as she drove slowly south looking for the right road.

Twenty years ago Anthony had lived here. He and Rebecca and Seth. It was possible that after school Gail had walked with her friends to the little deli on Main Highway to buy a soda. Anthony might have been standing in line ahead of her, his long hair waving past the collar of his green army jacket. He might have paid for his beer and, as he turned to leave, glanced without interest at the skinny fourteen-year-old girls chattering behind him, wearing their Ransom-Everglades uniforms, neat little sky-blue jumpers. Girls heading for deb parties and class trips to Paris, daughters of Miami's late-seventies social elite. What would he have thought if someone had told him he would someday fall in love with one of these girls? Or how would the girl have reacted, looking up into that bearded face, those angry black eyes?

The number for Seth Greer's house was tacked to a sabal palm tree, and under the sign, a stern warning from Brinks Home Security. The driveway was unpaved and overgrown into a tunnel of foliage that opened up to reveal a low, rectilinear house with overhanging eaves. Through glass panels under the flat roof, Gail could see the top of a stone chimney and an open-beam ceiling. A dense stand of bamboo threatened to take over what little yard remained. In the gravel turnaround were two cars — a small black BMW and a silver Jaguar.

In the fading daylight Gail walked across a mildewy plank porch. A wind chime of temple bells, green and pitted with age, tinkled softly from the far corner. Gail pressed the doorbell. She waited. Beside the door was a yellowing fiberglass panel with a Japanese design of twisted pine boughs and a snow-capped mountain. A shadow in the shape of a person moved across it. Probably checking her out through the peephole. The shape went back in the other direction. She pressed the bell again. Waited some more. Then heard shoes on a floor. She wondered what he had been wearing — or not — the first time.

The door opened. Seth Greer in business shirt and gray slacks. Not happy to see her, but smiling anyway, pretending she couldn't have noticed Rebecca Dixon's car in his driveway. "Well. Hello, Gail." He was not inviting her in.

"I don't want to disturb you —"

"No, it's okay." Then he dropped his forehead onto extended fingers. "Oh, Christ. The research."

"Your secretary said you might have taken it home."

"I'm sorry. Something came up and I don't have it finished. But look. I can courier it to your office by noon tomorrow. All right?"

"Oh, great. The appointment is in the morning."

"The morning? You should have told me."

"I did. Seth, you wanted to help out. That's why I called you."

He held up his hands. "All right. I'll go downtown early and get it from the law library."

"No, never mind." She could do that much herself. Or not do it at all.

Over his shoulder she noticed that Rebecca Dixon had come into the entrance hall. The little luncheon suit was gone, replaced by stretch pants and a black sweater. "Seth, for heaven's sake, don't keep Gail out there on the porch."

"I was just leaving," Gail said.

"No, you don't." Rebecca reached past Seth to tug on her wrist. "I have something to say to you. Come in here for a minute."

Seth stepped back and lifted an arm. "Please."

The living room had a conversation pit, an architectural touch Gail had not seen since her childhood. The furniture was a weird combination of oriental and unadorned modern, and the walls were done in rice paper. Sliding glass doors opened onto a wood deck under a vine-draped trellis. A pool pump hummed in the gathering darkness, then shut off.

Rebecca took the two steps down to a U-shaped arrangement of leather sofas, moving carefully, keeping her balance. "Seth, fix Gail a drink."

"I can't stay long. My daughter has a soccer game."

"You can stay five minutes." Rebecca

sank into a corner and curled her legs to one side. She was barefoot.

"What would you like, Gail?" Seth asked.

"Nothing. Thanks." She sat down and put her purse on the coffee table — a black lacquered square with dragon's-claw feet and a scaly bas-relief tail around the perimeter.

With one elbow on the sofa, Rebecca rested her head in her hand. Heavy bangs and the black sweater framed her pale face. Her mascara was smudged. "I want to apologize for my behavior today outside the opera. I am not normally a rude person. I feel so bad."

"Please. There's nothing to apologize for," Gail said.

Rebecca reached for her drink, a red concoction in a big martini glass. Her long nails grazed the stem and sent the liquid sloshing close to the rim. She settled back with the drink on her angled knee. "Are you shocked and scandalized, finding me here?"

"You said you and Seth were friends, so I don't think anything about it."

"Very diplomatic of you. I don't do this very often. Whenever I need cheering up. Good old Seth."

"Don't let your coach turn into a pumpkin," Gail said.

It took Rebecca a second to figure that out. She made a soundless laugh. "Lloyd's in Cuba."

"Cuba?"

"I thought you'd get a kick out of that."

"What's he doing in Cuba?"

Her eyes closed for the length of a little shrug. "No idea."

She didn't know or wouldn't say? Gail would have pressed to find out, but Seth returned with his drink, something in a rocks glass. He remained standing, either for the sake of not appearing too chummy with Rebecca or because he did not want to encourage Gail to linger.

Gail would have said good night, but there was another issue to take care of. "Rebecca, I talked to Tom this afternoon about Felix Castillo being his bodyguard. He said you'd told him about Castillo's past in Cuba. I don't know exactly what you said, or how accurate it was, but you really shouldn't have. If it became public knowledge, Castillo could have some trouble."

"God forbid," murmured Rebecca, her lips at the rim of her glass.

Seth asked, "Is Tom going to use him?"

"I'm not sure. I gave him Castillo's business card, and he said he'd call him."

"What would it take to unhire Felix

Castillo and find someone else?"

"Why would we do that?"

"Are you serious? Becky called me up. I couldn't believe it. Could not believe it."

Gail looked at Rebecca. "I asked you. I said if you don't want Castillo, say so."

"It doesn't matter. Seth, please —"

"No, let me talk." His attention was still on Gail. "I assume by now that Anthony filled you in on our little sojourn to Central America."

"Yes, he told me. Felix was there as an advisor from Cuba working for the rebels. That was twenty years ago. He's like Anthony — he stays out of politics now, and I think that's what we need. I'm sure he'll do a good job."

As if she had spoken in Chinese, Seth stared at her from the other side of his black dragon coffee table. "You know about the girl who was with us?"

"Yes." Gail said slowly, "Anthony told me what happened to her. She was shot by the Sandinistas — by a man named Pablo. And after . . . her burial, you escaped."

"Jesus H. Christ!" Seth put his hands to his head. "How can you be so goddamn insensitive? You don't think it *matters* that Felix was there? That he knows who we are?"

Gail stared back at him. "He was there . . . when she died?"

"Yes! He came with Pablo!" Dropping his arms by his sides, he said, "Oopsie. Looks like Quintana missed that one little detail. He called me, you know. Called both of us. Said, 'I'm going to tell Gail about Los Pozos. I'd appreciate it if you didn't talk to her yourself.' Well, you just tell him I fucked up here. Sorry, Tony."

Still trying to make sense of this, Gail said, "I — I'm sure Felix won't talk about it to anyone. Anthony wouldn't use him as an investigator if he weren't discreet."

A soft laugh came from the corner of the sofa. Rebecca said, "We should have a party, Seth. A twenty-year reunion party."

"Come on, Becky."

"Oh, we should. All of us together — Almost all of us." She laughed again, more like a hiccup. But it wasn't a laugh. She was crying. Seth put down his drink and rushed over to her. "Don't. Becky. Sweetheart." He put his arms around her head and kissed her hair. She leaned against his chest.

Gail stood. "I think I should go." Neither of them seemed to notice.

Daylight had diminished to a faint wash of gray through the trees. Gail was unlocking her car when Seth called to her from the porch. If his tone had been hostile, she might have fled.

Gail waited. "Is Rebecca all right?"

"Sure. She said I ought to walk you out. Sorry for yelling at you, Gail. It's not your fault. I'm going crazy with this."

"What should I do?" she asked. "My God, I feel so terrible. If I'd known —"

Seth took her hand and patted it. "Don't worry. Like you said, Castillo has no profit in bringing it up. We could do the same to him, right? I bet the exiles would have him for lunch."

"He wanted Emily Davis *dead?* He knew she was Anthony's girlfriend, didn't he?"

His face tightening as if in pain, Seth said, "There wasn't a whole lot anybody could do about it. Not even Felix. It's not one of my favorite topics of conversation. Do you mind?"

"Oh, God, what a situation," Gail said. "Are you sure Rebecca's okay?"

"Yes." Then he shook his head. "No, she isn't. If I could get her out of Miami, it would help. But there are a few complications, including the fact that the lady is married."

Gail had heard nothing further from Rebecca about wanting the name of a divorce lawyer. She said, "Rebecca mentioned just now that Lloyd went to Cuba. You don't happen to know why, do you?"

He made a short laugh. "Maybe for the women. They hang around the tourist hotels. Supposedly they'll do anything if you take them to a dollar store for a pair of shoes."

"You don't believe that's why he went," Gail said. "Rebecca really doesn't know?"

"She doesn't tell me everything," Seth said.

"Did she ever mention that Lloyd knows Octavio Reyes?"

"Reyes is a customer, I know that much. Is there more?"

"I'm not sure."

Seth laughed. "Wouldn't that be a news flash on Octavio Reyes's radio show? Damn. You know, I've been thinking of going on the air. He's been asking for one of us to debate him. I could tell his listening audience that he's a hypocritical blowhard."

"You bet," Gail said.

"I mean it. Somebody should stand up to him. My Spanish is still good enough."

"No, Seth. Absolutely not. Jeffrey Hopkins is handling all media relations — if you can call Octavio Reyes a serious member of the media. Tell me you won't."

"It was a thought." He looked up at the pallid sky. The bamboo swayed and whispered in a faint breeze, and the wind chime answered from the porch. "If not for now, when do we live? Socrates said that, for what it's worth. It seemed to make sense when everything I owned would fit into my Volkswagen Beetle."

Gail said, "Maybe you should talk to Rebecca. It's not too late for either of you, Seth. People can start over."

"Sho nuff?" He laughed. He was angry, but not, Gail was certain, angry at her. "No, I think Los Pozos might've done us in. We were okay — more or less — before that. What we had is buried right along with Emily Davis." He patted Gail's shoulder. "That's what Becky thinks, and if she thinks, therefore it is. I can't get her to accept that Emily's death wasn't her fault."

"Why would she blame herself?"

"Because she's the one who reported her. She saw her with the American agent. We were friends with some of the men who died, so Rebecca was furious. She talked to the other nurse in the clinic, and then the rebels heard about it." Seth's glasses lifted when he rubbed his eyes. "Can I say this? The problem was, and is, that Emily should never have gone with us. She was a dumb, sweet kid. She couldn't take it, she wanted out, and Quintana wouldn't let her go."

Gail frowned. "He said there wasn't money to pay her airfare back to Miami."

"Oh, bullshit. All he had to do was phone home from La Vigia. Eat a little crow, beg a little bread to get her out of there. What happened to her, I blame Anthony Quintana. She was a toy to him. He didn't care."

"That's not true." Gail could remember clearly what Anthony had told her about Los Pozos. He had not mentioned Felix, but his anguish over Emily Davis had been real.

Seth was smiling again, that thin cover for anger. "Why do you think he brought her along?"

"He isn't like that at all."

"You did not know the man then, Gail. I did. Here's how he met Emily Davis. We saw her jogging on campus. She was a cute girl with a great body. A nice girl, you know? She had long blond hair and loads of freckles. He had a thing about American women, his little joke. He said it was his way of screwing the U.S. We had a standard bet, twenty bucks if he could get the girl into bed within two days. He lost with Emily. It took him a week."

Turning away, Gail leaned on her car. "All right. As a young man he was generally pissed off about everything —"

"Yeah, Gail, I'm sure that's what it was. Rebecca and I were living together over on Elizabeth Street. I was practicing law, she was in pre-med. We had a nice little apartment. When Tony got into trouble with his granddad, I let him stay with us. One day I came home early, they're going at it in the bedroom. I tried to be cool about it. In the seventies, people weren't as uptight as now. We never heard of AIDS, and sex was actually fun. Anyway. He moved out, she went with him, and I said, Becky, when it's over, call me. Tony had no guilt about it. He dumped her inside a month. She came back, and Tony and I made up. We were fairly progressive in those days."

Struggling not to show a reaction, Gail stared straight into Seth's face.

He seemed to crumple. "Jesus, what am I doing? I'm sorry, I'm sorry, sorry, sorry." With each word he hit his forehead lightly with the heel of his hand. "You didn't need to hear that. I swear to you, I don't mean to bash the man. He saved my life, mine and Becky's. He got us out of there, and God knows I couldn't have done it." Hands on his hips, his face ragged with fatigue, he looked back at the house. "I should go check on her."

Seth opened Gail's door and made sure she knew which way to turn at the end of the driveway. "Good night, kid."

On the field behind Biscayne Academy, blazing lights made an island of color and motion. Children raced across the field in their yellow or red jerseys. Cleated shoes thundered over the ground and kicked up bits of grass, and the soccer ball shot ahead, a dizzy spin of black and white.

Biscayne made the goal and the parents whistled and cheered. Gail waited for Karen to look her way, then waved and gave a thumbs-up. Karen grinned, bounced up and down excitedly in her big yellow jersey, then spun around to line up with the rest of her team. She had fallen down a few times. Her knees were scraped.

Dressed in jeans and sneakers, Gail walked along the sidelines, avoiding conversations with other parents. She was waiting for Anthony to return her call. Five minutes ago she had left a message on his beeper. He might be at dinner with a client or another lawyer in his firm. He would feel the beeper at his belt, glance at the number, then excuse himself to find a phone. And Gail would say, *Anthony, I'm so sorry. This isn't a good night for you to come over. The soccer game started late, and Karen just told me she has a book report to do.* A lie, but she didn't particularly care if he believed her or not, the mood she was in.

On the field the children ran past in a huffing mass of arms and legs. Karen played halfback, and she was poised, shifting foot to foot, arms out for balance. When the ball got within range she rushed at it, and Gail heard the thump of a shoe hitting a shin guard and high-pitched yells to kick it here, kick it here.

As she kept an eye on the action — trying to — she heard piano music in the back of her mind. Mozart, played by the accompanist from Tom Nolan's master class. Nolan had walked slowly around the young soprano, who blushed as he held out his hand and sang in that incredibly rich voice. But it wasn't Nolan she was seeing. It was Anthony.

FIFTEEN

Sometimes after a game, team parents let themselves be talked into going by the Pizza Hut near the soccer field. Gail often said *no* for any of several good reasons: it's a school night, you have homework, I have a trial to prepare for — But tonight she gave in. Biscayne had won. But more than that, Gail needed the babble and laughter of a room full of fifth-graders. Anthony had accepted without question her flimsy excuse for not seeing him tonight, and his understanding had made her feel even worse.

On the way to the car Karen skipped, still buoyant from victory. She wanted to know if Gail had seen her make the assist on the winning goal. The coach had said he would put her in the starting lineup for the next game. They followed the other cars out of the parking lot, and Karen scooted down in the seat with her leg in the air to pull off cleats and shin pads, then lace up her sneakers.

Karen had made it known that wherever they moved to, it had better be close to their present neighborhood so she wouldn't lose her friends. Anthony had talked about looking at more houses this weekend with that in mind.

Pacing up and down the sidelines at the soccer field, Gail had felt sick with the realization that there was no point in looking at houses this weekend; their marriage was sure to fail if Anthony was the kind of man Seth had portrayed. Then her thoughts whirled in the other direction: Seth had lied. Holding a grudge for twenty years, Seth wanted revenge.

Or maybe not. Maybe the facts were right, but Seth's conclusions had been wrong.

Maybe Anthony had slept with Rebecca, and he had made bets on seducing American girls — but so what? He had been so young, living in another era, as Seth had said. The late seventies. Gail had come of age in the eighties, with its own way of looking at things.

Facts and conclusions. In her law practice Gail had heard different witnesses interpret the same set of facts and reach wildly diverging conclusions. Each had sworn to tell the truth, and each appeared to be sincere. According to Seth, Anthony had taken Emily Davis along for sex. She'd been a sweet, dumb kid. Anthony had said Emily wanted to go along, then when she got there, she turned into a complainer.

Gail's blinker ticked as she waited for a light to turn green. She thought of her mother's bridge games, the endless stories about the people they knew, how the truth went round and round. What was true? And who was Anthony? Why had he gone to Nicaragua? For justice? To prove his manhood? Or to recover what he had lost — his idyllic life in Camagüey? Whether it had actually been so idyllic didn't matter. The image mattered. For whatever reason he had gone to Nicaragua, he had come back injured in his soul. Seth had said his and Rebecca's love had died with Emily Davis. Something in Anthony had died as well: his certainty. There were no good guys anymore. No good, no bad. Everyone equally lost.

Turning into the lot at the Pizza Hut, she heard a muffled jangle and at the same time, Karen's voice. "Mom! Mom, aren't you going to answer it?"

Gail glanced at her purse. She hesitated, then flipped open the phone. "Hello."

"Hey, counselor!" It was Seth Greer, sounding strangely upbeat. "I tried your house, then I remembered you had a game to go to. Are you in your car? Turn on your radio to AM eight-seventy."

"WRCL? What's up?" Gail punched the preset button and heard an orchestra with a Latin beat, probably pre-revolution. "What am I supposed to be listening to?"

"They'll announce it any minute now. Seth Greer live at nine o'clock. I'm going to do it, Gail. I'm getting into the ring with *el rey del comentario,* the King of Crap."

"Oh, my God." Gail quickly found a parking space. A nasal-voiced ballad singer crooned along in Spanish with the orchestra.

"Mom, what's that stuff?"

Gail waved her quiet. "Seth? What the hell are you telling me?"

"Does that mean you disapprove? Well, Gail, that's too bad. Sorry if that sounds uppity. They've already announced my appearance. In fact, they've already broadcast some of the comments I made when I called up the station and said I was going to take Reyes on."

As Seth talked, the song ended and a Toyota ad began.

"Mom!" Karen was on her knees looking through the back window. "They're going in!"

Glancing around, Gail said, "Go ahead, honey. I'll be there in a minute. Seth, the executive committee will have a fit if they

245

hear about this — and they will. You could get kicked off the board."

"Not to worry. How many of them listen to Cuban radio?"

Karen's door slammed.

"Seth, don't do this. You have not been authorized by the opera —"

"I'm not going as a representative of the opera. Quiet, it's coming on. Listen!"

A man's voice, an announcer. Gail heard Thomas Nolan's name, then the words *el regimen de Castro.* He had sung for the regime — Then the voice of a man speaking Spanish with an American accent.

"Seth, what did you say? I didn't understand —"

"Let's see. How would I translate that? It's like . . . the battle is over, folks. Fidel won. Deal with it."

She yelled into the phone, "Are you crazy?"

"Listen, Gail, I have to get ready to go. They want me there by eight-forty-five."

"Stop. Are we working together or not? You're not helping if you run off and do stupid things like this."

"Well, I haven't been much help so far, have I?"

"Wait. There's something you have to know."

A moment of silence. Then he said, "What is it?"

Her mind spun, grabbing for anything plausible. If she could talk to him for five minutes — Grab his arm. Beg him.

"Gail?"

Her engine was still idling. She said, "It's too sensitive to discuss on a cell phone. I'll come by your house."

"There's no time. It's eight-fifteen. Meet me outside the station, Coral Way and Twentieth. In fact, you should join me in the studio."

"Wait for me," she said. "Promise you won't go on the air till we talk."

"Well, you'd better hurry."

Gail tossed the phone to the passenger seat. "Dammit!" She put the car in reverse. accelerated, then hit the brakes, went forward, and parked again. She rushed inside the restaurant and found Karen at a table with her best friend, Molly Perlmutter. Gail smiled at the girls, then went around to speak to Molly's mother. They lived down the street.

So sorry. An emergency with a client. An hour or so, not more than that. She would pick Karen up at Molly's house. She gave Karen ten dollars, kissed her, and was out the door. It would take fifteen minutes to get there. Gail gunned the car up U.S. 1. The station would be just east of Coral Gables.

With the interior light on, she flipped through her address book for Felix Castillo's pager, the only way to contact him. "Felix, this is Gail Connor. We have a loose cannon from the opera on his way to WRCL — Seth Greer. I'm going to try to persuade him not to go on the air, but just in case, would you please be available for Tom Nolan? He might need you later on tonight or tomorrow. I'm going to tell him to contact you. Thanks."

Next she punched in Tom Nolan's number in Miami Beach. Five rings, then his voice mail. Gail took a breath to sound completely relaxed. "Hi, Tom. This is Gail Connor. Don't worry, it's probably fine, but Octavio Reyes is on the warpath again tonight. I've left a message with Felix Castillo to expect your call, so go ahead and beep him."

She stopped herself before mentioning Seth Greer. Instead she signed off with Castillo's pager number and a cheerful "Talk to you soon. Bye."

Coral Way was an old street, two lanes divided by banyan trees, with small shops on either side. Traffic was not heavy at this time of night. Through the trees, then more clearly, she saw a blue backlit outline of Cuba, then across that at an angle the letters WRCL in white neon.

The building rested on concrete pillars and a small cube that contained a lobby, a guard's desk, and elevators. Gail got a glimpse inside as she turned into the parking lot. A tile walkway between low hedges led to the street. Gail parked in one of the visitors' spaces at the side. The antique shop next door was closed, as were the other small businesses in the strip. Beauty shop, pet store —

Seth's BMW was nowhere in sight. A chain-link fence and electronic gate protected the parking lot behind the building, but he wouldn't have the gate opener to get in there. Apparently she had arrived first.

This was not a dangerous area, she reminded herself. A couple strolled along the sidewalk. Gail got out of her car. There was an all-night restaurant across the street with plenty of people inside. She glanced over her shoulder at the studios of WRCL. On the second floor, light came weakly through tinted glass and closed miniblinds. Octavio Reyes was up there preparing to eviscerate Seth Greer.

With a shiver that came more from nerves than the chilly night air, Gail got back inside her car and hit the locks. A minute later a BMW turned off the street and parked next to the sidewalk. Its headlights went off. With a little sigh of relief, Gail watched Seth Greer get out, buttoning his suit jacket over his tie, smoothing his hair. Dressed for battle. He walked around the rear of Gail's car. She pressed the button to lower her window.

"My fan club is here," he said, reaching through to pinch her cheek.

"Is Rebecca still at your house?" Gail asked.

"No, she left a couple of hours ago, not long after you did. She took a cab. I'll get her car back to her tomorrow."

"God, Seth. Does she know what you're doing?"

"Sure. I called her." Seth laughed. "She told me to have a good time. Come on, lady. Smile." He had just shaved and put on cologne. His face glowed.

"Get in," she said. "I need to talk to you."

Seth planted his hands on the open window. "I have to go upstairs."

"You promised you'd talk to me first," she said.

He checked his watch, looked over at the building, then back at Gail. "Okay, give me the short version."

"Listen, Seth. You say you're not representing the opera, but Reyes won't see it that way. I heard your remarks on the radio. People will assume you're a spokesman, even if you deny it."

"I'll make it clear to him —"

"Nobody will believe you. Whatever you say — and what I heard was pretty damned inflammatory — will reflect on the Miami Opera and everyone connected to it."

"All right, it was a little strong." He shrugged. "You watch. I'll be a model of reasoned debate."

"Reyes will goad you into losing your temper."

"Not a chance." Grinning, he said, "I plan to be on the air long enough to point out that his company does business with a big fan of Thomas Nolan."

"It's not exactly a secret."

"Oh, but it's so sweet. I want to hear him explain why he's involved with Lloyd Dixon." When Seth backed away from the window, Gail quickly got out of the car.

"Would you *listen?*" Gail slammed her door. "It doesn't matter what you say to Octavio Reyes, he'll twist it around. Tomorrow morning I have to try to persuade the city manager that we don't have a problem. If you go on the air, I guarantee another concrete block through the door. Or worse. What might happen to Tom Nolan? Or the other cast members, or the employees? Or to you?"

His eyes were closed. "Gail — Gail, please. Somebody has to take a stand. Reyes is using mob tactics to control who can and can't perform or speak out in this city. It's wrong. It's not democratic. They're doing what they say they're against."

"But you're going to make it *worse.*"

"Everybody is afraid to stand up for what's right. That's the problem —"

"Who are you doing this for, Seth?" Gail was his height, looking straight into his eyes. "It's for Rebecca, isn't it? You want to prove something to Rebecca. This isn't the way to do it! Not by putting her and everyone in the opera in danger."

He looked around at the building. "I have to go. They're expecting me."

She grabbed at his coat and got hold of his cuff. "Screw Reyes. If you don't go on, he'll be embarrassed. He can call you a coward, but you're not. Seth, you're not."

He was wavering.

"Come with me to the city manager's office tomorrow. Say what you have to there, where it might do some good."

As she spoke, Gail noticed an odd flash of light on the dark lapel of his jacket, a small red dot. It moved sideways, brightening for an instant on his white shirt. Seth looked past her toward the parking lot next door. He frowned in puzzlement.

There was a muffled pop. Gail felt the fabric of Seth's sleeve pull from her grasp, and at the same moment the breath whooshed out of his mouth as if he'd been punched. An instant later a star appeared in the windshield. More pops. Seth stumbled and hung onto the side mirror.

The ground shifted and Gail put her hands out to stop her fall. Seth's shirt was turning red. Then his throat seemed to explode, and blood sprayed in the air like mist. His glasses clattered onto the pavement.

Gail heard screams — her own. She rolled underneath the rear of her car. Time seemed to drag out, and she observed her body reacting as if it were a separate being, calculating what had happened and how to get away, dragging her along, no thought to it, only motion and instinct. On hands and knees, crawling into the space between her car and Seth's. Rolling through the hedge, then scrambling to the sidewalk, tripping on the curb. The pavement rushing up to meet her.

Lights in her face. The scream of tires. A door opening.

People running toward her.

"Please help," she gasped. "Someone's been shot."

SIXTEEN

The paramedics let Gail sit on the back bumper of their truck to tape her left hand and wrist. She leaned numbly against the open door. The knee of her jeans had been ripped on a rebar sticking out of a parking bumper, luckily missing the flesh underneath. Blue and red lights flashed everywhere, moving in regular pulses across the building. A crowd stared from the sidewalk, kept back by crime scene tape and uniformed officers. People had come downstairs from the radio station as well.

A Miami police sergeant had taken Gail's statement, then told her to wait there for the lead homicide detective. From where she sat, Gail could not see past the walkway that divided the parking lot in half. Seth still lay on the other side, next to her car. He had been hit three times. One of the bullets, perhaps the one that had gone through his hand, had angled through the open driver's-side window and hit the windshield.

The security guard at the desk inside the lobby had a view of only the walkway. A passerby across the street had seen Seth fall.

The bullets had come from the tree-shaded darkness of the parking lot next door. No one had seen the shooter.

The paramedic, a young woman in a gray uniform, smoothed some tape over the gauze to hold it. "You can get this cut looked at tomorrow. The wrist is sprained, but I'm pretty sure it's not broken." She smiled at Gail gently, then started putting the equipment away.

"Thank you. Could I have some water?" Gail took the paper cup and swallowed painfully. Her screams had made her voice husky. "What time is it?"

The woman checked her watch. "Nine-forty."

"I have to call home."

She saw out of the corner of her eye a man's gray suit coat and turned her head. Octavio Reyes had separated himself from the knot of people standing in the lobby. She had noticed him over there a while ago and had pretended not to see him.

He bent down a little to look more closely at her. "Ms. Connor — Gail — Are you all right?"

"Bruises and a sprained wrist. Otherwise, yes."

"This is terrible. A terrible thing. I don't know who could have done this."

"Oh, you don't."

Blue and red lights flashed in his glasses. "I assure you, it wasn't an exile act. It couldn't have been."

"Who, then?" she demanded. "A provocateur from Havana?"

He made no answer to that, only turned and signaled to one of the people behind him. A woman hurried over. Reyes asked Gail if she wanted anything. Coffee, a soda? Maybe she would like to clean up in the ladies' room, to have help to wash her face and hands —

"I need to call home . . . my daughter." She coughed and swallowed. Her phone was still in her car, along with her purse and keys.

Octavio Reyes was in the middle of telling the woman to bring a telephone when he stopped and focused on someone sprinting toward them.

"Gail!"

Anthony was there. His eyes were wide, his face pale. His hands slowly went out, touching her face, then taking her upper arms. Gail stood up and leaned against him, felt him shaking.

"I'm okay," she said. "I wasn't hurt."

With one arm around Gail, Anthony turned his back on his brother-in-law. "I spoke to the police, and they let me through. Did you make a statement? Can you leave?" Despite the tension in his body, his voice was calm and steady.

"I spoke to a sergeant. He said to wait for the homicide detective."

Anthony looked around. "Let me see what I can do."

It took him five minutes. He knew the lead detective and arranged for Gail to speak to them tomorrow. He retrieved her purse and her house keys. The police would return her car keys later, as the technicians had not finished with the crime scene.

Anthony told her to wait with the police until she saw his car come to the curb. Two minutes later he was there, flashers on. He opened the passenger door, put her inside, then went around. Gail noticed his pistol on the seat between them, out of its holster. He checked the rearview mirror, then accelerated. Gail felt herself being pressed back into soft leather. She let her head fall against the headrest.

"Thank you."

He reached for her hand. She pulled her left one away and he took the other. He raised it briefly to his lips, then held it on her thigh. He must have come from home, she thought. He was dressed for home —

soft khaki pants and an old cashmere sweater without a shirt underneath. Slip-on shoes but no socks. Not the sort of thing he would ever wear in public.

A few blocks away from the area, he looked in the mirror again before pulling into a well-lighted lot in front of a super-market. He cut the engine and took her in his arms. He murmured words in Spanish that she didn't understand, then pulled back far enough to look at her closely, to kiss her, to touch her face again, and the bandage on her injured hand.

At the scene he had been calm. Now the relief took over. "You're all right. You're certain?"

Gail nodded. "I'm so glad you're here. Anthony, how did you know?"

"You left a message with Felix and he called me at home as soon as he could. He was on a job and couldn't get to his phone right away. He said you were on your way to the radio station, trying to stop Seth Greer from going on the air. I asked him to see about it, but he was too far away, so I came as fast as I could. Then I saw the police lights. Oh, my God, what I thought." He kissed her again, three hard kisses, holding onto her face. The day's stubble around his mouth scratched her skin.

She pushed away a little. "I need to call Karen. She's probably at Molly's house wondering why in the world I haven't shown up."

Anthony dialed the number on his car phone, and Gail explained to Molly's mother that she'd been involved in an accident, but she was all right. They would pick up Karen on the way home.

When she hung up, Anthony turned to face her. "They said he got away, whoever it was. They don't have any witnesses. They found some cartridge casings beside the building next door."

"How many? I remember hearing pops. I don't know how many shots there were. They asked me and I couldn't tell them." Her laugh came out as a sigh. "Before you get into a situation like this, you think you'll be a good witness, but right now I can hardly remember anything."

"There were five shots fired. *Five*. The police think someone was waiting for him."

"Waiting?"

"That's what they told me." Anthony stared at her disbelievingly. "Why did you go after him? It didn't occur to you that he could be a target?"

"No. He hadn't been on the air yet. I was going to talk him out of it."

"But he had been announced. People knew he was coming to the station. Seth Greer from the Miami Opera is going to appear to debate Octavio Reyes. Maybe he wasn't the only target. You're the lawyer for the opera." Anthony's voice was rising. "Maybe one of those bullets was for you, Gail."

She closed her eyes, feeling suddenly sick.

"You remember what we were talking about? That you never think first?"

Her eyes burned. She sobbed and the pain already in her throat made it worse.

"*Ay, Diós mio.*" Anthony reached for her, stroked her head. "Sweetheart, don't cry. I'm sorry. I was so afraid for you."

When Karen had gone to bed, Anthony taped a plastic bag around Gail's injured hand so she could take a shower. He helped her undress, and Gail got a look at herself in the bathroom mirror. Her face was all right, but bruises darkened her skin in odd places, as if she had rolled down a rocky hillside. Anthony pointed them out. Embarrassed, she told him to please leave her alone. Go fix her a double brandy and find the pain reliever in the kitchen, if he wanted to be helpful.

She came out in a robe and found Anthony sitting on a stool at the counter. She rested her head on his for a moment, a mute apology. He slid a brandy glass and a couple of pills toward her and patted her back.

"I should call Rebecca. It's almost eleven o'clock. Maybe she knows already, but if not, I don't want her to hear about it on the news." Gail downed half the brandy, then coughed slightly and pressed her fingers to the notch in her collarbone, breathing out through an open mouth.

"Rebecca was at Seth's house tonight. I went by there around six o'clock to pick up some legal papers — which he didn't have ready for me — and she was there. Barefoot and drunk. I didn't mention this to the police. I'd rather not. She consulted me about a divorce."

"They were having an affair," Anthony concluded.

"That's a reasonable assumption." Gail stopped the brandy on its way to her lips. "Oh, no. Rebecca left her car in Seth's driveway. He told me she took a cab home."

"Then the police will find her car where she left it," Anthony said. "What they think about it — or what her husband thinks — is another matter. You don't have any control over that."

The telephone hung on the wall by the

counter. Gail looked at it. "I don't know what to say to her." She finished her brandy, poured herself some more, and sipped it while finding Rebecca's number in her address book. She dialed. Waited. The voice on the other end of the line startled her. Gail had expected Rebecca or at least the housekeeper. It was Lloyd Dixon.

When he boomed out hello for the second time, Gail looked at Anthony, then said, "Lloyd, this is Gail Connor. I'm sorry to be calling so late. I have some bad news. Seth Greer was killed tonight, shot outside the studios of WRCL. Is Rebecca in? . . . They don't know who did it. . . . I really don't have many details, Lloyd. Could I talk to Rebecca? . . . I see. Will you tell her? . . . Good night."

Gail hung up. "Rebecca was asleep. Lloyd was there."

"Where else would he be?"

"In Cuba. Rebecca told me that he was in Cuba."

"Why?"

"I don't know." Gail took another sip of brandy and found that her hand was shaking. She laughed and her voice shook, too. "Seth and Rebecca and I had some pretty interesting conversations tonight."

"What about?"

She shook her head. "I don't want to talk about it now." She stared at the telephone. "I should call my mother. If I don't, she'll never speak to me again. Then I want to go to sleep. Can you wait for me in my room?"

She found Anthony watching the news. He was fully dressed on top of the comforter, legs crossed at the ankles. His shoes were by the bed. When Gail came in, he aimed the remote and the TV went dark.

"Did they mention me?" she asked.

"No." He swung his feet to the floor and sat with his hands loosely clasped, looking up at her. His eyes were dark and shadowed. "Do you want me to stay?"

Gail set her refilled brandy glass on the nightstand. It caught the edge of the clock radio and nearly overturned. "Of course I want you to stay." She dropped her robe on the floor and got into bed in her nightgown. Careful not to jostle her left hand, she moved over to make room for him on her right. She lay flat and closed her eyes.

"My mother wanted to know every last damned detail. She cried. She was going to come over, but I told her you were here. Yes, Mother, I'm fine. Anthony, hand me my drink, would you?"

"No, you've had enough."

She looked up at him, but he was opening her door. "I'll be right back." Then she heard Karen's door close softly down the hall. When he returned, he closed her door and turned the lock, then turned off the reading lamp on the nightstand. Dots of color swam in the darkness, then faded.

Moonlight shone faintly through the curtains. Anthony pulled his shirt over his head. Then there was the sound of a zipper, the shifting of cloth. He laid his clothes on the armchair.

Cool air when he lifted the blankets, then the heat of his body. She turned on her side away from him. He curled around her back, only her thin cotton nightgown between them. His hand slid down her stomach, pressed for a moment between her legs, then went under her gown.

"Anthony, I can't."

He turned her over.

"I can't. I'm so numb."

His warm breath in her ear was so soft she barely heard him. His lips moved on her skin. Speaking Spanish. The words he said to her sometimes. She had never asked — had never wanted — to know what they meant.

She wept soundlessly. He kissed the corners of her eyes — gently, not to scratch her skin. When he kissed her mouth she tasted salt on his tongue.

He knew how to touch her, taking his time. As if from the depths of a lake she rose slowly to the surface into a burst of heat and light that swept away everything else. She knew that this was what she needed from him — what he was now. Here and now. Whatever had happened before didn't matter.

Several times through the night she heard the sound of gunfire. Saw Seth hanging on, trying to stay upright, blood exploding from his throat, the clatter of his glasses hitting the pavement. Then the deeper thud of his body —

Whenever her eyes flew open and she woke up trembling, Anthony's arms tightened around her.

SEVENTEEN

Eleven A.M. found Gail at her desk. Her body ached, but staying home would have been worse. She had sent Karen off on the school bus with a hug, then had let Anthony drive her to a car rental agency. At some point her Buick would be towed to a body shop for repair — or possibly sold. Gail did not think she could bear to see it again.

Her first task was to phone the city manager's office to postpone the meeting until tomorrow. Before she dared to argue the unlikelihood of protesters on opening night of *Don Giovanni*, Gail wanted to know who might have murdered Seth Greer. The police would show up in the early afternoon to talk to her. She would ask them for an opinion. Had this been an act of political terrorism? Or were they following some other lead?

She knew what was being said in the media. She had turned on the television at home while getting dressed. The story had been briefly mentioned on NBC as "possibly related to Cuban exile violence, which has tapered off in recent years." Local stations covered it more extensively. Gail saw her own car, then flipped the channel before they zoomed in on the pool of blood and the tarp covering the body. She scanned the newspaper over coffee and toast. OPERA SPOKESMAN KILLED OUTSIDE EXILE RADIO STATION. Subhead: CUBAN COMMUNITY DISMAYED. In the body of the article, a quote: *WRCL commentator Octavio Reyes said, "This act of barbarity was not perpetrated by any of us. We should look to Havana for answers."*

Her name had been mentioned. *Miami Opera attorney Gail A. Connor, 34, was talking to Greer outside the station when the shooting took place. According to police, Connor was attempting to dissuade Greer from appearing on the air.* A related story detailed other incidents in the past few years having to do with exile protests against musicians who had appeared in Cuba before coming to perform in Miami.

Anthony had barely glanced at the newspaper. He had held his coffee mug and stared grimly out the kitchen window, his face a mask of fatigue and frustration. The assumptions had already been made: The exiles had done this. Whether an organized group or one lunatic inspired by twisted no-

268

tions of patriotism, the Miami Cubans were at it again.

Other motives would be proposed. The talk stations, both English and Spanish, would crackle with rumors: As a CPA, Seth Greer had been laundering money for the mob. He'd been killed by drug dealers, loan sharks, a jealous husband, a gay lover, a client. But always the talk would come back to the exiles.

When Gail arrived at her office, Miriam handed her a stack of new messages from the media, none of which Gail planned to return, and another stack from friends, which she might get to later. There were a few others from clients or fellow lawyers — ordinary matters related to their cases, which Gail gratefully set about dealing with. "If anyone outside of my mother, Karen, Anthony, or God Almighty asks for me," she had told Miriam, "I am *not here.*"

Sometimes between phone calls, Seth Greer's face would appear in her mind — the curly gray hair and wire-rimmed glasses, and the eyes that had suddenly lit up with such fire. She tried to keep that image. That, and not the other — the bloody horror of his death.

Gail looked up from a file when Miriam came in with a cardboard banker's box, her thin arms extended by the weight. Swinging it back for a good start, she heaved it onto the desk. Her corkscrew hair bounced on her shoulders.

"My God, what's that? More phone messages?"

"You don't remember? You wanted me to research exile terrorism. There's also stuff on Cuba — history, politics, involvement in other revolutions —"

"So much?" Gail came around to peer into the box.

Miriam lifted out a dozen library books and a foot-high stack of photocopies from magazines and newspapers. "Well, a lot of it is redundant," she explained. "You know, like, two or three articles on the same topic? Oh, Gail." Miriam's eyes glimmered with tears. "Why do people do this? You were almost killed. My mother was crying on the phone this morning. She said Papi is so angry, and she feels so . . . *ashamed*. Whoever did this, I pray to God he was American. Is that a horrible thing to wish for?"

Gail put an arm around her. "Yes, but I understand." Miriam, who had been born here, had never before talked about *us* and *them*. Gail was at a loss, not knowing what to say.

The phone rang in the outer office; Gail

had turned off her ringer. Miriam snatched up the extension on her desk. In one quick breath — she must have said it fifty times this morning — Miriam said, "Law offices of Gail Connor, may I help you? . . . I'm sorry, she's not in . . . Well, she still isn't in —" Miriam glared at the receiver, then hung up. "*That* was rude. Rebecca Dixon said she knows you're here, and she wants to talk to you. She's on her way."

Hidden behind her gold-trimmed tortoiseshell sunglasses, Rebecca walked slowly alongside Gail toward her office at the end of the hall. Her voice was low and calm, not a tremor. "The funeral will be on Thursday. All of us from the opera will be there. The other major cultural organizations will be represented, too. You'll come, won't you?"

"Of course I will." Gail closed the door. "How are you, Rebecca? I called last night. Lloyd said you were asleep."

"He woke me up to tell me. I couldn't believe it. Poor, poor Seth. Poor, brave, foolish man."

"Please. Sit down." Gail gestured toward the loveseat.

Rebecca seemed to float across the room. She turned and sat in one smooth motion, tucking the hem of her short black shirt under her thighs, a rustle of fabric, a whisper of sheer black hose as one leg slid over the other. Her jewelry was simple today, only a circle of gold at her neck, matching gold earrings, a lizard-strap Cartier tank watch, and her wedding band, but not the flashy diamond that went with it. She pressed a tissue to the outer corners of her eyes without removing her sunglasses.

Gail sat beside her. "I'm so sorry, Rebecca. You've lost a wonderful friend."

"I know. He called me last night to see if I'd made it home okay. He told me what he wanted to do. Just before he hung up he said, 'Becky, I love you.' He'd never said it like that before. I couldn't say anything. Lloyd was home. I just said . . . 'Bye, Seth.' And he'll never know . . . that I loved him, too."

"Lloyd was home? You told me he was in Cuba."

"He was. He came home."

"Does he know about you and Seth?"

She lifted one hand and dropped it on Gail's arm. "You know, the oddest thing happened this morning. Juanita brought me my breakfast, and opened the curtains, and the sunlight just poured into the room. My bedroom is white and yellow, so the light was intense. I put on my robe and walked out on the patio with my juice, and the colors were so amazing, with the sun just coming up, and pink clouds way out over the ocean. I saw a seagull flying past — just one — and I knew, all of a sudden, that Seth was free. Not only Seth, both of us. We were so trapped in the past. He was a very sad man, Gail. You don't know. But then, to leave the world when he did, in a moment of hope. When he called me he sounded . . . so happy."

Her mouth trembled, and she pressed the handkerchief to her eyes again.

Gail stared at her, trying to decide how she felt. Sympathetic, bewildered, or horrified? As for Rebecca — the woman was undeniably, without a doubt, medicated.

"Oh!" Rebecca lightly touched Gail's left wrist. "You're injured. Is it from last night?"

"It's nothing — a cut and a slightly sprained wrist."

"That's awful. You were there. Oh, Gail. I hope they catch this person and give him the electric chair." Rebecca finally took off her sunglasses and folded them in slow motion. "Have you talked to the police yet?"

"Just a brief statement at the scene. They're coming this afternoon."

"They were at my door at nine-thirty this

morning. Security didn't even alert me. Lloyd had just left, thank heaven. They said they found my car at Seth's."

"What did you tell Lloyd?"

"That it wouldn't start," Rebecca said. "That's what I told the police, too. And I told them that I was at Seth's house for a meeting about opera business, and that you were there."

Gail said, "That's . . . not entirely accurate."

"Well, it isn't a *lie*. We had a meeting. Seth and I discussed the opera. And you came by for some papers. All true." Rebecca's eyes drifted up to Gail's. "I don't want people to think we were having an *affair*."

"Weren't you?"

"No. Not . . . whoopee and good times. We hardly ever had sex. We were friends. Basically, that's what we had. I went to Seth for companionship and comfort."

"Hhhmmmm," was the only response Gail trusted herself to make. She doubted that Seth Greer had understood the nature of his relationship with Rebecca. Smoothing the elastic bandage on her wrist, Gail asked, "Did you tell Lloyd that Seth was going on WRCL?"

"Yes. I told him. He wanted to know why Seth had called."

"What time did Seth call?"

"I'd just walked in the door. The police asked me that. It was about seven-thirty."

"And what time did you go to bed?"

The only irritation allowed by whatever chemical might be floating through her bloodstream was the appearance of two small creases between Rebecca's artfully penciled brows. "I know what you're thinking. Lloyd never left the house. Seth was murdered by a Cuban exile."

"You're sure about that."

"Yes. Who else? You don't want to believe it because you're engaged to Anthony Quintana. Yes, yes, yes," Rebecca said when Gail began to object. "You want to believe it's anybody but a Cuban. But they did it." She clasped her hands under her chin as if in prayer. "You know, I just thought of something. Seth died for us. He was a martyr. That's so like Seth."

"I doubt that's what he intended." Gail dropped her forehead into her palm. "Seth said he was going to go on the air and tell everyone that Reyes was one of Lloyd's customers. Is there anything else, Rebecca? You're sure they don't know each other?"

"They don't. They're business acquaintances." Rebecca let her head fall back, and her hair swung away from her face. "Oh. I also told the police that I met Seth through the opera. I would appreciate it if you didn't contradict me. Why bring it up. Right?"

"Bring what up? Nicaragua?"

The brown eyes turned to Gail. "Reporters like to poke around in your past, especially if you've got money or status. If they find out that Seth and I were members of socialist organizations in college — I can't believe I ever did that. And Anthony — he was a Marxist head to toe. How would that look for any of us, Gail? Not good. And not good for the opera in the present situation. You have to agree."

Too agitated to sit any longer, Gail got up and paced across her office. She noticed the box of material about political terrorism on her desk and came back a few steps. "Nobody's going to ask about Nicaragua. Why should they?"

"But if they do, they might ask about the girl who went with us. Her aunt might be alive. What if she contacts an investigative reporter? Oh, my little Emily went to Nicaragua with that woman, and she never came back. Then the reporter asks me, and I say, oh, she fell in love with one of the men in the village, and we couldn't talk her into coming with us." Rebecca smiled. "I used to dream about her when it rained. She would be at my window tapping on the glass. You know. Lightning flashes, and you can see her face sort of rotted away, and her hair hanging in her eyes. Ooooo. Why did you leave me?" Rebecca laughed, but her placid mannequin's expression did not change. "Silly dreams. Gail, please. As a friend, don't say how Seth and I knew each other."

Still thinking of the dream, Gail struggled not to shudder. "I'll avoid it if I can."

"Do try. Anthony's name would have to come into it, and neither of you would like that. I'd have to mention Felix Castillo, too. God help us."

Annoyed, Gail said, "So what if it does come out? It wasn't your fault. Seth said you blame yourself. Rebecca, you should talk to someone who can help you resolve this. All of you were caught in the same nightmare, but it was Pablo who shot her."

"Pablo?"

"The rebel leader. The Sandinista." When Rebecca continued to look at her, Gail added, "In Los Pozos."

"I know who Pablo was, Gail. And you don't know what you think you do."

"What does that mean?"

"Nothing. This conversation is so depressing." Rebecca was looking for her sunglasses, finding them on her lap, uncrossing her legs to stand up. She slid the strap of her tasseled black bag over her shoulder. "I have to fly. I'm meeting Jeffrey Hopkins at the opera. I told him I'd help him call all our board members. Keeping busy is the best thing, I suppose. Let's stay in touch." She pressed her cheek to Gail's.

"Rebecca." Gail stopped her halfway across her office. "I can't lie for you. I won't volunteer any information, but I won't lie to the police."

"I never asked you to lie." Rebecca's face was obscured by the glasses. "I'm sorry you see it that way. I was not having an affair with Seth Greer. We developed a friendship through our work in the opera, and I'm going to miss him. The last time we spoke — after the meeting last night — was by telephone, when he told me that he planned to go on radio. I advised him against it, but he went ahead, and they shot him." Rebecca made a quick, sad smile, then went out the door.

The offices of Ferrer and Quintana, civil and criminal practice, were located in Coral Gables, just off a street called Miracle Mile. The building was upscale modern Mediterranean, with a courtyard entrance and a private atrium for each of the partners.

It was the fountain and ferny rocks that Anthony gazed at while Gail told him about her conversation with Rebecca Dixon. "I thought it was mutual," Gail said, "but Seth was the one in love. Rebecca allowed him to love her because he needed her, and she needed the adoration. Or am I wrong?"

Anthony continued to stand by the glass door with his arms crossed. "I remember Rebecca could be that way. Manipulative. But a man doesn't allow himself to be used unless he wants it. I think they were trapped in the same dance."

"How should I handle the police?"

"You don't handle them, you tell them the truth. I don't want to defend you on charges of perjury." He smiled and reached out to pull her closer. "Don't speculate. Okay? If they ask you to speculate, say you'd rather not. Just answer the questions. If the police choose to follow up with Dixon, that's his problem."

Gail slid the back of her hand down Anthony's tie, a lustrous gray and burgundy that matched the subtle lines of color in his suit. "I'm more interested in knowing whether Octavio was afraid of what Seth might say. The police think someone was waiting for Seth. That's what they told you, isn't it?"

"Gail —"

"Seth told me he was going to talk about Octavio's business relationship with Lloyd Dixon. Rebecca confirmed they knew each other, then later she denied it. What was the nature of this relationship? Was it only that King Furniture used Dixon Air to ship to its customers out of the country?"

Anthony was looking at her, eyebrows raised enough to create horizontal lines in his forehead. "I will handle this."

"Meaning you want me to stay out of it."

"Don't put it that way, Gail. This relates to my family. It's a delicate matter. I will keep you informed. All right?"

"Okay, fine."

"Listen to me." Anthony took her shoulders. "If there's anything going on, I will find out. When you speak to the police, I don't want you to mention Octavio and Lloyd Dixon. The police have no reason to think there is a connection, so they won't ask. If they don't ask, don't volunteer."

"Let's see if I have this," Gail said. "Rebecca doesn't want me to mention how she met Seth or that she was having an affair with him. You don't want me to mention that Seth might have known something about your brother-in-law."

He gave her a warning look. "I didn't say that. I said don't speculate."

"Just the facts," she said.

"Exactly." Anthony put an arm around her. "How are you feeling? Better? Did you get your hand looked at?"

"I will. Don't fuss."

"You know what I want to do this weekend? Pick out a ring for you. Look at some more houses. Silvia Sanchez called me with a new list. Can you do that on Saturday?"

Gail smiled at him. "I would love to."

"My grandmother called me this morning to find out if you were all right. They were worried. She said Ernesto wants us to come for a visit some evening. What do you think?"

"Of course we have to go. Are you and your grandfather building some bridges?"

"I don't know."

"Well, don't you want to?"

"Of course I do, but it won't happen until Thomas Nolan leaves town. Not with Octavio stirring it up. What a two-headed snake. If my grandfather were stronger, he would see this. He would never have let Octavio so close to him."

"Sweetheart, I hate to question your view of Octavio, but he was very nice to me outside the station last night."

"He had a guilty conscience," Anthony retorted.

"Are you going to be like this when we visit your grandparents?"

"I am capable, Gail, of great feats of forbearance." He kissed her quickly and looked at his watch. "I have to be in court at one o'clock. Talk to me while I get ready."

She followed him to his desk, a black triangle cantilevered out from a base near the wall. The room was all ebony and leather with accents of red and silver, illuminated by tiny halogen lamps suspended on thin wires from the ceiling. Only the law books and case files gave away Anthony Quintana's profession.

He set a briefcase on the desk and clicked open the latches, then gathered some papers from his credenza. Gail sat in a low-slung leather-and-chrome chair watching him move, gauging her own reactions. The lamps made pools of light that played on his hair, turning it a rich mahogany. Under the lawyer costume he had the body of a dancer — slender and hard, with lines of muscle down his back and an ass she could grab onto to pull him tighter. She wanted to lock his office door and unbutton her blouse. Watch his eyes dilate to black.

Making love with him last night had erased every question she had. There was nothing beyond the immediacy of desire, then the sweet fade into sleep. He had entered her so slowly, watching it happen, holding back until she was there, too. She had needed this, to fall asleep on these thoughts and not on the others. But moonlight through the bedroom window only lasted so long.

"Anthony, I have a question. If the answer is yes, I don't really care. But I would like to know why you didn't tell me. I think that's what I really want to know."

Frowning in puzzlement, he looked around from his credenza. "What's the question?"

"Did you have an affair with Rebecca while she was living with Seth?"

Anthony selected several files, one at a time, from a stack of them. "Did Rebecca say that?"

"No. Seth told me last night."

"I should have guessed, from the way the question was phrased. Betrayal is to be inferred." Anthony dropped the files into his briefcase. "What good would it have done, Gail, if I had told you?"

"It would have been some kind of assurance that you don't hide things from me."

"I don't hide anything that you need — *need* — to know. Some things cause more hurt than illumination."

"That's rather patronizing."

"Well, we disagree." He reached into his breast pocket to see if his Mont Blanc was there. He put it back. Opened his center desk drawer. Shifted some things inside.

"I have another question. It's about Felix Castillo. Was he at the scene when Emily Davis died?"

Still looking into the drawer, Anthony smiled slightly. "Seth again?"

"He told me that Felix came with Pablo. Why did you leave that out?"

The drawer slid shut. Anthony tossed a calculator into his briefcase. "Because it would have colored your judgment of him. Made you think of him in a way that isn't relevant to what he is now."

"What way is that? Rebecca just told me that Pablo didn't shoot Emily. That leads me to the question, who did? Felix?"

Not a flicker of reaction. "What did Rebecca say?"

"No, why don't you just tell me what Felix was doing there?"

The remoteness in his expression floated across the desk as if someone had opened the door to a freezer. Calmly, clearly, Anthony said, "I don't like to be questioned like this. Not by you. I told you what happened in Los Pozos. I don't care what Seth told you or what Rebecca said. Pablo was responsible for Emily's death. That's all I'm going to say about it. Ever. Don't bring it up again. All right?" He closed the lid of his briefcase and clicked the latches. "I have to go to court."

In nine years as a lawyer, Gail had questioned witnesses hundreds of times. She had seen other lawyers do it. Witnesses in interviews or under oath in depositions and on the stand. Facing the two City of Miami detectives across her desk, she felt an odd reversal of roles.

The police, she assumed, had more experience than she in interviewing witnesses who consciously lied. Perhaps they had sensors like bat sonar. Gail knew that she was prepared to be evasive on certain topics, and it made her nervous.

The detectives were Hispanic, not a surprise in the city police force. Fernandez was forty or so, with prematurely gray hair that touched the collar of his jacket. There was a small diamond in his left earlobe. The other man, Delgado, was older, and spoke with an accent.

The preliminaries were quick. They asked how she was feeling. She said she was still quite shaky over the incident. Fernandez apologized for putting her through this again, but he wanted her to describe everything that had happened. He gave her a drawing and she pointed out where she and Seth Greer had been standing.

She repeated their conversation without reference to what Seth might have known about Octavio Reyes. *Don't speculate.* "Mr. Greer was convinced he could take Mr. Reyes on in a debate. I told him that it would be harmful to the opera, and I think he was on the point of changing his mind when he was killed."

"Was he in any disagreements with anyone in the opera?"

"Not that I know of."

"You know of anyone who might have wanted to harm him?"

"No, I don't. I'm afraid to ask this, but were there any bullets where I had been standing? I fell down. Maybe that saved my life."

"I don't think he was after you. Unless you have any enemies?" When Gail shook her head, he went on, "The shooter had good aim, and he was using a laser sight to make sure. You fell, but he had a clear shot, if he'd wanted to take it. Bear in mind you can pick up a laser sight anywhere for about a hundred bucks. It doesn't mean a professional hit was involved here."

"Did you find any evidence around the other building? I know there were cartridge casings."

"Five Remington center-fire .223s. Common as dirt."

"That's it? No footprints? Nothing?"

"How I wish."

Delgado asked how long she had known Mr. Greer.

"I met him less than two weeks ago. He was on the board of the opera. We didn't know each other well."

"Why did he call you in particular, before he went over to the station?"

"I think because earlier in the evening Seth had mentioned doing this, and I advised him against it. I'd gone to his house to discuss possible legal action against the city. They've threatened to pull our permit unless we provide heavy security."

"Who else was at this meeting?"

In an instant Gail registered this fact: The police apparently believed that it had been a formal meeting. She replied, "The president of the board, Rebecca Dixon, was also there."

"What time did you leave?"

"I'd say around six o'clock. I went home, took my daughter to her soccer game, and then Seth called me on my portable phone around eight-fifteen. I left my daughter with one of the other parents." Gail felt out of breath. "I'm sorry, this has got me so rattled. Do you have any idea who shot him?"

"We're working on it." Fernandez had been writing in a small notebook propped on his knee. He flipped it shut. Gail followed its progress into the breast pocket of his suit coat. There had been no questions about Rebecca and Seth. None about Lloyd.

Gail said, "I'd like your opinion. You're aware of the controversy over Thomas Nolan. I have an appointment tomorrow with the city manager, and I need to know whether this murder was likely to have been an act of political terrorism. I need to know if Mr. Nolan is in danger."

Fernandez looked over at the other detective. "This one's for you. Lieutenant Delgado has been on the anti-terrorist task force for . . . how long, Bill?"

"Twenty-six years." Delgado laughed. "Long time. Too long. They put me on this case because of questions like yours, Ms.

Connor, but we don't think it's a political act."

"You seem pretty sure."

"I am sure. First thing, the victim wasn't known. You commit murder to make a statement, it has to be somebody that people know, okay?"

"Seth was going to go on the air."

Delgado waved a hand. "He was not important. To his family and friends, sure, but to the Cuban community? No. There's not one incident on record — not one — where a non-Cuban was ever assassinated for speaking his mind. Okay? Second thing. They announced that he'd be on the air forty minutes before he was shot. Not enough time for somebody to say, Hey, I ought to get this guy — and I don't even know who he is — then to load his weapon and get into position. Third. How did the shooter recognize the victim? Greer comes into the parking lot, could be anybody. And the last reason, probably the most important. There has been no communiqué."

"What is that?"

"Communiqué? There's been no letter delivered to the radio stations, no phone call, nobody saying, Look, we did it because this guy was an enemy of the Cuban people for such and such a reason. Maybe something will come today, but I won't bet on it."

Gail said, "Unless you count a phone message, there was no communiqué after the concrete block went through the glass door at the opera."

"No, that was probably some kid. It was petty. Not like murder. If they really wanted to make a statement, they'd have used a pipe bomb." Then Delgado laughed, but without much humor. "Pipe bombs are as Cuban as the royal palm tree."

For a few seconds Gail let this information settle into place. She said, "Do you believe in provocateurs? Or am I asking about the bogeyman?"

"They exist. Absolutely. A couple of years ago one of the members of Brothers to the Rescue was encouraging the pilots to get a little closer to Cuba on their next flight looking for rafters. Then the Cuban air force shoots down two of the planes, and the man defects back to Cuba. He was a spy. The situation is very complicated."

Again Gail felt that sliding sense of unease that she had noticed sitting on Felix Castillo's sofa listening to him and Anthony talk casually of spies and of people with indeterminate agendas.

"What do you think, Lieutenant? Could

there be a provocateur here?"

His hands went palms-up, a substitute for a shrug.

"I don't know what to tell Thomas Nolan."

"It's a complicated situation," Delgado said again.

EIGHTEEN

Gail telephoned the opera's general manager, Jeffrey Hopkins, to report on her meeting with the city manager of Miami the day before.

"This wasn't a meeting, Jeffrey. It was Alberto Estrada playing politician. We go into his office, there are five other people waiting for us — a city commissioner, an assistant city attorney who sat in the back taking notes, and somebody from the permitting department — the same one who told you we needed a hundred off-duty police officers if Tom Nolan remained in the cast. Estrada also invited what he called 'interested parties in the community,' meaning the president of the Cuban municipalities in exile and, finally, the programming manager from WRCL. I suppose Estrada wanted an audience.

"I wasn't completely outnumbered, because a friend of Seth Greer's from the ACLU heard about the meeting and wanted to sit in. His name is José de la Paz — also a Cuban, which goes to show something or other. He kept rolling his eyes whenever the talk went over the edge.

"For example: Just as I sat down, Commissioner Valdez jumped out of his chair and said, 'What are you really doing here, and who are you working for?' Jeffrey, I swear I am not making that up. I smiled at him and said, 'Well, Mr. Valdez, I'm the attorney for the Miami Opera, and I came here to speak to Mr. Estrada on behalf of my client.' And he said, 'No, you have an agenda — to embarrass the Cubans in the city administration.' And I said, 'You don't need me for that, Mr. Valdez.' I heard José de la Paz laugh, but Valdez starts screaming, 'You people do not own the theater. It is not yours. It belongs to the city of Miami, and we can decide if you can put on one of your shows.' I sat there smiling — it doesn't do any good to argue — and thinking to myself, 'Damn, I wish I had my tape recorder, nobody's going to believe this.'

"Finally Al Estrada calmed him down. So I said, 'Mr. Estrada, I wish to state the Miami Opera's position on the security requirement that your office is demanding. We believe that it's not only unnecessary, it's illegal. It's unconstitutional. It appears, in fact, to be political harassment motivated by some people in your administration who don't like the fact that someone in the cast of *Don Giovanni* performed in Cuba.'

"Of course Estrada had to say, 'Ms. Connor, I am insulted that you accuse the city of harassment. If an event is a threat to public safety, we can prohibit it from taking place.' So we go around and around about how much of a threat there is. I told him that since Seth Greer's murder, the verbal attacks on the radio have stopped, and there have been only a handful of threatening phone calls. Then the president of the municipalities objected to my saying that because it tends to blame the exiles, when everybody knows that provocateurs are to blame. He said, 'A Castro agent pulled the trigger to make us look bad.' I had to bite my lips not to say, 'You gave him the rifle.'

"Unfortunately, most of the people in the meeting were too committed to their positions to give an inch. I hoped the assistant city attorney would help out, but he said he had to discuss it with his boss. I knew it was hopeless at that point. I stood up and said, 'Mr. Estrada, thank you for your time. I hope we can resolve this, but if not, my only course of action is to file a lawsuit in federal court. Miami is already under scrutiny because of bribes and kickbacks in the previous administration. If you try to censor the opera, you're going to have the international press on your head, and nobody will be happier than the guy in Havana. Why don't you take the weekend to think about it and call me by five P.M. on Monday. Otherwise, on Tuesday morning I'll be holding a press conference on the steps of the federal courthouse.'

"You know, Jeffrey, I think Estrada might go our way. He just can't come out and say so right now. It's politics. He was appointed to his job by the city commission, and I've heard that he wants to run for mayor next year. Anyway, he walked me to the elevator, and as soon as we were out of earshot of Valdez and the others, he became a normal, rational human being. He wanted to know what *Don Giovanni* was about. I said it's the Don Juan story, the great lover no woman could resist. Estrada said it sounded pretty hot, maybe he'd take his wife to see it. I offered to get him tickets, but he said no, he couldn't accept gifts."

Glancing at her watch, Gail swiveled her chair toward the telephone and stood up. "I have to run. I promised Tom Nolan I'd drop by his place for lunch and explain what's going on."

She heard Jeffrey Hopkins wishing her good luck — and telling her to keep her windows rolled up and her doors locked.

★ ★ ★

Thomas Nolan rented a guest cottage on the grounds of a mansion on the bay side of Miami Beach. The place was secluded and quiet, with a grand piano and a view through wide French doors of landscaped lawn, shady trees, and sparkling water. The weather had warmed up to the high seventies, and the sky was perfectly blue.

Nolan had already made sandwiches, which he took outdoors on a tray with a soda for Gail and a pot of hot tea for himself. They sat in painted white metal lawn chairs facing the bay, a small table between them. Water splashed over the age-blackened rocks of a small fountain in the center of the patio, and from a banyan tree drooped an enormous staghorn fern. Two plastic flamingos posed stiff-legged in the flower bed, a joke made of a cliché.

Seth Greer's funeral would be held this afternoon, Gail remembered, then pushed the thought from her mind.

Sunlight poured onto the patio through an opening in the trees. It played on Tom Nolan's hair, which had been washed so recently as to still be damp at the crown. The rest of it was unbound, a pale blond mass of unruly curls that the wind would occasionally tease across his face. He kicked his heavy sandals aside and stretched out his long legs. His T-shirt said EDINBURGH FESTIVAL 1995.

He dropped an ice cube into his teacup, then poured. When he saw Gail watching, he said, "I have to be careful with my throat. Once I burned the roof of my mouth on hot cheese pizza and missed a dress rehearsal."

"Are all singers so sensitive?"

"No. We're picky, though. Superstitious. Sopranos and tenors are the worst, of course." He measured a precise teaspoon of sugar. "I know one singer who ate at McDonald's before a successful audition for the Met, and now he has to have his Big Mac before every performance. Some people say don't eat nuts or chocolate, but that's an old wives' tale. If I shout too loudly, that could keep me from singing the next day."

Nolan sipped his tea. "Some singers can smoke and drink and party and nothing happens, but I'm not that lucky. I work at staying in shape. I've studied acting and dance. The body has to look good on stage. I know Italian, German, and French. My manager wants me to try out for *Boris Gudonov* in San Francisco, so I'll have to learn to pronounce Russian. And then there are the new roles to add to the repertoire as well as keeping current on the old ones. I'm on the road about nine months out of the year." He laughed in his odd way, a soft rumble deep in his chest. "There you have it. The life of an opera singer."

"Do you have a girlfriend or . . . whatever?"

"Or whatever?" He smiled. "No, I don't have a girlfriend. It's hard to maintain personal relationships traveling so much."

"Your old piano teacher is in Miami," Gail remembered.

"Miss Wells. She travels a lot these days," he said. "I see her when I can. We're very close."

"Oh, yes. The lady who said you had no talent for classical piano. Sing, Tom, sing." Gail watched the water in the fountain splashing down the rocks into the basin that surrounded it. Goldfish darted underneath the lily pads. "You don't have any family left in Miami?"

"My parents were both from somewhere else. My father died when I was eleven, and my mother eventually decided to move back to Virginia, where she had grown up."

Gail took another quarter of a ham sandwich. "No brothers or sisters?"

"I was an only child." Apparently reluctant to talk about his personal life, Tom No-lan said, "Tell me about your meeting yesterday with the city. What's going to happen?"

She gave him the conclusion, not the details. If they forced the opera to pay for heavy security, a lawsuit would be filed in federal court.

"Can they shut us down?"

"Of course not. We'll either pay for the extra security or the court will say we don't have to. Don't worry." She smiled across the little table at him. "When they say they'll revoke our permit, that's only if we don't meet their demands. There is no way, Tom, that we will not produce this opera."

He settled back, holding his cup in both hands on his chest. "You know what's funny? My manager called me yesterday. Opera companies are asking him when I'm available. Usually he's out there chasing down jobs. The news media are interested, too. They're calling me for interviews."

"Don't do that till we hear from the city," Gail said. "Things are a little quieter since Seth Greer's death. I'd like to keep it that way."

Nolan asked, "Are you going to the funeral?"

"Yes, are you?"

"If I'd known him I would, but we're on a tight schedule, with opening night only ten days away."

The show must go on, Gail thought. Seth Greer's wide smile came into her mind, then a quick image of a gravesite, rows of chairs, a coffin heaped with flowers. How much Valium would Rebecca Dixon require to get through it? Assuming she went. What would Anthony be thinking under his impenetrable facade?

Tom Nolan took another sandwich and bit the corner off. "I heard on the news this morning that the police don't think the exiles shot him. How can they be sure?"

"What they know, or what they assume, is that it wasn't done as a political statement. A lone crazy acting on his own isn't likely, either: How would he have recognized Seth when he arrived? They assume it's someone Seth knew, and that this person was following him or knew where he was going." Gail recounted her conversation with Detective Delgado two days ago, explaining why the police were ruling out an organized group of militants.

"I see. Well, that's a relief. I've been so tense it was showing in my performance. Everyone in the cast and crew has been tense. I guess we can stop worrying." Nolan looked at Gail for confirmation. The sunlight cut across the sharp planes of his face.

She took a few seconds to answer. "I think you're probably all right."

"But?"

"This is a remote possibility — a provocateur who wasn't clear on the rules of how to lay blame on the exiles. Cuba has people here."

"You're kidding. To commit murder?"

"Usually nothing that extreme. That's why I think you're probably all right."

"Unless somebody puts a bomb under my bed. The police don't have any suspects?"

"Not so far," Gail said. "All they've got is a handful of brass cartridge casings."

"You must've been scared," Nolan said. "He could have hit you, too."

"He had a laser sight and good aim. If he'd wanted me dead, I wouldn't be here now." She took another bite of sandwich. "How's Felix Castillo working out? Did you call him?"

"Yes, the next day. I think this is more of a bother than it's worth. Before I left for rehearsal yesterday he checked out my car, followed me to the opera, and we went through the same drill on the way back. I refuse to let him drive me. He wanted to go through my house before I came inside.

I told him to forget it." Tom Nolan flexed his fingers. "What happened to his hand?"

"Someone went after him with a machete," Gail said. "Luckily, Felix had a gun."

Through a grimace, Nolan said, "He showed me two of them. One under his coat and one on his ankle. He's a scary dude." A gust of wind blew the napkin off his lap. As he leaned over to pick it up, his hair swung forward, covering his profile, leaving only the triangle of his nose. There was an odd bump on the bridge. A memory stirred at the back of Gail's mind. A skinny boy in a plain blue short-sleeved shirt, walking alone across campus at Ransom-Everglades, blond hair hanging in his face.

Tom Nolan sat back in his chair, finished off his sandwich, and balled the napkin in one large, bony hand.

"Can I ask you something?"

He picked up his tea. "Sure."

"You're going to be singing at a dinner party at Lloyd Dixon's place. Would you happen to know who his guests are?" She smiled at him. "I'm just curious."

"No, I don't."

"I was just wondering if there were any local businessmen on the guest list."

The blue eyes settled on her. Several long

seconds passed. "You seem awfully interested in Lloyd Dixon. You were watching him through the window at the rehearsal hall. Don't deny it."

Gail replied with a slight shrug and said that he needn't talk about Lloyd Dixon if he preferred not to.

"I don't mind." He lifted the top off a sandwich and went over to the fountain, throwing crumbs to the goldfish. "Here's my opinion about this meeting. Lloyd wants to expand his business into Cuba when it opens up to Americans. That's what I think because some of his guests heard me in Havana two years ago — according to Lloyd."

"You didn't tell me that the last time we talked."

He aimed a little ball of bread and flicked his long, graceful fingers. The bread bobbed on the surface before vanishing with a tiny smacking noise into the mouth of a fish. "I didn't want to talk about Havana."

Gail dusted her hands over the napkin on her lap. "You invited Lloyd Dixon and his wife to hear you sing in Germany because you wanted to be hired for the lead in *Don Giovanni*. Then you went to Cuba. I happen to know that Dixon goes to Cuba occasionally — a fact that you shouldn't spread around. Did he suggest the trip to you?"

After a moment Nolan released a small sigh and turned around. "This is what happened. Lloyd and Rebecca Dixon came to the opening night of *Lucia di Lammermoor*, and I invited them to the party afterward. I don't remember how, but it came up that some of the other cast members — not Americans — were going to the music festival in Cuba, and their bass was ill. Lloyd said I ought to do it. He said I wouldn't get into trouble as long as I came in through a third country. How wrong he was. Lloyd's apologetic about it. He even wanted to pay me for singing for his dinner guests, but of course I said no."

Gail looked at Nolan, then said, "You didn't by any chance see Lloyd Dixon in Cuba, did you?"

The thin lips curled into a smile. "Yes. I did."

"Was he there for the investment conference?"

"What's that?"

"At the Hotel Las Americas. Some Cuban VIPs spoke there, which is the reason we're in this mess."

Nolan finger-combed his hair off his forehead. "I don't think he was there for that reason, but I can't say for sure. When my friends and I got to the hotel, things were running late, so we went outside to the pool bar to have a drink. Somebody tapped me on the shoulder, and I turned around and there was Lloyd Dixon. He was dressed like a tourist, not a business-man. He said he had come down to do some fishing. I didn't ask about the invest-ment conference. It didn't enter my mind."

"Where was he staying? At the Las Americas?"

"He didn't say."

"Did you see him with anyone else?"

"No. He said his wife was in Miami. We spoke for a few minutes, then he left."

"What did you talk about?"

Nolan let out a small breath and walked back across the patio. "Oh, what was it? Had we been sightseeing? Had we seen Er-nest Hemingway's house? Did we like Cu-ban music? Things like that."

"Was that the only conversation you had with him?"

"Yes, there by the pool. I didn't see him again till I got here to Miami two years later." Nolan looked down at Gail in her chair.

Gail shaded her eyes. "Rebecca Dixon said she didn't know you had performed in Cuba. She was horrified. So I thought."

"She knew he'd *suggested* that I go," Nolan corrected. "He may not have told her that he saw me there."

Gail added silently, Or else Lloyd Dixon had taken off on another of his adventure trips without telling Rebecca where he was going.

The wind shifted the branches of the tree, and light flickered on Thomas Nolan's hair, turning it into a froth of pale gold. In the shadow cast across his face, his eyes danced with amusement. "Now I have a question for you. How did you become engaged to a Latino?"

"He asked me and I said yes."

"Dark, handsome, and irresistible? Were you overcome?" Nolan's laugh rumbled in his throat. He spread his arms with a flourish. "I have to play Don Giovanni. I guess I'd like to know if it's true what they say."

Gail smiled back. "Absolutely."

"Would he shoot me if he knew I invited you here for lunch?"

"No, don't be silly. This is business."

"So he'd shoot me if it weren't business."

She laughed. "We'd both be goners."

His eyes stayed with her a second before he stuck his hands in his pockets and gazed out toward the bay, where a sailboat was just passing out of view, hidden by trees at the edge of the property. "Just teasing. I was thinking the other day, it's funny how life brings you around to places you never thought you'd be in. I never thought I'd be back in Miami, but here I am talking to Gail Connor. I didn't remember you at first, but I do now. In high school you were one of those cheerleader types who never noticed anybody but the jocks."

Momentarily confused, Gail said, "I was never a cheerleader."

He seemed not to hear her. "You were going with that kid — what was his name? Ronnie Bertram. His family made yachts. He had sun-bleached hair and a new Trans Am. Played tennis — naturally."

"We went together for a month," Gail said.

In profile, his face half-hidden by his hair, Tom Nolan smiled. "And you don't remember me at all."

"I'm sorry, I don't."

"Don't apologize." He shrugged. "I was not a memorable guy."

But of course Gail did remember — not perfectly, but in hazy shadows cast by events far past recollection. Tommy Nolan, walking alone across campus, head down, hair over his eyes, as if his loneliness were an affliction that could be hidden from the other students.

Against his protestations that she not bother, Gail helped him carry the remains of their lunch back inside the cottage. In the living room, the piano lid was up, and his music littered the worn oriental rug. Compact discs of operas were stacked by the stereo. There was only one pillow askew on the sofa, only his sweater on the rack by the door. For all his acclaim and the money he had to be making, and the career that was taking off, he seemed so alone.

Then Gail considered that this view of Thomas Nolan could be skewed by her memory, which might be faulty. She could be wrong about him, just as Thomas Nolan had been wrong about her. A cheerleader type? Each of them looking at the other from his or her own peculiar, imperfect teenage perspective. And yet . . .

And yet.

She could not dismiss the sense of unbearable loss. Something had happened to make him drop out of school halfway through the spring semester of 1979, but like a remnant of a dream, the memory whirled beyond reach.

Just before noon on Tuesday, the day after Seth Greer's murder, Irene Connor had received on her answering machine at home a message from Glasgow, Scotland. She had jotted down the number and brought it along when she came to Gail's house to check on her injured hand and, more important, her emotional state after having seen a man shot to death an arm's length away. Gail had left the piece of paper folded in her purse.

Stopping down the street from Tom Nolan's cottage, she pulled it out, along with her telephone, and caught Jane Fyfield just as she was getting dressed to leave for the opera house in Glasgow. She would be singing the title role in *Norma* for another week, then on to Sydney, Australia, to rehearse *I Puritani*.

She spoke quickly, in a light, clear voice. "I don't have much time. Sorry. I'm in a bit of a rush. Your mother — Irene, was it? Yes. She explained your situation. Good lord. What a bizarre city. I've never been to Miami. Not sure I want to go after hearing this."

Jane Fyfield confirmed the basic facts of the trip to Havana. "Tom decided to go with us, a last-minute replacement, really. . . . No, we didn't get paid, but we had a nice holiday. . . . He said I was *married?* Oh, really."

Then Gail explained the reason for her

phone call, and if Ms. Fyfield could indulge her a moment longer —

"Let me think. Lloyd Dixon. Big man, white hair — Yes, of course. I saw him in Dortmund with his wife. It was he who suggested that Tom go with us. . . . You're right, he did appear in Havana, too, but he didn't call himself Dixon. I've forgotten what he called himself, but it was a false name. He said it was the only way he could get into the country. . . . I can't recall what they talked about. Wait. He told Tom that he had arranged for him to do *Don Giovanni*. That made Tom happy. . . .

"Only that one time, yes. . . . Except I seem to recall that Tom left with him. . . . No, not that night, a couple of days later, before our last performance. We were scheduled for the amphitheater on the beach, and we had to rearrange the music. It was rude of him to leave us in the lurch. The baritone had to fill in. . . . Tom said that the American — Dixon, correct? — Mr. Dixon was going to give him a lift in his airplane to . . . oh, where was it? Central America. One of those countries. . . . I can't remember. That stuck in my mind because it was so extravagant — his own airplane. He must be quite wealthy.

"I can't remember, it's been so long. . . .

Costa Rica! . . . Positive. . . . I've no idea why. . . . I'm sorry, that's all I know about it. Tell Tom I'm still annoyed with him for leaving. . . . He didn't call me after that, even to say thanks for the great time. Well, it wasn't so great, actually. . . . Tom was, shall we say, a letdown.

"Oh, God, sorry, I've got to go or I'll be late. . . . Yes, of course, call again if you like."

NINETEEN

A huge fan in a steel cage revolved slowly at the far end of the hangar. One of several doors had been shoved open, sliding along a track in the concrete. Gail walked inside. There were three aircraft, the nearest of which was a cargo jet with a scaffold under one of its engines. The cowling was off, revealing tilted blades and more wiring than she wanted to know about. The mechanic turned around when he heard her footsteps.

"Excuse me. Where can I find Lloyd Dixon?"

"In the office." He tilted his head toward the other end of the hangar. She went around the nose of the plane and crossed the cavernous space toward the glass-enclosed room on the other side.

Dixon was talking to somebody at one of the desks. No leather jacket today. He wore a dark suit, probably for Seth Greer's funeral, which would start in a couple of hours. He saw her through the window and came to the door. His crooked smile showed some puzzlement. "Ms. Connor." He stood aside. The other two men in the room looked back at her.

"Hello, Lloyd." She didn't come in. "I wonder if I could talk to you for a few minutes."

He told the men to finish working up the figures, then said, "Walk outside with me. I have to speak to one of my pilots. It won't take long."

They went out an exit door to the field. Private aircraft were parked in rows extending from the high chain-link fence to the concrete apron that led to the main landing strip. A small passenger jet took off, rattling the air.

Lloyd Dixon strode toward a cargo plane with blue stripes and the Dixon Air insignia on the tail. A truck was backing up, and men waited by the cargo bay. Another started the engine of a forklift. Dixon hauled himself halfway up the ladder to the cockpit and had a conversation through the open door.

When he walked back toward her, Gail asked him how many planes he had.

"Seventeen. Most of them are en route somewhere or other. The operations manager keeps up with them." He looked at her. "What brings you?"

Gail had already decided to get straight to it. "I talked to Jane Fyfield by telephone an hour ago. She's the soprano who sang *Lucia* in Germany, then went to Cuba with Tom Nolan. She saw you there. Tom says the same thing, but don't blame him for telling me. It came up in conversation. I thought I'd ask you about it."

"What do you want me to do, admit I went? The answer's yes. Cuba is one of the few places you can go that's not overrun with American tourists."

She said, "Why am I only now finding out about this?"

"You sound pissed off, Gail."

"Annoyed. I'd say I'm annoyed. Did you attend the international investment conference at the Hotel Las Americas that week?"

He crossed heavy arms over his chest, which had the effect of making his neck seem even thicker. "Isn't this a little outside the scope of your duties as our lawyer?"

"On Tuesday morning," she said, "unless the permitting department of the city of Miami cuts us some slack, I'm going to file a federal lawsuit. The opera is going to be in the spotlight. I hate to think what would happen if somebody finds out that one of our major donors is making — even contemplating — investments in Cuba."

With a barely audible chuckle, Lloyd Dixon watched his men load crates through the cargo bay of his airplane. "My name was not on the attendee list, so don't worry about it."

"Did you use another name?" When Dixon looked at her, she added, "Jane Fyfield said you used a false name in Havana."

"Isn't she a fountain of information," Dixon said. "Am I investing in Cuba? No. It can be done if a person is creative, but it's just not a good risk right now. Soon as the embargo is lifted it'll be a different story. When Fidel falls, you're going to hear this big sucking sound — all the money in Miami flowing south. Construction, transportation, health care, tourism — name it."

"Air freight," she said.

He smiled. "There you go."

She asked, "Are you working with Octavio Reyes?"

The sunlight made Dixon squint, closing his eyes to slits through which showed a glimmer of gray. "In 1994 the University of Miami sponsored a weekend seminar called 'Investing in a Post-Castro Economy.' That was an optimistic year. Forty thousand rafters floated across the straits, and it really seemed that the regime was going belly-up. Didn't happen, but there was a bunch of activity on this side of the water. Reyes attended the seminar, and we got to talking.

His company was already shipping on Dixon Air, and we'd met a couple of times. I know several people who are seriously looking at possibilities in Cuba. He's one of them. And I'm asking you, what's the problem?"

"You denied knowing him."

"Imagine that."

Gail laughed. "This is such massive hypocrisy. Both of you! He singlehandedly made Thomas Nolan into a flashpoint in this town, and you let him get away with it."

"I didn't expect the Cubans to make a big deal out of it," Dixon said. "Who pays attention to opera? I had a talk with Reyes. He's got a new enemy now — provocateurs. Don't worry about it, Gail. The city's going to drag this decision out to the last minute, but they'll come around. They don't want another black eye."

"Don't worry," she repeated. A four-engine propeller aircraft thundered past them and angled upward. Some high cirrus clouds were moving in from the north. When the roar had diminished, she said, "Seth Greer is dead. I keep thinking, maybe the person who did it was after me, too, but I fell and rolled under the car. He was afraid to show himself, so he's saving me for another time. This goes through my mind. I replay it at night in my sleep."

"I've been shot at," Dixon said. "It gives you a new perspective on things, doesn't it?"

"Yes. You put up with less bullshit."

He laughed. "This is true. Very true."

Gail said, "Maybe something Seth knew got him killed. I wonder about Octavio Reyes. He was the only one who knew far enough in advance that Seth would be at the radio station."

"What did Seth know?" The amusement on Lloyd Dixon's face said he liked playing games.

"That Reyes was involved with you."

"Involved? We talked. That's it."

"The exile community thrives on rumors. Reyes could be ruined if they so much as *thought* he was putting money into the Castro regime. When Seth called to say he would go on the air to debate him, Reyes was upstairs in the studio, but he could have made a phone call to one of his extremist friends and told him God knows what."

Dixon eyed her steadily. "Extremist friends?"

"He has them," Gail said. "He probably goes target-shooting on weekends with Alpha 66."

"They aren't hit men, Gail. All right. Say that Seth was going to run his mouth. How would Reyes have known this in advance?"

"Seth could have told him when he called the station."

"Then Reyes would've been crazy to let him go on the air!"

"He lured him there and had someone waiting for him," Gail suggested.

"No. If you want somebody eliminated, you don't have it done in your own parking lot — unless you think it's going to make you look innocent." Dixon chuckled. "I'll show you how crazy this gets. I listen to the Spanish stations. Some people are saying the job was done by a Castro agent who knew that if he made it look like an exile act no one would believe it, so he intentionally made it *not* to look like the exiles did it, so the police would wonder if they *did*. If you follow that logic. Provocateurs have the wits of a fox."

Gail shook her head. "The police believe he was killed for personal, not political reasons."

"You'd like to nail Reyes, wouldn't you?" Dixon gave her a conspirator's grin. "He's in a good place, married to old man Pedrosa's granddaughter. He thinks your fiancé is the black-sheep commie in the

Pedrosa clan. I'd watch my back."

Angrily Gail said, "How can you associate yourself with him?"

The grin grew wider. "We're not pals. Besides, it's interesting to watch events unfold." He said, "I've got a bone to pick with you, lady. What was the meaning of that advice you gave Seth Greer, he should talk Rebecca into leaving me?"

Gail could only stare back at him.

"The night he died, you were at his house. So was my wife. She came home in a taxi, too drunk to drive her own car home. Seth called to see if she was okay. He thought I was out of town. I happened to pick up the extension in the kitchen. Oh, Becky, marry me. It was meant to be. Gail Connor says so. We can start over, roll back the years —"

"I never told him that!"

"— be happy together. You should have married me twenty years ago."

"I did not say that." Gail took a breath, staying calm. "I said he should be honest with her about how he felt. Look, I don't want to get involved in your marital problems."

"Be honest about his feelings. Jesus. That kind of talk makes me queasy. People start being totally honest with each other, they wind up wanting to choke somebody. And then you show up playing Dear Abby."

"That's enough," she said.

They looked at each other.

Lloyd Dixon's smile lifted one side of his mouth. "You think I shot him?"

"You had a motive."

"Uh-uh. She wasn't in love with Seth — so she said, and I believe her. Don't speak ill of the dead, but Seth Greer couldn't have kept up with Rebecca. She's an expensive lady. I'm not complaining about it. I knew that when I married her."

"Another motive," Gail said. "You knew Rebecca was talking to Seth. Maybe she told him too much."

Dixon was enjoying this. "The police asked me about Seth. They found my wife's car in his driveway. I told them to check with the ferry master. I didn't leave the island. They keep a list of names, people going in and out."

"Unless a person leaves by boat."

"Takes too long. And the dock master keeps a list, too. I was home with my wife."

Gail made a slight shrug. "To answer your question — No. I don't think you shot him."

They turned to walk back toward the hangar. On the way out they had passed a sleek little twin-engine jet with a long nose and swept-back wings. This one had no markings other than its FAA numbers on the tail.

Gail said, "Did you fly to Cuba in this?"

"Jesus, no. U.S. Customs and the Navy track the position of every airplane in the Caribbean. I leave it in Mexico or Jamaica, then go from there."

"With your false identity papers. You aren't afraid of getting arrested or shot?"

"That's what makes it fun."

Without saying so, Gail began to see how Rebecca Dixon had grown tired of her husband's adventures — if that's what they were. She stopped walking. "One more question?"

A few paces past her, Dixon checked his watch. "One more."

"Why did you and Thomas Nolan go to Costa Rica?"

There was a brief moment of puzzlement, then it hit him. "And where did you get that?"

"Jane Fyfield. Tom was explaining to her why he had to leave Havana ahead of schedule."

"I gave him a ride," Dixon said. "He asked if I could take him to Costa Rica. He'd been there the year before on vacation and inadvertently left a suitcase. A friend was keeping it for him. So we went over to Mexico, picked up the plane, then headed south."

"A little out of the way for you, wasn't it?"

"Not cruising at five hundred knots."

"The friend couldn't ship the suitcase back?"

"Tom said no."

"What was in there?" Gail asked.

Dixon grinned at her. "I think we're on question four already. I waited at the bar in the airport in San José for a couple of hours till Tom came back. He didn't say, I didn't ask. We refueled and got back to Miami the same day we left Havana. He said thank you, goodbye, see you for *Don Giovanni*, and that was that."

"You helped him smuggle something into the U.S.," Gail said.

"That implies contraband. I don't know what was in there, and I respected the man's privacy."

"How do you know it wasn't drugs?"

"He's not the type."

"What about Customs? Don't they usually ask?"

"If they see it."

"What does that mean?"

"It means nothing. I took him to Costa

Rica as a favor, and he brought back something that belonged to him. I don't inquire into private matters that are none of my business." Dixon raised his white eyebrows at her, then glanced at his watch. "I've got to pick up Rebecca. We have a funeral to go to."

Gail sat in her car in the parking lot of the Miami Opera wondering if Thomas Nolan would arrive before she had to leave. The funeral home was less than ten minutes away, and she had planned to meet Anthony there.

She sat in her car because she hadn't decided yet what she would say, or if she would speak to him at all.

It was not, technically, her car but the Ford sedan she was renting while her own car was in the body shop. She had decided to fix it, then buy something else. Even if a new windshield were installed and the bullet holes were puttied up and painted over, she still wouldn't be able to get into it without seeing Seth Greer hanging for one hideous moment on the outside mirror, his breath wheezing through a bloody and shattered throat.

Gail scooted further down in the seat and rested her head on the headrest.

Lloyd Dixon had just handed her a suitcase full of BS, she was sure of it. And by now, more likely than not, he would have called Tom Nolan and told him to lie, just as he had told Tom Nolan to lie the first time Gail had spoken to him. Speaking to Nolan might not produce any answers, but Gail wanted to look in his face and see how he responded.

She did not know if the suitcase had been real or fictitious. If real, Lloyd Dixon would have insisted on knowing what it contained. He was not stupid. Customs would have confiscated his airplane for smuggling. But only if the contents had been contraband. Which meant that they weren't.

Unless Lloyd Dixon had done it for fun. Quite possible.

The more Gail thought about it, the more certain she became of not getting an answer. What she wanted from Tom Nolan was not to know what was in the damned suitcase, but what Lloyd Dixon had really been doing in Cuba, and whether Octavio Reyes had been there, too.

She saw a gray van come across the parking lot. They went through the drill. Van pulling up to the side door of the rehearsal hall, driver's side toward the street. Bodyguard getting out, going around. Only the top of the rehearsal hall door was showing. It opened. Then closed. Felix Castillo reappeared. He was dressed for the role — dark suit, a black collarless shirt, and rubber-soled black shoes.

He did not, however, get back inside the van, but started coming across the parking lot toward Gail. It took her a minute to realize what was different about his left hand — there were five fingers on it. As he got closer, she could see that it was some kind of prosthetic device worn like a glove.

He leaned down to her window to see in. His heavy gray mustache had been trimmed, showing more of his crooked teeth when he smiled at her.

"Hello, Gail. Are you looking for me?"

"Not really. I was going to speak to Tom Nolan, but I chickened out." She told him where she had just come from, the Dixon Air Transport hangar at Tamiami Airport. "I just found out from Lloyd Dixon that he and Octavio Reyes are planning to do business in Cuba — when the regime falls. That could be next week or beyond our lifetimes. I don't know how patient they are. It might be a good idea to find out if they're doing more than talking about it."

"Did he give you any details?"

"They attended a University of Miami

seminar on the topic, and Dixon was in Cuba during the investment conference two years ago." Gail paused, then said, "This isn't news to you, is it?"

He shrugged a little. "I might have heard something."

"Where?"

"You know. Around."

"What else have you found out from . . . around?"

Castillo shrugged. "You should probably talk to Tony about that."

"Why?"

"Well. You know. It's his deal now."

"His deal? Whatever that means. How did you find out about Reyes and Dixon?" But Castillo straightened up from the window. "Felix, I asked you to look into this, remember? Octavio Reyes is the one causing grief for the opera. My client? I'd like to know what you found out in case I have to lean on him."

"You should talk to Anthony about it."

"I *will*, Felix. Anything to do with Octavio I run by Anthony, but that doesn't mean you have to leave me in the dark."

"Well, it's not up to me."

"Anthony told you not to tell me anything, didn't he?"

Castillo made a vague salute with his half-prosthetic hand and smiled at her again. "Nice to see you, Gail." He walked back to his van. She watched him open the door and step up to the driver's seat, the hem of his pants rising just enough to show the gun strapped to his left ankle.

TWENTY

A canopy had been erected over the gravesite. Mourners filled the space underneath and spilled out onto the grass in rows six deep. Gusts of wind played with the ribbons on flower arrangements laid across the coffin.

From where she stood with Anthony behind the last row of chairs, Gail estimated that two hundred people had followed the hearse from the funeral chapel to the cemetery. Seth Greer's elderly parents sat weeping between his sister and brother. Friends and associates at his accounting firm stared numbly ahead, unable to accept what had happened. Behind them stood members of every cultural and political organization in the city, as well as a couple of hundred miscellaneous onlookers.

Camera crews had filmed the arrival of city manager Alberto Estrada. Noticing the video cameras, Estrada had gone over to make the expected statement about tragedies bringing the community together. Uniformed police were keeping reporters away from the gravesite itself until the service was over.

Gail held onto Anthony's arm, feeling the tension in his body. Rebecca Dixon stood beside her husband in the crowd on the other side of the coffin. Slightly parted lips gave the impression that behind the dark glasses her eyes were closed.

Lloyd Dixon's aviator-style sunglasses turned slightly in Gail's direction, and she averted her eyes.

Were you really at home with your wife when Seth Greer was shot to death so close to me that I found his blood on my clothes?

If the exiles hadn't killed Seth, and Octavio hadn't done it, and a provocateur was an insane suggestion, then who had? Seth Greer had been well liked, hadn't gambled or done drugs, and the books at his accounting office were in order. But he was having an affair with a married woman. A woman whose husband picked up the extension and heard that her lover would soon be debating Octavio Reyes on the air. The exiles would be blamed if the lover died outside the studios. Men like Lloyd Dixon would know how to have certain things done.

Did he love Rebecca enough to kill for her? Gail wondered if he knew the truth about her past. Rebecca had said that she had told him about Los Pozos. Had she told him about accusing Emily Davis of being a spy for the CIA? Or brushing the mud off Emily's face and closing her eyes? Lloyd could be right: Too much honesty and someone will wind up wanting to choke you.

Gail took another glance at Rebecca. She was leaning against her husband. How many milligrams of what kind of tranquilizer were deadening her response to the sight of her lover's grave?

The burial in Los Pozos had been nothing like this. Not this blue and sunny day, these neat rows of chairs, and a coffin laden with fresh flowers. Here the dirt taken out of the earth was under a green covering made to look like grass. At some distance was a high hedge of glossy green legustrum, and just beyond it, a shed. The backhoe and shovels would be inside. When everyone was gone, cemetery workers would lower the coffin, erect a stone, and lay sod.

Moving her gaze over the crowd, Gail noticed among the people outside the canopy a man in a dark suit and black shirt. He wore sunglasses and a tweed cap with a small bill. The gray mustache gave him away.

Felix Castillo.

She nearly smiled at the awful irony of it. Those who had survived Los Pozos were all here in this cemetery, one of them dead as the girl they had left there.

Felix Castillo had seen Emily die. Anthony had not told her that. *Because it would have colored your judgment of him.* He didn't want her to know the truth.

Hearing Anthony's story about Los Pozos, Gail had believed him completely. He had said that Pablo took Emily from the house, made her kneel, then shot her in the back of the head. But confronted with what Rebecca had said, and asked the question directly — *Who shot Emily?* — Anthony had replied, *Pablo is responsible.* He had not said, *Pablo shot her.* Then he had forbidden Gail to raise the subject again.

Two days ago at Gail's office, Rebecca had said, *You don't know what you think you do.*

Felix had come with the Sandinistas, according to Seth. He had come with Pablo, whose weapons cache had been hit by government troops. Some of the rebels had been killed outright. Others had been taken, interrogated, and tortured. Their mutilated bodies had been dumped on a road outside the village.

You don't know what you think you do.

Pablo had come looking for Emily. Twenty years old. A pretty girl with long blond hair and freckles.

331

Emily in the bedroom on one of the folding cots, crying. The three others waiting for the rain to stop. It falls on the tin roof and drips off the eaves in long silvery streams. They are sitting at the table talking. On the wall is a picture of Jesus with his heart in flames.

Perhaps they are talking about what to do. Anthony was too proud to beg money from his grandfather to send her home. The others were too angry with Emily to care about the consequences of what she did. Or they didn't see the danger. Either way, they have all waited too long.

The rebel soldiers arrive, and Felix is with them, a young man with black hair and all of his fingers. He carries an AK-47. He knows that somebody has screwed up, and his superiors in Havana will ask questions. His friend, the exile, the grandson of a wealthy banker, has a woman who betrayed them.

The men's boots thump on the wooden porch as they come in out of the rain. Their green ponchos are dripping. Under camouflage hats their wide, dark faces show Indian blood. Pablo is in his late twenties, with lank black hair and a thin beard and mustache. He carries a U.S.

Army Colt .45 in a holster.

Commotion. The Americans don't know what to do. One of Pablo's men brings Emily out, and Pablo speaks to her gently. She confesses. The man in La Vigia promised her a ticket back to Miami. She wanted to go home.

But it isn't Pablo who shoots her.

Felix doesn't want Pablo to think he is on Anthony's side. He takes Emily into the yard and makes her kneel. It is over quickly. He uses his rifle. One shot into her head. She jerks forward and slumps into the dirt, and her blood swirls down the muddy slope, mixing with the rain. The gunshot echoes, then fades into the thickly forested hills.

Why aren't the other Americans executed? Instead of bullets, they are given shovels. The men dig the hole. Rebecca closes Emily's eyes and brushes the dirt away. Then they lower her body into the grave.

With a sudden tremor, Gail pressed her forehead against Anthony's shoulder and squeezed her eyes shut. If Felix Castillo had shot this girl, had murdered her, how could Anthony bear to speak to him? How could they have remained friends? Felix couldn't have done this. But Anthony had lied about it. Why?

She felt Anthony's hand on her cheek, then his arm went around her.

Recovering herself, she took a breath and opened her eyes.

He said softly, "It's okay."

Some people lingered in conversations, but most drifted toward the cars that lined the road. The funeral home attendants were already folding the chairs. The coffin still lay under its blanket of flowers. Camera crews were beginning to close in on the city officials again.

Gail took her mother's arm, talking as they went. Anthony listened for a while, then said he had to speak to someone, would they excuse him for a moment? Gail watched him go through the dwindling crowd in the direction she had last seen Felix Castillo.

When Gail turned back to her mother, she noticed Rebecca Dixon heading toward them, hips swaying, balancing on her toes to keep her heels from sinking into the grass. Behind Rebecca, her husband stood by their car. He called to her. Still walking, Rebecca turned her head. "I said just a minute!"

She stepped over a border of small white flowers onto the path where Gail and Irene stood waiting. Gail had seen her weeping during the services, but doubted that her tears had really been for Seth.

Rebecca's hand went around Irene's wrist. The heavy diamonds glittered. "Irene, I have to talk to Gail, but don't leave. I can trust you not to say anything, can't I?"

Irene's blue eyes shifted to Gail for a second. "Of course."

"I told Lloyd I wanted to come say hello. Gail, what we were discussing before about a divorce attorney? I'm ready. I'd like to talk to someone as soon as possible."

"All right."

Rebecca drew closer. "I'm sorry I didn't tell you the truth about Octavio Reyes. Lloyd said you talked to him about it. God, so many lies. I'm going crazy." She glanced back toward her husband and smiled, holding up one finger to signal she'd be right there. "To hell with that simple life in the country. Reading books. Tending a garden. Did I ever say that?" She turned and made her way back across the grass, long legs in black hose.

After her mother had left, Gail spotted Anthony standing with Felix Castillo in one of the grave sections, headstones going away from them in ragged patterns across the grass. One man taller and slender, the other heavy in the shoulders, dressed in black. Anthony had put his sunglasses on.

She could guess what they were talking about. On the way to the cemetery, she had told Anthony everything she had learned.

Already the sun was slanting westward. Gail checked her watch, then followed the path to the section where they stood. They watched her coming toward them.

Castillo held out an arm. She let him kiss her cheek, and his mustache tickled her skin. "Such a sad day," he said.

"Yes, it is," she replied. "Seth mentioned that you and he were acquainted."

He smiled, showing crooked teeth stained with nicotine. "Well. You know."

Then he looked past her shoulder and made a single nod of his head. Anthony glanced around. Camera crews and reporters were heading their way. Felix said, "I'll be seeing you." He smiled once more at Gail, then maneuvered between two headstones to take another path to the main road.

Anthony took Gail's arm. "Let's go."

The reporters intercepted them halfway to his car. They kept walking slowly as a man in jeans hoisted a video camera to his shoulder. A boom mike was attached to the front of the camera, and a young man in a suit carried another microphone in his hand like a cone of ice cream.

"Gail Connor, you're the attorney for the Miami Opera. What effect will the violent murder of a prominent board member have on the lawsuit you plan to file against the city?" He glanced backward to make sure he wasn't tripping over his cord.

She said she was hopeful that the opera and the city could work out security arrangements. Other than that, she preferred not to comment about the pending lawsuit. They surrounded her, stood in her way.

Anthony said, "Excuse us, please," and gently shouldered through, his hand on Gail's elbow.

She smiled at the next question, then said, "No, this is absolutely not a fight with the exile community."

A woman reporter told her cameraman to get a wide shot. She shouted, "Ms. Connor, you're engaged to Anthony Quintana, one of Miami's top criminal lawyers, a Cuban exile himself. How do you feel about it? Is this a Romeo and Juliet story?"

Gail glanced at Anthony. He kept moving, his slight smile in place and his sunglasses on.

She said, "We're engaged. That's all I have to tell you."

A microphone was shoved at Anthony. "Noted criminal attorney Anthony Quintana is the grandson of Ernesto Pedrosa, a militant anti-Castro exile, and the brother-in-law of WRCL commentator Octavio Reyes, a harsh critic of the Miami Opera —"

"I have no comment."

"— who was about to debate Seth Greer on the air when Mr. Greer was shot to death in the parking lot of the studio. Who do you think is responsible?"

"I don't know."

"Have you discussed this with leaders in the exile community?"

"No."

He opened the passenger door of his Cadillac for Gail. The reporters pursued him around the other side. Anthony got in and closed his door, started the engine, and slowly pulled onto the road leading out of the cemetery.

"What insulting questions," Gail said. "You were amazingly calm. I would have told him to get the hell out of my face."

"No, you wouldn't. They would have put it on the six o'clock news. It's best to say nothing." At a stop sign he unbuttoned his collar and took off his tie. He reached around to lay it across the backseat. He was smiling. "So. Do you feel like Juliet?"

"Much more wicked than Juliet — and twice as old." She leaned over to nuzzle her nose under his ear. He must have shaved in his office before coming to the funeral; his skin was satiny, and he smelled delicious.

He gave her a quick kiss on the mouth, then returned his attention to the road. They would take the expressway south to Coral Gables, where his grandparents would be at home expecting them. Irene had already agreed to pick up Karen from school.

Gail watched traffic for a while, then said, "I have a question. How did Felix find out about Lloyd Dixon?"

The car accelerated around a semitrailer. "He talked to one of Lloyd Dixon's employees."

"You mean bribed him?" When Anthony nodded, Gail said, "How much did it cost you?"

"A thousand dollars."

"I hope it's worth it."

"Not yet." When Gail asked why not, he said, "What's it worth to know that some-day, maybe, if things change in Cuba, my brother-in-law might have a chain of furniture stores from Pinar del Rio to Santiago de Cuba?" Anthony held up his thumb and forefinger in a circle. "*No vale nada.* Zip."

"Why did you tell Felix not to talk to me?"

He laughed softly. "It's not like that. I don't want you to get information from Felix, then you come ask me, then you talk to Felix again. It's simpler this way, if I tell you."

"If in fact you do tell me," Gail said.

"What do you mean, I don't keep you informed?"

"Would you have told me about Dixon and your brother-in-law if I hadn't found out for myself?"

"Of course I would have." He reached for her hand, then turned it palm up. "How is this? Did you see a doctor?"

"Don't change the subject. It's fine. I want to know these things because it could have some bearing on my negotiations with the city. Think about it. If Octavio Reyes — our major critic — is involved with somebody on the opera board —"

"Where is the evidence of that?" Anthony said. "All we know is that they have talked about doing business in Cuba. That's it."

"All right, but say that Lloyd Dixon is currently investing in Cuba. I don't mean planning to, but doing it now through an offshore corporation or financial manipulations, of which he is manifestly capable. And let's assume that Octavio is in with him —"

"Gail, that is not possible."

"Why not?"

"Because —" He exhaled. "Octavio would never do that! Not only would he be cutting his own throat if someone found out, he wouldn't do it because he despises the Cuban regime. He's too much of a patriot. He and my grandfather think alike in that regard. *La causa* above everything."

"You called him a two-headed snake."

"He is. But on the question of Cuba, he's a patriot. I don't agree with his brand of patriotism. I think he's wrong, but Gail, he is sincere about it." Then Anthony added, "That's what makes him dangerous. People who like easy solutions believe what he tells them on the radio."

Gail sat sideways to look at him. "If it isn't possible that Octavio and Lloyd Dixon are doing business, so to speak, why did you spend a thousand dollars to bribe one of Lloyd Dixon's employees?"

The answer took time coming. "Felix thinks you could be right. Not that there is a conspiracy or a business arrangement between Octavio and Lloyd Dixon, as such,

341

but perhaps . . ." The speculation ended in a shrug. "I don't know. We'll see." Anthony guided the car off the expressway and sped through a left turn under a yellow light. They headed east toward Coral Gables.

Gail said, "Will you tell me what Felix finds out?"

"Sure."

"Will you?"

"I said yes."

She made a weary laugh. "You tell me what you want to tell me."

The sunglasses turned toward her. "What do you mean?"

"I mean you hide things."

"Nothing important," he said.

She said quietly, "You didn't tell me about your affair with Rebecca."

He laughed. "Is that why you're mad?"

"It's an example, Anthony."

"More than twenty years ago! How is it important now? I didn't lie. I admitted it when you asked. Stupid thing to do." He added under his breath, "Women never forgive old affairs."

"Are you trying to miss the point, or can't you see it? I don't *care* if you slept with Rebecca, but you gave me such a bullshit reason for not telling me. You didn't want to hurt me? No, you were covering your butt."

His voice rose. "What are you doing, picking a fight on the way to my grandparents' house?"

With an elbow on the window frame, she pushed her fingers into her hair and watched the road.

The car slowed down. He pulled onto a shady side street and turned off the engine. Under the heavy foliage, the sunlight faded. Anthony pulled off his sunglasses and tossed them onto the dashboard.

But when he turned to her, there was no anger in his face. "I'm not going to fight with you, Gail. If we have disagreements, we'll work them out, but not that way." He looked at her awhile, his dark eyes moving back and forth to meet hers. "Okay?"

She nodded. "You're right."

He put a hand on her cheek and leaned over to kiss her softly on the mouth. She smoothed the lapel of his jacket. "You have to talk to me," she said. "You have to trust me, Anthony. We have to be open with each other. About everything. You can't pick and choose what you want me to know about you. Or your past. You know what I'm talking about."

He let out a breath. "It's not that easy, Gail."

"I understand, I know what you've been

through. I love you."

His eyes were closed, his face so close to hers it was out of focus. "I hope you do."

"How can I help myself?" She smiled and said, *"Te quiero."*

"Te quiero más." He unfolded her hand, gave it an open-mouthed kiss, and pressed it between his legs.

A rush of heat expanded in her chest and came out in a ragged laugh. "Is that for me?"

"If you're very good."

"Yes. I can be. Very good."

"I can't touch you without wanting to make love to you." He held her face tightly, fingers clenched in her hair. His tongue moved inside her mouth. He moaned when her hand tightened on him. Then he kissed under her jaw and down her neck to the hollow at the base of her throat. Finally he dropped his forehead on her shoulder and drew in a breath. "Wait. Don't move. Gail, stop."

"If you wanted me to . . . I would do anything." She held perfectly still. "Right here on a public street." Her voice came out in a whisper, and she felt dizzy from wanting him.

TWENTY-ONE

The housekeeper, Fermina, gray-haired and plump, lifted her arms with a cry of delight at the door. Anthony bent to embrace her. In Spanish, Fermina told them that everyone else was out of the house — except for *los viejos,* the old couple, who were upstairs. Digna was helping *el señor* dress, and they would be down soon.

With a gasp, she remembered that she had left something in the oven. Her voice diminished as she hurried away, and Gail missed the rest of it.

Just past the entrance from the foyer, Anthony rested his hand for a moment on the carved back of an antique Spanish chair, then came further into the living room. Over the coral rock fireplace a clock ticked on a mantel crowded with family mementos. A last bit of sunlight flickered through the wooden blinds at the windows and gleamed on the floor. A potted plant was positioned between two of the windows. Gail thought of the dark-eyed, laughing boy at the house in Vedado. The photograph had shown areca palms in planters on shiny tile floors. The boy stood on a wicker sofa and beside him, nearly out of view, was the arm of a man in a white linen suit. A slight turn of history, and the boy would have grown up to live in that house, would have followed the man's path in Havana. The years in Camagüey would never have happened, nor the rage at being dragged into a foreign country, nor the rebellion that led to Los Pozos.

How well he fits here, she thought. Anthony Quintana Pedrosa walked through the rooms of this house as if he owned them. He was not impressed by the wealth. Gail had once believed — because he had said so — that he did not want it. She was beginning to see another interpretation: A man need not desire what is already his by birth. Anthony had spent his years thirteen to twenty here, before the break with his grandfather. The ties of blood were strong. In his heart, he had never left.

Gail asked, "What did your grandmother say, Anthony? Why did she want us to come?"

"To visit. To get to know you, I suppose."

She bit her lower lip, thinking about that, then went to check herself in the gilded wall mirror at the other end of the room. She had not worn a somber color to the funeral, knowing she would be coming here afterward. She smoothed the jacket of her royal blue suit over her hips. It fastened up one side with shiny black buttons. She fluffed her hair. "Do I look all right?"

"You're beautiful." He smiled at her in the mirror.

She whispered, "I'll bet he wants me to explain why I'm going to sue the city. He'll yell at me, and I won't know what to say to him."

Laughing, Anthony pulled her closer. "No. He only yells at me."

Fermina came back in, clearing her throat. *La señora de Pedrosa* had rung down to say they would meet Anthony and Gail in the sitting room. She bustled away again to open a bottle of wine.

They walked down the hallway with its arched ceiling and pools of light. "Nena will probably invite us to stay for dinner," he said. "It's her way. We could tell her we have plans."

"Do you want to stay? Karen's at my mother's house. Maybe we should."

"I thought you were nervous."

"I can be brave if you can."

"We'll see how it goes," Anthony said.

She kept her voice low. "How long has it

been since you've had dinner here with your grandparents? No fair counting family dinners."

He thought about it. "I don't remember."

"Shame on you. We should stay."

"Only if my grandfather asks."

"Why wouldn't he?"

"Don't count on it."

She took his arm. "And don't you be so pessimistic."

The sitting room was on the west side of the house, an intimate room with brocade furniture and small oil paintings decorating the walls. Rugs brightened the terra cotta floor. The sun was a sliver of gold in the trees, which cast deep shadows across the yard. Floor-to-ceiling windows gave a view of a grassy circle around a bronze statue of a laughing cherub. Gail asked about it, and Anthony said, "That was my grandmother's flower garden. She doesn't have the strength for it anymore. You should have seen it. So many colors."

The sunlight through the trees winked out.

Anthony had told her his first clear memory — his grandfather taking him to the bank. Only him, none of the others. Ernesto Pedrosa had worn a white linen suit — it must have been summer — and they rode in the back of a long black Chrysler.

He smells of cologne. Guerlain. His hands are spotless, the nails pink and clean. He wears a hat and two-toned shoes. His pocket handkerchief is heavy silk, the same blue polka dot design as his tie. The driver follows a route that Anthony will later, as an adult, map out. Fifteenth Street to Paseo, then to Twenty-third, then the Malecón, which curves along the sea, then south on Galiano a few blocks. The driver stops the car, opens the rear door.

Anthony reaches up to take his grandfather's hand. He sees the underside of his chin and the straw brim of the hat. They walk across the sidewalk in the fierce sunlight. Shiny gold letters are embedded in the concrete. Carved stone portals, immense wooden doors. A black man in uniform pushes one open. The lobby echoes with voices and footsteps. People are smiling down at the boy. His grandfather puts his hands under his arms and lifts him up, up. The counter is marble, cold on the backs of his legs, which are bare in his short pants. His hair is combed with violet water. Pedrosa announces, Este es mi nieto. *His grandson sits at eye level with the people who gather around to see him.* Que machito. Que lindo el nené. *Already this boy has a look about him. He knows who he is.*

He runs his fingers up and down the turned brass bars of the teller's cage. On the wall there is a huge black-handed clock, and the second hand is sweeping around.

A shuffling footstep at the door drew Gail's attention, then Anthony turned from the window. Digna Pedrosa was entering slowly to accommodate her husband's slow pace. Her eyes widened and she cooed happily, as if surprised to find visitors here. Ernesto Pedrosa's posture was as erect as eighty-four years would allow, and he pretended to use his cane more for effect than necessity. Both he and his wife were dressed for company, she in an ivory wool crepe dress with a string of pearls, and he in a dark suit and tie.

The old man kissed Gail's cheek and patted her hand, then held his arm out to Anthony and allowed himself to be embraced. With Digna's subtle assistance, Pedrosa steadied himself over the armchair, then sank into it.

Sherry and coffee were brought, and a

tray of pastries, chocolates, and cheeses. Inquiries were made about Gail's health, the health of her mother and daughter, and the rest of the family. How was Doris, the aunt who is learning Spanish? And the lovely cousins. They must all come here again, anytime.

This visit was not simply to get to know the prospective granddaughter-in-law, Gail realized. Digna Betancourt de Pedrosa wanted to bind up the wounds in her family. It was she who pushed her husband along in the conversation, who laughed, who brought up the sweetest remembrances of the past. The two men said little at first, but gradually they talked about Anthony's children — a safe topic. They would of course come down for the wedding. Digna asked why the children could not stay here while their father was on his honeymoon. What do you think, Ernesto?

Ernesto Pedrosa agreed. He sipped his sherry and said his grandson had some sense after all, to have chosen such a beautiful and intelligent woman, who was kind to have taken pity on him. Using Gail as a focal point, they talked of the differences between American and Cuban weddings. The old man said they should bring back the guitarists for the reception. He had enjoyed them so much. Gail inquired about the little seascape on the wall, and he braced himself on his cane and got up to show it to her. Anthony said he had never noticed this painting, and Pedrosa said he had not opened his eyes. It had been done by Ernesto Pedrosa's own mother as a girl on vacation in Majorca in 1882 — he pointed at the date. Older even than I am, he said with a laugh. He pretended astonishment that Gail had never seen Spain. You must! Go there on your honeymoon. Yes. The Prado is what you want to see in Madrid. Then go south to the coast. See the Alhambra. He asked Digna if she remembered the Alhambra.

Then Pedrosa said he had to sit down. He went back to his chair and let Anthony help him. Still standing, Anthony took the bottle of sherry to his grandmother on the sofa and filled her glass till she waggled a finger to stop.

Pedrosa leaned toward the ottoman where Gail sat and squeezed her hand. The pouches under his eyes were deeply shadowed. He took a breath. "You should see Cuba, too. *La isla mas bella del mundo.* That's what Cristóbal Colon — Columbus — said when he saw it. The most beautiful island in the world."

"I would like to go someday," Gail said.

"You will." His lined face lifted into a smile. "So will I."

"*Si Diós quiere,*" murmured Digna.

He waved a hand. "If God wishes? No. We wish it. It will happen. You should see our farm in the country. Incredible, incredible place. Look, there by the window, the photograph, you see? The house with the royal palms leading to it, and the poinciana tree on the side."

"*Framboyán,*" Gail said.

"Ah! Very good. It was bright red, but the picture doesn't show the color. That's our country house. I'll spend my last days there, and I want to be buried on the hill overlooking the farm." He patted her hand again. "What do you think? Isn't it beautiful?"

"It is, yes." She exchanged a glance with Anthony. He had already told her that the country estate had been turned into a citrus grove, and that the house had been bulldozed for a processing plant, which now had fallen into ruin for lack of parts.

Pedrosa said, "It's still there, isn't it? Or have they torn it down?"

"It's there," Anthony said. "I saw it on my last trip."

"It's there? And they haven't torn it down?"

"No, *abuelo*. It's the same." Anthony looked into his glass of sherry, swirling it slowly. His grandmother tugged on the hem of his jacket, and he sat next to her.

Pedrosa leaned on the arm of his chair. "Gail, you will see it soon. The regime won't last much longer."

"Fidel can't live forever," Gail said, a response that anyone in Miami could safely give.

"They won't wait for Fidel. The people will rise up." The old man's voice dropped to a whisper. "Not from outside. No. We tried that. Washington betrayed us. They never wanted a coup to take place. We were tricked. In 1961 they gave away Cuba to the Russians in exchange for peace. Today Washington won't allow a coup because they're afraid of immigration. The only hope of change is the Cuban people themselves, who hate the dictatorship."

"I see."

"It's the only way. Attack from within. The people will rise up if given the means to do so."

Gail thought of the men in the shadows at Ernesto Pedrosa's birthday party, talking with Octavio on the front porch. Members of militant organizations. Which ones? Alpha 66, Omega 7, others without names —

Desperate to get off this topic, Gail said, "Did you keep horses at the farm? You once told me you had stables."

Digna called out, "Ernesto, tell her about our racehorses."

But Pedrosa leaned even closer. "It's already happening. Hotels have been bombed. The Hotel Nacional, the Capri. A year. You will see Cuba free within a year, I guarantee this."

Anthony shook his head. "You said that when the Berlin Wall came down."

Pedrosa looked around at him. "He doesn't agree with me. He wants Cuba to stay the way it is."

Digna clicked her tongue. "Ernesto."

"No, let him answer. Let him tell us what he thinks about the bombings."

Anthony said quietly, "I think the regime will use them as an excuse to tighten its grip. Two generations have lived under that system. They don't want violent change, and even if there is change, the country would never go back to what it was. Nor should it."

"You know nothing. You believe in nothing."

Digna went over to put a hand on her husband's shoulder. "Ernesto, please. We have a guest. Gail doesn't want to hear talk like this."

His chest rose and fell with his breathing. "I apologize. My wife is right, of course." He turned his head to smile up at Digna. "You're a tyrant."

On the sofa Anthony was leaning on an elbow, rubbing his forehead.

"Digna, more sherry, *mi vida*." She refilled his glass and he touched her arm lovingly. He said to Gail, "I am sorry about the man who died. I read in the paper his funeral was today."

"Seth Greer," she said.

"Was he a friend of yours?"

"Not a close friend, but we knew each other."

"And you weren't hurt." He was frowning, wanting to be sure.

"I'm perfectly fine."

"Thanks be to God." His face sagged for a moment, then he gestured with his glass. "This other man, the one who is going to sing in the opera. What is his name?"

"Thomas Nolan."

"Octavio says he is a communist. Is this true?"

"Ernesto!" said Digna quietly.

"No, it's not true," Gail said. "Tom Nolan has no political agenda. He stumbled into this. He went to Cuba with his friends not knowing anything about the country."

"Is that so?" Pedrosa frowned. "How could he not know?"

"Most people don't. He spends his life singing. That's all he does. He doesn't watch the news, he doesn't listen to radio, and he isn't interested in politics."

"How can a man have no politics?" Pedrosa asked. "A man without politics is a man without passion."

"But Thomas Nolan has his own kind of passion — his music."

From a distance came the shouts of children, the thudding of footsteps. Somewhere a door slammed. Digna looked into the hall. "Who is that? Oh! Alicia!"

Anthony's sister came in, saying hello. She leaned over to kiss her grandfather, then went to give her brother a hug. "What a surprise! I saw your car outside. Hi, Gail." The two women brushed cheeks.

Glancing again at Anthony, Alicia said, "We dropped by to take the measurements for the party." She gestured toward the hall. "I told Octavio to take the kids to the game room. They are so noisy!"

Which was not, Gail knew, the real reason Alicia had sent her husband with the children. She wanted to keep him and Anthony apart. Gail wondered if Octavio had ever told his wife what Anthony had done to him outside the guest house.

Still smiling, Alicia said to Gail, "We're having a party here in two weeks for Maddie. She'll be twelve. You have to come. Bring Karen, too."

"Thanks. I'll see what we're doing that weekend." Both of them knew the chances of Gail and Karen showing up. Gail felt a twinge of annoyance that Alicia could simply drop by unannounced, while Anthony waited for an invitation. In the next instant she was ashamed of her jealousy. Anthony kept himself aloof; Alicia did not.

Digna said, "Alicia, you are eating dinner with us, no?"

"Of course."

Then Octavio appeared at the door in a sport shirt and yellow golf sweater that made his skin sallow and added twenty pounds. His eyes moved around the room. He didn't come in until he had located Anthony.

"Hello, Gail. How is your injury?"

"Much better, thank you."

"I'm glad to hear it."

Anthony set his glass of sherry on the tray. "Gail and I were just leaving."

"No, please," Digna said, taking his arm. "We have the most wonderful swordfish tonight."

"Please," Alicia repeated. "Why don't

you and Gail stay?"

Octavio said, "They probably have things to do, Alicia."

For a second Anthony looked at his grandfather, but Ernesto Pedrosa sat silently resting his hands on his cane. His thick gray brows rose slowly, as if asking Anthony what he intended to do next.

He said to his sister, "Thank you, Alicia, but you know if we stayed no one would have much of an appetite."

"Oh, don't be that way. You can't go."

Octavio sighed with more than a hint of regret. "We'll wait for another occasion. You know, Anthony, you're welcome here anytime."

Color flooded into Anthony's cheeks, and he made a single exhalation that could have passed for a laugh. "This is your house now?"

Digna put her hand on his arm again, tugging till he looked at her. "Alicia and Octavio and the children are going to live with us. They will move in as soon as they sell their house."

"What?"

Alicia twisted her hands together. "It's my fault. I was supposed to talk to you about it. Nena can't run this house by herself anymore."

Anthony stared across the room.

Octavio looked back at him over the top of his glasses, then spoke calmly in Spanish. Gail struggled to pick it up. Something about helping Ernesto with the businesses.

Then Anthony asking whose decision this had been. He turned to his grandfather.

Ernesto lifted his head and tiredly replied, "He's a good businessman."

"You have managers for all your companies," Anthony said. "They do an excellent job. I don't understand this."

"*Los* managers *no son familia,*" Octavio said.

"Neither are you. You're in the family because you married my sister. You sell furniture. What do you know besides bed frames and cheap sofas?"

"Anthony, *por favor,*" Digna said.

Unable to look at the others, Gail put a hand on his shoulder and said in a low voice, "We should go."

For a long moment he seemed frozen, staring at Octavio Reyes as if Reyes had struck him across the face. Then he let out a breath. "Yes. We should." He glanced at his watch. "Nena, thank you for inviting us. Grandfather." He made a slight nod in the old man's direction. Ernesto Pedrosa did not reply.

Passing by his chair, Gail stopped to say, "Thank you."

His pale blue eyes lifted to meet hers, and he took her hand. "Come back to see us anytime."

Her heart beating erratically, she glanced around the room. "I hope to see you again soon. I'll tell my mother that you asked about her." Her gaze seemed to snag on Octavio Reyes just long enough for her to see the quick smile of satisfaction that vanished back in like the tongue of a snake. She knew that he had taken only the first step to destroy Anthony Quintana, and that his revenge would be total.

In the hallway, Gail had to hurry to keep up with Anthony's fast pace. She told him to slow down, but he seemed not to hear her. A vein stood out in his forehead. His skin seemed drawn to the bones of his face as if pulled from inside. They had reached the front door when they heard someone calling his name.

Alicia ran into the foyer. She went around him and leaned on the door. "Anthony, please."

He said quietly, "Get out of the way, Alicia."

"Don't leave like this. They're getting so old. It was my idea to help them. Mine.

Please don't leave until you tell me it's all right."

His laugh ended in a sigh. "It wasn't your idea. I know whose it was. And why are you asking me now? You could have asked beforehand, if it mattered."

"It does! I didn't think you would care." She moaned. "Oh, my God, I saw your face when Nena told you —"

He held up his hands and spoke in a low, calm voice. "Do what you want. But don't expect to see me walk through that door as long as Octavio Reyes lives here."

Alicia stared at him. "Why?"

He smiled. "Would I be welcome?"

"You're crazy. You hate Octavio so much you'll hurt everyone else. How do I tell Nena? What are you going to do when your children come for Christmas? Drop them off and wait outside?"

He studied his car keys. "All right. I will come in and speak to the family as long as Octavio is not here at the time."

She was close to tears. "I can't tell my husband to get out whenever you decide to come over."

"That's up to you. Alicia, move out of the way, please."

Gail felt ill. "Anthony —"

"No. He won't listen to anyone!" Alicia

pushed herself away from the door, broke into sobs, and fled down the hall.

They drove the few miles to Gail's house in near-total silence. Her head was a storm of emotion, and her chest was so tight it hurt to breathe. She glanced at Anthony from time to time. He seemed deep in thought but otherwise unaffected by what had occurred. She was afraid to speak until she had decided what to say.

He wheeled into her driveway and turned off the engine. "Did you say that Karen is with your mother tonight?"

"Yes. She has a school holiday tomorrow."

"Good. Let's have a drink. We'll have some dinner and go to bed early."

She felt her head pounding as she got out of the car. He locked it, and they went inside. The house was eerily quiet.

He took off his jacket and hung it neatly on the back of a chair at the table, then took a bottle of white wine from the refrigerator and the opener from a drawer. Expertly he cut the foil off the top of the bottle, then twisted in the corkscrew. "What do you want to eat? We could go out or have something delivered."

Rubbing her temple, Gail set her purse on the kitchen counter and opened the cabinet for the bottle of pain reliever. "Look and see if there's some frozen lobster."

He left the corkscrew half in the cork and opened the freezer door. She heard the rustling of packages.

At the sink she tossed back two pills and drank some water. Her hands were shaking. "Let me say just one thing, Anthony, then I won't say anything else about it tonight. I hope you can calm down enough to reconsider what you said to Alicia. She was right. If you cut yourself out of your family, everyone will be hurt. Everyone but Octavio."

"I am calm." He frowned at the instructions on a package of frozen lobster tails. "And I'll say one thing, too, then maybe we can enjoy the rest of the evening. My grandfather is letting Octavio in for a reason. He is still punishing me for the past. It has become part of his character, and he is too old to change. I won't keep slamming my head against a wall. If my kids want to go over there, I have no objection. And that's all we need to say about it." He read the other side of the bag.

Gail grabbed the wine bottle by the neck to finish opening it. "Oh, I see. He's punishing you for the past. And you aren't doing the same?"

Anthony tossed the lobster into the sink,

where it hit with a clunk. He unfastened his gold cuff links and rolled up his sleeves, each fold quick and precise. "What else should we have with this? Potato? A salad?"

Twisting the corkscrew, Gail said, "Really, it's a mutual misery society. For years you and Ernesto have held grudges for sins in the past. In some weird way maybe you both enjoy it. It's how you get to each other. But if he lives another year, it will be a miracle. Then what? You've just walked away, and I don't think he's going to beg you to come back."

Hand on his hip, Anthony looked at her for a while, then said, "Are you finished?"

"Yes."

"Good." He took the wine bottle from her and levered out the corkscrew, which ripped through the cork. *Coño cara'o.*

"Octavio can slide in there like the snake he is because you left a vacuum. He's going to take everything, and you don't care?"

Anthony poked at the cork. "Is that what you want, Gail? The house? All that money?"

"Dammit! How could you — I don't *care* about that, and you know it!" She leaned against the sink.

He closed his eyes. "I know. I'm sorry I said that to you." He touched her shoulder and let his hand slide off. "We shouldn't talk about this tonight."

"What I want —" She grabbed a paper towel and blew her nose. "I want you and your grandfather to get along. That's all. Forget Octavio, if he lives there or doesn't. This is your *family*. Don't pretend they don't mean anything to you. Until you fix what's broken, you will never have anything right with them. And maybe not right with us, either."

"Until *I* fix it? You saw how he is." Anthony set the bottle down so hard the toaster oven clattered.

"He's an old man! The past is all he has. What do you want him to do, say he's sorry? He won't. He will grow old and die and you'll keep insisting it's up to him. That is so *selfish!* You're blaming him for sins he committed when you were thirteen years old — taking you out of Cuba! He did it because he loved you. And now — oh, yes, he's as much of an idiot as you are — he blames you for going to fight for the Sandinistas." She laughed. "I mean, it's all so incredibly stupid."

Anthony smiled at her. "Have you said everything now?"

"You want me to ignore it, don't you? Just be a good girl and agree with you."

"Right now, yes, that would be very nice."

She felt herself sliding toward the edge. "Well, I won't. That is not who I am. I do not ignore things —" Her throat ached. "— that matter to me . . . and to the people I care about. I don't understand how you can. Ernesto doesn't know what really happened in Nicaragua, does he? You gave him the censored version. You're afraid to admit that somebody died. You took your girlfriend to Los Pozos and she was murdered. You wouldn't let her go home, and you think you're responsible."

His black eyes narrowed to slits. "I told you not to bring that up again."

"Why? Because you don't have the guts to face the truth?"

He pointed at her. "Don't."

"You know what Rebecca said? The bones are rising from the earth. You can't keep them buried. They haunt you." She followed him to the chair where he had hung his coat. "I want to know who shot her. Tell me the truth."

He leaned on a hand braced on the back of the chair. His knuckles were bloodless.

"It wasn't Pablo, was it?"

He shook his head.

"Then who? Oh, God. Did you —"

"No. It was Felix." He squinted as if the kitchen was too bright, and held his hand over his eyes. "Pablo wanted to kill all of us. Felix convinced him that Emily was to blame. Seth broke down crying. He fell on the ground and shit his pants. Rebecca was screaming. And I . . . couldn't . . . do anything."

Gail looked at him for a few moments, then asked, "Are you telling me the truth?"

"What the hell do you want me to do, get down on my knees and beg you to believe me?"

"I just need to know I can trust you."

"Trust?" His face was red and twisted, a man she didn't recognize. *"Tú hablas* all that bullshit about trust and feeling. You want control, *esto es lo que tú quieres* — a man you can control. *No soy americano como tu esposo.* I will never be an American, forget it, I don't take this shit from a woman. I am what I am. Okay? *¡Yo soy como soy!* If you don't like it, too fucking bad. *¡No me hace falta esa mierda o tú tampoco!"*

"Great. You don't need me? Then leave!" Gail screamed back at him. "Go find yourself a nice little *cubana* like you had before, who couldn't stand being married to you."

Panting for breath, he stared at her a moment longer, grabbed his coat, and walked out of the kitchen. The front door slammed.

TWENTY-TWO

Irene Connor's house was just north of downtown in Belle Mar, a waterfront area that looked out on the islands between the city and Miami Beach. A girl Karen's age lived across the street, which gave Karen someone to play with. While Gail lay on a lounge chair, the two girls swam in the pool. Shrieking happily, they made cannonball dives, and Gail would flinch at the occasional drops of cold water that hit the backs of her legs. She had untied the top of her swimsuit and propped herself on her elbows to read.

Along with a suitcase for the weekend, she had brought all her files relating to *Miami Opera, Inc.* v. *City of Miami.* Gail had spent yesterday drafting the complaint. There would be an emergency hearing in front of whatever judge might be assigned to the case — if it were filed. That was looking less likely. The mayor was on the opera's side. A local TV station had conducted a poll, and respondents — those who recognized the name Thomas Nolan — voted five to one that he had a right to sing in

Miami. A Little Havana civic leader had been interviewed: "It is unfair that a few troublemakers can create a bad image for all of us."

She lay on the lounge chair reading old newspaper articles about exile terrorism that her secretary had copied from library microfilm. The purpose had been to give some background to the lawsuit. Gail had not used the research after all, but flipping through it on Friday had piqued her interest. Today, reading about bombings and assassinations suited the bleak mood she was in.

She had read that in 1975, the publisher of *Réplica*, a Spanish-language magazine in Miami, had the nerve to suggest working with Cubans inside Cuba, even participating in elections if they were held. He was gunned down outside a children's hospital.

A radio commentator preached against such violence. When he left the studio and started his car in the parking lot, a stick of dynamite tore off his legs.

Raids were planned. Men trained in paramilitary camps in the Everglades. Armed militants were arrested by the FBI or Customs on their way to Cuba in boats riding low in the water. Weapons were seized.

The name Ernesto José Pedrosa Masvidal

had appeared several times, referred to variously as exile leader, hard-liner, right-winger, extremist. Suspected of financing terrorist acts, Ernesto Pedrosa had been investigated by the FBI. This image did not fit the old man Gail had seen the other night, who had dreamily gazed at a faded photograph of a house in the country.

If Anthony had wanted to be cruel, he would have said, Sorry, *abuelo,* your country estate was paved over, and the *framboyán* tree is gone. But he let his grandfather believe in a gentle lie. Gail had loved him at that moment. Then he had closed up entirely, shut her out, and screamed at her for pushing to know the truth.

Gail jerked when a splash of cold water hit her back. She held a towel to her front, turned around, and yelled, "Karen! Lisa! Stop that!" Two faces appeared grinning, their owners dog-paddling in the sparkling pool. Giggles. There was another face, too — a fifty-nine-year-old woman in a swim cap with yellow daisies.

"Mother, what are you doing?"

"Come in with us, you grouch."

"I'm working."

She put her sunglasses on, fastened her top, rearranged the towel, and sat down. Reaching into the box on the patio, she pulled out a book titled *The Exile: Cubans in the Heart of Miami*. She tossed it back, not in the mood to read another word about Cubans in the heart of anything. She suddenly longed for a romance novel set in Montana. The hero would have cool blue eyes and a monosyllabic name. Jake. Ted. Luke.

She heard the patter of wet footsteps. Her mother hurried across the patio in her sea blue swimsuit with the little skirt, pulling off her swim cap, fluffing her red hair. Her skin — once so luminous and smooth — was sagging at thigh and upper arm, and her petite torso had thickened. How sad, thought Gail. Or maybe it wasn't sad at all, but a liberation from the demands of the flesh.

"Brrrrr, that was invigorating." Irene dried herself off and tucked in the towel at her bosom. "Are you still reading those depressing newspaper stories?"

Gail said, "It was pretty exciting around here in the seventies. I was in high school, then I went away to college, so I don't remember very much. Do you?"

"Not clearly," Irene said. "It was mostly in Little Havana, and nobody I knew was affected. There wasn't as much violence as those articles make out, but a lot of my friends left Miami during those years. They said the city had been ruined. It wasn't, of course."

"We should have gone, too," Gail said. "Put one of those bumper stickers on the U-Haul. 'WILL THE LAST AMERICAN LEAVING MIAMI PLEASE BRING THE FLAG.' "

"What a thing to say!"

"Why didn't you and Dad leave?"

"This is our home," her mother said.

Gail stretched her arms over her head. "Last time I saw Ernesto Pedrosa he was talking about those Cuban tourist hotels that were bombed last summer. He says the people will rise up. He thinks he's going to make it back home."

"Maybe he will."

"He could go if he wanted. He's just stubborn and contrary."

"He's very old, Gail. You're in a mood, aren't you?"

"I've had a hard week."

Slipping into her sandals, her mother said, "I'm going to get dressed and make some fruit daiquiris. We'll get our vitamins."

In 1978 Ernesto Pedrosa had been investigated by the FBI for funding sabotage raids, the same year that Pedrosa's eldest grandson, whom he had rescued or kidnapped from Cuba, depending on one's view of it, had gone to Nicaragua to fight with the leftists and get the innocence blasted out of him for good.

The telephone in the kitchen rang. Gail stopped breathing. When her mother didn't lean out the door to call to her, she pushed her sunglasses up into her hair and lay down. Spots of color swam in the darkness like miniature fireworks. She dozed.

There was a thump of a tray being set on the metal table. Gail ratcheted up the back of her lounge chair and felt the prickle of a sunburn. Her mother, dressed now in white slacks and a bright green T-shirt, filled two tumblers with frothy pink liquid. She had put on fresh lipstick and mascara.

After handing Gail her drink, Irene went to the edge of the pool. "Little mermaids! Little mermaids, time to grow legs and come out of the water. Cookies and juice." Dripping and shivering, the girls wrapped themselves in colorful beach towels that hung to their ankles. Irene gave them a bag of bread and told them to carry their snacks to the seawall and throw crumbs to the fish.

Then she stood at the foot of Gail's lounge chair, stirring her frozen daiquiri with a cocktail straw. "Jeffrey Hopkins called just now looking for you. He wanted to know if you had seen the interview on Channel Seven last night with Tom Nolan. He tried to reach you at home."

"Oh, God. What happened?"

"Well —" Irene made a little smile. "Tom said he was happy to have sung in Havana. The U.S. embargo is causing all the problems down there. Washington is afraid of the exile lobby. What else? Oh, yes. Fidel has done more for the Cuban people than the exiles ever would have, if they'd stayed."

Gail took a long breath in, then let it slowly out. "I'm going to kill him. I'll tear out his tongue. Does Jeffrey want me to call back? He has got to be boiling." She imagined his smooth cheeks flaming over his bow tie.

"You can call later," Irene said. "He was on his way out. Who you should call is Tom Nolan before he makes it any worse. I have his number in my address book by the phone."

Knotting her towel at her hip, Gail strode barefoot into the kitchen. She grabbed the phone off the wall and punched in the numbers.

Four rings. Then an answering machine. Then a soft, deep voice informing her that no one was home. "Tom, this is Gail Connor. Are you screening your calls? If so, please pick up." Silence. "I suppose you're at rehearsal. I hope you made it there without being shot at. I heard about your interview on Channel Seven last night. How can I put this without being rude? I can't. That was so incredibly *stupid*. We agreed, *no interviews!*" She paused for a breath. "All we can do now is pray that nothing happens. And meanwhile, if anyone asks, would you *please* say it was a joke, a misunderstanding, you lost your marbles, you didn't mean it. And call me immediately. I'm at my mother's house, Irene Connor."

She left the number and hung up. "Dammit!"

At the table outside, she gulped down half her frozen daiquiri, then felt the ache grab her throat. "Shit." She held her mouth open and breathed in some warm air. "*Idiot. What is he doing this for, the publicity? I'm going to kill him.*"

The phone rang again. Gail glared in the direction of the kitchen, then feared that it might be Anthony. She had not told her mother anything about their argument.

The phone was still ringing. "Do you want me to get it?" Irene asked.

He was not likely to call there, Gail decided. "No, I'll do it."

Rebecca Dixon was on the other end of

the line. Yes, she had heard about Tom Nolan's interview, wasn't it awful?

"My maid, Juanita, just told me that Octavio Reyes made another of his vicious commentaries this morning. He even played some of Tom's remarks on the air and translated them into Spanish. All the other stations are talking about it, too."

Leaning her forehead against the cabinet over the sink, Gail said, "Rebecca, if you expect me to have a solution to this mess because I'm a lawyer, prepare to be disappointed. I don't know what the hell to do now."

"Lloyd said he's going to have a talk with him."

"Who, Tom?"

"No. Octavio Reyes." Rebecca spoke as if she were afraid of being overheard. "He's coming here tonight, and Lloyd's going to talk to him."

"Lloyd asked him to come to your *house?*" Gail found this incredible. "And Octavio Reyes is going to be there? Are you sure?"

"Yes. I'm sorry I didn't tell you this before. Lloyd is having some people over for dinner, and Reyes is on the guest list."

"The dinner party where *Tom Nolan* is going to sing? How is that possible?"

"Mr. Reyes doesn't know about it. It's

Lloyd's little joke. He says it's payback for all the trouble he caused us. He wants to see his reaction. He thinks it's funny."

Gail stood up straight, still not believing this. "What is going on, Rebecca? What are they doing?"

She heard a little laugh on the other end. "These people at the party are acquaintances of Lloyd's. They have money, and they're going to invest it in Cuba as soon as the opportunity arises. It's not legal now, you know, but Lloyd says that luck comes to those who prepare for it."

"And Octavio Reyes is one of his friends," Gail said.

"Not *friends,* per se. They don't socialize or anything. Octavio Reyes has been to the house, but not while I was here. I wouldn't recognize the man if he walked into my bedroom this minute. I'm sorry. Lloyd told me to stay out of it, so I kept quiet. Maybe you should tell Anthony."

"He already knows about it, Rebecca. Not that Reyes is going to show up at your house tonight, no, but the rest of it he's aware of."

There was a long pause. Then Rebecca said, "How does he know?"

"Felix Castillo. Anthony hired him to look into it."

"Oh." A laugh came over the line. "Well, Anthony's always a step ahead of us."

Hanging up the phone, Gail thought for only a moment about calling Anthony to report all this. But he knew about it. What was the point? What Anthony did not know was that his brother-in-law was more of a snake than he had ever imagined.

Outside on the patio she finished her daiquiri, refilled her glass, then sat down and told her mother that the call was from Rebecca Dixon, wanting to talk about Tom Nolan's interview. She did not mention the rest of it. All roads led to Anthony.

Irene's arms shone with sunscreen, and she had put on a big straw hat. From the shade of its brim she said, "I've been thinking about what Tom might have brought back from Costa Rica in that suitcase."

"Your guess is as good as mine." Gail reached for another of the articles on exile terrorism.

"I think it was ancient musical instruments. Mayan or . . . what kind of Indians did they have in Central America? A musician would want souvenirs like that. Tom could never have gotten pre-Columbian artifacts into this country legally, so he had to ask Lloyd Dixon to smuggle them in. What instruments did the Indians play before the Spaniards got there?"

"I don't know, Mom." Gail flipped another page, looking at a photograph of the smoking ruins of a cigar factory. The owner had been suspected of traveling to Havana.

A minute later her mother asked, "Are you going to tell me what's going on with you and Anthony or not?"

Gail kept her eyes on the page. "Well, I didn't really want to bring it up this weekend, but it's pretty much over."

"Oh, no. You can't mean that."

"Afraid so. You were right when you warned me about him six months ago."

Irene scooted her chair around to face Gail. "You said he made you happy."

"Sometimes he does, but sometimes isn't enough. The moment we disagree — *kaboom!* He has a horrible temper."

"Oh, Gail. He isn't violent, is he?"

"No." She thought of Octavio Reyes gagging after a punch to the stomach. "Never with me."

"Darling, all couples have their disagreements and sore spots."

"It's more than that. I've talked to Cuban women, so this isn't just my politically incorrect opinion here, all right? They've told me, Cuban men tend to be selfish, domineering peacocks, and they expect the

380

woman to take a secondary role. It's a cultural thing. I don't blame Anthony. He can't help the way he was brought up."

"But he was brought up in Miami, not Cuba."

"Is there a difference?"

"What does he ask you to *do* that you don't like?"

Gail tossed the stack of papers back into the box and reached for her drink. "Mother, why do you make everything sound so trivial? It's basically — and you will bug me until I tell you — an inability to open up. He is an emotionally closed man."

"Anthony?"

"There are important issues that he refuses to deal with. And I can't discuss them, so please don't ask me."

"Well, I think it's his gender more than his culture. Your father and I went round and round, fighting about every little thing. You don't remember because you were so young when he died. I have learned since then how much wiser it is just to be quiet and listen. Try to understand. If you become angry and insist on your way, you might end up losing what you want to save. You have to be subtle and patient."

"*Yo soy como soy.*" She saluted with her glass. "It means, I am what I am."

Irene stirred her daiquiri. "You know, darling, you could look in the mirror when you accuse someone of having a temper."

Gail was silent for a while, then held out her arms. "I'm sorry." She put her head on her mother's shoulder. "Please don't tell anyone, especially not Karen. She likes him so much. I don't know what to do. Oh, Mom, I can't talk about it anymore now."

When Irene went to see how the girls were doing, Gail cried for a few minutes into a corner of her towel. Sick of her own self-pity, she blew her nose and picked up another newspaper article at random.

In 1986, at the Torch of Friendship in downtown Miami, two hundred liberal protesters had gathered to sing folk songs and make speeches against U.S. aid to the Nicaraguan contras. On the other side of police barricades, two thousand screaming exiles waved American and Cuban flags and threw eggs. Inevitably, the crowd broke through and police had to get the peace protesters out of there.

Scanning the article again, Gail recalled that the contras had been fighting the Sandinistas. Curious when that had started, she rummaged in the box for a book she had seen on socialist movements in Latin America. She opened it on her lap.

In 1979, the corrupt dictator General Anastasio Somoza had fled Nicaragua, and the Sandinistas took over. The contras had launched a counterrevolution to oust them.

In 1985, with Reagan in the White House, a group of Cuban exiles went to Nicaragua to fight with the contras. The exiles had trained at a secret base in the Everglades operated by Brigade 2506 — the same Brigade that had been defeated at the Bay of Pigs in 1961.

Gail remembered having seen on the wall of Ernesto Pedrosa's study a flag of Brigade 2506, and alongside it, a framed black-and-white photo of men in fatigues. She did not know that Cuban exiles had gone to Nicaragua. Seven years before that, Anthony had been there, age twenty-two, with a beard and long hair, carrying an AK-47 lent to him by Felix Castillo, the spy from Havana.

The Cuban exiles had gone to Nicaragua in 1985, she assumed, to do there what they could not do in Cuba: Kick some communist ass. There had been a slogan: Today Nicaragua, tomorrow Cuba.

She rummaged through the box, found a book on the CIA in Central America, and opened it on her lap.

The United States undertook to supply the contras with arms and ammunition.

Reagan had said we wouldn't walk away from this one — referring, perhaps, to the fact that the U.S. had walked away from Cuba. When Congress voted to cut off anything but humanitarian aid, ways were found to keep the guns flowing. Working with the CIA, Lieutenant Colonel Oliver North set up a secret supply route. Cargo planes flew from bases in El Salvador and Costa Rica and dropped weapons to the contras on the ground. Laws were broken at the highest levels. The White House was implicated.

When the scandal broke in 1987, the participants were forced to give testimony before a U.S. Congressional committee. Gail had been in law school, and the subject had been a hot topic on campus. Oliver North defiantly admitted that he had lied.

Gail had forgotten that many of the weapons had been purchased and prepared for shipment in Miami, and that an air cargo company based in Miami had actually been owned by the CIA, and that one of its planes had been shot down over Nicaragua in 1986.

Cuban exiles had raised money for the contras. Gail would bet that Ernesto Pedrosa had kicked in with a substantial contribution to Oliver North and company.

And during all this, Anthony had been safely away in New York, practicing law in the federal public defender's office, married with two kids.

Swinging her legs off the lounge chair, Gail stood up to refill her glass. With the book open on the table, she read that Colonel North had turned the operation over to Major General Richard Secord, who acquired five aircraft, built airstrips and warehouses, and hired pilots to fly the missions.

From March to October 1986, Secord's Operation Enterprise flew over forty missions into Nicaragua, dropping pallets with machine guns, rocket launchers, mortar shells, grenades, rifles, C-4 plastic explosives, detonators, fuses, parachutes and rigging, and various forms of ammunition and other supplies. The party ended on October 5 when a Sandinista SAM-7 missile brought down a C-123 transport plane over Nicaraguan territory. The Reagan administration denied all knowledge of the flights.

Gail flipped to an appendix at the back of the book listing the types of airplanes: C-123, C-7 Caribou, L-100. She did not know what they looked like, but imagined dark gray, propeller-driven aircraft flying at low altitude over the hills at midnight, the pilots watching for a signal from the ground, their faces illuminated by the instrument panels, and the pallets stacked next to an open cargo door, ready to be shoved out or however they managed it. She turned a page and read a list of pilots, flight crew, and ground support.

She reached for her glass, then froze with it suspended in midair. She let it down slowly, as if to do otherwise might jostle the print.

A voice seemed to come from far away. "Gail, I said what do you want for lunch? Gail? Are you all right?"

Slowly she looked around at her mother. "Guess what Lloyd Dixon was doing in 1986."

Irene hesitated. "I don't know, dear. What?"

"Flying a C-123 cargo plane out of secret air bases at Ilopango, El Salvador, and western Costa Rica, dropping weapons to the Nicaraguan contras." Gail closed the book. "I wonder if you could do me a favor. Call Rebecca's house? If Lloyd picks up the phone, I don't want him to know it's me."

TWENTY-THREE

The last light had faded when Gail drove her car off the ferry onto Fisher Island. She spotted a golf cart waiting by the main road, and a woman at the wheel. The guard checked her name off a list, then said that Mrs. Dixon had already arranged to show her the way. Gail blinked her lights. The cart did a quick U-turn and Gail followed. They went past the marina, then around the golf course, the same route she and Anthony had taken after Thomas Nolan's recital at the clubhouse.

A curving driveway went under the portico of the building where the Dixons lived, but Rebecca swerved left into the small parking lot for visitors, vanishing for a moment behind the thickly planted tropical landscaping. She stopped the cart at the back of the lot.

Gail got out of her car and heard Rebecca's soft laugh. "Your *hair*. I didn't recognize you."

"It's a wig. Am I Fisher Island enough?"

Rebecca took a look at Gail's black cashmere tunic and loose trousers. "Not nearly enough jewelry, and I don't see a face-lift, but it's a start." She patted the seat beside her. "This seems like a lot of trouble to take a picture."

"I don't want Octavio to recognize me." Gail put her shoulder bag on the floor of the cart and got in.

"But why do this at all?" Rebecca tossed her hair back, and long pearl earrings swung. "Lloyd can be very persuasive. He'll say . . . Octavio, if you don't stop attacking the Miami Opera, I'll take you up in my airplane and kick you out over Havana. Oh, come on, Gail. Laugh, will you?"

"I'm too wound up," Gail said. "No, I want a photo. The city is close to making us lose tens of thousands of dollars, and the lawsuit could go either way. And maybe Lloyd doesn't really care if Octavio stops. I want a picture of the King of Commentary, WRCL, going into the apartment where Thomas Nolan is singing. It would be too, too sweet."

Rebecca turned around in the seat to look at Gail directly. Her coat fell open to reveal a slim black dress with silver beading around the low neckline. "Something tells me," she said, "that this is personal. You're out to get him. Admit it."

Gail let out a breath. "Well . . . not out

to get him, exactly. I wouldn't put it like that, but in a way I feel responsible for what's been happening. Octavio started this, but only because I was involved with the opera. He's using the issue to drive a wedge between Anthony and his grandfather."

"Ahhh. Ernesto Pedrosa. Lloyd says he's worth over two hundred million dollars. Oh, yes, I would think that's highly personal."

"Look, Rebecca. Anthony doesn't want the money —"

She laughed.

"He *doesn't*. He has his own money. He wants his place in the family. I can tell you this because you'll understand. Anthony's grandfather still holds it against him that he wanted to join the Sandinistas, and Anthony never told him what really happened. Their relationship is fragile, Octavio knows it, and he'll do whatever it takes to ruin it completely, or at least keep them from reconciliation till Pedrosa is dead."

Rebecca's mouth was a perfectly outlined and lipsticked O of wicked delight. "God, would this make a good opera. Somebody's got to die in the end. Who do we pick? Octavio, naturally. Then you and Anthony take the throne in the last act —"

"Rebecca, please." Gail let out a breath. "Anthony and I are having some problems right now. I don't know what's going to happen."

"Is it bad?"

She nodded. "It's tied up with his grand-father and Octavio, and so much crap in the past to deal with. You know about that. Then we've got our own differences on top of it. I'm not doing such a good job." She waved it away. "Never mind."

Rebecca scooted over and gave her a squeeze. "I'll help you with Octavio. His head on a pike."

Gail laughed. "No. Just a few pictures."

Reaching to turn on the battery in the golf cart, Rebecca said, "Why did you tell me not to say anything to Lloyd? He'd get a kick out of it, you lurking around in the bushes."

They started forward with a little jerk, moving silently across the parking lot. Gail said, "No, let's leave Lloyd out of it. What do you know about these men coming to-night? Who are they?"

Rebecca had already told Gail there would be eight, including Lloyd. Rebecca would have cocktails with them and listen to Thomas Nolan and the others sing, but then she was expected to quietly disappear to her own part of the apartment. The caterers would take care of serving and cleaning up.

"They're Lloyd's friends. I might remember a few names, but that's it. Lloyd never talks about them."

"Could you find out who they are? What they do?"

The golf cart suddenly slowed, its fat tires skidding a little on the pavement just at the edge of the parking lot. Rebecca turned off the key. "Why? There's something else going on. What is it?"

Gail didn't want to lay it all out. She had only suspicions, not evidence. Octavio Reyes and the others had not come for a chat about future investment opportunities in Cuba, but to plan more serious moves.

"You got me onto Fisher Island, so let's leave it at that," Gail said.

"I can turn around and take you back to the ferry, too. What's going on? I'm getting a divorce, so don't be afraid I'll run to Lloyd with anything you tell me."

"Fine. I think those men could be planning a coup against Fidel Castro. I'm not certain, but that's my guess. Lloyd's in on it."

That brought a stare of astonishment. "Lloyd?"

"How much do you know about his past? Do you know that in 1986 he was flying secret missions for Oliver North and Richard Secord, resupplying the contras in Nicaragua?"

"Yes, I know about it. He told me."

Gail asked, "Is he still involved with the CIA? What about his dinner guests?"

"They're businessmen."

"You're sure."

"Gail, really."

There was silence. Then Gail said, "Are you going to get the names for me? You don't have to."

"Yes, of course." Rebecca turned the key, and the cart moved silently around a row of cars, then out of the parking lot. They went across the road and past the portico, heading for a garage entrance.

But at the last moment Rebecca turned away, went fifty yards farther on, and parked in an area where thick trees cut the illumination from streetlamps. Rebecca's black coat drew her further into the gloom.

She spoke softly. "Okay. You're right. Lloyd did know some people with the CIA. I'm not sure if he still does. As I told you before, the boys get together for fun and games, and I'm not supposed to ask. After we got married — when I was at the clinic in England getting my head fixed — I told Lloyd about . . . Nicaragua. I was worried whether anything had ever come out. Lloyd said he knew some people in the CIA he could ask."

"The CIA made a report?"

"That girl's aunt wrote to the State Department, so they looked into it."

"What did they say? If you don't mind telling me."

"Lloyd got a copy. It was pretty vague. They had all our names listed as American volunteers for the church. Isn't that wild?"

"What about Emily Davis?"

Beyond the trees Gail could see the glint of the ocean, and Rebecca seemed to be staring at it, deciding what to say. "They sent a man up to Los Pozos. He got conflicting stories. She was alive, she was dead, the National Guard killed her, she left for Managua. The local bureau decided that she was officially missing and presumed dead. They sent the report to her aunt. Case closed." Rebecca took a breath that lifted her chin and exposed a long line of pale throat. "Want to know why they closed it? Emily was nobody. Emily was a scholarship student. She gave piano lessons to earn spending money. If she had been you or I, the government would have found out what happened. They would have stuck with it. But Emily's family accepted what we, and then the CIA, told her. Lucky for us. No problem."

"No problem," Gail repeated. "But it won't go away. Not for Anthony, either."

"Let's not get into that." Rebecca turned the key.

The wheels of the golf cart kicked up some gravel making a sharp turn in the road. Rebecca said, "I'll get you the ferry records showing Octavio Reyes's previous visits. I'm a resident here. I have a right to see them."

"Be careful, though. Don't mention his name."

"Please. I'm so good with the staff. They love me. Do you have a phone with you? Write down your number." While Gail jotted it on a page of her memo book, Rebecca explained, "The desk downstairs lets us know who's coming. I'll call when Octavio is on his way."

Gail hung on as they took the turn into the parking garage under the building. The only noise was the high-pitched whine of the golf cart as they passed rows of luxury cars and sports models. Several more carts were tethered to electrical outlets. Rebecca stopped between her Jaguar and her husband's Lincoln. She lifted a panel on the side of the cart, plugged in the cord, then nodded toward the elevators. Gail followed her in, and Rebecca pressed the button for the sixth floor.

"Are you nervous?"

"God, yes, I'm sweating," Gail said.

"Don't worry. Our neighbors are gone, but Octavio won't know that, so you can stand on the walkway in front of their door. You'll be backlit, so he won't see your face."

"Okay." She took a breath and counted the numbers going up.

The elevator opened onto the sixth floor terrace, a wide area of decorative planters and benches. A cool breeze came through the tops of palm trees a few feet past the railing. They turned left and walked with some distance between them until Rebecca reached the carved double doors of her apartment. "Bright enough?" Rebecca whispered. Light came from twin lamps beside the doors and from a spotlight overhead. She smiled and went inside.

Gail set her camera exposure and took a shot of the door. Number Three.

The terrace took a turn, putting the next apartment at right angles, so that Gail could stand at the railing and look across at the Dixons' apartment. The palm fronds rustled just below her. Gail did not like standing in the light, but it came from behind her. She knew that anyone entering the Dixons' apartment would see only the outline of a tall brunette woman in black enjoying the night air before going back inside.

She set her camera on the flat top of the carved limestone railing and aimed the adjustable zoom lens at the Dixons' door. The camera would be shielded from view by her body. Under the wig, sweat tickled her scalp.

From around the corner she heard the elevator bell. She leaned an elbow on the railing and put her cheek in her palm, waiting, covering the camera with her other arm. Four men in suits appeared. She hit the shutter. The automatic advance sounded hideously loud. She got all four of them, whoever they were, as the door opened, then shut.

A minute later her phone rang. Rebecca said that Octavio Reyes was on his way. Forcing herself to breathe slowly, Gail rechecked her camera, squinting through the viewfinder to make sure nothing had moved. Then she waited. Heard the bell. She leaned casually on the railing as if she were looking out over the island.

There he was — a stocky man with gray hair and glasses, moving quickly through pools of light. His gaze seemed to reach across to the railing where she stood.

He stepped into the light at the Dixons'

door and turned his back.

Gail breathed out a soft curse. "Turn around." He pressed the door bell. Gail hit the shutter. The door opened and he was gone.

It occurred to her that he might have wondered why a woman was standing alone, looking in his direction. Maybe he'd seen a glint of light on the lens. He would come out for another look. She had wanted to get Thomas Nolan as well, but without a photo of Reyes, it would be useless. Gail dropped her camera into the bag and took the stairs at the corner. Catching her breath at the bottom, she eased open the security door, then came into the light of the portico as if she preferred to take the stairs for her health.

She crossed the road and casually walked to the visitor's parking lot. It took her a few minutes to find Reyes's car, a burgundy red Lexus. With the flash attached, she dared one shot of the license plate.

She waited for Nolan to appear. Five minutes later a taxi pulled up under the portico. A man in the backseat had a blond ponytail. Staying just behind the trees across the road, Gail zoomed in on the taxi. The first person to get out was the Asian accompanist she had seen at the recital. He extended a hand to assist the soprano, who wore a long gown. Tom Nolan and the tenor came out the other side in their tuxedos. She got a good shot of his face with the doors of the condominium in the background.

She was retreating into the shadows when her phone rang again.

Rebecca said, "The desk just called. Tom and the others are on their way. Where are you?"

"In the parking lot," Gail said. "I think I missed Octavio. He turned his back."

There was a silence, then Rebecca said, "I'll get him myself."

"Rebecca, no —"

But she was gone.

The phone rang again in less than a minute.

"What are you doing?" Gail whispered.

"I'm on the terrace outside the living room. Walk around to the south side. I'll wave to you. The lights are off out here, so they can't see me, or if they do, they'll think I'm talking to one of my friends. I'm smiling, I'm laughing, I can see everything. Octavio Reyes is right there. It's so bright in the living room I don't need a flash."

"Don't let them see the camera!" Like one of the residents out for a walk, Gail went around the building. She looked up toward the arches along the terraces and the various angles of the roof. She put the phone to her ear. "Okay, I'm down here."

She heard Rebecca laugh. "They're coming in. Oh, God, this is hilarious. Octavio doesn't recognize Tom. Lloyd is introducing everybody. Tom is staring at Octavio. He's being a nice guy, holding out his hand. Wait."

There was a long silence. Gail stood on the grass next to a palm tree, seeing lights on in the apartments above her. A few people were out on their terraces, talking and holding drinks. She heard music from somewhere.

"Octavio is just furious. He's walking out."

"Don't take any more pictures. Rebecca —"

"He wants to leave, but Lloyd is laughing. He's pulling on his arm. Now they've gone down the hall. I guess they went to Lloyd's study. Can you see me from there?" Gail had been staring up the whole time. A woman appeared on the topmost terrace, waving a pale, bare arm. Over the phone Rebecca said, "I'm going to throw the film to you."

She leaned over the railing, extending her

arm. The film cartridge, a dot of black, hurtled downward, hit Gail's arm, and bounced to the grass. She found it and waved toward the terrace.

Rebecca waved back and disappeared. Gail dropped the film into her bag and hurried across the lawn of the building, staying close to the shadows cast by the bushes and trees.

She heard the quick footsteps in the grass a split second before she felt the hand over her mouth.

Her feet left the ground. Somebody was dragging her backward. She kicked and twisted, flailing her legs, digging her fingers into the hand. It was not flesh, she realized. A glove. But too hard to be a glove.

A voice hissed into her ear. "Shhh, it's me, Felix. Be quiet!" He pulled her behind some bushes. "A security guard is coming." He crouched, drawing her down beside him. "Be still." Gail was still shaking, breathing open-mouthed, trying to make no sound. Her heart slammed at her ribs.

Felix Castillo held up a hand, signaling her to wait. He stood up just far enough to see through the top of the hedge, then sat back down.

She whispered, "You scared the shit out of me! What did you do that for? Security doesn't care if people take a walk at night!"

"Shhh. I saw one of them watching you. Do you want him to ask what you're doing here?"

"And what are *you* doing here, Felix?"

"Just looking around. You know."

"Following Octavio Reyes, aren't you?"

"No, I came with Tom as his bodyguard."

"You're lying. He came in a taxi." In the starlight she could see a smile: teeth appearing under a mustache. Gail said, "How did you get on the island?"

"Some bullshit story, and I gave the ferry captain a hundred dollars." He grinned again. "I'll put it on Anthony's bill."

"I suppose you're going to tell Anthony you saw me."

"I suppose so." Castillo tugged on her hair. "You look better as a blond. You could get into trouble, what you're doing."

"How did you know it was me?" Gail pulled off the wig and shook out her hair.

"Who else? I saw you when you took a flash picture of his license plate." He took a tiny camera out of a pocket. "This is easier. Infrared film." He showed her another small camera and a long lens. "Be prepared." He stowed the parts back inside his coat. "What were you and Rebecca Dixon talking about on the telephone?"

Gail told him about the scene Rebecca had described to her. "Having Tom here was a joke Lloyd Dixon played on Octavio."

"I don't get it," Castillo said.

"I know. I don't, either. Lloyd has a weird sense of humor. Rebecca says he's going to make Octavio stop his attacks on the opera. That's not going to be easy after Tom said what he did on TV last night. Did you see it?"

"Why did he do that?"

"Because he's stupid."

"You think so? I talked to him. I think he's a very smart guy." Easing to a crouch, Castillo stood up to see past the bushes. "Okay, it's clear. Come on. I'll take you to your car." He extended his elbow. "Nobody will notice two people together. We make a nice couple, you think?" He led her to a lighted pathway that curved toward the road.

"There wasn't a security guard, was there?"

He smiled again. "There could have been. You should be careful."

Gail stopped. "I have to talk to you, Felix. It's important."

"Okay." He nodded toward the beach. Starlight picked up a curve of white in the darkness. With water too shallow for waves, the ocean lapped softly onshore.

They sat on the ends of wooden beach loungers. Key Biscayne lay to the east. Straight ahead, the darkness was unbroken except for the running lights of boats still out at this hour.

"This may sound strange, but I think Lloyd Dixon and his friends — including Octavio Reyes — are planning a counter-revolution in Cuba. It's possible that the CIA is either involved directly or at least aware of it."

Castillo looked at her from under half-lowered eyelids, not sure if she was kidding. He reached into his jacket for cigarettes and a lighter. The cigarette bobbled between his lips when he said, "Tell me why you think this." His hands cupped a flare of orange that picked up the lines in his face and his thick gray mustache.

Then darkness again.

Gail said, "All I have to go on are a lot of unrelated facts. I could be wrong. Lloyd Dixon admitted to me that he and a group of investors want to do business in Cuba. The country is a huge market on our doorstep. It's closed now, but someday that will change. Let's say they're impatient. They believe that if the regime is given a push, it will fall. Let me tell you what I just learned about Dixon." She told Castillo about the flights to arm the contras.

Smoke curled upward. Castillo held the cigarette low to the ground, his hands between his knees. A careful man.

Gail told him about Dixon's trips to Cuba under a false name. Had he been looking for places to leave C-4 explosive and a timer? Hotels had been bombed already, and those responsible had not been found. Gail mentioned the men she had seen with Octavio Reyes in the shadows during Ernesto Pedrosa's birthday party.

For a while Gail sat in silence. "You know about Anthony's grandfather, don't you? His family history?"

Castillo exhaled smoke toward the ground. "Yes. He told me."

"I don't like talking about his family, but consider this." She told him about Pedrosa's history of financing raids on Cuba. The investigation by the FBI. The ties to the CIA that had probably saved Pedrosa from indictment as a terrorist. Recounting her visit to the Pedrosa house, Gail told Felix how wine and nostalgia had led the old man to talk about Cuba. The old man wanted to go home, to die in his native land and be buried there, not in this cold foreign earth. *You will see Cuba free within a year, I guarantee this.*

"I didn't pay any attention to what Ernesto was saying at the time. We were having a good visit till Octavio came in and announced that he's going to be managing some of Ernesto's businesses. Worse than that, Octavio and Alicia are moving into the house. He's taking over by dividing the family and making Ernesto believe that Anthony doesn't care about what they have lost in exile."

Sifting sand through her fingers, Gail let a handful of it trickle into a pile. "Octavio is caught in a bind. He wants to do business with the guys upstairs, but he wants to get tough with the opera for hiring Thomas Nolan. That's another way to get to Anthony, you see? He's using me, and I resent that. At first Lloyd Dixon didn't think anything would come of Octavio's rantings on the air, but now he has to tell him to stop. We'll see what happens. I don't know, Felix. I could be so far off about overthrowing the regime. It does sound far-fetched. But I am sure that Octavio Reyes is moving in on Anthony's grandfather, and that poor old man wants to go home so badly that he would believe anything."

She drew a slow circle, watching how the

sand drifted back into the trough. "I'd like you to tell Anthony what I just told you."

"You should do it." She could feel Felix Castillo's eyes on her. "Okay, he doesn't like to talk about his brother-in-law with you, but this is different."

"Well, we're not currently speaking to each other on any topic."

"Why?"

She only shrugged. "I don't know. We had a fight. Don't ask."

"I'm sorry to hear that," he said. "Very sorry."

Gail sat up straight, dusting the sand off her fingers. "Here's another odd piece of information. Thomas Nolan and Lloyd Dixon flew to Costa Rica two years ago, after Dixon showed up in Havana. Dixon told me he was doing a favor for Tom, bringing back a suitcase Tom had left there by accident. Dixon claimed not to know what was in it. Maybe it was jewelry for Rebecca."

Castillo brought the cigarette to his lips, holding it between thumb and middle finger, the glowing ember out of sight. "Could have been weapons."

"Smuggling weapons *into* the United States?"

He blew smoke toward the water. "A rifle

and scope would fit in a suitcase."

Gail looked at him. "Meaning what?"

"How long have Dixon and Thomas Nolan known each other? I'm thinking, Dixon and Nolan in Germany at the same time. Then in Havana. They fly to Costa Rica. Dixon travels a lot. So does Nolan."

"What are you saying, Felix?"

"Where was Nolan the night Seth Greer was shot?"

"I don't know. Rehearsing, probably."

"I called him like you asked me to. I got no answer, and there was no rehearsal that night."

Gail let out a laugh of utter surprise. "Thomas Nolan is a hit man for Lloyd Dixon?"

"For anyone. The CIA. They have people they use."

"Felix, whenever I talk to you I start believing in conspiracy theories. I could believe the Cubans and the Mafia were behind the assassination of President Kennedy."

He smiled and took a last puff of his cigarette. He dug a hole, dropped in the butt, and smoothed the sand over it. "It's time to go." He rose and extended a hand to help her up. When she didn't move, he asked, "Is there something else?"

"A question." She hesitated. "It's about

Nicaragua. Los Pozos."

"Why ask me?"

"I have to know about the girl who died. Seth Greer said you were there when it happened, so please don't tell me you weren't. Who killed her, Felix?"

"You don't need to worry yourself with that. It's a long, long time in the past." He began to walk toward the parking lot, following the shoreline rather than the main road.

Gail followed him down the gentle slope, the sand getting firmer. The shallow water rose and fell on the sand as if it were alive, breathing. "Anthony won't talk about it, either. It's a barrier I can't get through. He tries to forget what happened there, but he can't, and it's tearing him apart. Emily Davis's ghost won't leave him alone. Please tell me, or all I can think is the worst."

Castillo stopped walking. "You think he killed her."

This was exactly what she had feared without consciously realizing it. She waited for Castillo to speak. He was a silhouette against a backdrop of stars. "No, it was me that shot her. She didn't suffer any. It was fast."

Gail let out a low moan and hugged her arms to her chest.

Castillo said quietly, "Emily Davis caused the death of eleven men."

"She couldn't have intended that. She didn't know. My God. She was so young."

"The men were young, too. One was fifteen, two others were seventeen. In a war there aren't any kids. They were men." The shore turned gently north, and Gail followed Felix Castillo as he resumed walking. "They wanted justice. A piece of land for their families. The Somozas and their friends owned everything. These people had nothing. You can't imagine how poor they were. This woman betrayed them."

"So she had to die. This *woman*, twenty years old."

Castillo made no response.

"Did Pablo make you do it?"

"No. It was my decision."

"Yours? Was it easy for you?"

"It had to be done."

Her voice broke. "How can Anthony speak to you after what you did?"

Castillo said, "He knows how it was."

They had reached the low wall marking the end of the beach. "How ugly this is. How horrible. I'm sick of thinking about it!"

"People in this country don't have to think about it. You're lucky." His voice was sad beyond measure. "Be seeing you." He disappeared into the darkness.

Fifteen minutes later, halfway across the channel from Fisher Island, Gail reached into her bag for the film that Rebecca had dropped to her.

It was gone.

TWENTY-FOUR

Listening to Jeffrey Hopkins, watching his face turn pink with indignation, Gail wondered if he was deliberately insulting Thomas Nolan. Provoking him. Expecting him to leap up and scream across the desk, *Who do you think you are, the fucking Metropolitan Opera? I'm out of here.* Replacing the star of an opera to open in two weeks would not be, Hopkins might reason, as difficult as suffering the consequences of keeping him.

Tom Nolan sat impassively, looking back at the general manager from under the sharp ridge of his brows. He seemed perfectly at ease. Legs crossed. Hands clasped loosely on his lap. But Gail could see the vein that pulsed in his hollow temple.

Pausing for breath, Hopkins jerked his chin to one side as if his green paisley bow tie were too tight.

Nolan said quietly, "The answer is yes. Of course I want to stay."

"Then you will make a statement to the media." Hopkins planted an elbow on his desk and counted off his fingers. "First, you will apologize to the Cuban exile community for your insensitive remarks. You will confess your ignorance of their history and their current political situation. You will beg forgiveness. You will have no — absolutely no — further contact with any reporter whatsoever outside my presence."

A chuckle resonated in Tom Nolan's chest. "Are you serious?"

"It's your decision. We can use the understudy."

"He isn't good enough for this role."

"At this point, Mr. Nolan, I do not care." Hopkins's eyes narrowed. "Ms. Connor, explain our legal position."

With no more than a shift of deep-set blue eyes, Thomas Nolan looked at her.

Gail said, "You have exposed us to potential losses of thousands of dollars per performance in additional security costs. Before your interview on television, I was confident that the controversy had died down. This morning I received a phone call from the city manager, who said that in view of your remarks the city of Miami cannot waive its demands. Radio commentators are calling for a mass demonstration on opening night. It's my opinion that we have grounds to fire you for cause. However, we hope that some intensive PR will mitigate the damage.

We're willing to try, but unless you assure us of your cooperation, we have no choice but to replace you." She added, "One point your attorney should consider. If you sue us, the lawsuit would be filed in Miami — with a Miami judge and jury."

Jeffrey Hopkins made an elaborate nod.

Nolan shifted in the chair. Pulled his fingers through his ponytail. Let out a breath. "I've never made a statement to the press. What do you want me to say?"

"That's up to you," Hopkins said. "Jot down some ideas over your lunch hour and let me see them. The reporters and cameramen will be here at five o'clock."

"Rehearsal isn't over till six."

"I've spoken to the director. You'll finish early and come straight here. Do we understand each other?"

"Yes. All right." At the door Tom Nolan turned stiffly around. "This is so damned unprofessional. You could have worked this out with my manager. The tension is going to affect my voice."

Hopkins gave him a mean little smile. "Be a trooper, Tom."

Hurrying after Thomas Nolan in the corridor that led to the theater, Gail heard him before she saw him. He was vocalizing, the

413

sound coming through his nose. *Ying-yang-ying-ing-ing.* Then his voice dropped to the bottom. He sucked in some long breaths, hands on his hips. Then arpeggios. *Ah-ah-ah-AH-ah-ah-ahhh.* Up an octave, then down in a different series of notes, then another, then down again, then a change of key, going faster. His voice leaped and soared and reverberated on the concrete walls and against metal doors.

"Tom!"

Still walking, he glanced at her. "What is it? I have to get to rehearsal." He dug his fingers into the back of his neck and rotated his head.

"I'm sorry we had to do this," she said.

"Please do not preach at me."

"No, Jeffrey did that already. I thought you might want some help deciding what to say to the media."

"Probably. Yes."

"They'll ask questions, too, and we should discuss some responses. When you break for lunch, call me at my office."

"Thanks." He pinched his nose. *Waa-waa-waaaa.*

Gail waited for two men to pass carrying a sheet of plywood. "Tell me, how was the party last night at Lloyd Dixon's place?"

"Oh!" Nolan abruptly stopped walking

and pulled her away from an open door. He leaned closer. "You won't guess in a million years who was there. Octavio Reyes."

"What?" Gail let her eyes go wide.

"As God is my witness. I didn't want to say anything in front of Jeffrey back there, because Lloyd Dixon said he would talk to him today. Reyes is a customer of Lloyd's." When Gail nodded, Nolan made a small laugh of surprise. "You're aware of this? What is going on?"

"I don't know, Tom. Tell me what happened. Did you speak to Reyes yourself?"

"No, he and Lloyd went into another room to talk, and five minutes later Lloyd came back in and said Octavio Reyes had gone. He was, quote, insulted by my presence. I didn't take offense because it was funny, in context. Reyes came expecting a business dinner, and he got me. Lloyd said that Reyes had promised to take it easy on us from now on, though, so it turned out all right. His commentary today didn't mention me or the opera. We're not in such bad shape as Jeffrey makes out."

"Except for the other four or five radio commentators that want to lynch you," Gail said. "What do you mean, Reyes expected a business dinner? Who were those men you sang for? What did they talk about?"

"They were . . . businesspeople. They have money. I don't know who they were."

Gail looked away, thinking, then said, "Have you seen Felix Castillo?"

"No. Why?"

"I'm trying to find him. He hasn't returned my calls."

"Mine either. Where is he? I could be shot dead on my way home tonight. Come on, they're expecting me in the theater."

Opening his mouth as if in a yawn, then setting his teeth together, he let his voice drop to a dark rumble. He glanced at Gail. "That was about an E. I can't do it in performance. My bottom note is a G. It's the high register that kills you, but I've got good technique."

They walked down an incline, the corridor opening up to the backstage area. The double metal doors were propped open, and beyond them Gail could see scaffolding and lights, everything painted black. The lights were on, harsh white illumination coming straight down. A woman with a clipboard backtracked and came out. "Tom! Where've you been? Martin's looking for you."

He waved a hand at her. "Be right there." To Gail he said, "Martin's the director. Do you want to watch for a while? I'll take you out front." He led her along a narrow passage to a carpeted area, then to a door that opened noiselessly into the auditorium.

The red-upholstered seats seemed to stretch upward to infinity, with boxes on the sides and an immense spiraling chandelier in the ceiling. The house lights were on. About halfway back a table had been set up over the seats to hold a computer and microphones. There was no orchestra, only a pianist in the pit talking to a chubby woman in black jeans leaning over the edge of the stage.

The woman looked at Tom Nolan and tapped her watch.

"Coming!"

Onstage the lights brightened, then dimmed. A bluish spotlight illuminated a two-story set with a red tile roof and an ornate balcony outside someone's window.

Gail asked what they would be rehearsing.

"We'll skip around, but we'll start with act one, scene one." Thomas Nolan extended his arm toward the stage. "Nighttime, outside the house of Donna Anna. Giovanni is inside, and his manservant, Leporello, is pacing back and forth with a lantern, waiting for him. Suddenly Giovanni appears at the door, pursued by Donna Anna, screaming that he has seduced her by force. *Traditore!* Betrayer! The lady's father, a commandant in the army, comes out and demands that Giovanni defend himself. They draw their swords. They fight. The old man dies. So the opera begins with a rape and a murder."

"Murder or self-defense?"

Tom Nolan smiled. "Spoken like a lawyer. Whatever it was, the Commendatore comes back from the dead to give Giovanni one last chance to repent. Giovanni refuses and demons drag him down to hell."

Gail said, "I remember. You sang that part with one of your students in the stairwell at the School of the Arts."

"A good memory." Nolan glanced toward the stage. "Well, if you'll excuse me —"

"Wait. I have one more question."

"If it's fast."

Gail came closer, speaking quietly. "You told me you saw Lloyd Dixon in Havana." Nolan nodded. "It wasn't just that one time at the Hotel Las Americas, was it? Dixon says that you and he flew to Costa Rica. What's the story on that?"

"The story?"

"Why did you and Dixon go to Costa Rica?"

She got a blank stare. Nolan said, "What's that got to do with anything?"

"I don't know. And that's my problem with it. If you'd told me everything from the beginning, we wouldn't be in this mess."

He smiled. "Gail, this isn't your concern."

"Lloyd Dixon says you picked up a suitcase in San José that you didn't take through Customs on the way back." Gail dropped her voice further. "What were you doing, Tom? I have a right to know. I'm not likely to tell anyone, am I?"

His cheeks became concave when he pursed his lips. "It wasn't mine. It belonged to a friend."

"Who?"

She counted off four long seconds before he said, "Miss Wells. My former piano teacher. She'd been in Costa Rica a few years ago doing missionary work, and she accidentally left it there. I called her and asked if she'd like me to pick it up for her."

"Really. Who paid for the jet fuel to Costa Rica and back?"

"I did. It was extravagant, but I had the money."

Gail closed her eyes. "That is such BS."

Someone shouted from the stage, "Places, Tom!"

"All right!" He looked back at Gail. "I'll call you at your office at noon." He strode toward the stage door, discernible in the wood paneling only by virtue of its hinges and doorknob.

Gail followed. "What was in the suitcase?"

"Oh, a few kilos of cocaine." He opened the door, then stopped and looked around at her. "It was clothing. What did you expect?" The door closed behind him.

That afternoon Gail spent an hour with a reporter from the *New York Times* who had flown down to do an article on the controversy for the Sunday magazine. When he finally left, with photographer, her head felt like somebody was driving a chisel into her eye sockets.

"Oh, God," she moaned to her secretary. "Aspirin." She went into the tiny kitchen, took two extra-strength, and pressed a glass of ice water to her temple.

Miriam had some papers for her to sign. The complaint for injunction in the federal lawsuit had been printed out on crisp white paper. There was a summons for Albert Estrada as city manager. Estrada had called her with his regrets. Not a bad guy. He had suggested it would be good to get all this out in the open. The media would be at the courthouse at ten in the morning to film the festivities. Gail expected that the emergency hearing would take place the next day, or the day after. She hoped that Thomas Nolan's interview would help. She had decided not to be at the opera this afternoon, but to watch the press conference on television from home. Her presence might suggest that someone was holding a gun in his ribs.

He had called at noon, as promised. Not being much help. Expecting her to do it. Long silences, then Gail suggesting this or that phrase, and Nolan saying sure, sure, whatever. At one point she had yelled at him. *This is supposed to sound sincere, dammit.* And he had laughed, that deep chuckle. *Don't worry. I make my living onstage.* Gail had given the notes to Miriam. Miriam had typed them up, then faxed the statement to Jeffrey Hopkins. Done.

Sitting in the extra chair in Miriam's office, Gail slid the signed papers for the federal lawsuit back across the desk.

She tapped the pen in a rhythm and stared at the telephone. She had left four beeper messages for Felix Castillo, progressively more irate. The first had been on the Fisher Island Ferry last night, asking if he had noticed a film canister that might have fallen from her bag when he grabbed her and pulled her into the bushes. Assuming he hadn't been able to get to a phone, she had let it ride until midnight, then called him before going to bed, asking if he had received her previous message, and *please call no matter how late*. By morning, she wanted to know, *Where is the film, Felix?* Driving to the opera, she had spoken through clenched teeth. *I want the damned film.*

And where might it be now? Her anger was fueled by knowing exactly where it was. Converted to four by six prints already, in a photo finisher's envelope on Anthony Quintana's desk. If she called him, he would deny it.

Gail rubbed her forehead with the heel of her hand, then picked up the telephone. She had another call to make.

Information gave her the number of Ransom-Everglades High School, the main office. When someone answered Gail said who she was, a former graduate of the school with a question about the teaching staff. "Do you have in the music department a teacher by the name of Wells? A woman. She's probably around fifty. . . . No, I'm sorry, I don't. Just Wells. . . . Perhaps back in 1979? She would have been a classically trained pianist." Gail held on while the woman went to ask someone else, a person who had been in the office at Ransom for thirty years. She heard voices. Footsteps coming back. The woman said that no one by the name of Wells had ever taught at the school.

Gail thanked her and hung up.

From the copy machine Miriam asked, "What was that?"

"I'm on the trail of a suitcase from Costa Rica." Without getting into the details, Gail explained that Thomas Nolan had picked it up two years ago and delivered it — so he said — to his piano teacher, whom he still visited whenever he came through Miami.

Miriam laid out copies on her desk and picked up her stapler. "Why do you care about it?"

"Because he's lying to me, *chica,* and with everything else going on, it makes me nervous. I hate to be lied to. I thought she might have taught at Ransom-Everglades. They say they never heard of her."

The stapler bit through the copies. Click. Click. Click. "I bet we could find her."

"I bet we could," Gail said. "How does one find a piano teacher? She could be retired. Call the music schools. They might have professional associations —"

As she wrote a list, the front door opened.

The bell tinkled on the counter outside the small frosted window, and Miriam slid back the glass. Gail heard a male voice say he had a delivery for Ms. Connor.

Miriam let him in, a muscular man in walking shorts and sunglasses. There was a pen stuck in his Afro. The cardboard box was about two feet square. It did not seem heavy when he dropped it onto the work table, but Gail felt a tremor of skittish, irrational fear, imagining a package bomb. "Who's it from?"

"Says here Quintana. I picked it up at a law office in Coral Gables."

The man whipped out his pen and Miriam signed the receipt. When the man was gone, Miriam rushed back to the box. Her brown eyes sparkled. "Is it a present?"

The box was sealed tightly with tape. Marked *Personal, Gail Connor only*.

Gail picked it up. "I don't know, Miriam. I'll take it home and find out."

"Aren't you going to open it now?"

"No." She headed for her office.

"Why not?"

"Miriam, please." The tone had been too sharp. "I'm sorry. I'll be in a better mood when all this is over." Gail shoved her door closed with her foot. She didn't have to open the box to guess what it contained.

For several minutes she stared at it on the end of her desk. Finally she used a letter opener to slit the tape. She folded back the flaps. There was an envelope on top, which she set aside. She saw her brown cashmere sweater, neatly folded. A negligee, a pair of jeans, some lacy underthings she had only worn at his house. Cosmetics and shampoo in plastic bags. Her hair dryer. Some paperbacks. A pair of shoes at the bottom. And throughout, the faint scent of his bedroom, his closet, the cologne he used.

Pressing her lips together, she took a big breath. Then another, refusing to cry.

The business-size, cream-colored envelope was sealed. Ferrer & Quintana, Attorneys at Law, P.A. Her name written in black ink, a line under it. *Gail.*

She slowly tore the unopened envelope and the note inside into pieces.

Karen had a soccer game at seven o'clock. At 6:10, Gail was sitting on the edge of her bed tying her sneakers when she heard the TV anchorman mention the words *Miami Opera.*

Gail stood up and pointed the remote to raise the volume.

There was the recorded image of Thomas Nolan, talking about how sorry he was. He was magnificent. His deep clear voice, the carefully enunciated words. *Like many others in this country I was unaware of the tragic history of the exile community . . . the anguish of a people divided, brother from brother . . . a country betrayed . . . if this could bring understanding . . .*

A perfect combination of dignity, shame, and repentance. When the reporters shouted questions, he was thoughtful and patient. The brow furrowing just right. There was a snippet of interview with Albert Estrada, then some on-the-street quotes from citizens, Hispanic and otherwise. Most of them said the issue was an embarrassment. One woman said Nolan should be put in jail.

Gail hit the remote and the screen went dark. What Thomas Nolan was sorry about was having to do this at all.

She went into her closet for a sweater and had to step around the box that Anthony had sent.

In a sudden rush of anger, she kicked it, then flipped it upside down, shoving her clothes into a corner. Into the empty box she pitched Anthony's shoes, a shiny pair of tasseled loafers. Took some shirts off hangers, his luxurious monogrammed shirts with four initials, ALQP. Two pairs of slacks. A jacket. She wanted them out of her sight.

A Florida Marlins baseball cap. Three silk ties. A heavy robe that slithered off the padded hanger.

She resented the impersonality of receiving a box at her office. He had used a delivery man. No phone call first, nothing. It was rude. Petty.

Into the bathroom. Pulling things off a shelf in the cabinet, tossing them into a shoebox — cologne, razors, aftershave, whitening toothpaste, his toothbrush. Then to the drawer in her dresser where he kept underwear.

What could have been in the note? She imagined the words, *I'm sorry. I still love you.* She laughed aloud. No, he had probably written, *This is to request that you return my possessions forthwith.*

"Fine. Take them."

Gail went back into the closet, dumped everything into the box, then leaned on it, interweaving the flaps to keep them closed. There was a roll of wide packing tape in the garage. Passing Karen's door, she called out automatically, "Hurry up, sweetie. We have to leave in fifteen minutes, turn off the TV, get dressed."

In the garage, heading back from the

kitchen, tape in hand, Gail noticed the old packing boxes on the metal shelves past the washer and dryer. One of them contained memorabilia from her high school days, including, she was certain, her yearbooks. She hesitated, then pulled the box down and set it on the dryer.

The yearbook for 1979 had a cloth cover, a silhouette of trees. The school was on a shady waterfront campus in Coconut Grove. The seniors had pages to themselves. The younger students were posed in groups, sitting or standing by the water, or on the steps of the library, or under a tree. She flipped to the tenth grade class photos and found herself in a minidress. Long straight hair, like most of the other girls. The boys' haircuts were shaggy, and their pantlegs were flared.

She turned pages till she found the photos of the junior class. Turned another page, looking for Thomas Nolan. He stood with a dozen others on the porch of the old wooden building constructed at the turn of the century, when Ransom School for Boys had taught sailing to the sons of the northeastern elite. Tommy Nolan in the back row in a plain shirt, his blond hair combed to one side, the forced smile of a loner.

Then Gail remembered. "Oh, my God."

There had been at Ransom-Everglades a small wood-frame cottage, painted green, overgrown with vines, and used at that time to store band instruments. Late one spring afternoon in 1979, when most of the other students had gone home, Tommy Nolan had been found unconscious in the band-master's cottage, one end of a rope tied to a beam, and the other around his neck.

Gail looked down at the small face in the photograph. For a while there had been speculation. Why had he done it? He didn't have a girlfriend who had just broken up with him. Everybody agreed he wasn't a queer — what they called it then. His grades weren't bad enough that he would get kicked out. They quickly lost interest. He hadn't come back after that, and anyway, he hadn't been one of the popular kids.

Why had he done it? Gail sat on the step to the kitchen, piecing a story together. His father had died when he was eleven years old. Then his mother had decided, when Tom was sixteen, to move back to Virginia. How inconsiderate, even cruel, to take her son out of school his junior year, and worse, to do it a few short weeks before the end of the term — after he'd been told he didn't have enough talent for the piano, but before he really believed in himself as a singer. He must have been devastated.

He had tried to kill himself. Except for a custodian's fortuitous intervention, he would have succeeded. With his life ripped from its moorings, the words of one teacher were all he had to sustain him: *You should sing.* And he had done it, had given himself to music. He had no wife, no children, only this one consuming passion.

Closing the yearbook, she thought of Anthony again. No wife, his children far away. In the space of one hour last Thursday night he had walked away from his family and ended his engagement. She wondered what he had done all weekend. Gotten drunk? Gone home with the first *latina* he could lay his hands on? Would he one day drive to Key West, sit alone in his car gazing toward Cuba, and put his pistol to his temple? Better to have stayed there and married Yolanda, his first girlfriend. In his memory she, like his childhood, remained virginal, innocent, and lost.

Gail had called him a coward. *How brave am I?* she wondered. *How loving and wise?* Her mother had been right. He was who he was because of his history, not his culture. Because of what he had loved that was lost forever.

Her fault. She had not loved him enough.

She put her forehead on her knees and sobbed.

The telephone in the kitchen rang. She ignored it. It stopped.

Then Karen's voice. "Mom! Mom, where are you? Phone!"

Wiping her eyes, Gail cleared her throat. "I'm out here. Coming." She tossed the yearbook back in the box and came inside.

It was Rebecca Dixon.

She had some things to give Gail, very important. Could she drop by the opera?

TWENTY-FIVE

The business offices of the Miami Opera were around the corner from the auditorium itself, whose grand windows faced Biscayne Boulevard. Gail came in the side entrance and found the staff parking lot full. This meant that the orchestra was rehearsing tonight. The musicians had taken every space.

In a hurry, she squeezed her rental car between the sidewalk and a tree. Rebecca had said there would be an executive board meeting at eight o'clock, so please arrive as soon as possible. Gail had begged help from Marilyn Perlmutter down the street, whose daughter played on Karen's team. Karen could hitch a ride to the game, and Gail would buy them pizza afterward. It had been the only way to uncross Karen's arms and get the scowl off her face.

The glass doors to the reception area were dark, but lights shone in the windows of the boardroom. Farther along the side of the building, a guard sat by the rear entrance, his chair holding open the metal door. He looked up from the sports pages. Gail explained who she was, and that Mrs. Dixon was expecting her in the office.

Entering the wide corridor, she heard the orchestra and assumed *Don Giovanni*. Bright violins punctuated by darker chords from cellos and basses followed her toward the offices, gradually fading. She had purchased a tape of the opera and had listened to some of it in the rental car on the way home. The music had seemed too cheerful for the terrible acts of lust and betrayal that Thomas Nolan had described.

She turned a corner and opened the door to the carpeted administrative area. Surprised, she found Nolan himself in the boardroom. He and Rebecca Dixon sat talking in one corner, each in a modular upholstered chair. Nolan sat back with his legs casually crossed. Rebecca perched forward, making notes.

Facing the door, Tom Nolan noticed Gail first and broke off in the middle of a sentence. His pale brows rose a fraction. Rebecca smiled at her. "Hi, Gail. Come in. Tom's giving me some ideas for a fundraising party before opening night — a lecture about the opera, the story behind it. He's an angel, donating his time like this."

Nolan waved away the compliment. He remained seated, his eyes shifting upward as Gail crossed the room. "Are you here for the board meeting?"

Gail glanced at Rebecca. "No, I came to pick up some papers."

"Tom, I need to talk to Gail for a minute."

"Not to be rude," he said, "but how long will this take? We need to finish so you can present this to the board in half an hour —"

"I can't stay," Gail said, "My daughter's expecting me at her soccer game."

Rebecca reached over to pat his arm. "Sit right here. We'll go out to the lobby."

"Please, don't bother." Nolan pushed himself out of the chair, his long, lanky frame seeming to rise in stages. "I've got to speak to the conductor about something. We're rehearsing with the orchestra tomorrow." At the door he said to Gail, "What did you think of the press conference?"

"You were great."

"Now what do we do?"

She turned her hands palms up. "I'm filing the lawsuit tomorrow at ten. If I hear from the city before that, hooray, but I'm not holding my breath."

Rebecca waited for him to go, then closed the door. She was Madame President tonight in a navy pinstripe jacket and white turtleneck. Her shoes were two-tone lace-up oxfords that Gail had seen at Nieman-

Marcus for three hundred bucks and promptly put back on the display table.

"How did it go after I left last night?" Gail asked. "Tom told me that Octavio Reyes walked out. Did Lloyd get a chance to talk to him first?"

"Yes. We'll see if it does any good." Distracted by other things on her mind, Rebecca strode toward the conference table, where a big Louis Vuitton tote bag lay on its side. She rummaged through it, pulling out some membership brochures, a notebook, and file folders that pertained to the opera. "I wrote down the names of our guests last night, as you asked me to."

"What do you think?" Gail asked.

"I think you're crazy, but I'm nobody's judge of sanity. By the way, I had the appointment with Charlene Marks today. Thanks for recommending her. She's a bitch, just what I need." Finally a stack of three or four small mailing envelopes came out of the tote bag, and Rebecca straightened the prongs that held the first one shut. "I told Charlene everything — I hope you don't mind. It will take me a few days, but by the weekend, I'll be staying with some friends in Ft. Lauderdale. This morning I went into Lloyd's study. He keeps it locked, but a long time ago I found the key and made a copy. It pays to know your husband's assets. Don't forget that after you're married. I made copies for the attorney, and thought, well, let's just see if there's anything Gail could use. Anything related to our favorite radio host, Octavio Reyes."

Rebecca was speaking quickly, and from time to time she would glance toward the door. She spread out the papers on the conference table. One page contained a list of names written in her slanted script — the men who had attended Lloyd's dinner party last night. She opened two other envelopes and explained what else she had found.

"These pages are from his appointment book, wherever I saw the initials 'O.R.' Some have the phone number. You can check it out. I went back to last summer and forward a month. These pages are the ferry records. You'll see Octavio's name three times. These are from a corporation called DSA — that's Lloyd and two other men — Santangelo and Atkins. They're into hotels. Octavio Reyes is one of the shareholders. Let's see. Here are some letters and notes to or from Reyes. A memo of understanding regarding future investment . . . Dixon Air to provide all air shipment —"

Gail touched the pages as if they weren't quite real. She scanned a letter in which

Octavio Reyes stated his intention of providing up to ten million dollars in capital. He didn't have that kind of money. But Ernesto Pedrosa did. She wondered if Reyes planned to wait until the old man was dead or loot his businesses while he was still breathing.

"Rebecca, this is incredible. I could hang Octavio up by the *cojones*."

"Have at it," she said, "but it won't do any good. The exiles in general are so angry at Tom that Octavio could retract everything he ever said, and it wouldn't make any difference. Gail, you'd better not read all this now. We don't have time."

"Of course." They gathered the papers and folded them into the envelopes. Gail said, "I promise you, Rebecca, this will not be made public. I refuse to put you in jeopardy."

"Thanks, but I don't worry too much about Lloyd finding out. That man always lands on his feet." She put a hand on Gail's arm. "How did the photos come out? Did you get them developed?"

"Mine are useless, and yours, I am sorry to say, are gone. I saw Felix Castillo last night on the island. I put the film in my bag after you threw it to me. Then Felix appeared and dragged me into some bushes claiming a security guard was coming. Later on, I couldn't find the film. I know he took it, the bastard. I didn't see any security guard."

Twirling her gold chain around one finger, Rebecca said, "Why was he there?"

"Anthony hired him to follow Octavio. That tells me where the film is."

She twisted the chain the other way. "He used to be a Cuban agent. What if he still is?"

"No," Gail said. "Anthony would know if he were, believe me."

"I used to think that a lunatic exile murdered Seth, but whoever shot him was ice cold. The police don't have any leads. The man got away so cleanly. What kind of person could do that?" Rebecca looked at Gail. "I'm going as crazy as you, aren't I? You got me started with all this talk of spies."

Before last night, Gail would have dismissed this suggestion at once. Anthony trusted Felix Castillo, and therefore so did she. She did not know why Anthony maintained a friendship with Castillo, but the fact remained, this was a man who had shot a young woman in cold blood.

"Maybe it isn't so crazy," she said. "Felix Castillo is capable of murder. Last night he admitted what he did to Emily Davis."

Rebecca stopped twisting her gold chain. She seemed to freeze into position staring at Gail.

"I'm sorry," Gail said. "I didn't mean to bring it up."

"Felix said . . . he did it?"

"Yes. I wouldn't have asked him, but you told me last week that the rebel leader didn't do it. Anthony said Felix did. I wanted to be sure, so I asked Felix." Gail's words became slower. "And . . . he admitted it. Why are you looking at me like that?"

Rebecca laughed and put a hand on her forehead. "I'm sorry. Oh, Gail."

The room seemed to tilt. Gail put both hands on the table. Better to turn around now and walk out. A person didn't have to know everything. *Some things*, Anthony had said, *cause more hurt than illumination.*

Rebecca leaned against her shoulder and put an arm lightly around Gail's waist. "Listen to me. You can't hate him for it. I did, for a long time. It was horrible and ruthless, what he did, but I'm alive because of it. When Pablo came to interrogate Emily, he thought we were protecting her. Pablo said we had to prove we weren't working for the CIA. If one of us executed the spy, he would let us go. His men were armed with rifles. He tied her hands with electrical wire and made her kneel, and he held onto her hair. She was crying. Pablo took his gun out of his holster and told one of us to take it. Oh, Gail, this is so hard."

She pressed her cheek to Gail's and closed her eyes. "I didn't want to tell you. Anthony knew what would happen. They would have tortured her before they killed her, and they would have done the same to us. We were such fools. Such children. I've been hiding all my life, you know that? Seth is gone now. I miss him, but oh God, he was such a reminder of everything I wanted to forget. Charlene Marks told me today, Get out, start a new life. I'm going to do it." She hugged Gail, laughing softly. "Expect a postcard from Hong Kong."

They remained still for a few seconds. Someone was knocking on the door. As if waking, Rebecca looked around. "Tom."

Gail nodded. "I have to go." She picked up the envelopes from the stack of folders on the table.

When Rebecca opened the door, Tom Nolan stood there with a sour expression. "Excuse me for interrupting, but we don't have much time."

"I'm sorry, Tom." Gail looked over her shoulder. "Good night, Rebecca."

"Call me," Rebecca said.

"Gail!" Tom Nolan came a few steps after her. "Felix Castillo never showed up. That guard down there is going to escort me home. I wouldn't bother you with this, but you hired Felix. I think we should find someone else."

"Fine. I'll see about it tomorrow morning, before I go to the courthouse."

He gave her a guilty smile. "I'm sorry for adding to your problems. Go home, get some rest."

"Good night," she said.

The music of Mozart flooded the corridor when Gail pushed open the door. A harpsichord, then strings. The brass came in. Tympani. Such divine precision, every note exactly where it should be. Human affairs were never so perfect. Anthony had seduced Emily — if it had been seduction — after an affair with Rebecca. But whose fault was that? Rebecca had wanted him. Seth had forgiven. Or perhaps he hadn't. In Los Pozos they had all stumbled into a swamp of arrogance and jealousy. A power struggle between the men. The project stalled for lack of funds. The women hating each other. Then Emily hating Anthony for not begging money from his grandfather to buy her a plane ticket home. And all culminating in tragedy, with a burden of guilt for every one of them to carry back. Every one but Emily. Anthony had put a bullet in her brain. Or maybe not. Maybe Rebecca had been lying. Somebody was, that much was perfectly clear.

In her car, Gail stuffed the envelopes into her purse and counted only three of them. There had been four, she was certain. She turned on the interior lights, looked inside them. The copies of pages from Lloyd Dixon's appointment book were missing.

Grabbing her purse, she locked the car, then sprinted across the parking lot. She told the guard, "I was just here. I left something in the boardroom."

"Yeah, okay. Go ahead." He waved her ahead and went back to his newspaper.

The music faded out again as Gail hurried along the corridor and pushed through the door to the offices. She wanted to retrieve the envelope before one of the board members due to arrive at eight o'clock picked it up and looked inside, wondering what it was. The consequences of that made her shudder.

She heard Thomas Nolan's voice, but it seemed to come from farther along the hall. Lights were on in the lobby. She could see the reception desk, a chair, a vase of flowers. Tom Nolan and Rebecca had to be just out of sight around the corner.

Nolan laughed at something. Then he said to Rebecca, "You take care. I've got to be going now."

Gail went inside the boardroom. The envelope was there on the table. She had missed it before among Rebecca's other papers. She folded it and stuck it into her purse with the others.

Stepping into the hall, she automatically looked toward the lobby.

Time expanded, and what happened next seemed to take forever. A brilliant white light, too sharp and brilliant to be real. Everything making weird shadows. A shadow cast by the clock on the wall. The looming shadows of the vase of flowers. The light seemed at the same instant to go through her and lift her into the air.

The brilliance turned physical, a force that hurled her into the wall where the corridor turned. She observed all this as if detached from it. She saw in the same split second a desk tumbling across the lobby. A body hitting the wall. Dimly it registered in Gail's mind that she didn't know who it was. The front of it was gone, nothing left but red.

A crash of glass.

A billow of black with tongues of red and orange boiling toward her, then an icy feel on her face and arms.

Snow floated down. Bits of white falling from the ceiling, gently drifting. White fog everywhere. She couldn't see past her knees.

She heard Tom Nolan say again, *I've got to be going now.*

We'll have to use the understudy.

He isn't good enough for this role.

Slowly she slid over to the carpet, and seemed to keep falling and falling, spiraling downward until everything went white.

TWENTY-SIX

Faces floated like untethered balloons. Mouths opened and sounds came out. Gail could not understand them. Didn't care to. Lights flashed in her eyes. Dimly she was aware of pain, but the pain was separate from her body. Then it settled down on her like a heavy beast with claws. She escaped into whiteness, felt nothing. Hands prodded. She heard voices in the distance. Saw a woman with red hair. Her mother, she thought. Tried to speak, but her mouth wouldn't work. She drifted, then woke. Saw two images, couldn't bring them together. A man's face came closer. Dark brown eyes. She felt her hand being lifted, felt the warmth of his lips. Heard him saying her name.

Too hard to keep her eyes open.

Gail found herself flat on her back in a hospital bed, feeling like someone had dropped her over the side of a building. She saw Anthony slumped in an armchair by the window, eyes closed, head propped on his fist, the shadow of beard on his jaw. The curtains were drawn, but bright sunlight leaked through.

A small cool hand touched her face, and she turned her head. Her mother smiled down at her. "Welcome back." She kissed Gail's cheek. Smoothed her hair.

With great effort, Gail said, "What time is it?"

"Almost nine in the morning. Anthony and I have been here all night. I called him. You don't mind, do you? He fell asleep a little while ago. I took a nap earlier."

"Where's Karen?" Gail whispered.

"With Molly's family. She's waiting for you to call her. Are you in pain, darling?"

Gail nodded. "Everything hurts. My ears feel like I'm underwater." Then she remembered the flash, the hideous noise. "Rebecca's dead, isn't she? And Tom."

"She's gone. Tom's going to be all right. The security guard found you in time." Irene grabbed for a tissue. "Oh, I'm getting weepy again."

In the chair Anthony shifted, getting comfortable. His eyes opened, then focused on Gail. He pushed himself out of the chair. "How long has she been awake?"

"Just now," Irene said.

Gail tried to smile. "Yay. I'm alive." She held up her arms and grimaced at the pain of being embraced, but held on tightly.

The nurse had told them to notify her when Gail woke up. She came in and went through the routine of blood pressure and temperature check, then gave her a couple of high-octane Tylenols. It would be up to the doctor when Gail could leave, she said, and he would come by shortly. Other than some bruises and minor burns, she was all right.

Anthony helped Gail stand up, and her stomach heaved. Irene got behind her and held her gown closed. In the bathroom she told them both to leave, please. She took a look in the mirror, squinting. "Oh, Jesus." The flash of heat had crinkled her hair and eyebrows, her eyelashes were stumps. Her nose and cheeks looked like she had stayed out in the sun too long.

When the toilet finished flushing, she cracked open the door. "Mom, where's my purse?"

Irene brought it — the paramedics had given it to the hospital staff, who had put it in Gail's room. Looking for her brush, Gail found four small-size mailing envelopes. She had to concentrate to remember what they were. Tensing against the pain, she brushed her teeth and did what she could with lipstick and powder. Out of breath, she leaned against the sink and called for Anthony.

Once she was in bed again, Anthony told her what he knew about the bombing, most of which he had read in the paper at five o'clock this morning or watched on television. A pipe bomb had been placed along an inner wall of the lobby, probably under a small table between two chairs. Rebecca Dixon had been sitting in one of them. The blast killed her instantly and destroyed the lobby and boardroom. Standing in the corridor, Gail had escaped the major force of the explosion. Thomas Nolan had gone to the next room to make a phone call and was likewise protected. He and Gail had been rushed to Jackson Memorial.

All the national networks had shown footage of shattered glass doors, overturned furniture, and blackened ceiling and walls. Everyone interviewed in Miami, from whatever group, expressed disbelief and outrage. There were no suspects. No one had claimed responsibility. Even so, CNN had made the usual assumption: *In Miami last night, opera star Thomas Nolan, recently criticized by the Cuban exile community for a performance in Havana two years ago, was injured in what police say could have been a terrorist bomb attack —*

The telephone in Gail's room rang, and

Irene picked it up. "No, Ms. Connor is not available. . . . Yes, she is going to be fine. . . . This is her mother. . . . No, I don't think that's possible." Hanging up, Irene said, "That was a reporter for Channel Seven."

"I don't want to see *anyone*," Gail said.

The doctor came in, a small dark man named Mohammad Patel, one of the staff residents at Jackson, and had Gail sit up so he could put a stethoscope on her back and hear her breathe. She had been lucky as hell, he said. Any closer to the lobby, they would be picking shrapnel out of her skull. He wrote in the chart. "I'm going to come by again about two o'clock. You can probably go after that."

Gail asked about Thomas Nolan.

"He's getting out, too." The doctor put away his pen. "Damned bad luck for a singer. The smoke got to his lungs. He sounds like a frog. Take care of yourself, Ms. Connor. By the way, the police want to talk to you. I think they're on their way."

Then Irene called the Perlmutter house and handed Gail the telephone so she could speak to Karen. Molly's mother had let her stay out of school today. Karen demanded to be brought to the hospital, but Gail promised her she was all right. She would be home this afternoon, and Karen could be her nurse.

Gail managed to eat half a blueberry muffin before feeling sick again and letting her head fall to the pillow. Irene left to bring back some clothes Gail could wear home. Her own smelled of smoke and something else that Gail couldn't place. Cordite, Anthony said. Gunpowder.

The telephone rang. Another reporter. Anthony said no. After the third inquiry, he unplugged the line.

He closed the door. Finally the room was quiet. He stood by her bed. They looked at each other without speaking. Too much had to be said.

She touched his arm. He wore a business shirt with the sleeves rolled up. He might have had it on since yesterday morning, she thought. He was rarely this rumpled. She looked up at him and his image wavered. "Anthony, I'm so sorry." The tears spilled over, hot on her burned skin. "I shouldn't have pushed you to tell me about Nicaragua. Not after what happened at your grandfather's house. How thoughtless —"

"No." He leaned over her. The light from the window dimmed, and she could feel the warmth of his body. "Don't blame yourself. I went crazy." He kissed her, and his lips trembled. "When I saw you here, lying so still — If you had died — And the last thing you believed was that I didn't love you —"

She put an arm around his neck and pulled him closer. How familiar and compelling, the textures and weight, his taste and his scent. His kisses were soft and quenching as rain.

She knew that the hands that touched her so gently might have ended a young woman's life. Might have. Rebecca could have been mistaken. Or lying. And Felix Castillo had confessed.

With Anthony lifting her close to him, and his tears on her neck, Gail was aware that her mind was simultaneously erasing possibilities of his guilt and rationalizing his reasons for pulling the trigger, if he was guilty. An odd sensation, like watching footprints obliterated by a wave sheeting across the sand. She observed, unable to stop. She wanted only to feel his arms around her. To hear him say he loved her. *Te quiero, te amo, no puedo vivir sin ti.* He could not live without her. She held his face, kissed his mouth, and finally, weak from even this exertion, had to lie down again.

As he poured her some water from the plastic pitcher on the bedside table, she said, "Anthony, I need to talk to you before the police get here. Did Felix tell you about Saturday night?"

"He told me he saw you on Fisher Island in a disguise, playing detective, taking pictures of Octavio." Anthony put a straw in the cup. "Very foolish, *bonboncita*."

"Did he give you the film he stole from me?"

"No. What do you mean, 'stole'?"

"Rebecca was on her terrace taking photos of your brother-in-law with Lloyd Dixon and his guests. Tom Nolan was there, too. She threw the film down to me. Felix was watching. He distracted me, then stole it out of my bag. Where is he? I've left messages."

"I don't know." Anthony was puzzled. "Why was Tom Nolan there?"

"He was hired to sing, and Octavio didn't know he was coming. Lloyd Dixon's idea of a joke. Did Felix tell you what we talked about?"

Anthony sat on the edge of the bed with one foot on the floor. "Cuba, you mean. Yes. I have to tell you, Gail, this is very improbable. Lloyd Dixon has been to Cuba. He has to know that the regime is thoroughly entrenched. Fidel is an icon. If Dixon thinks he can get weapons into Cuba and start an uprising, he's out of touch. The people don't want to revolt. They're waiting for Fidel to die, then they want to make some slow changes."

"You told me there's a Cuban underground," Gail said.

"Very small and very underground," he said. "You get the death penalty for that."

"But if they had enough weapons to make a statement? Dixon likes to take risks. If he and his group — Octavio included — could disrupt the tourist industry, changes might come more quickly. One push. A little bit of C-4 at a big hotel."

"Mmmnnn." Anthony took another minute to think about it. "It's impossible to get weapons there in sufficient quantities. There isn't one group that hasn't been infiltrated."

"Dixon isn't Cuban," Gail said, "and his dinner guests aren't your garden-variety militant exiles. Go get my purse." She pointed at the counter next to the sink, then dropped her arm, too tired to hold it up. "Look inside. There are four envelopes. Rebecca gave me those last night."

Anthony slid some folded papers out of one of the envelopes. His eyes moved quickly over the lines. "Memorandum of understanding . . . Octavio Reyes and DSA Corporation . . . ten million dollars?" He stared at the pages. *"Ay, Diós. Octavio, ¿qué haces?"*

She took a breath and shifted to ease a pain in her back. "Rebecca saw a divorce lawyer. She copied all Lloyd's financial records, and if there was anything relating to Octavio, she made another copy for me. It's to show that Octavio and Lloyd are planning to do business in Cuba. I was going to use it to embarrass Octavio if he kept causing us problems."

Anthony shuffled through pages and opened more envelopes. "Anything in here about weapons? Sabotage?"

"I don't know. I didn't have time to look."

"My grandfather can't be involved in this. It's impossible." Anthony made a short laugh. "I also said it was impossible that Octavio would be involved with Lloyd Dixon."

"Maybe Octavio didn't tell your grandfather." Gail closed her eyes, wanting to go back to sleep. "If I were Octavio, I'd tell him about overthrowing Castro, but I wouldn't tell him that Dixon was helping. Maybe it's all crap. I'm probably wrong."

There was a knock at the door. The papers were spread out on Gail's lap. Anthony folded them quickly. "If that's the police, I don't want them to hear about this. Let me review these first. If they ask, you went to speak to Rebecca concerning opera business — and you did." Anthony put the pages into the inside pocket of his suit coat, which hung on the back of a chair. "Gail, if by some remote possibility, knowingly or otherwise, my grandfather is financing the purchase of weapons to send to Cuba, he could be prosecuted for conspiracy. It would kill him. I can't allow that to happen." He stood calmly beside the bed, looking down at her with his dark, fathomless eyes. "Please."

The knock came again.

She nodded.

He went to the door. Thomas Nolan was turning away when it opened. He glanced at Anthony, then past him toward the bed where Gail lay. "I came to see how you are." He spoke in a husky whisper.

Gail said to come in, and he limped into the room. There was a bandage around his left forearm. She did the introductions. The men shook hands.

Nolan looked at Gail. He whispered, "Wow. You okay?"

"Bruises and some singed hair. I get paroled this afternoon."

"You were at the office when the bomb went off? Thought you'd gone."

"I came back for some papers I left in the boardroom. I was in the hall. How are you, Tom?"

"Not too bad. Twisted knee and some cuts. My ears are still ringing." He coughed, wincing. "Shit. My throat —" He coughed again. "My throat is trashed."

Gail reached for his hand. "Oh, Tom, your voice."

"Yeah. Bad luck."

Anthony said, "It's not permanent, is it?"

"They say not. Rebecca . . . got it worse." He closed his eyes for a second. There was a bruise on his cheekbone. "She was too close. Making notes for the party. I went to make a copy. The explosion knocked me down. So much smoke. No lights. I couldn't see. I got out through a window." He tensed against another cough. "It's my fault. What I said to the TV reporter. I wanted to tell you . . . I'm sorry."

"It isn't your fault," Gail said.

"Should I leave the opera? I don't want to give it to the bastards that did this, but if I'm putting everyone in danger . . . maybe I should go."

"Can you sing?"

"Maybe. We've got two weeks. Did you see Felix last night in the parking lot?"

"Felix? No."

"His van." Nolan shrugged his wide, bony shoulders, which were tilted as if he had a stitch in his side. "Maybe it wasn't his. I beeped him. I thought he finally showed up. Guess not." He squeezed her hand. "Take care. I promise. No more interviews."

"Do you have some help getting home?"

"About a dozen people downstairs. No problem." He nodded to Anthony. "See you."

The police detectives were the same men who had come to her office after Seth Greer's murder. Fernandez and Delgado, the latter being the older cop who had spent twenty-six years on the anti-terrorist task force.

Anthony introduced himself. Both men had heard of him. "Gail and I are engaged," he said, explaining his presence.

"Congratulations."

The detectives remained standing. Anthony took a chair near the foot of the bed. He had hung his jacket on a hanger behind the door.

The bomb, Delgado said, had been made with about a pound of black powder packed into a two-inch pipe, six inches long, with end caps screwed on. Wires came out a small hole, went to an electric match of the type used for model rockets, then to a digital timer and double-A battery. Components available anywhere. Black powder could be purchased without proof of ID in quantities up to five pounds. The bomb had gone off at 7:37 P.M., according to most witnesses.

It seemed unlikely that anyone in particular had been targeted. Thomas Nolan and Rebecca Dixon had been there by chance, and the board meeting had been called just hours before. At Nolan's press conference, dozens of people had wandered around. Anyone could have planted a small box under the table, half-hidden by an armchair. Staff members who locked up around six o'clock didn't see anything unusual, but they hadn't been looking for anything.

Detective Fernandez asked Gail what she remembered.

She felt Anthony's eyes on her. She spoke slowly, fatigue dragging on her words. "I arrived about seven-fifteen. Tom went to see the conductor while Rebecca and I talked for about ten or fifteen minutes in the boardroom, then I left. In the parking lot I remembered I'd left some papers, and I went back to get them. I heard Tom and Rebecca in the lobby, but I didn't see them.

I came out of the boardroom and the bomb went off."

No, she hadn't seen anything unusual in the parking lot, no one walking through.

Detective Fernandez turned to look at Anthony, who was slowly tapping his tented fingers on his chin. Fernandez was around forty, with prematurely gray hair that touched the collar of his suit jacket. "We're looking for Felix Castillo as a possible witness. He works for you as an investigator. You have any idea where to find him?"

Anthony lowered his hands to his lap. "What do you mean, witness?"

"He may have information relevant to the investigation."

He frowned. "Would you explain that?"

Fernandez ignored the question. "Where is he, do you know?"

"No, I don't. I saw him Saturday night, but not since then."

"What did you talk about?"

"I don't discuss my clients' business," Anthony said. "Did you go by his house?"

"Earlier this morning. No answer at the door. A neighbor saw his van around midnight Saturday, but it was gone on Sunday. She hasn't seen him or his girlfriend around. Does he have any friends or relatives in the area?"

"No relatives in Miami," Anthony said. "I don't know his friends. Who told you he has information about the bombing?"

"I'm not going to disclose that," Fernandez said. "Right now we just want to ask him some questions, okay? We're not saying he had anything to do with it."

Gail glanced at Anthony, reading nothing in his expression.

Fernandez asked her, "Ms. Connor, you hired Mr. Castillo to do some work for the opera, is that correct?"

"Yes. He was Mr. Nolan's bodyguard," she said.

From his chair Anthony said, "Thomas Nolan came by earlier. He mentioned that he might have seen a van like Felix Castillo's in the parking lot before the explosion. Is that the information you're going on?"

The older detective, Delgado, said, "Are you Castillo's lawyer?"

"If he asks me to be." A smile passed over his lips. "Look. If you think that Felix was involved in this, forget it. He's not political. He's not with any group. I know him well enough to be sure of that."

"We don't believe that an exile group did it. We get strong denials from all of them."

"Does this surprise you?" Anthony said. "Give me your opinion, Lieutenant. Who do you think is responsible?"

"What do I think? This might be payback for the hotels bombed in Havana last summer."

Anthony couldn't hold back a smile. "And you're looking for Felix?"

"Interesting fact we picked up about your friend Castillo. He came over in the Mariel boatlift. Before that, he was with Cuban State Security." Delgado waited for a response. When there was none, he said, "I know about G-2. *Me pusierson en el Boniato en una celda tapiada. Me torturaban. Llevo las cenizas, si quiere verlas.*" Gail could understand enough of it. Boniato was a prison. Delgado had been there, had been tortured, and he still had the scars.

Anthony said quietly, "Felix Castillo quit in 'seventy-nine, and they threw him in prison."

"What a shame."

With a small exhalation, Anthony planted his hands on the arms of the chair and stood up. "I think that's all, Lieutenant. Ms. Connor needs to rest."

The detectives passed a look between them. Fernandez said, "Mr. Quintana, let's go outside." He tilted his head toward the door.

"I want him to stay," Gail said.

"No, we're finished with you for now, Ms. Connor."

Delgado said, "Let's go." He opened the door.

Anthony stayed where he was. "What is this about?"

"We want to ask you about Felix Castillo."

"I told you, I don't know where he is."

"Then we'll just talk. Come on."

"You want to talk to me, make an appointment at my office." His attention was drawn by a movement at the door, and surprise flickered over his face.

The detectives turned around. They blocked Gail's view for a moment, then moved aside as an elegant white-haired woman came in carrying flowers.

Digna Pedrosa. She noticed Gail and smiled broadly. "We found you!" Outside, Ernesto Pedrosa sat in a wheelchair. With help from Alicia, he stood up and came into the room, leaning on her arm, steadying himself with a cane. He was too proud to sit in his chair.

His gaze fixed on the detectives, a look that both recognized who they were and dismissed them from further business here.

Delgado said to Anthony, "We'll be in touch."

When they had gone, Anthony closed the door. He watched, but said nothing to the three who had just come in, clustered now at Gail's bedside. From the women there were expressions of horror, inquiries about her wounds. Light kisses on her cheeks. Exclamations at the state of her hair, her eyelashes. Gail said she was in some pain and still a little dizzy, but that was passing. She thanked them for the flowers. Anthony stood just beyond the end of the bed with his hands in his trouser pockets, feigning disinterest.

During this, Ernesto Pedrosa gazed down at Gail through his thick glasses.

Alicia reached past her grandmother to touch Gail's hand. "We were frantic, calling the hospital, and they wouldn't tell us anything! I'm so sorry, Gail."

"If that's an apology," Anthony said, "it should be coming from your husband."

Gail gave him a warning look.

It was as though Ernesto Pedrosa had not heard this remark. He took Gail's hand. His trembled slightly, and the skin was papery dry. His voice had more strength in it, and the accent and cadence belonged to a man accustomed to power.

"*Pobrecita*. My heart aches, Gail. I would take your place if God let me. The death of your friend is a terrible thing. And the singer, Thomas Nolan — I think he was wrong to sing for the regime, but I am sorry, believe me, that he was hurt. When I heard about this bomb, I wanted to know, Who could have done this? Last night I talked with many people. Ooof! Hours on the telephone. Some people came to my house. And you know, usually there is talk. Usually someone has heard something. But with this bombing? Nothing, nothing, nothing. But this tells us who was *not* responsible."

Still holding her hand to his chest, Ernesto Pedrosa slowly patted it, emphasizing his words. "It was not one of us."

"Never one of us," Anthony muttered from the end of the bed. As if the room were pressing in on him, he turned to the window and held back the curtain far enough to look out. He squinted in the sudden light, which sharpened the lines at his eyes and mouth and made a white blaze of his shirt. "The radio hosts, the politicians, the writers of those cheap newspapers on every street corner and in every grocery store, breeding hatred, but when someone acts on that hatred, well, it was a Castro agent, a provocateur."

Without turning his head, Pedrosa lifted his ragged gray brows. "One must fight tyranny. Maybe, to some people, that is hatred. What should we do? Be quiet? Let conditions remain the same and hope they will change? No, speak out. A man must believe in something, and fight for it."

The light dimmed when Anthony let the curtain go. "And Rebecca Dixon was blown to bits. If we give a provocateur a reason to do it in our name, are we less guilty?"

"*¡Silencio!*" shouted Pedrosa, the warrior again. "I know this!" His wife closed her eyes. Alicia glared darkly at her brother. Turning back to Gail, Pedrosa said, "I have asked my friends with the radio stations what they think. They all agree. Forget about Thomas Nolan. He's probably a communist, but it doesn't matter."

Anthony leaned against the wall, wearily shaking his head.

Pedrosa's face softened. "Are they treating you well here?"

"Yes, but I'll be happy to leave," Gail said.

Digna patted her arm. "Do you have some help with your house?"

"My mother —"

"No, no. Your mother will take care of *you*. Let us send someone."

"You mustn't bother, really —"

With a finger in front of her pursed lips,

Digna said, "Shh. We want to help."

The old man leaned closer. He smelled lovely, and his cheeks had been freshly shaved. His suit was immaculate. "I don't like hospitals," he whispered.

"I don't either." She returned his smile.

He gently kissed her cheek, then said to Alicia, *"La silla, por favor."* He glanced past Anthony without seeing him. Alicia said goodbye to Gail, nodded to her brother, then went to turn down the footrests on the wheelchair. Digna stood for a long moment looking up at her grandson. Whatever she murmured in Spanish, Gail missed it. Anthony embraced her.

As soon as the three of them had gone out of sight, Gail felt her nose sting. Her eyes filled with tears, and she hiccuped a sob.

Anthony hurried to her. "What happened? What is it?"

"I don't know. I'm so tired. First Seth. Now Rebecca — Everything is so horrible."

He made quick shushing noises and stroked her hair. "Sweetheart. Don't cry. I'll get the nurse. Something for the pain. Giving you Tylenol is ridiculous."

She pushed his hand away. "Go after them. Go speak to your grandfather before he leaves. You didn't even say goodbye to him."

"Gail, please —"

"It isn't his fault that I'm here. Go, before it's too late."

"It's been too late for a long time."

"He's old and sick, and he's going to die soon. My sister died and we were on such awful terms with each other, and it wasn't until she was gone that I knew how much I loved her." Gail wept into the sheet, unable to stop.

"No. I won't leave you here like this. All right, I'll call him tonight. Stop crying."

"Anthony, for God's sake, how can you be so *stupid?* You don't know why your grandfather came, do you?"

He frowned, puzzled. "To see you. To explain. What do you mean?"

"He was talking to *you,* Anthony. God, it's so obvious. He needs you. You're his hope, don't you know that? Please don't walk away. You did that . . . with me, and . . . I wanted to die." She sucked in a breath and let it out in a long wail.

He stared at her for another moment, then got up and looked into the hall. "They're gone." He hit the door frame with his open palm. "What would I say to him? I'm sorry? Sorry for what?" He looked back at Gail, then let out a breath. "I'll be back."

His footsteps faded in the corridor.

Utterly spent, Gail closed her eyes, and her arms flopped to the mattress.

What would happen downstairs? His family would have reached the elevator already. She imagined Anthony running for it, seeing the silver wheels of his grandfather's chair roll inside, then the doors closing. Anthony backing up to see where the other two elevators were. What floors, how long a wait?

He goes for the stairwell, down four flights of stairs, then into the lobby, people rushing in every direction. Which of the many exits did they take?

His grandfather is waiting with Digna under the portico while Alicia goes to get the car. Anthony sees them through the glass doors. He slows down, catches his breath. How many years' worth of pain can be erased in a few minutes? None. But a start can be made.

They are looking up at him, waiting for him to speak.

TWENTY-SEVEN

A week later a memorial service was held for Rebecca Dixon, whose funeral had been private. Her husband had scattered the ashes over the Atlantic from ten thousand feet. The memorial ended at two o'clock, and Gail came straight home. She dumped bath salts into her tub and turned on the water full force to make a froth of bubbles.

Dropping her robe to the mat, she looked over her shoulder in the mirror. She had lost weight, and her ribs showed. On her pale skin, the bruises had faded a bit, now more yellow than purple. "Oh, you are so gorgeous." She hit the rheostat on the light switch, and the row of bulbs over the mirror dimmed to a soft glow. Steam was already obscuring her image. Gail tested the water with a toe, then carefully lowered herself into the tub. Her body still ached. The water was hot but not painful. She leaned back on the inflatable pillow. The bubbles reached to her chin. She inhaled a long, slow breath and floated, then reached for her wine.

Anthony had called her at work to say he

couldn't go with her, one of his trials taking longer than expected. He wanted to come by later for dinner. Of course he would expect to spend the night. And she would say yes, although she wasn't sure she wanted him to. Their fight, the bombing, her injuries — all were making her feel disconnected and subdued.

Over a thousand people had attended the service, held in the theater. The set for *Don Giovanni* had been rolled aside to make room for the orchestra on stage. The Philharmonic chorus had sung portions of Mozart's *Requiem*. There had been remembrances by Rebecca's friends. Lloyd had made a tribute to his wife, and his voice had trembled in places. Then the speeches by politicians. News cameras had filmed everything. Gail knew before she arrived and was ushered to the reserved seating down front that this event was never really about Rebecca Dixon.

Reporters in the lobby swooped like carrion birds. Gail had been able to avoid most of them until today. She endured several interviews. She shook hands with Alberto Estrada, the city manager. The city had dropped its demand for extra security for the run of the opera. No lawsuit would be filed.

For the exile community, the memorial had been a celebration of sorts, a sigh of relief. The bomber had been identified, and he was not, as Ernesto Pedrosa had said, one of us.

Based on Thomas Nolan's observation of what he thought was Felix Castillo's van in the opera parking lot the night of the bombing, police had obtained a search warrant for Castillo's house. Bingo.

His clothes were strewn about as if he had packed in a hurry. His personal papers were gone. His girlfriend, Daisy, was missing. There was nothing moving in the house but a cage full of hungry lovebirds. In the garage police had found wire, a soldering iron, and traces of black powder. Among ammunition left behind they found a box of .223 Remington center-fire cartridges, the same lot number as those picked up at the scene of Seth Greer's murder.

The day after the bombing, the Spanish edition of the *Miami Herald* and several of the Cuban radio stations had received in the mail a typed communiqué from a group calling itself F.L.C. — *Frente para la Liberación de Cuba* — announcing that the opera bombing would be the first strike against communists in the city of Miami. Unused sheets of the same paper had been found in the trash behind Castillo's house.

The City of Miami police chief stated in a press conference that Felix Castillo, former agent with Cuban State Security, was wanted for the murders of Seth Greer and Rebecca Dixon.

Obtained from his investigator's license, Castillo's photo appeared on television screens and on the front page of newspapers — an unsmiling, balding man with a gray Fu Manchu mustache. The flat lighting, narrowed eyes, and thick neck made him look like a thug. Sightings were reported from Key West to Atlanta. Rumors said he had gone back to Cuba. Others said he was still in the Miami area, planning his next attack.

Anthony had not wanted to talk about it, other than to tersely say, "Something is wrong. I think he was set up." Reluctantly Gail told him that on the night of Seth Greer's murder, she had left a message on Castillo's beeper that Seth was heading for WRCL. No one else knew but Rebecca and Lloyd Dixon, but they were too far away. Felix lived within a mile of the station. Plenty of time to get there. Hearing that, Anthony had become even more depressed, wondering how he could have misjudged Felix Castillo so completely.

Gail balanced her wine on her chest and inhaled. Her breasts appeared through the bubbles. Small rosy breasts. Anthony had said he liked them. *Un buchito*. A mouthful. She exhaled and sank.

After the memorial was over, she had noticed Lloyd Dixon among a group of opera friends in the lobby, one older woman sympathetically patting his arm. He stood with feet squarely planted, a big, ruddy-faced, white-haired man in a somber gray suit. He had not seemed overcome with grief, but then, he wasn't the type.

Yesterday Anthony had told her she'd been wrong about Dixon's dinner guests. He had given Rebecca's list to a private investigator, who had found nothing, not a hint, that any of them was other than what Rebecca had said they were — wealthy men with offshore business interests.

Today in the lobby Gail had asked Lloyd Dixon if she could speak to him privately for a moment. They went back into the theater and stood in the center aisle. Stagehands were clearing music stands and risers from the stage.

"Please forgive me, I know this isn't a good time," Gail said, "but I have reasons for wanting to know. You and Octavio Reyes were planning to make investments in Cuba at some point in the future. Are you still working with him on that?"

He gave her a long, appraising look before apparently concluding that it didn't matter if he told her. "I've withdrawn my participation in the group. Don't have the interest right now. As for Octavio, well, that's up to him. Why?"

After a moment, Gail shrugged and told the truth. "I like to keep up with what Octavio Reyes is doing. It affects me because it affects Anthony. I'm not sure I trust him."

A smile started on one side of Dixon's face and stayed there. "Reyes is all right, if you keep an eye on him."

Then Gail asked, "What's really going on with Felix Castillo? Do you know anything that the police aren't telling the rest of us?"

"Strange question."

She spoke quietly. "People have been used before as political scapegoats. How convenient to charge a man who used to be a Cuban spy. How solid is the case against him? Rebecca told me that you have friends who . . . How can I say this? You know people in agencies of the government that deal with foreign affairs. People who would be interested in Felix Castillo. I thought — because of Rebecca — that you might have asked about him. Maybe you know things concerning the investigation."

Dixon crossed his arms over his big chest and thrust out his chin. "Of course he's being used, but that doesn't mean he didn't do it. The police have no reason to frame Castillo."

Maybe Dixon needed Felix Castillo's guilt as much as everyone else seemed to. It tied up his wife's murder in a neat little package.

Onstage, men were throwing folding chairs onto a dolly. "Who's asking? You or Anthony Quintana?"

"I am, but Anthony has known Felix a long time. He is absolutely stunned that Felix Castillo is under suspicion."

"Stunned." The half-smile reappeared. "Twenty years ago, when Rebecca and Seth Greer and Anthony Quintana were in Nicaragua, Castillo was there, too, working for the Cubans. He and your fiancé were buddies."

"I know."

"According to my wife, Anthony Quintana could quote Karl Marx and Che Guevara. He was in Central America to fight Yankee imperialism, and he talked about giving up his U.S. citizenship and going back to Cuba. Things didn't work out down there for our happy little band of college radicals, but now your fiancé goes to Cuba a few times a year —"

"Wait a minute," Gail said.

"— where he visits his father — which we can understand — and his sister, who is a top official in the Ministry of Trade, and who — I am so stunned — happens to be married to a major in the Cuban army, intelligence division. Then Felix Castillo shows up as Tom Nolan's bodyguard. Two weeks later, the opera is bombed."

Gail made an exhalation of disbelief. "Felix spent time in a Cuban prison."

"That's what they all say, to get into this country." Dixon paused to see if any of this was sinking in. Gail only stared back at him. "Well, it's just something to consider." He started to go.

She grabbed his coat sleeve. "Lloyd, wait. Rebecca told me you saw a copy of the CIA report on what happened in Los Pozos. Was there anything about Emily Davis's death? Who killed her?"

Dixon had not answered. He had turned his shoulders away, then his face, and last, his eyes, breaking contact just before he strode up the aisle and out of the auditorium.

She had surprised herself, asking that question. She had promised herself not to think about Los Pozos anymore. The only way to resolve the conflict between two versions of the story was to ask Anthony again. She didn't know how to do that without risking another blowup. Their reestablished relationship was still fragile. Gail had told herself that even if Anthony had shot Emily Davis, he'd been forced to do it. What possible good would it do to drag those bones to the surface yet another time? Felix had confessed, and Rebecca Dixon had been mistaken or lying.

Floating in the bathtub, Gail heard the front door slam in that way Karen had of doing it, then her high voice. "Mom! Mom, where are youuuuuu?" Gail called back, and the sound of clogs thumped down the hall. Then a backpack hit the floor in Karen's room. Gail had left her bathroom door open, and Karen came in wearing polyester bell-bottom pants and a tight little shirt with horizontal stripes, everything retro.

The night Gail had come home from the hospital Karen had slept with her, curled up like a kitten against her side. The next morning she wouldn't let go of her hand. And she made her promise not to leave her with the Perlmutters again. *Every time you leave me with Molly's mother, you get hurt. Don't do it again!*

Karen scooped up some bubbles and made herself a beard. She announced she was going to watch Comedy Central for a while. Gail asked her to take the steaks out of the freezer. "Anthony's coming over later. Is that okay with you?"

"I guess. Are you going to stay in there all day?"

"Till I turn into an albino prune." Gail pulled her down for a kiss and got bubbles on her cheek. "The hot water is good for my back, sweetie."

Karen went out, then spun around and held onto the door frame, leaning over as if she were a ballerina, one leg extended. Her head was sideways and her hair hung straight down. "If Anthony wants to move in, it's okay with me."

Gail laughed. "Where did that come from? We were talking about finding a new house and not moving till the summer."

With a shrug, Karen vanished, and Gail picked up her wine. They were conspiring against her, those two. Subtly but thoroughly, in his understated way, Anthony Quintana had won Karen's heart, and this kid was no pushover.

Gail was beginning to think that the only sure way to harmony in a family was not to ask too many questions.

She'd had another question for Lloyd Dixon, which had remained unasked, since he had cut off the conversation so abruptly. *Lloyd, what were you and Thomas Nolan really doing in Costa Rica?*

Gail's mind had spun out all sorts of scenarios. Thomas Nolan as drug dealer. Thief of pre-Columbian art. Hit man. Felix Castillo had suggested that there had been a sniper's rifle inside the suitcase, and that Dixon had taken Nolan down there to do a job.

Had the suitcase actually existed? She did not believe Tom Nolan's story that he had gone to pick it up for his former piano teacher. It was also becoming more possible that the lady herself did not exist.

Gail had asked her secretary to find her. Yesterday, Monday, Miriam had come into Gail's office and announced she was giving up. There was no Wells in the telephone directory who had ever taught piano in 1979. Miriam held up a legal pad and flipped pages to show the phone calls she had made. Every music school and music store, every private school and college music department. The county school board, every church large enough to have a music director. Then the same routine in Fort Lauderdale and Palm Beach, in case the woman had moved north. Miriam suggested that if she had a first name, she could do a search of the Bureau of Vital Statistics for birth records, or the county records for real estate and criminal justice. If this woman had so much as a speeding ticket, Miriam could find her. But a first name would help. Or even better: "Why don't you just ask him where she lives?"

After the memorial service was over, Gail spotted blond hair in a halo of video camera lights, Tom Nolan being interviewed by TV reporters. He told them that his voice was improving, and he hoped to open in *Don Giovanni* at the end of next week.

Gail stood on the periphery of the little group. A reporter noticed her and one of the cameras spun around to record her reaction to the question, *How do you feel a week after the bombing?* She gave the expected reply — *I'm feeling much better* — then looked over at Tom Nolan. "Tom, someone just asked me and I was unable to tell them. What was the first name of your old piano teacher?"

He gave her an absolutely blank, hollow-cheeked stare.

Gail said, "Miss Wells's first name. You must have told me, but I forgot."

Nolan smiled slightly. "Elvira." He pronounced it *El-vee-ra*.

She said to one of the reporters, "That would be a great story. Thomas Nolan and Elvira Wells, the lady who inspired him to sing. She still lives in Miami."

The reporter asked Nolan how to get in touch with the woman.

Raising his hands, Tom Nolan shook his head and smiled, "No, she's retired now, a very private person. I won't allow her to be disturbed."

On the way home, Gail had put on *Don Giovanni*, her second go-through. The overture boomed out of the speakers, those ominous crashing chords, a foreshadowing of vengeance at the end. It had been the overture, oddly enough, that the Miami Opera orchestra had been playing as Gail entered the offices the night the bomb went off, and she could not hear it now without a shiver of premonitory fear.

After the overture came the comedic aria of the manservant, Leporello, as he waited for Giovanni to finish seducing Donna Anna. Gail had seen the cast rehearse that scene last week. In a swordfight, Giovanni killed Donna Anna's father, who had rushed to his daughter's defense.

Gail guided her car south on U.S. 1 in pre-rush afternoon traffic listening to

Donna Anna's fiancé swear revenge on the culprit. After Giovanni and his servant congratulated themselves on their escape, another soprano came on, a stunningly emotional aria. Her voice quivered with rage. At a stoplight, Gail flipped through the libretto with its minuscule print to see what the woman was shrieking about. *Gli vo' cavare il cor.* She wanted to tear out Giovanni's heart. One of his spurned lovers. Then Gail remembered the name of this poor unfortunate. A noblewoman, Donna Elvira.

"Elvira," Gail had repeated aloud. "Son of a bitch."

The horns had blared behind her and she had squealed her tires taking off.

Elvira Wells didn't exist. If Miss Wells didn't exist, then her suitcase didn't exist, either. Maybe. Had Lloyd Dixon been lying about bringing it back from Costa Rica? What else had he lied about?

Gail had assumed strange goings-on between Dixon and Tom Nolan, possibly as far back as Dortmund, Germany. In her more imaginative versions, she saw Nolan and Dixon going to Costa Rica to check it out as a stepping-off point for an invasion of Cuba. Dixon was familiar with the country. It was next door to Nicaragua, where he had dropped weapons to the contras.

That theory was blown to hell now, because the businessmen at Lloyd Dixon's dinner were, after all, only businessmen.

Sipping her wine, trying to figure this out, Gail heard the murmur of voices. A child. Then the deeper voice of a man. A cabinet door closing. The grind of ice cubes from the refrigerator door.

"Drat." Gail rubbed under her eyes to clear off the mascara that she knew must have run from her eyelashes. She was wearing it extra heavy these days, filling in where her own lashes were still growing back.

She sank further into the bubbles and watched the door, through which she could see her dresser and the end of the bed. Heard footsteps on the carpet.

Anthony appeared. He leaned a shoulder against the door frame. In the soft light his image was repeated in the mirror, a slender, dark-eyed man in a tawny gold shirt. He had taken off his tie and rolled back his cuffs.

"Hi." She smiled at him across the bubbles. "You're early."

"You should have a bigger bathtub," he said.

"Like the one at your house. You could come in with me."

That brought a slow smile. "If we were alone, I might try it." He set his drink on the vanity. "How was the memorial service?"

"Lovely, really. But the sideshows were tedious. Be glad you missed it." With a swoosh of water, she sat up. Lifting her hair with both hands, she said, "Do my back, and I'll tell you about Elvira, the incredible disappearing woman."

Anthony was watching the bubbles sliding slowly toward the water, leaving wet, bare skin. He glanced at the door, then closed it and turned the lock. He sat on the edge of the bathtub and picked up the sponge. "Who is Elvira?"

Gail had already told him about the suitcase from Costa Rica that Thomas Nolan had allegedly picked up for Miss Wells. The suitcase full of flowered shirtwaist dresses and sensible shoes and large-size women's cotton underwear, no doubt. And Bibles, since the lady had gone down there to do missionary work. But now it appeared that Miss Wells, and maybe the suitcase, didn't exist.

"Where does that leave you?" Anthony asked.

"Bothered. Annoyed. I hate it when people play games, and that's what he's doing."

She leaned her head on her knees as Anthony rinsed her back. "Oh, that feels wonderful." Her voice was muffled. "And in related news, Lloyd Dixon told me that he's given up his Cuba investment plans. He says he doesn't know what Octavio is doing."

Gail sat up straight. "I was looking over the copies from Dixon's appointment book today. There's an entry for this Thursday, Reyes. Then an address in south Hialeah. I looked it up. Sun Fashions. They make women's apparel. Since when does your brother-in-law have an interest in ladies' clothing — or maybe you know something about him I don't."

The sponge swept over her skin. "I saw the entry," Anthony said. "The owner is Cuban. Dixon's group was probably going to talk to him about investments. If Dixon isn't involved in that anymore, I'm going to forget about it. And you don't do anything on your own," he added firmly.

"Me? Like what?"

"Like driving to Hialeah to see what you could see."

"It hadn't crossed my mind. I was just mentioning it." Gail winced when Anthony hit a tender spot on her back.

"Sorry." He bent over and kissed it.

"Your bruises look better."

"No, they don't. In the words of my daughter, they're yucky."

Anthony took a sip of his drink, then set it on the bath mat. "Did she say that?"

"Unfortunately, Karen has been taught not to lie." Gail scratched a fingernail down his right forearm, the muscle hard under pale golden skin and smooth, dark hair. There was a gold bracelet on his wrist. He wore a man's diamond ring, nothing feminine about it. "I have heard," she said, "that Cubans like jewelry because they never know when they might have to go into exile again, and you can always carry what's on your body."

He laughed. "No kidding. I didn't know that. You think it's too much?"

"Not at all." She held his hand and looked at the ring on his little finger. "It's perfect. It's you. I love it."

The diamond sparkled when he moved his hand over her breasts, making the points tight as rocks. Glittered for a brief instant in the water before it disappeared under the bubbles.

"Anthony —"

He laughed softly, an exhalation against the back of her neck. He closed his other hand around her hair and eased her head back. His mouth opened, covering hers, more breath and heat than flesh. His tongue moved inside.

"Oh, God."

He pulled back. "Want me to stop?"

"No." She made a ragged laugh. "I could have sworn . . . I wasn't in the mood for this." Her fingers tightened on his arm. "Oh, my God —"

"Shhhh."

Finally she sagged against his arm, her forehead on his shoulder. Anthony took off his ring. "Give me your hand. Let's see if it fits." He slid it onto her third finger.

Still languid and loose-limbed, she blinked and focused on it. "Too big. Anyway, it's a man's ring."

"But it's a nice stone." When she agreed that it was, he said, "What do you think? An engagement ring for you? A solitaire?"

"No! It's yours."

He held the ring up between them. "But this one will have memories."

She smiled and looked away.

He dropped the ring into his shirt pocket. "Marry me," he said. "This weekend. Tomorrow, if we could do it."

"What?"

"I'm afraid to let you out of my sight." He held her face. "I almost lost you."

If there was a better opening for her to suggest that he move in, Gail did not know what it could be. She kissed him. "We agreed it's better for Karen if we wait." Someone in the back of her brain screamed, *Coward!* She leaned over and lifted the drain to let the water out. "Help me up."

He held her terry-cloth robe for her, then picked up his scotch. Gail tied the sash and walked into her bedroom.

Anthony followed. "They found Felix's van today in a canal west of the airport. I heard it on the news driving here. His girlfriend was inside. Tied up. She was probably alive when it went in."

"Oh, no." Gail turned around, searching his face. She knew that Anthony had hoped, against all logic, that someone with a political agenda had planted evidence in Felix Castillo's house. That hope was fading. She said, "No sign of Felix?"

"No."

Gail sat on the end of the bed and pulled Anthony down to sit with her. "I remember, when I was talking to Felix on Fisher Island, how careful he was. He was smoking, and he held his cigarette so the ember wouldn't show. When he finished he buried it in the sand. So . . . why did he leave so much evidence in his house?"

"You're thinking like a defense lawyer," Anthony said.

Gail loosened his tie. "How was lunch with your grandfather today?" Over the weekend, the Reyes family had moved in. Anthony was pretending he didn't care, but he had made sure that Octavio was at work before going to the house.

He seemed to smile into his glass before he took another sip of scotch. "Well, we discussed Felix Castillo."

Gail said, "Oh, no. Octavio has been telling him what good friends you are with a Castro agent."

"He's probably more subtle than that. Ernesto asked me how I had met Felix Castillo, and didn't I know what he was." Anthony rolled his glass slowly between his hands. "I said Felix had fooled me. I said I'd met him in Camagüey when I was a kid. It's what I told the family when Felix showed up in 1982 from Mariel, wanting a job. What else could I say?" Anthony leaned forward, elbows on his knees. "I don't know if he believed me or not."

Gail wondered how soon it would be before Anthony started believing in Felix's guilt, too, because it was easier that way. She pulled him around by his shoulder. "You have to tell your grandfather what happened. Everything. Everything you didn't tell him when you got back from Nicaragua twenty years ago."

As if she had pulled open a pit and expected him to jump in, Anthony rose to his feet and walked a few steps away. He drained his glass. "Go ahead and get dressed. I'll fix one more of these, then let's have dinner."

The door closed behind him.

She stood up to go to her closet, but her legs were too weak. Shaking, she sat back down on the bed, her hand clenched on her lap. A good effort, she thought. She had made a damned good effort to forget about Los Pozos, just as Anthony had. But it had failed. She knew that sooner or later she would ask him again. There was no choice. Even if Felix Castillo had done what he said, had put two bullets into Emily Davis's brain, Anthony was still carrying the burden of her death. The weight was starting to crush them both.

TWENTY-EIGHT

The last time Gail saw Felix Castillo, that night on Fisher Island, he had been using a miniature camera and zoom lens. With a few phone calls Gail located something similar downtown at the Spy Shop. After a hearing at the courthouse, she picked it up, a sophisticated little machine that set off warning bells on her MasterCard.

Anthony had gone back to his own place after a night at hers, so Gail had time to get familiar with the new toy. A couple of hours later she could aim and shoot without fumbling at the tiny controls.

At just past three o'clock on Thursday, Gail looked through the viewfinder at Sun Fashions, Inc., and pressed the shutter. *Click-whine.* The building was like dozens of others in this part of Hialeah — a flat-roofed, windowless warehouse. Gail had been lucky to find a visitor's space at a business across the street, her view obscured only by the trucks and step-vans clattering past.

From this angle she could see both the side of Sun Fashions with its open loading bays and the front entrance, which sported a phony mansard roof that overhung a glass door decorated with a yellow sun. To judge from the thickness of the grass, the only spot of green on this narrow, dusty street, business at Sun Fashions was good. The monotony of the long white facade was broken by the name of the company and two flagpoles. One flew the U.S. flag, and the other the flag of Cuba.

A few drops of rain hit the windshield. The flags lifted in a sudden breeze. Gail prayed that the clouds would pass over.

The entry in Lloyd Dixon's appointment book had put Octavio Reyes's initials by this address in Hialeah at 3:30 P.M. She was not sure what it would mean, exactly, if he showed up, or what she would do about it. She had given herself several good reasons to stay away, but none could overcome her anger. Rebecca Dixon and Seth Greer were dead. Gail did not believe that Felix Castillo had killed them. They had died for something they knew. Something that Felix might have found out. Felix was probably dead, too. And in all her dreams the dark face of Octavio Reyes appeared.

She despised him for what he had done to Anthony. She had no fear, only a humming alertness. To reduce the possibility of being recognized, she had put on the brunette wig and a pair of her mother's reading glasses. She felt capable of anything.

As Gail held the camera in her lap, a lunch truck — a roach coach — turned off the road, its horn playing the first two lines of "La Cucaracha." The driver got out and raised a panel on the side, making a little roof. At the same time, a dozen or more women came out the side door of the building and down a short flight of concrete steps — seamstresses on break. Gail could hear their voices, the quick patter of Spanish, as they clustered around to buy sodas and snacks.

Hialeah was a blue-collar grid of small streets on a relentlessly flat landscape. Its garment factories provided jobs where new immigrants could sit at sewing machines eight hours a day at cheap wages. As Gail watched, more seamstresses came out of the building and walked through the gate. She noticed a pickup truck waiting for them to move out of the way. Gail stared at it, a dark blue Ford 250 with tinted windows and a CB antenna. There was a small American flag on the bumper sticker. The pickup backed toward the loading bays and vanished, blocked by the women and the lunch truck.

Without hesitation Gail locked her car and walked across the street with her jacket draped over the camera. She had noticed the bus route sign attached to a concrete utility pole. A heavy middle-aged woman sat on the bus bench, arms crossed. She watched without much interest as Gail set the camera on the back of the bench, checked the viewfinder, then draped an arm over it and put her finger on the shutter.

The man getting out of the truck was not Lloyd Dixon. She was surprised by this, then recognized him as an employee, the mechanic she had seen on the scaffold at the Dixon Air hangar. Hispanic, around forty, brown slacks, windbreaker. She got him stepping up to the loading dock, then speaking to a man in a suit who came out of the building. The second man was older, mid-fifties, the type who would drive the Mercedes in the reserved spot by the front door.

Then a dark red Lexus with gold trim turned in from the street. The women were going back through the gate, and the car moved slowly, nosing up to the building. Gail rechecked the focus and pulled back the lens for a wider angle. She pretended to look in another direction and pressed the shutter, hearing the soft *click-whine* of the advance. Got Octavio Reyes coming out of the car. Straightening the jacket of his gray suit. Reaching back in for a small black gym bag. Up the stairs. Handshake with the man who had come out earlier. The driver of the pickup truck lighting a cigarette, not really part of this. But his eyes watched the street.

Seven seconds. Gail had already calculated how long it would take to walk casually across the street, get back into the car, and start the engine. Less time than it would take any of those men to spot a camera lens, jump off the loading dock, and come over to ask her what she was doing.

Reyes walked inside with the older man. Drops of rain hit the sidewalk, making dark circles in the dust. The last of the seamstresses hurried inside, and the driver of the lunch truck closed the side panel, got back in, and went on down the block. The woman on the other end of the bus bench popped open an umbrella.

Gail stayed where she was. Counted off four minutes on her watch. Five. Rain was coming a little faster, but not enough to send her running.

A forklift appeared in the open bay door, its metal arms holding a pallet with a blue plastic tarp wrapped tightly around a rectangular shape underneath. The driver from

Dixon Air jumped off the dock and lowered the gate on the pickup truck. Reyes and the other man came back out. Watched the forklift roll forward and place the pallet in the bed of the truck, which rocked, then settled on its springs.

Gail wrapped her jacket around the camera and ran for the car as the rain started falling in ragged gray sheets.

Dixon Air Transport shared a parking lot with a neighboring hangar. Gail found an empty space near the other building and put the VISITOR sign on the dashboard. The guard at the gate had given it to her when she showed her business card and said she had an appointment with Lloyd Dixon. She had noticed, last time she was here, that the guard had not called to get an okay. The main terminal entrance was through a gate some half-mile distant, where most of the private airplanes came and went on runways not shared by the cargo carriers on this side of the field.

Gail turned off the engine and sat for a few minutes listening to the rain tick on the roof. She had escaped Hialeah just before four o'clock, when workers started pouring out of the factories, locking up traffic. The pickup truck couldn't have been so lucky, but it would arrive soon enough. She had no doubt of its destination. And as for what was under the blue tarpaulin — not ladies' dresses, not the way that truck had settled under the weight. She didn't believe it was sewing machine parts, either. A routine pickup of cargo would not have been jotted down in the CEO's personal appointment book. She guessed that the CEO himself would be the pilot. Dixon in his leather bomber jacket. He had winked at her on his way out of the rehearsal hall after speaking with Tom Nolan. *Some fun, huh?*

The words DIXON AIR TRANSPORT marched across the side of the hangar in huge red letters. Her position gave her an angled view of the front. The door had been pulled halfway across the wide opening.

On the way here, she had thought about what to do next. There were no personal matters to handle. She had rescheduled an appointment with a client. Karen had soccer practice, but Irene had agreed to take her. With the rain, they would probably stay home and play cards. Anthony had a trial this afternoon, but if he finished early, Miriam would say that Ms. Connor was in court. A lie. She intended to apologize later, if he found out.

People came and went, hurrying with umbrellas held close or coats thrown over their heads. A jet took off, thundering overhead. Gail felt the first stirring of unease. No danger sitting here in her car, but if she went inside, then what?

She shivered, suddenly aware of how foolish this was. Insane, sitting here in the rain-faded light of late afternoon, the parking lot slowly emptying out.

If those weapons made it to Cuba — where else would they be going? — then maybe Ernesto Pedrosa's prediction would come true. Cuba free within a year. But Anthony had said it couldn't happen. Nobody there wanted a bloody counterrevolution.

Rain slid down the windshield, making the hangar's red letters move. She noticed a small sign on the wall indicating a reserved parking place. DIXON. The space was empty. A metal exit door opened, and a thin fiftyish woman came through it, her skirt fluttering as she ran toward her car. Windshield wipers went on. She drove away. A minute later two men in dark blue jumpsuits came out — mechanics, Gail assumed. Quitting time.

The apprehension passed. No one knew what she was doing here. No one would give a flip if the opera's lawyer came in looking for Lloyd Dixon. Gail tore off the wig and stuffed it under the seat. Combed her hair and put on lipstick. A salon had done a good job cutting off the singed parts, giving her a short blond layered look. In her navy-and-tan tweed jacket, even with jeans, she was a lawyer taking an afternoon away from the office.

The camera fitted in separate pieces — lens and body — inside an inner pocket of her shoulder bag. She did not expect to use it. She expected to snap a mental picture of what was on the other side of the hangar door. If the pickup truck arrived — and if Octavio Reyes followed close behind — so much the better. She wanted to see his reaction. Wanted him to know that if he trashed Anthony, she would ask him, in front of Ernesto Pedrosa, what he'd been doing at Lloyd Dixon's place of business. Dixon, the opera donor who supported the commie singer, Thomas Nolan.

Smiling with anticipated triumph, Gail strode toward the hangar, entering on the near side, where the hangar door was open. She brushed the drizzle off her sleeves. The wet soles of her shoes squeaked on the concrete. There were three airplanes inside, one of them Dixon's own jet, the white Citation, then two cargo jets, both in stages of repair. The planes had been turned at an angle so their wings would fit, and a scaffold was in place beside one of them. With the heavy overcast, the skylights gave little illumination. Big work lights hung from trusses in the high ceiling, but they were turned off. The gloom was relieved only by what light came through the door. There was a fluorescent glow from the glassed-in office on the far side of the hangar.

Coming closer, she saw three men standing inside talking. They did not look like office workers. Her steps slowed. Unobserved from ten yards away, she studied the faces of these men, trying to decide if she had seen them before. Perhaps in the shadows on Ernesto Pedrosa's front porch, talking to Octavio Reyes.

The implications of what she was doing suddenly hit her like a cold wind, and a shudder ran across her chest. Very bad, to be caught here without a reasonable explanation. Gail Connor, lawyer for the opera, engaged to Anthony Quintana, whose friend Felix Castillo was accused of being an agent for the regime. Caught here with a miniature camera, which already held shots of a pallet being loaded onto a pickup truck. She took a step backward.

From behind her she heard the growl of an engine, the squeal of tires on slick concrete. Gail hurried to hide behind the landing gear of the middle cargo plane. Huddled on the floor, she could see under the belly of Dixon's personal jet. A Ford pickup braked to a stop beyond the tail. Then a Lexus appeared in the open hangar door and stopped near the cockpit. Headlights went off. A car door slammed. Reyes's gray trouser legs appeared.

Voices came from behind her. Gail spun around. If they walked this way, they would see her immediately. She glanced through the scaffold toward the darkness at the rear of the hangar, fifty yards away. Too far. If she ran, they would hear her.

Crouched behind the big wheels under the wing, she swiveled as the men passed by. Her wet footprints were directly in their path, but they hurried by without noticing. Her heart pulsed wildly in her chest.

She came out far enough to look up at the scaffolding. One side gave access to the engine, the other to the cockpit. The door was open. Gail put the strap of her shoulder bag crossways over her chest and began to climb, stealthily as a cat. The fuselage protected her from view. Octavio Reyes and the other men were on the far side of the hangar, talking so loudly they would not hear the hollow shift of pipe or squeak of metal.

Shaking, she pulled herself up the bars, then to the metal mesh floor, and then, at last, she crept into the airplane.

Her legs gave out and she sat on the floor trembling, able to see nothing but dim shapes. The door to the cockpit was closed. The windows admitted pale gray light. There were only six seats before the cabin ended at another door, beyond which she assumed was cargo space. Silently she felt for a seat and pulled herself into it. She dared not sit next to a window.

Forcing herself to breathe slowly, she said over and over, *They don't know you're here. You're perfectly safe. When they leave, you can go.*

Rain beat down harder on the high metal roof. A diesel engine started. A high-pitched *beep-beep-beep* told her it was probably a forklift backing up. The noises went on for a few minutes, then the engine shut off. Men's voices again. A few minutes later, the restrained purr of a car engine. That would be Reyes's Lexus. Tires squeaking, then the engine fading. Gone. There would be four men left in the hangar. She waited for the pickup truck to leave. It didn't.

An electric motor cut on, and at the same time the hangar door began to shut with a squeal of metal and rattle of wheels and pulleys. "Oh, damn," Gail breathed. The light faded further.

Footsteps and voices came nearer, then passed by. Inside the airplane, she could not make out the words. She crept across the aisle and stood up far enough to see out the window. Four men walked past the nose of the other cargo plane, going toward the office.

Gail heard the sound of a push bar on a metal door, voices getting fainter, then cutting off as the door swung solidly shut behind them. She waited, wondering how many had left. At least two. They had probably parked just outside the office, not in the lot where she had left her car.

A minute later she heard the other two men start a discussion about what to eat. "¿Qué quieres comer?" "No me importa." He didn't care. Gail cursed silently. Were they staying all night? They argued the quality of Pollo Tropical versus KFC. They agreed on pizza. And bring some beer. Footsteps to the side door. The push bar. Then the door clicking shut. That left one man. She heard the murmur of his voice, then realized he was making a phone call.

Unable to see her watch, she guessed the time at six o'clock. Panic gradually subsided, and Gail considered the alternatives.

It would be no difficult matter to sit in this airplane all night, except that her absence would not go unnoticed. Her mother might get Karen put to bed, but after that, she would call Anthony. He would be beyond frantic. She had to find a way to get the hell out of here before the other man came back.

She heard conversation in Spanish, then music. A commercial. He was watching television. Gail slowly stood up. Panic danced down her spine, but she forced herself to be calm. This would be simple. Go down the scaffolding, walk to the door in the far corner. She had seen people coming out that way going to the parking lot. Three airplanes blocked his view. With the television on, he wasn't likely to hear her. If he did hear the door shut and ran across the hangar, he'd see nothing but taillights.

Over the muffled sound of the television she heard the drone of a small plane going over. Rain on the metal roof. Water splattering in a downspout. She slowly stood up. Her eyes were adjusted to the darkness in the cabin, and she could see her way. At the door she looked out. Nothing moved. Light gleamed faintly on the wings and fuselages of the aircraft. A bright glow came from the direction of the office. She could not see, but visualized, the door in the far corner of the hangar, a red exit sign glowing like a beacon. She slid her purse around so it was on her back, out of the way, then stepped carefully onto the mesh floor of the scaffolding.

Lightning flickered faintly through the skylights, sharpening her vision. Thunder rolled a few seconds later. She grasped the frame and felt with her foot for the next horizontal bar. Then heard an odd click of metal. Not from the scaffold but from the office area. She waited. Heard a soft squeak. Then another metallic click, as if someone had come in through the door. But no one called out. The television was still on, same volume.

Several long seconds passed. Her arms were starting to quiver. The noise might have been the dripping of rain. She went down another step. Then another.

She heard an electronic ringing noise, then another. Then two more. Her portable phone. It seemed as loud as a fire bell, and there was no way to reach it. She hooked an elbow around one of the bars and fumbled her purse around. Opened the flap. The ringing was louder. She pulled out the telephone, hit the off button, and the thing spun out of her hands. She grabbed, missed.

It dropped ten feet, the sound echoing on concrete and metal.

The television went off.

Silence, except for the light patter of rain.

Gail clung to the scaffold, every muscle tense. Footsteps came out of the office. Paused. He had to be standing in the doorway listening. If he came around the front of the other cargo plane he would see her.

Thunder grumbled in the distance. No, not thunder. A jet taking off, the noise coming closer. Quickly Gail came down off the scaffold, picked up her telephone, which had cracked into pieces. She ran alongside the fuselage, her pace spurred by raw fear.

A shout boomed out behind her. "Hey! *¿Quién es? ¡Parate!*"

Feet pounding, Gail sped under the tail of the cargo plane. Past the Citation. Swerved around Dixon's pickup truck. Only a few more yards to go.

Conscious thought vanished under the will to escape. Her eyes fixed on the exit door. Steel-caged storage areas to one side, stacks of wooden boxes on the other. The red glow. As she opened her hands to push through the door, the pieces of her telephone dropped. Then she saw the heavy chain wrapped around the push bar, securing it to a ring in the block wall.

With a cry of panic she spun around, calculating the distance to the other door, realizing immediately it was too far. Her eyes darted about, looking for a way to defend herself. Boxes, crates stacked against the wall. Vast cabinets of tools. She would grab a wrench, anything —

Footsteps thudded closer. The man appeared. There was enough light for her to see the gun. He was screaming at her to stop. She launched herself toward the shadows. The gun fired, creating a flare of light and sharp explosion of noise. Wood cracked just over her head. She dove behind the boxes.

Then heard a thud, a grunt, a great clatter of something tipping over. Metal crashed to the floor.

Two voices, not one.

Gail peered out. Saw dark figures struggling on the floor. A gun a few feet away. They rolled toward it. An arm came out, reaching. The man on top clubbed the other with something in his hand. Then again.

There was a moan. The arm went still.

Breathing hard, the other man braced himself on a knee. Slowly stood up. He was holding a pistol.

He turned around and came toward the boxes.

In the gloom of the hangar, and on the edge of panic, it took Gail a while to arrange his features into a recognizable face.

"Gail, come out of there."

TWENTY-NINE

She stared at him, unable to move, hearing the rasping of her own breath.

Anthony put his pistol inside his black zippered jacket. He walked around the boxes and reached down to grasp her arm. His voice was low and insistent. "We have to go. *Now.*"

Numbly she said, "How did you —"

"I took the keys from a guy leaving. He's in the trunk of his car."

"But what —"

He caught her when her legs went weak. He walked backward, dragging her along. "Gail, stand up! *Jesucristo, ¿qué me haces?*"

She regained her balance, then saw the body on the floor. "Oh, my God. Is he dead?"

"No, but he won't be out forever." Anthony kicked the man's gun into the shadows.

"My telephone," Gail whispered. "Over there."

He stared at her. "That was *yours?* You left your telephone on?" He spun around and spotted the pieces near an oil drum.

Gail followed him, whispering, "Anthony, I had no idea these people were in here, and then Octavio came, and I had to hide —"

"I don't want to hear it."

"Octavio was at Sun Fashions," she said. "He gave the owner a gym bag, then a forklift loaded some boxes onto Lloyd Dixon's pickup truck. Dixon wasn't there. I guessed that they were coming to the hangar, so I got here first —"

He grabbed her wrist and pulled her along. "Amazing to be in two places at once. Your secretary said you were with a client. You who value truth so highly."

Gail ran to keep up. "*Your* secretary said you were in trial this afternoon. What were you doing, following me?"

"No. Dixon. He stayed in his office, so I went to Hialeah and got there in time to see Octavio leaving with the truck. I was waiting in the parking lot deciding what to do next when I noticed a rental car. I said to myself, Oh, that looks so familiar. But no, it couldn't be Gail. Not even Gail would be that foolish."

They passed behind the middle cargo plane, moving toward the offices.

"Anthony, wait!" She jerked free. Opening her purse, she ran back the way they had come, her footsteps echoing.

He caught up. "What the hell are you doing?"

She pulled out the camera and lens. The staggering fear had gone, leaving nothing but an anger so cold her teeth were chattering. "I want to know what's under that tarp. Somebody tried to kill me, and by *God* I'm coming away from here with pictures."

Speeding past the figure still lying prone, then past the pickup truck, she spotted an empty wooden pallet, then a blue tarpaulin with three rectangular shapes underneath. "Look under that tarp!" The lens snapped onto the camera. She popped open the flash.

"There isn't time! The others could come back."

"Thirty seconds."

Anthony produced a small flashlight. The beam hit the tarpaulin, and bright blue surged from the darkness. He pulled back the tarp, revealing three heavy black plastic boxes with rounded corners, each about three feet wide, two deep, and six feet long. Handles were inset along the sides, and latches fastened the lids with spinning nuts that locked into place.

Squatting down, Anthony moved the beam of light along the edge of the first box.

Shadows danced on the floor. "They're designed to be waterproof."

Gail told him to move back, to look away. There was a flare of white. Then again at another angle. "Open it."

The men had left the lid unlatched. Anthony raised it and blew out a breath. "Look at this." The beam of the flashlight passed over military rifles with folding front grips. From the other end of the box he lifted a pistol. The light gleamed on the dull gray metal. "Makarov. It's Russian. There are at least a dozen in here. Get a closeup." He wiped off his fingerprints, then laid the handgun on top of the rifles.

Gail spoke from behind her camera. "Why would they send Russian guns?"

"Because they fit the ammunition already in Cuba. You bring in American weapons, what happens when you run out?" He shielded his eyes.

Click-whine. Click-whine. "How can these be enough weapons for a counterrevolution?"

"It's more than enough to cause some serious problems." A moan came from the darkness. Anthony rose silently, listened for a few seconds, then said, "We should hurry."

The second box contained survival equipment — small stoves, tents, rope, knives, shovels — along with medical supplies. By the time they got to the third, she could see the sweat on Anthony's forehead, and her fingers were shaking. The flashlight picked up more handguns. Metal boxes of ammunition. He pointed to a rectangular gray shape wrapped in clear plastic. "C-4. Plastique. Thirty . . . forty kilos, at least. And here are fuses, timers, detonators. Over here, some two-way radios. Batteries, various sizes."

Gail took the pictures. "Do you think they're flying this stuff out tonight?"

"I doubt it. There's a storm front moving through. In any event, they won't fly over Cuba. They'd be spotted. Both the Cubans and the Americans track everything in the western Caribbean. I think they'll land somewhere else."

"Costa Rica?" she suggested.

"Why do you say that? Ah. Because Lloyd Dixon went there with Tom Nolan two years ago. No, it's too far. What he might do is fly that little jet to an island somewhere. They could take the boxes in on a fishing boat. Or they could get the boat close to shore, then clip the boxes to underwater cables, and someone pulls them in."

She looked at him. "Has anyone ever really done that?"

"I've heard stories. What's this?" He pulled out a small black bag.

Gail came closer. "That looks like the bag Octavio gave the owner of Sun Fashions."

Anthony unzipped it and shook out U.S. currency in rubber-banded stacks. "Take a picture. That's about fifty thousand dollars. Maybe they *are* flying out tonight. They wouldn't leave this much cash around during the day." He moved back, and Gail zoomed in for a closeup. "The owner of Sun Fashions is a man named Bernard Levy. He's a Cuban Jew who travels frequently to the Middle East. A friend of mine in the federal public defender's office told me."

"Levy is an arms dealer?"

"Let's say he has connections." Anthony stuffed the money back into the bag and zipped it closed. He slammed it into the box.

"Anthony?"

"I didn't expect this. I don't know what to do." He stood with one hand on his hip, the other raking through his hair.

"You're thinking of your grandfather," she said. "He may not know about it."

"Oh, I'm sure he does. He probably paid for it. God *damn* it." He let out a breath.

"Come on. Help me put everything back the way it was." They snapped the lids on and threw the tarp over the boxes. The circle of light swept the floor, looking for anything they might have dropped, then moved ahead of Anthony as he went back to the man he had knocked out. "Here. Hold the flashlight."

She looked away from the man's head. There was a gash over his ear leaking blood on the floor.

Anthony turned him over, found his wallet, and shuffled through the papers and cards inside. "Rodriguez. Okay, *señor,* I see you have no objection." He put the driver's license on the man's forehead and told Gail to get a closeup. This was a heavy-featured man with black hair, a thick mustache, and a purpling bruise around his left eye.

"Oh, great," she muttered, hoping that the flash wouldn't wake him up. It didn't.

Anthony returned the license and wallet. "Let's go."

Silently they ran across the hangar to the other exit door. Hand on the pistol inside his jacket, he looked through the small window, pushed on the bar, then motioned for Gail to follow. They walked out into the yellowish glow of security lights along the fence. Thumps and muffled yells were coming from the back of a Chevy sedan parked by the wall.

A mile or two past the gates, heading east toward Miami, Gail saw Anthony's right blinker flashing. She followed onto a smaller cross street, then into the driveway of a Catholic church parking lot. He was not driving his Eldorado, but a borrowed Camaro. Tires splashed through a puddle and the headlights went out. The rain had stopped, leaving a chilly mist in the air.

Anthony got out and came to sit in Gail's car. They had parked at the side of the lot under some trees, and drops of water fell at irregular intervals on the roof and windshield. A twig stuck to the glass.

He reached for her, and for several minutes they embraced without speaking. Then he asked if she was all right. She said she was. "Gail, what in the name of God were you thinking of?"

"I wanted to catch Octavio at something." Gail laughed. "I'll bet he wet his pants when he found out that Lloyd flew missions to resupply the contras. Octavio, all his life selling discount furniture, the Furniture King. Cowardly son of a bitch. I hate him for what he's done to you. Not just to you. He pulled your grandfather into this mess."

"Don't underestimate my grandfather. He's a smart old bastard — as long as he knows what's going on. I'm not sure how much Octavio has told him."

"What are you going to do?" she asked.

"I'm not sure."

"Please be careful. Seth and Rebecca are dead. They must have known what Octavio and Lloyd were doing."

"Why are you assuming that they would commit murder? That's a leap." Anthony shook his head. "Listen, what Octavio wants is to free Cuba. That doesn't make him a killer."

"Then what about Lloyd?"

"Because he flew some missions for the CIA?"

"Anthony, if the CIA is involved, this is bigger than we think it is."

The tapping on the roof came faster, and silvery flashes of rain appeared around the streetlights.

"Did any of those men recognize you?" Anthony asked. "Is there any possibility?"

"No. The one who chased me couldn't have seen my face clearly."

"What about at Sun Fashions?"

"I was wearing a dark wig and glasses."

"Diós mio." Anthony let out a slow breath and stared through the windshield. "It

wouldn't do any good to yell at you for this."

"No, please don't." Gail leaned her head on the headrest. "Oh. The guard. I left my name with the guard at the gate."

"Okay. I'll take care of it."

"How?"

"I'll bribe him. I'll give him some story. Listen to me. I'll make sure you get home, then I have to go somewhere. I'll be back later, okay?"

"Where are you going?"

"We'll talk about it later. Gail, I'm going to need the film." When she stared back at him, he said, "Also the pictures you took at Sun Fashions."

"What are you going to do with it?"

"Please don't argue with me." He picked up her purse from between the seats and gave it to her.

She dropped her hand on it. "After what I've been through, you can at least give me one simple explanation."

"Okay. The explanation is, it's dangerous. I don't want you to get hurt."

She laughed. "Really. I just got shot at."

"Exactly. You could have been killed. I'm not going to let that happen to you."

"I know you want me to be safe," she said, "and I love you for that. But why can't you talk to me?"

He touched her cheek. "All right. I want to get the film developed, see what there is, and then — maybe — talk to Lloyd Dixon."

"Oh, my God. Why don't you go straight to the police?"

"What if my grandfather is involved, Gail? If U.S. Customs busts this group and he's part of it, it could kill him. It would destroy my family."

She nodded. "Okay. The film is yours."

Anthony clicked on his flashlight, shielding the beam to a small point. Gail slid the cartridge from the camera and gave him two others. "There. That's all."

He put the film into his jacket pocket. "I should have told you this already. Felix gave me the film from Rebecca's camera."

Gail said, "I figured that. Where is he, Anthony?"

"I don't know. We talked for a couple of hours at my house. He left around ten-thirty, and I haven't seen him since."

"Anthony, listen. He's your friend, but maybe he didn't tell you everything. Isn't it possible that he really did plant the bomb that killed Rebecca?"

"No." Anthony's voice was deadly calm. "He was framed by someone. He was used. Someone drove his van by the opera before the bomb went off, assuming it would be seen. The van was pulled out of a canal with Daisy's body inside it, but not Felix. Maybe he's still alive. If he is dead, and I find out who did it, don't ever ask me what happened to that person."

He took his car keys out of his jacket pocket. "I'll follow you home and make sure everything is all right. I'm sure it is, but I need to see for myself."

She put her arms around him. "Please be careful."

"I will. I promise." He held her tightly, then reached for the door handle. He let go and turned back around to look at her. "When Felix came over, the last time I saw him, he said you and he had talked about Los Pozos. I'm sorry it took me so long to tell you about it myself."

"Me, too. Felix's was the fourth version I've heard."

Anthony looked at her.

She said quietly, "Two are from you — Pablo did it. Felix did it. Then Felix told me it had to be done because Emily cost the lives of eleven men. The night of the bombing, Rebecca gave me one more version. She said you did it."

"No. That's not true."

"She said you had to. Pablo threatened to kill all four of you unless one of you executed Emily Davis. Rebecca didn't say it was your *fault*. That's what you told me, too. That Pablo was responsible."

"Gail, she lied to you."

"Why? What motive would she have?"

Instead of anger, a great weariness seemed to have settled on Anthony, and he made no movement except for the slight rise and fall of his chest. "I told you the truth. Felix shot Emily. I don't know why Rebecca lied to you. Maybe . . . she hated me. She wanted to cause trouble."

"But why?" Gail could not see his face clearly, could not read his expression. "Felix had a reason to lie. He owed you a lot, and he knew I wanted an answer. So he gave me one."

"You believe Rebecca Dixon instead of me. You have my word, and you have Felix's, and you believe her. Is that how it is between us? You have no trust in me, do you? None."

"Trust *me*, Anthony. Tell me what happened."

"I didn't do it!"

There was silence except for the rain whispering in the trees. A car went by on the street.

"A technicality. I didn't do it. I am technically innocent, Your Honor." Anthony put an elbow on the window frame and rested his forehead on his fingers.

"Emily didn't want to go, but I talked her into it. When Rebecca told me that she had seen Emily talking to a CIA agent in La Vigia, I didn't believe it. And then when Emily said it was true, I told her nothing would happen. So. Pablo and his men came. They marched us outside. He tied Emily's hands and made her kneel, then he held his gun out, the butt of it toward us, and said we had to choose. If not, we would all die. I knew he meant it for me. Not for Seth and Rebecca. For me. It was about power. Who was I? An American college student pretending to be a Cuban guerrilla. I had challenged him too many times. I took the gun. My hands shook so badly I almost dropped it. I thought of killing myself. Or Pablo. Emily was begging me. Crying for me not to do it. Then Felix shot her."

Gail touched Anthony's arm. He was trembling. "That's enough."

He seemed not to hear her, and the quiet words went on. "For a second I thought my gun went off by itself, but I looked around, and Felix was putting his pistol away. He told Pablo I would have missed. He said, 'Make them bury her. It's raining, let's go inside and get dry.' Then he hit me across the face. Called me a coward, a poor excuse for a man. I figured out, somewhere on the road to Managua, that he had to say something like that to save his own ass. Pablo knew we were friends."

Gail said, "Maybe that's why Felix killed her. He did it for you and the others."

"We never talked about it," Anthony said, "so I don't know. And I don't know if I would have shot Emily. I will never know."

"But you didn't."

Slowly his head turned toward her. "That's what you wanted. The answer. Okay, there it is."

"Anthony, it wasn't your fault. You had no choice."

"But won't you wonder?" There was enough light to see him smile, a glint of light on his teeth. "Sooner or later, won't you ask yourself, what would I have done?"

"No."

"You will."

"Stop it! I don't *care*. I love you. Whatever happened in Los Pozos, whatever you've done or seen or have been in your life, I know who you are, and I love you."

"That sounds very pretty."

She drew in a breath as if he had slapped her. The windshield, the streetlights, and his silhouette wavered.

"Oh, my God. Gail —" He pulled her close. "I didn't mean that. Forgive me, sweetheart, please." He held her tightly and murmured, "*Perdóname. Tú sabes que te quiero tanto, tanto.* Why do I make you cry? I'm sorry."

It had been Irene whose call had interrupted Gail's climb down the scaffolding. Her note was stuck to the refrigerator with a magnet made to look like a miniature orange. Gail read it after Anthony had checked the house, then had driven away.

Karen and I have gone to a movie. Be back about eight-thirty. Tried to call you. Love, Mom.

Gail looked at her watch. 8:20. Days seemed to have passed since she had walked into the Dixon Air Transport hangar. She fixed a sandwich and a glass of milk and sat at the kitchen counter, but her appetite was off.

Leaning her cheek on her palm, Gail thought again of the ladies in Irene Connor's bridge club. How many versions of a story, and which could you really believe?

She heard her mother's car in the driveway. In a few seconds there would be voices on the porch. Comments on the movie. Irene shaking off her umbrella. The door opening. Karen running into the kitchen.

Irene appearing a moment later, bustling around to make some hot tea, saying it is just *awful* out there, and how was your evening, darling?

And then later — much later — Gail would hear her bedroom door open. Anthony would come tonight. Gail had no doubt of that. He would have been out doing whatever it was he said he had to take care of. He would come, and they would hold each other and go to sleep, but she was not sure they could survive Los Pozos.

THIRTY

On Donor Day, the Miami Opera allowed board members and major donors to attend the technical dress rehearsal. The action would pause if the set or lighting director needed to make an adjustment. An immense number of details had to come together before *Don Giovanni* opened on Thursday. Irene Connor talked Gail into taking Karen out of school early. *Oh, come on, every kid needs to play hooky once in a while. So do you.* Gail had given in when Irene slyly mentioned the educational value of looking behind the scenes.

Most of the audience clustered down front, their faces turned expectantly toward the stage while the orchestra tuned up.

Lloyd Dixon was not in attendance. He had told his friends he intended to take an extended vacation, but no one seemed to know where he was going. Irene had told Gail *she* had heard that Lloyd Dixon intended to move to South America with the housekeeper, Juanita, and don't you just know something is going on there?

The house lights dimmed. Gail squeezed

Karen's hand. The conductor raised his arms, paused, and then the overture began, the long dark chords that signaled disaster in the final act.

The curtains parted, and moonlight shone on the house of Donna Anna with its balcony and red tile roof. Don Giovanni would be inside seducing the lady. Karen tapped on Gail's arm and whispered, "Who's that?" Gail answered, "Giovanni's servant. He's waiting for him. Shhh." She pointed to the surtitles projected above the stage. "Read that."

The door to the house burst open, and a man in a cape came out, trying to get away from a woman in a nightdress screaming for help. They threw insults at each other. Gail recognized Thomas Nolan's voice, but could not see him clearly. His cape swirled, and a white-plumed hat hid his face. The servant, Leporello, ran about helplessly. Gail glanced at Karen, whose eyes were wide, taking it all in — the father demanding that Giovanni defend himself, the swordfight that ended in death.

When Thomas Nolan swept off his hat, Gail let out a breath of surprise. He was not blond, but dark. A wig, of course. The hair was combed straight off his forehead, thick and wavy, tied in a bow at the nape of his neck. Makeup had given him dark eyes and brows, a straight, narrow nose, and a fuller, more sensuous mouth. For a second Gail had seen Anthony Quintana. Somehow he had walked onstage in this costume. In the next moment the man was Thomas Nolan again, and Gail relaxed in her seat, laughing at herself as if an illusionist had shown her a magic trick.

Karen tapped her arm. Gail leaned over to explain that the tenor who had come back with Anna was in love with her, and he promised to avenge her father's death.

There was a glitch in the scene change, and the stage manager conferred with the director. The curtains closed, the conductor once again tapped his baton on his music stand, and the orchestra began scene two. Giovanni strolled past an inn with his servant, plotting to make another conquest before dawn. Suddenly a disheveled woman appeared, her hair flying about her face. Gail recognized the aria. This was Donna Elvira, who wanted to tear out Giovanni's heart for deserting her.

Giovanni escaped, and Leporello assured the woman that she was not Giovanni's first victim or his last. *"Madamina, il catalogo è questo, delle belle che amò il padron mio . . ."* The audience laughed when he pulled out a roll of paper that hit the floor and unrolled toward the orchestra pit.

Gail whispered to Karen, "Don Giovanni had more than two thousand girlfriends. Elvira was one of them. He dumped her but she's still in love with him."

"*I* think she's crazy," Karen whispered back.

"Well, she can't help herself, he's so charming and handsome."

Anthony had come back from his visit with Lloyd Dixon telling Gail that everything had been worked out. The boxes would go back to Sun Fashions and the money returned. Dixon had taken a look at the photos and laughed. *No skin off my nose, buddy.* Gail had asked Anthony if he intended to let Octavio walk away from this. He said he had to think about it.

Onstage Don Giovanni was singing to a young peasant girl, persuading her to go with him to his villa. Gail smiled. She had seen Tom Nolan show this one to the students in his master class. His velvet voice wrapped around the girl, and her lovely soprano quivered with uncertainty, then desire.

Watching this, Gail again experienced the odd sensation of seeing Anthony onstage. His dark eyes fixed on the girl, and his hand lightly touched her cheek. The same day Gail had visited the master class, Seth Greer had told her about Emily Davis. She hadn't wanted to go to Nicaragua, but Anthony had talked her into it. She had followed him believing he loved her, but at twenty-two, Anthony still had too much of his father in him, a *machista* for whom love was a useful word.

Enter Donna Elvira to save the girl from ruin. But a few scenes later Giovanni was ordering his servant to make preparations for a party, at which he would seduce at least ten more.

The music whirled and danced, and Thomas Nolan ran from one spot to another, miming how he would flirt with so many women. His sprained knee had apparently healed. His voice was leaping, too, easily taking the fast turns of a difficult aria. Nailing every note. When he finished, the audience shouted "Bravo!" and applauded and whistled. Nolan made a deep bow.

Exit stage left.

Gail's eyes were directed at the stage, but she didn't register the next scene. She was wondering how he had recovered so completely in less than two weeks. His voice had come back from a ragged, painful whisper, and there was not the slightest sign of a limp. She recalled he had been in the work-room making a photocopy when the bomb went off. Closer to the bomb than she herself, standing around a corner in the hall. The door to the workroom would have been open, of course, because Rebecca Dixon was waiting for him in the lobby. She had been sitting next to a small table with a lamp on it, and the bomb had been under the table in a cardboard box. The explosion had thrown her across the room. If Nolan had been where he said he'd been, the fire-ball would have fried his ponytail into a crew cut.

Possibly he had gone into the supply closet for more paper. Or even into the next room, a small conference area outside Jeffrey Hopkins's office. No reason to go that far, but if he had — Gail counted three turns and two walls between him and the blast.

Strange that Rebecca had sat in that particular chair waiting for him to make a photocopy. They had been talking in the boardroom. Why not wait there? No, Rebecca wouldn't have let him make the copy at all. She would have done it. She knew where the machine was. Thomas Nolan was the opera star. He should have been sitting in that chair.

Gail had told the police she had heard them talking in the lobby. But no. Not both of them. She had heard only Nolan's voice. He had laughed, then said, *Take care. I've got to be going now.*

That wasn't, *Let me make a copy, I'll be right back.* It was . . . *Goodbye.*

In the lobby at intermission, Karen finished her cup of soda and asked Gail if she could go to the topmost balcony. "All right. I'll go with you." Gail was too tense to sit still.

Up and up the silent, carpeted stairs, trying not to lose sight of Karen, who knew this theater's secret hiding places and could move like a cat in her sneakers and jeans. "Wait for me!" Gail trotted behind in her pumps and the tailored dress she had worn to the office this morning.

Her eyes were on Karen, but her mind was constructing the case against Thomas Nolan.

Point one. He could not have been standing at the copy machine. Point two. Most singers arrived three weeks before opening night for rehearsals, then left after closing. Nolan had arrived just after Christmas and would be here through the semester. Time to plot murder.

Point three. There was only one reasonable way he could have known that Seth Greer was heading for WRCL the night he was killed. Lloyd Dixon had told him. Nolan had said he'd been out with friends. Assume a beeper. Assume a return telephone call to Lloyd Dixon, who had overheard Seth Greer telling Rebecca where he was going.

The shiny brass railing turned up another level, the stairs getting narrower. Gail saw the flash of Karen's sneakers in the dim light. "Would you slow down?"

Nolan had to be working for Lloyd Dixon. Perhaps it had been Dixon who suggested using the controversy with the exiles. That would explain why Dixon had apparently not been worried about it. He had let the situation continue in order to make murder look like political terrorism.

But the police had not been fooled. Detective Delgado had explained to Gail why they did not suspect the exiles. There was no communiqué. In addition, the method was wrong. If a killer had really wanted to make Seth Greer's murder look like a political act, he would have used a pipe bomb. *Pipe bombs are as Cuban as the royal palm tree.* And Gail had sat with Tom Nolan on his patio having sandwiches, telling him everything.

Holding onto the railing, Gail sank down on a step. Her legs were shaking. Even now, two weeks after the bombing, her body had not completely recovered, but it wasn't just that. She was staggered by the knowledge that she might have enabled Rebecca Dixon's death.

Nolan had made the bombing look like an attack on the opera. He had somehow maneuvered Rebecca into position and set the timer. Gail remembered how annoyed he had been that she had unexpectedly showed up. *We don't have much time.* He waited for her to leave, then knocked Rebecca unconscious. Possibly strangled her. A blow to the head or bruises on her neck would hardly show after a pipe bomb explosion.

How easy. Put Rebecca in the chair, put the bomb under the table. Set the timer for ten or fifteen seconds, run through the workroom, around the corner, crouch behind Jeffrey Hopkins's desk. Hands over the ears, eyes closed. Then come out limping and roll in the ashes. A cut to the arm and a bump on the head for good measure.

After the shocked silence following Seth Greer's murder, Thomas Nolan had been ordered not to talk to the press, not to stir things up again, but he had made some outrageous statements, setting off the controversy all over again. The bombing was at first assumed to be the work of militant exiles, right down to the communiqué from a phony anti-Castro group. Until the announcement that Felix Castillo was wanted for murder.

Still clinging to the brass balustrade, Gail lowered her forehead to her hand. Point four. Thomas Nolan was the one who had reported seeing Felix Castillo's van driving through the parking lot before the bombing. It had been his tip that sent the police to Castillo's house, finding the black powder and bullets like those that had killed Seth.

Gail heard music and remembered Karen. She ran up the remaining stairs, coming out in the top balcony.

The second act had begun. She found Karen with her chin on the railing, a small solitary figure among all the empty seats. Gail hugged her and sat down.

She barely took note of what was going on in the opera. Giovanni attempting to seduce Elvira once again, only to trick her and laugh about it. Then disguising himself as his own servant.

Felix Castillo had suggested Thomas Nolan was a hit man, and Gail hadn't listened. Castillo had suggested that a sniper's rifle would fit in that suitcase Nolan had brought back from Costa Rica. A contract killer in the disguise of an opera singer.

From this angle the street scene on the stage looked like a doll's village, and the singers were two inches tall. A group of men was preparing to capture Giovanni, but he sent them off in all directions. He tricked the leader into handing over his musket and pistol, then beat him up. A clever, ruthless man.

Why had Lloyd Dixon hired Thomas Nolan? A jealous husband, getting rid of his adulterous wife and her lover. No, that didn't fit. Rebecca had said that Lloyd knew about her affair and tolerated it, as long as she was discreet.

Second possibility: Rebecca and Seth had found out too much about the weapons. That made more sense. Or did it? Lloyd hadn't seemed so bothered when Anthony put a stop to the arms deal. *No skin off my nose, buddy.*

Octavio knew that Seth was coming to WRCL. Maybe he had hired Nolan. But was Octavio smart enough to orchestrate two murders and blame them on Felix Castillo? Anthony had been certain that Octavio was not a killer. He only wanted to overthrow the regime. But if the CIA were involved — if big American business interests were at stake —

Reaching into her purse, Gail remembered that her portable phone was still being repaired. She found a quarter and told Karen not to move, she'd be right back. The telephone was down two levels outside the ladies' room.

Anthony's secretary told her he was still in court, and she didn't really expect him back in the office, because he was meeting a client for dinner at seven o'clock.

"Oh, yes. He mentioned something about that. Tell, tell him —" Gail looped the steel phone cord around her hand. The party after the dress rehearsal would last until six. "Tell him to call me at home later. Thanks."

She hung up and leaned against the wall. *Anthony, I think Thomas Nolan was hired to shoot Seth Greer and set off the bomb that killed Rebecca.* How insane, to make a statement like that on no evidence whatsoever.

What if she was wrong? As a criminal defense attorney, Anthony Quintana had a funny quirk — he wanted evidence of guilt. She closed her eyes and thought of the argument Anthony might make to a jury on Thomas Nolan's behalf. Ladies and gentlemen, the prosecutor has produced *no* evidence that Rebecca Dixon and Seth Greer knew *anything* about Lloyd Dixon's activities. Second. Do you really believe that Thomas Nolan would have put himself anywhere near a *bomb?* To risk his hearing? His voice? Never. Third point. We know who did it. Felix Castillo. Bomb-making materials were found in his house. His fingerprints were on cartridges matching those at the scene of Seth Greer's murder. What has the prosecutor shown you from Thomas Nolan's house? Nothing.

Gail went back up the stairs.

As she walked along the front row, the curtains parted on a graveyard. Fog drifted among headstones and statues of the departed. Don Giovanni appeared, climbing a tree, then dropping over the wall, another narrow escape. He laughed with his servant about it. Then a deep, hollow voice came from somewhere, and Giovanni drew his sword.

"Wow," said Karen. "Mom, look!"

One of the statues was moving. Gail said, "That's the Commendatore, the man Giovanni killed at the beginning. He says, 'You'll have your last laugh soon.' But Giovanni's not afraid. He invites him to dinner. 'Will you come or not?' "

"The statue is nodding!" Karen said.

Looking over the rail, Gail could see her mother sitting with some friends. She tugged on Karen's hand. "Come on, let's go back down. Gramma will think we deserted her."

Karen was bored with the next scenes — until the ghost of the Commendatore showed up in the dining room at Giovanni's villa. The statue demanded repentance. Giovanni refused, and the pits of hell opened up. Hunchbacked demons swarmed out with pitchforks. Whatever the set designer had used for flames looked frighteningly real, and steam hissed from hidden vents in the stage. The music reached a crescendo, Giovanni screamed, and an elevator under the stage lowered him down.

Then, in Mozart's odd way of joining frivolity to tragedy, the music was suddenly uptempo, everyone happy again, the remaining characters coming on to deliver the moral of the story — evildoers get what they deserve.

Gail's spirits were not lifted.

She had not intended to stay for the donor party, but Karen wanted to, so they joined the crowd in the rehearsal hall. Gail heard someone say, "If you ask me, Giovanni is the only one with any spunk.

Nobody else knows how to have a good time."

The hall buzzed with congratulations. The orchestra had played wonderfully. The cast had been brilliant. The opera would be a smash. Jeffrey Hopkins gave Thomas Nolan a hug, careful not to touch the makeup on his face. Standing closer, Gail could see the fine net of the wig, which had been crafted of real human hair. For the last scene he had worn a loose white shirt with lace at the cuffs and a red embroidered vest over black satin knee pants and white hose. The heels on his shoes gave him another inch in height. He towered.

"Congratulations," Gail said. "A terrific performance."

He made a slight bow.

"Your voice seems to have recovered."

He spoke softly. "I was lucky. So were you." He smiled at a woman handing him a glass of champagne. The woman started to speak, but Gail beat her to it and said she needed to borrow Mr. Nolan for a minute. She maneuvered him so their backs were to the crowd.

"So your piano teacher's first name is Elvira. What a coincidence. Does Miss Wells really exist, or did you make her up, too?" Gail looked straight at him.

The makeup gave him such odd eyes, pale blue outlined in dark brown. One black eyebrow was painted higher than the other in permanent ironic jest. His face was several shades darker than normal. "All the world's a stage, Gail, and reality is what you think it is."

"What is that supposed to mean?"

He saluted with his champagne. "Whatever you want it to mean. Excuse me, I've got to get cleaned up, then make happy talk for an hour. It comes with the job."

She watched him go toward the dressing rooms, having to stop several times, people smiling up at him. She heard his deep laughter, his modest expression of thanks. She tried to imagine him standing in the shadows of the building next door to WRCL. Pulling out his sniper's rifle, sighting the laser on Seth Greer's chest.

If Lloyd or Octavio had not hired Thomas Nolan, then who had? Some group that knew about Castillo's background as a spy, and was powerful enough to convince local police he was responsible for two murders.

The same people would want to know why the shipment of weapons to Cuba had never been made. Lloyd Dixon, whereabouts unknown, would give up Anthony

Quintana in a heartbeat.

Gail wanted out of here. Too many people and too much noise. Too many mouths open in laughter. She looked around for Karen and found her in serious conversation with one of the little horned demons, a woman not much taller than Karen. "Go already? Mom!"

Irene agreed to take Karen home with her after the party. She looked at her watch. "Well, I suppose we'll be here till six or so. Where are you going?"

"I have to deliver something for a client."

"You look so pale. Are you all right?"

"I'm fine. I'll meet you at your house. We'll go out to dinner, my treat."

Curtains were drawn in the mansion at the front of the property. Gail hoped the owners were still out of town. She looked both ways, then turned quickly into the driveway, stopping her car behind some hedges where it could not be seen from the street. She got out and walked to the rear entrance of Tom Nolan's cottage. The green grass, dappled with shade, stretched to the bay.

She had tried to call Anthony again before leaving the theater, but he had still not returned to his office. She could not afford to wait by the pay phone in the lobby.

Gail shaded a glass pane in the French door and looked through, seeing the evidence of a musician's life. Grand piano, scores, sheet music, and classical CDs by the dozens. How irrational it seemed, thinking of Thomas Nolan as anything more than an opera singer or that a sniper's rifle was being aimed at Anthony because of what he knew. *Reality is what you think it is.*

There was only one way to find out.

Gail checked her watch. 5:20. She did not expect to be here longer than ten minutes. On her previous visit, she had not noticed a burglar alarm. No security company stickers in the window, no wires. Her hand was poised over the doorknob on one of the French doors. She hoped there was not a deadbolt requiring a key from the other side.

Behind her, water splashed in the coral rock fountain.

She stared at the glass. She looked at her watch again. 5:24.

"Oh, just do it and get it over with." She spotted a piece of scalloped edging stone in the flowerbed. After a glance toward both sides of the property, she picked it up. Touched it to the glass pane beside the doorknob. Swung it back, then forward. The glass shattered like a sonic boom passing over. Gail flung away the stone, sat in one of the metal chairs, and crossed her legs. She waited for barking dogs or someone wanting to know what the hell that noise was.

After a minute she patted the stone back into the flowerbed. The lock did not need a key. She turned the bolt and went inside.

A dish towel hung from the oven, and she borrowed it to wipe off her fingerprints. There were dishes in the sink. Carryout containers in the trash. A big ice chest on the counter, which seemed odd. She opened it and saw milk, orange juice, Swiss cheese, and three bottles of beer. She looked in all the cabinets, seeing nothing out of the ordinary.

She made a quick tour of the living room. Nothing behind the sofa but dust. Nothing under the sofa cushions, in the piano bench, or in the closet by the front door. The dining area near the kitchen had an oak table and four chairs.

In the hall she opened a door, saw linens and cleaning supplies. Nothing under the towels or behind the vacuum cleaner.

5:28. The bathroom. Blond hair in the shower stall. A dozen kinds of shampoo and conditioner. Cleaning supplies under the cabinet. The usual razor, aftershave, dental floss, et cetera behind the mirror. She opened the hamper and found dirty clothes.

Then to the bedroom. Light flooded in through the closed windows, which faced west. The room felt hot and short of oxygen, but Gail knew it was only her nervousness beginning to bite. Plenty of time, she told herself. Bed unmade, pillows askew at the head. Blue sheets, matching duvet. Nightstand with telephone, score to *Boris Gudonov*, several colored markers, and a Russian dictionary. Drawer contained porno videos. Gail pushed it shut.

She looked at her watch again. Only 5:30. The closet contained clothing — big surprise. Two tuxedos in garment bags. Likewise pleated shirts. Leather shoes, running shoes, boots, sandals. An empty suit bag. And a suitcase. Gail stared up at it. She could hear her breath rushing in and out of her lungs. She reached up carefully and poked it to see if anything was inside. It felt light. She brought it down and unzipped it anyway. No rifle. No scope or silencer. No bomb parts.

The realization was starting to dawn that she had committed a felony with nothing to show for it. She went to the bureau and opened drawers. Shirts, sweaters, workout clothes. Nothing. She looked at her watch. Told herself to relax.

To the dresser. A television and VCR sat on one corner. Top drawer. Bills, envelopes, checkbook, some cash. A few personal photos. Friends skiing. A postcard from Milan, someone named Fredericka. A small frame that opened up to show a three-by-five color snapshot, teenaged Tom Nolan at a piano with a blond girl standing behind him, probably another student. Gail knew it was Nolan only because she had seen the same face in her high school yearbook. She looked through some bills. Letters from friends. Nothing with Dixon's or Reyes's name on it. She glanced through his checkbook. No unusual deposits. Neat handwriting. Balance $4,389.18. Found an appointment book, flipped through it. Rehearsal schedules. Phone numbers. Dixon or Reyes not listed.

She pushed the drawer shut. She had been wrong. Glanced at her watch. 5:35.

With one last look around, she wiped the doorknob and went back down the hall, wanting only to get the hell out. She hung the dish towel back on the oven handle.

Shards of glass glittered on the wood floor in the living room. Through the broken pane she heard the fountain. Water splashed into the basin below.

What a weird feeling, she thought. As if

suddenly she were standing by the seawall looking back at the cottage. Seeing a woman at the door, a grand piano behind her. The woman looking through broken glass at a fountain, the water gushing out.

She heard Anthony's voice. *Los Pozos is a small village in the hills . . . covered in mist and rain, and the earth is red. . . . We lived . . . in a house that belonged to the church . . . no plumbing, but there was a well. "Pozos" means "wells," so at least we had plenty of fresh water.*

Gail could see the woman in the doorway backing up, disappearing into the cottage.

Moving down the hallway again, hurrying before the thought disappeared. As if coming out of a dream, wanting to hang onto it before it vanished like mist.

To the bedroom, open the top dresser drawer. And lift out the frame with the snapshot. Unfold it.

Gail stared down at Tommy Nolan, then the blond girl. The freckles on her face had thrown Gail off at first, but the girl was not a teenager. *When I was young, I wanted to be a concert pianist. Miss Wells — my teacher — said no. You should sing. I owe everything to her.*

Rebecca had said, *Emily was a scholarship student. She gave piano lessons to earn spending money.*

How had Seth described Emily Davis? *A pretty girl, loads of freckles.*

Gail heard her own low moan as she put the picture back. "Oh, no. Oh, my God." She closed the drawer with the tip of her finger. She felt a chill so intense the hair on her arms stood up.

She looked in the mirror, seeing the woman again, such a pale face, then behind her the mussed bed with the duvet hanging off the end of it. She turned slowly around.

Kneeling on the carpet, she lifted the hem of the duvet, and bent over to peer underneath the bed.

It was as if she had known all along it would be there. No surprise.

She slid it out. An expensive Hartmann, tweed with brown leather trim. Not new. There was something inside, but not a great deal of weight. She ran her hand over the surface.

In her intense concentration, with every sense focused on the zipper rasping smoothly around a corner of the suitcase, Gail did not register the other sound until a second after it had occurred: the creak of wood in the doorway.

By then it was too late.

Thomas Nolan had come home.

THIRTY-ONE

"What are you doing here?"

Nolan spoke in nearly a whisper, not believing what he saw — Gail Connor kneeling at the foot of his bed unzipping a small brown suitcase.

In those few seconds she managed to find in his expression more astonishment than anger. "Oh, Tom. I'm really sorry. I wanted to — to see your house. That's all." Legs shaking, she stood up. She found her breath again. "I mean — I'm such a fan. I wanted something of yours. A memento."

Looking at her sideways as if studying an apparition whose reality was still not certain, he moved slowly into the room. A blue denim shirt was tucked neatly into black jeans. His hair was free, curling past wide shoulders, and the stage makeup was gone. Once more the eyebrows were only vague arches on the bony ridge over deep-set eyes. His lips had vanished entirely, sucked inward as he continued to watch her.

"I thought . . . a shirt . . . some pages from a piano score. You were at the party."

"So you decided to burglarize my house."

"Please don't have me arrested. I'll leave. You'll never see me again." With a foot she shoved the suitcase under the bed.

"Why were you opening that?"

"I wasn't. I didn't actually open it."

He stooped to check the zipper.

"I'll pay for the glass I broke. And the bother." She moved toward the door. "Whatever you want."

His eyes fixed on her. "Did you come looking for this?"

"Tom, I don't know what it is, and I don't care."

He came across the room. "What else did you look at? What did you touch?"

"Nothing." She was walking backward in the hall. "I'm really sorry."

She whirled around and ran. Fingers slid off her shoulder as if a cat had swiped at her. The heels of her pumps pounded out of the hall, across the living room, everything a blur, then toward the open French door.

Across the patio. She lost a shoe taking the turn around the cottage. A scream for help died in her throat when trees and sky whirled and the grass rushed toward her. She put out her arms and rolled.

Tom Nolan's hand became a fist. In the next instant her head exploded. The light wavered and went out.

Gail came slowly out of the darkness, and for a while she drifted. Then the pain dragged her into full consciousness. It burned down the side of her head into her neck. She shifted her jaw. Nothing broken. Her eyes opened. She saw a grand piano. A worn oriental rug prickled her cheek.

Then she felt the constriction around her wrists and ankles. She was bound with rope and lying on the floor in Thomas Nolan's cottage. The window behind the piano showed a colorless sky. The light was fading. The curtains across the French doors were drawn shut.

Music soared from the stereo on the bookcase opposite the sofa. An opera. Wagner. Then a deep voice from somewhere behind her joined in. *Tristan und Isolde.* Gail concentrated to orient herself. Her back was to the kitchen. She heard a cabinet drawer shut.

She shifted. Her hands were tied behind her, numb and tingling. The blood came back into the arm she lay on, and she grimaced. With effort she twisted around. Saw the dining area between herself and the kitchen. Everything at a crazy angle, the lamp hanging sideways, the table coming from the other direction to meet it. The

French doors were closed. Someone in a blue shirt stood in the kitchen doorway on long black legs.

She turned her head and the world righted itself. Tom Nolan said, "How could you screw things up like this?" She didn't know if he was talking to her or to himself.

"What are you going to do?" she asked.

He squatted down beside her and flipped his hair over his shoulder. "Where are you supposed to be right now?"

"My mother's house. She's expecting me. My daughter — Karen —"

"Do they know where you are?"

The *yes* caught in her mouth. If she said it, then what? Would he go and find them? She shook her head. "I didn't tell anyone."

"Where is Anthony Quintana?" Nolan poked her shoulder when Gail felt dizzy and closed her eyes. "Where is he?"

"Having dinner with a client."

"Does he have a portable telephone? How do you get in touch with him?"

Hesitantly she asked, "Why do you want to know?"

Nolan exhaled, then said patiently, "I want him to come and take you out of here. If he gives me any trouble, I'll call the police and press charges against you."

"Call his voice mail. He has a beeper."

Gail gave Nolan the number. When he stood up, she started trembling with relief. Nolan didn't know. He didn't know what she had found in the drawer. He didn't know why she had come.

Her eyes followed him across the room to the stereo. The Wagner went off, and the room was silent. "Tom, untie me. My arms hurt. I won't run away."

He held up a hand — wait — and picked up the cordless telephone by the sofa. After a few seconds, he said, "Hi. Mr. Quintana, this is Tom Nolan. I've run into a problem. You're probably busy, but this is extremely urgent. Could you call me back as soon as you get this message?" He left his own number and hit the button for disconnect.

With a bubble of fear rising in her chest, Gail said, "Why didn't you mention me?"

Nolan hung up the phone. "When he gets here, you can go."

"Please don't hurt him."

"Why would I hurt him? And I'm not going to untie you. Just lie there and be quiet." He sat in the armchair and tapped tented fingers on his forehead in a steady rhythm. "I have to think."

When the telephone rang, Nolan slowly lowered his hands. It rang again. He picked up the handset and carried it down the hall into his bedroom. The door closed.

Gail rolled against the sofa and used it to get herself on her knees. Pressing her lips together not to let out a sound, she walked herself across the rug. The skin on her knees burned through torn hose. She would somehow get to her feet, maneuver through the curtains, and turn the doorknob on the French doors. She swept the curtain aside with a shoulder and saw that the hurricane shutters had been rolled across the doors. She collapsed to a sitting position, then struggled up and went toward the kitchen.

A knife. She could visualize it. Heavy, sharp, with a wooden handle. Somehow get to her feet. Open a drawer. Sit down. Wedge the knife between her heels, cut the rope on her wrists. There had to be a way. There was time. Anthony was with a client. He wouldn't want to come. Nolan would have to convince him.

The ice chest was on the kitchen floor. Gail dropped her shoulder on it, intending to lever herself to a standing position. Her knee dragged through a puddle of water. Gasping for breath, she got up halfway and saw a man lying next to the cabinets. The water had run from his clothing.

As if in slow motion her mind pulled in the details: rumpled black clothing, gray mustache, close-cropped graying hair. Everything gray. The face. The hands. He lay on his side. Arms crossed on his chest and tied in place. The rope around his knees was looped around his neck, pulling him into a tight package.

Gail noticed that the left hand had only a thumb and two fingers. It was Felix. She let out a scream of horror and rage. Now she knew how his fingerprints had been placed on the evidence. The night the bomb went off, Felix was already dead. She knew where Nolan had kept him.

A few seconds later Tom Nolan was dragging her by an elbow to the middle of the living room. He dropped her, then pushed a hand through his hair to get it off his face. "I told you to stay where you were."

Gail was shaking with terror. "Anthony —"

"He's on his way. I told him the police were about to arrest me for beating up a member of the crew. I had just hung up when you screamed." Nolan pulled back his cuff to see his watch. "He said he'd be here in half an hour."

Numbly Gail said, "Seth and Rebecca

and Felix. Now you want Anthony. Please don't. Please."

Nolan stared down at her.

"I know everything, Tom. Your piano teacher. Miss Wells. Oh, my God. It was there all the time. Los Pozos. Emily Davis went to Los Pozos in 1978. You left school in the spring semester of 1979. I never connected the two. Is that why you tried to kill yourself? I remember they found you in the bandmaster's cottage."

Gail twisted to a sitting position and leaned on the sofa. "The State Department sent a report to Emily's aunt. Did she show it to you?"

"Yes. It had all their names."

"Anthony didn't kill Emily Davis! Neither did Seth or Rebecca. Tom, please. It was Felix Castillo. Felix confessed to me."

"What do you mean? Felix wasn't there. His name wasn't in the report."

"Of course not. He was a Cuban spy."

Nolan bent down to look into her face, and his hair swung forward. He slowly enunciated every word. "Felix Castillo was in Cuba until 1980. Rebecca Dixon told me that. Oh, very good, Gail. Blame Emily's murder on a man who wasn't there."

"But he was there. He shot her because she spied for the CIA."

"*Emily?* That's ridiculous."

Gail shouted at him, "If Felix wasn't there, then why did you kill him?"

"He was asking me questions. Where had I been the night Seth died? What friends had I been with? Where did we go? I came home late after the recital at the Dixons' apartment. I beeped Felix and said someone had just threatened to come over and kill me. Felix arrived and I shot him as he got out of his van."

"You vicious, heartless son of a bitch," Gail said between clenched teeth. "Why did you have to kill his girlfriend, too?"

"I'm sorry about her, but she started screaming. I had to go to Felix's house, and I didn't expect her to be there."

The tears were rising again, and Gail forced herself to hold them back. "How did you know Seth was going to WRCL?"

"I was following him. I had planned to do it that night at his house, but Rebecca came over, and then you. When the two of you had left, I followed him to the radio station. A stroke of luck."

Laughing, Gail lowered her head to the sofa cushion. "I thought — at one point — that you were working for Lloyd Dixon. And then I thought you did it for the CIA, and the CIA had framed Felix Castillo."

Nolan narrowed his eyes, studying her in that sideways fashion. "The CIA again. You're raving." He walked to the bookcase.

"Tom, please don't hurt Anthony. He didn't do anything to her, I swear it."

From behind a row of books he pulled out a red metal can and a small cardboard box. "You've been seduced by a master. I tried to warn you several times, but it went right over your head. Too bad you're not more observant."

"Tom, he didn't do it! None of them did!"

With slow deliberation he set the box and metal gasoline can on the table. The hanging lamp made his hair into a penumbra of light. "They destroyed the most beautiful creature — the sweetest, most gentle — They took her to that backward, violent, filthy place, murdered her, and left her there."

"But *why?*"

"Why? Because she discovered the real purpose of their trip — to establish a connection for illegal drugs — and they thought she would tell the authorities."

Gail wavered on the edge of hysteria. Version number five. She thought she might lose her sanity. "Where did you hear that?"

With slow paces he walked across the

room, his soft-soled boots making no sound. "Emily told me she was involved with a Cuban named Tony. She said he wanted her to go with him to Nicaragua. I begged her not to. She said, 'Oh, it's only for the summer. I promise I'll be back. I'm going to be your accompanist. You'll be a great opera singer someday.' She kissed me. She said . . . I was the one she would always love. Then she was gone."

Nolan paused to get his voice under control. "Three months later this same Tony informed Emily's aunt that she had fallen in love with one of the men in the town. That was impossible. Emily had such talent, such beauty and promise. When I read the report from the State Department — Emily was presumed dead — I fell into despair. I tried to kill myself. Later, I vowed to find out what had happened to her. There was civil unrest in Nicaragua until 1991. In 1992 I spent a week in Los Pozos. People remembered the four Americans, one of whom called himself a Cuban. They remembered Emily. They called her *la rubia* — the blonde. Her friends made connections with a supplier. *La rubia* found out and tried to leave. They killed her."

He now stood so close that Gail was forced to look up the length of black jeans and blue denim torso. His nose projected like the beak of a bird of prey. "I have planned this for a long time. I learned all about them. Their history, their habits. I even know about you. No, I don't know which one of them killed her, but they're all guilty — Anthony Quintana the most culpable of all." Nolan laughed. "And now he defends criminals. Drug dealers and murderers. He hasn't changed."

Gail leaned against Tom Nolan's legs and wept. "Please, you don't know him at all. He isn't what you think. We're engaged to be married. I love him!"

Tom pushed her away, and she toppled over. "Where's your purse? I need your keys to move your car."

"Please don't do this. Please!"

He grabbed her shoulders and shook her, and pain rocketed through her head. "The keys."

"In my pocket," she gasped.

He patted her skirt pockets and found the keys. Then went to get more rope. He bound her knees together, then looped a line through her wrists to her ankles.

"You were fifteen years old! She was being nice to you. Tom, think!"

From his pocket Nolan pulled a handkerchief and tried to cram it into Gail's mouth while she writhed on the floor. She bit him. He slapped her. She tasted blood. Softly he said, "Gail. Don't make this difficult. You have to be quiet." He tied another handkerchief around her head to hold the first one. She thought she might vomit. She pushed with her tongue, then choked and coughed on saliva. Nolan rechecked all the knots.

Sitting on his heels, he looked at her, his features softening. "I'm sorry. I really am." He patted her shoulder and stood up. He looked around the room. "Felix will show up to kill me while Anthony is here. Gunshots are exchanged. The bomb goes off accidentally. No. That won't work."

He took the gasoline and box off the table and took them into the kitchen. Gail heard him talking to himself. "You and I are having an affair? Anthony arrives to kill us both. He gets you, I get him — But that doesn't take care of Felix."

Nolan came out again and crossed the room to lift the lid on the grand piano. "I think Felix is holding me prisoner when you and Anthony show up. Felix shoots both of you, but gunfire ignites the gasoline." From inside the piano Nolan took a pair of latex gloves and snapped them on. Then he lifted out a longish black plastic case. He lowered the piano lid, set the case on top, and clicked open the latches. "This is Felix's rifle. At least, it has his fingerprints on it."

On the floor Gail moaned and choked. Her nose was clogged from crying, and she couldn't get enough air.

The barrel screwed into the breech. The scope clicked into the barrel. Nolan attached a silencer. "The fire is necessary because of Felix. He's starting to decompose. I'll be in the bedroom. There's a fire extinguisher in the hall closet I can use, so I'll be safe." Cartridges clicked into the magazine. "Safe enough."

The barrel pointed at the floor as Nolan came over to stand beside Gail. "Try to breathe slowly." He checked his watch, then went out the front door.

Gail prayed to go deaf rather than lie helplessly waiting to hear the pop of a silenced rifle. Her lungs burned. She wiped her nose on her shoulder and concentrated on breathing slowly. Slowly. Gradually the panic lifted. Anthony would never leave a client in the middle of dinner to advise Tom Nolan on an assault and battery case. What egotism to think a criminal lawyer would drop everything and rush right over. If Anthony had said he would come, he had to suspect something. He would come with the police.

The windows were losing light quickly. Gail lay on the floor no longer thinking of the pain in her body, but of Karen. Her energy, her sweet, mischievous smile. How little time they had spent together lately. Gail vowed to change. But her thoughts kept going to Anthony. *Please let him know it's a trap.* She thought of their arguments. How petty and selfish she had been. She swore never to be cross with him again. She would be patient and kind. Always gentle.

There was a thud at the door and Gail stiffened. The door flew inward, then Tom Nolan appeared, leaning over, the rifle across his back on its shoulder strap.

He was dragging Anthony inside. Gail heard her own muffled cry of anguish.

"He arrived early, and as I thought —" Tom pulled Anthony's .45 pistol out of the holster under his jacket. "He arrived armed."

Anthony lay facedown on the rug ten feet away from her with his arms curved above his head. Gail strained to see him. His back slowly rose and fell. He was alive. She saw no blood.

Tom Nolan closed the door. "I need to think. I need to set all this up first. I haven't decided yet how to do it." He lay the pistol and rifle on the lid of the grand piano.

She watched him go into the kitchen and come out with rope and a knife. Within five minutes he had Anthony tied up in the same manner he had used on her. Then he went down the hall toward the bedroom. A drawer opened and shut. Anthony was lying motionless on his side. Gail scooted nearer. She yearned to touch him. To say his name. *Anthony, I love you.* Tears leaked out of her eyes and ran into her hair.

Nolan returned and knelt to stuff one handkerchief into Anthony's mouth and tie it in with another. Anthony made a muffled moan and coughed. When Nolan had gone into the kitchen, Gail moved closer. Their knees were touching, and she could look into his face. She pressed her forehead to his chest and felt the steady beating of his heart.

Something thudded onto wood. She twisted her head around. Nolan was setting the table for dinner. Three place settings. Three wine glasses. A bowl of fruit. The meaning of this slammed into her mind. The ghost of the Commendatore had interrupted Don Giovanni's dinner to give him one last chance to repent. Tom Nolan was playing the part of avenger — but this Commendatore offered no mercy.

Nolan came out with a pitcher and filled

water glasses. A muffled wail stuck in Gail's throat. She wheezed, dizzy for breath, for air. She began to feel faint. It would be better, she thought, to die now, and quickly.

Then the gag was jerked down over her chin. Nolan pulled out the handkerchief. "If you scream," he said, "I'll put it back in."

Coughing, she shook her head. "Tom —" She took a breath and lay still, twisted on her back, lying halfway on her hands. "Please do me one favor." He sat on his haunches and looked at her. "If you're going to . . . kill him, please don't let him wake up first and see me."

"I don't know. It depends." Tom shook his hair back.

"One other thing. Do you have a CD of *Aïda*? You must have. Please put on the last scene." She took another deep breath, then whispered, "That's all I ask."

He put his hands on his knees and pushed himself up. At the stereo he clicked through his CD collection. She asked if he had ever performed in that opera. "I sang Ramphis in Chicago," he said. "The high priest." He smiled. "The man who condemns Radames to death."

He aimed his remote at the stereo, and a tenor voice soared from the speakers. Radames, sealed in the tomb, aware of his fate, praying that Aïda never knows of his death. But to his horror, she has hidden herself in the same tomb. They will perish together.

Beyond tears or pain, Gail said, "Tom. You were right. I'm sorry I lied. Felix wasn't in Nicaragua."

He glanced up from the libretto. "I know that."

She said, "The real story was too complicated. I don't know why the people in Los Pozos told you those things, but I can guess. They were afraid. Anything was better than the truth."

Tom Nolan looked at her.

"I was looking for the truth, too," she said. "Anthony asked me to marry him, and I said yes, but there was a darkness in his past that he wouldn't talk about. I knew a little. When he got back from Nicaragua, he spent two weeks in a mental hospital. When he got out he went to New York, got his law degree, married, and had children. His marriage failed. I knew something tragic had happened, but I didn't know what.

"I asked Rebecca and Seth for help. They didn't want to talk about it either, but finally they did. We talked the night I went to Seth's house. Before . . . he died."

Behind her, a muffled moan came from Anthony. Nolan's eyes flicked toward him.

Gail projected her voice just over the music. "I read the same report you did, but I had more. A CIA report. Lloyd Dixon gave it to me after the memorial service for Rebecca. Lloyd has contacts. He was with the CIA in Nicaragua in 1986, flying missions for Oliver North. When you went to his apartment last week, who was there? Octavio Reyes. What do you think they were doing? Those men weren't just investors. They were plotting the overthrow of Castro, and the U.S. government knows about it. Felix Castillo told me about all this. When he disappeared, I thought the CIA had done it, and you were working for them."

Thomas Nolan tossed the CD case back onto the shelf. "This is insane."

"People cover things up, Tom. The people in Los Pozos were protecting themselves. What did they tell you about Pablo?"

"I never heard of this."

"Of course you didn't. Pablo Bermudez. Commandante Zero, a captain in Somoza's army. They were brutal. Anyone suspected of working for the rebels would be brutalized, tortured, murdered. Rebecca told me about seeing bodies lying by the side of the road. It was horrible."

Anthony shifted. Moaned again.

Gail spoke more quickly. "They went

there out of idealism. Seth as a carpenter, Rebecca as a nurse. Anthony and Emily wanted to teach. Oh, Tom. They were in love. He adored her. Emily's aunt hated him because he was Cuban. She tried to keep them apart, but when Anthony asked Emily to go with him, she said yes. She believed in his ideals. Anthony talked about how poor these people were. They had no land, nothing. Somoza and his friends owned everything. It's true that Anthony met the Sandinistas while he was there. He wasn't afraid. He'd grown up in Cuba. Seth and Rebecca warned him to stay away, but he was young and naive and confident of his own power."

On the stereo, the chorus of Egyptians began to sing slowly. Chanting, invoking the gods.

"One day Pablo, the army captain, invited the Americans to his house in the hills overlooking Los Pozos. He had a piano that his wife had used before her death, and he wanted to hear music again. After dinner Emily played for him. He immediately fell in love with her. He wanted her, but she wouldn't have anything to do with him, of course. So Pablo had someone accuse Anthony of working with the Sandinistas. Anthony was thrown into a jail cell in La Vigia.

He was tortured, but he refused to confess to something he hadn't done. Pablo told Emily he would let Anthony go if she gave herself to him. Otherwise, Anthony and all the others would be taken into the jungle and shot. Emily knew that Pablo meant what he said.

"When Anthony was let out of jail, he went to Pablo's house, but Emily had to tell him she had gone willingly with Pablo. Rebecca and Seth convinced him to leave with them. They left the country. And here the story runs out. Emily disappeared. I believe that she either killed herself or she tried to escape, and Pablo had her shot. What I read in the CIA report matches everything I heard from Anthony, Rebecca, and Seth. If the people told you anything else, it was because they didn't dare accuse Pablo. He's a high official in the government now. They had to blame somebody. You suggested the Americans, and the most logical crime to throw at them was dealing drugs. Tom, it wasn't true."

Tom Nolan had sat on the sofa as Gail spoke. His hands dangled between his knees, and his hair fell to cover his face.

"That was the darkness that Anthony has been trying to escape. Emily saved him, but at what cost? When he found out that she was missing, presumed dead, he nearly lost his mind with grief. They were all ruined. Rebecca took pills to forget. Seth couldn't forget, and he lost his faith and his courage. He was on his way to WRCL that night to regain his self-respect when he was shot. Before she died, Rebecca told me she couldn't go on without Seth.

"Oh, Tom, you've been lied to. I consider you innocent because you didn't know, but now you do. Please don't do this anymore. I beg you for mercy. They've all suffered, just as you have. I beg you for his life."

Aïda's ethereal soprano floated through the room. *O terra, addio. Addio, valle di pianti* . . . Farewell to earth, farewell vale of tears —

Gail said, "He loved her. He never meant to take her away from you. She died, and he has suffered as much as you have, Tom."

A noi si schiude il ciel e l'alme errante, volano al raggio dell'eterno di. The heavens open and our souls escape to the rays of eternal day.

He went to the table and picked up the pistol. Gail leaned back against Anthony and felt his warmth.

Nolan stood over them. "There is no forgiveness. *Pace t'imploro.*"

Gail closed her eyes.

Then heard footsteps retreating down the hall. She looked to see the bedroom door closing.

The last bars of the opera were soaring from the speakers. The chorus invoking God. Aïda's rival, Amneris, begging the spirits for peace. *Pace t'imploro . . . pace . . . pace.* And above them all the fading voices of the doomed lovers.

Like their breath running out in the sealed tomb, the last notes faded away.

There was silence. Then Gail heard a gunshot.

Shortly thereafter, when Anthony awoke, Gail tugged at his gag with her teeth. Quickly she explained what had happened. Her words — and her tears — poured out. Maneuvering around so that he could feel the rope that bound her wrists, he loosened them, and in this way they freed themselves.

Anthony picked up the rifle, not expecting to need it. He led the way down the hall and pushed open the door with the barrel.

A lamp was on by the bed.

The pistol had dropped near Thomas Nolan's hand. He lay with a framed photograph on his chest. His other hand rested on a small brown suitcase.

Lowering the rifle, Anthony went across the room. He touched the suitcase. "What's this?"

Gail said, "No. Don't open it. I can tell you what's inside."

THIRTY-TWO

Thomas Nolan was buried in Miami, his place of birth. At the funeral his friends mourned, the curious came by the hundreds, and no one knew whether to be horrified or saddened. They preferred not to believe that Nolan had been crazy, except in the operatic manner of *Otello* or of Don José in *Carmen*. That he had committed four murders was, if not excused, at least understood in the elevated context of great passion. Anthony commented to Gail that if Thomas Nolan had been one of his clients, a murderer of no particular distinction, Nolan and his crimes would have been deplored.

The Miami Opera had been forced to scramble to find a replacement to sing the lead in *Don Giovanni*. Even with a few glaring gaffes on opening night, the public clamored for tickets. The opera sold out every performance, and two more were added.

After closing night, when media attention had moved on — and when certain bureaucratic difficulties had been taken care of —

another internment took place in the same cemetery.

A week or so later, on a warm sunny afternoon in mid-February, Anthony asked Gail if she would go with him to take flowers. The headstone had just been put in place.

It was a quiet, shady spot. Mockingbirds sang in nearby trees. Nolan's headstone, paid for by donations from friends, was an ornate affair of white marble. The other was simple. *Emily Davis, 1958–1978. At peace with God.*

Her aunt had passed away several years before, and her father could not be located. By choice more than by default, Anthony had taken over the arrangements. It had been suggested that both bodies be placed in the same coffin, or at least that their names be carved into the same stone, but Anthony did not think Emily would have wanted that. He had finally decided to purchase a site just across the walkway from Nolan's.

If Anthony had asked her to, Gail would have told the police that she had no idea whose remains were in the suitcase or why Thomas Nolan had turned homicidal, but Anthony was determined that Emily be buried properly. Gail had countered that revealing every last detail would accomplish nothing but to turn Anthony Quintana into an object of curiosity. They had finally agreed on what to say: With all his teenage passion, Thomas Nolan had loved Emily Davis, his young piano teacher. She and three friends had gone to Los Pozos as volunteers. She decided to stay and never came back. Nolan found her grave, then got it into his head that her friends were responsible for her death. Nolan killed Felix Castillo, who had become suspicious. Daisy had been in the way. Anthony was to have been the last victim, but for some reason or other Nolan changed his mind and committed suicide.

Later, Gail told Anthony the elaborate story she had spun for Tom Nolan — which in its way held more truth for him than the actual events. Nolan had wanted a story of passion and self-sacrifice. Gail had taken a chance, asking him to put on the last scene in *Aïda*, the story of an Ethiopian princess forced into slavery in the Egyptian court, beloved by Radames, himself betrothed to Amneris. He betrayed his country to save Aïda, but rather than escape, she chose to die with him. Amneris wanted vengeance, but as the lovers slowly suffocated, she stood outside the tomb praying for peace.

Pace t'imploro. At the end Thomas Nolan may have seen himself as Amneris. He had said, "There is no forgiveness." He meant none for himself. All he could ask for was mercy and peace.

These things went through Gail's mind as she stood with Anthony at the site of Emily's grave. She glanced at him. He had not spoken for several minutes, lost in his own thoughts.

He crossed himself, then leaned down to place the flowers on the grave. He looked at them for another moment, then turned and smiled at Gail. Hand in hand, they left the cemetery.

The Pedrosa house was not precisely on the way home, but Gail suggested they drop in to say hello. Until recently Anthony would never have considered such a thing, at least not without calling first.

Turning through the iron gates into the circular driveway, he put on his brakes. Gail saw a dark red Lexus parked near the front entrance. As far as she knew, Octavio Reyes had decided to move to Texas, taking the family with him.

"Did you know Octavio would be here?" she asked.

"No." His face wore that cool, impenetrable expression that she recognized as a mask for anger.

Gail said, "Let's not go in."

But he finished the turn and parked behind the Lexus.

Octavio Reyes had not been seen in public lately. He had been fired from WRCL, and his furniture business was up for sale. Bricks had been thrown through the plate glass windows of the showroom. It was said that Reyes had tricked Ernesto Pedrosa — a respected but elderly man — into supplying money and arms for a Cuban underground that did not in fact exist. Even worse, Reyes had already skimmed hundreds of thousands of dollars from Pedrosa's businesses to invest in the Cuban tourist industry.

Gail had been as shocked as anyone else, but Lloyd Dixon, in an interview with the *Miami Herald*, had sworn it was true. She had worried that someone might kill Octavio, but Anthony had said no, Octavio would be all right — as long as he stayed out of Miami. Feeling bad for Anthony's sister, Alicia, Gail had called to talk, but Alicia had refused to come to the telephone.

When the old aunt who served as housekeeper opened the door, Anthony asked if his grandfather was at home. His aunt said yes, his grandfather was in the study with *los* Reyes, and *la dama* was upstairs resting. *Los* Reyes. Meaning more than one. Gail assumed both Octavio and Alicia were speaking with Ernesto Pedrosa about some family matter.

When the aunt had left them, Gail said to Anthony, "What do you think?"

"I don't know." Stony-faced, he walked out of the foyer into the wide tiled hall that would take him to his grandfather's study. Gail followed, knowing that it was probably Alicia's presence that had prevented Anthony from asking her to wait in the living room.

Heavy wood muffled Octavio's angry voice. Anthony knocked, then opened the door. Gail saw past him — Ernesto Pedrosa seated on one end of the leather sofa, Alicia beside him crying, Octavio standing over both of them. They all looked around at Anthony, still in the hall.

In Spanish, Anthony asked his grandfather if everything was all right. The old man seemed tired, Gail thought. He leaned on the arm of the sofa, and his eyes were shadowed. Gail could guess what was going on. Octavio had asked Alicia to come plead his case. The old man was caught in the middle.

Anthony said quietly to Octavio, "You should go."

The look that passed between them was acid. Then Octavio made a stiff bow to Ernesto Pedrosa. He said that he and Alicia had to leave now, but wished both him and Digna good health.

"*Gracias,*" Pedrosa said. He held out an arm to Alicia. She kissed him goodbye.

Anthony told his grandfather he would be only a moment escorting Octavio to the door. Gail would wait with him.

The Reyeses came out, but before Gail could go in, Alicia closed the door. She brushed past Gail without acknowledging that she was there. She walked over to her brother and tried to slap him. Anthony jerked aside and caught her wrist in time.

She sobbed, "How? How could you do this?"

Anthony said nothing.

But Alicia continued to weep angry tears. "We lost our home, everything! We have to leave Miami!"

Anthony said, "No one is going to let you and the children starve, Alicia. You can stay here if you want. You don't have to go with him."

She drew in a ragged breath. "He's my husband!"

Octavio turned her away and told her to forget it. "Alicia, *olvídalo*."

Gail looked from one to the other in confusion. Alicia grabbed her arm. "Do you know what my brother is? Do you know the kind of man you want to marry?"

Anthony said, "Alicia —"

"No! Let me tell her. He's a liar! He's doing this because he hates my husband. Lloyd Dixon's mechanic told Octavio the truth. Anthony blackmailed Lloyd Dixon. He threatened to show photographs to the FBI unless Dixon told lies about Octavio. He never stole money from my grandfather. Never! He would never put money into Cuba. Anthony has turned everyone against us. My children are taunted at school."

Alicia brought her fists down on Anthony's chest. "How could you?" He tried to embrace her. She sobbed for a moment into his shoulder, then pushed him away. Quietly Anthony said to Octavio, "Take her out of here. She's upset."

In the foyer, Anthony stood by the front door until they had gone through it. He pushed the door shut, then stared at the dark carved wood.

Gail said, "Did you do that? Did you do what she said?"

Fiercely Anthony said, "He would have

destroyed this family, Gail. He would have brought the FBI here. They've been looking for a way to get to my grandfather for years. One of the men working at Sun Fashions is an FBI informant."

"What will happen to Alicia?"

"She made her choice." Then took a breath, no longer angry. "I won't let anything happen to her. Whatever she and the children need, they can have it."

Gail continued to look at him. "You didn't tell me."

"No, I didn't." He offered no apology.

There were shuffling footsteps in the hall. The soft thud of a cane. Ernesto Pedrosa had come out of his study.

The two men looked at each other. Anthony said formally, *"Señor, ¿cómo está?"*

Pedrosa lifted an arm and Anthony stepped forward to embrace him. *Un abrazo fuerte* — the embrace of respect and affection.

He knows, Gail thought to herself. The old man knew exactly what Anthony had done. He approved. Gail herself was not really surprised that Anthony's actions had been so devious, brutal, and complete. At the crude burial site in Los Pozos, he had killed a rebel soldier with a shovel to save himself and two friends.

Watching Anthony gently kiss his grandfather, she realized that she had barely begun to learn who he was.

Then Ernesto Pedrosa smiled at her and held out his arms.

THIRTY-THREE

"This house was built in 1927, very strong construction of coral rock and Dade County pine, which will last forever. It came through Hurricane Andrew perfectly — only some roof tiles blew off. Look at this beautiful porch, so shady. The house is on the historic register."

The realtor unlocked the front door and led them inside. Their footsteps echoed on wood floors. Gail and Anthony looked around at the fireplace, the Art Deco curves, the beamed ceiling. Karen ran for the stairs to see what was up there.

Silvia Sanchez was still talking. "Three bedrooms, three baths, and a study downstairs. The kitchen is charming."

Gail smiled at her. "You mean it's small?"

"No, *charming.*" She led the way through the dining room. "You must see it. Look. Room for a big table. An eat-in kitchen, perfect for a family. Don't you love the wood windows? They crank out, very historical."

Anthony muttered, "They stick in humid weather."

Gail opened a door and found a pantry. "This is nice. You don't see pantries anymore. Where are the washer and dryer?" When Mrs. Sanchez told her they were in the garage, which one could get to by going outside, Gail rolled her eyes.

The realtor only waved a hand. "This is no problem! You put them in the pantry. Remodeling is so easy."

Gail and Anthony glanced at each other. They obediently followed Mrs. Sanchez through the rear door of the kitchen onto an enclosed patio with a terra cotta floor. The floor had settled, and the tiles were cracked with age. They could not see through the windows for the untrimmed plants pressing against the glass, which was clouded with mildew and algae.

"Historical," whispered Anthony, "means you don't repaint even a closet without permission from bureaucrats on three different preservation boards."

Karen's clogs thudded across the living room, then she herself appeared, pushing open the French doors. Her face was flushed. "Mom! Anthony! Come upstairs! You have to see my room! There's a window that sticks out over the roof —"

"Dormer windows," said the realtor. "Four of them."

"And your and Anthony's room has a fireplace!"

Gail glanced at Mrs. Sanchez, then said quietly to Karen, "Sweetie, we're just looking right now."

"We've seen five houses today! This one is so cute."

The realtor was shoving against the back door with a shoulder, but it was stuck. Anthony said he would do it. The wood creaked, then the door flew open. Gail whispered, "There would be so much to do to this house."

"Mom, there's a park down the street."

"We'll see."

Karen gave her a look. "That means no."

When Gail turned around, she saw Anthony staring into the backyard as if the door had snapped back and hit him in the head. He slowly moved down the steps into the sparse and weedy grass. Wind sighed in the trees, and birds chirped.

A brick walkway led to a gazebo on one side, an overgrown rose garden on the other. Decades ago someone with a sense of harmony and balance had laid out the backyard. The wide, shady lawn sloped gently to an inlet that lapped at the seawall. The realtor's brochure had said the property backed up to a canal, but this was no canal.

Gail could see how the land curved out to the bay.

"I told you," Karen said. She flew off the steps and ran toward the gazebo, where she tried out the glider.

Anthony kept walking until he stood on the seawall.

Mrs. Sanchez folded her hands at her waist. She smiled at Gail.

Gail said, "I don't think so."

"It's a very nice property."

"Yes, well . . ." She sighed. "Let me go talk to him."

At the seawall Gail slid her hand into his. He had lost that stunned look, and now a smile had worked its way onto his lips. She said, "You like it, don't you?"

The smile disappeared. "It's an old house. They require a lot of work. On the other hand, it has character. It's not like the others we've seen. With a few touches here and there, I think it has possibility. But if you don't agree, we'll keep looking."

Gail shaded her eyes. "You can see Camagüey from here."

He made a soft laugh. "Do you think I want to go back?"

She raised a shoulder.

"Gail, I would never go back. I told you that."

"Maybe not being able to have something makes people want it more," she said.

"No. Everything I have — everything I want is here."

"I'll never be Cuban," she said. "Prepare yourself. I can't cook and I don't even want to learn. I like making my own living. And I have a rotten temper — which I promise to work on."

"Gail, one reason I love you is because you *aren't* Cuban. When I was married before — I don't mean to bring that up, but — she was so traditional I lost a sense of myself. With you, I feel . . ." His hands moved as if he could find words in the air.

"Confused?" Gail tugged on the lapels of his jacket. The diamond on her finger sparkled. It had looked good on his hand. She liked it better on hers.

"I feel . . . like myself." He laughed. "Whatever that is. My grandfather accuses me of being too American. Your relatives think of me as one hundred percent *cubano*. But I'm neither. Or maybe I'm both."

Gail lightly kissed him on the lips. "You still haven't told me what you said to your grandfather about Nicaragua. Not now. It's just a reminder."

Anthony had spent an evening with Ernesto Pedrosa last week, coming home past midnight. He had been too sleepy to talk about it then, and Gail had not wanted to push him.

He shrugged. "There isn't much to report. I said that I had something to tell him, a story that started when I was a kid living in Camagüey with my father. I told him things I'd forgotten I knew about. Then I told him what happened in Los Pozos. Everything, Gail. I didn't leave out any of it. I talked for more than three hours. I thought now and then that he might be asleep, but he would open his eyes and tell me to go on."

"What did he say?"

"Nothing. He asked me to pour us some brandy. We talked about . . . I don't know. The leak in the roof. His new dentist. Where my daughter wants to go to college in the fall. Then I helped him stand up. He embraced me and went upstairs to bed."

"I guess what I want to know," she said, "is what you're going to do now. He wanted to turn over his businesses to you, didn't he?"

"Ah." Anthony smiled. "I said no. Do you mind?"

"Mind? I am so relieved!"

Anthony amended, "Of course I'll help, but I made it clear I don't want to follow in his path. He understands. I'm a lawyer. I like what I do, and I don't want to give it up."

Gail laughed. "He *understands?*"

"Well . . . a little fight keeps the old man alive."

"He'll never see home again, will he?"

Anthony put an arm around her. "He sees it more clearly now than ever, you'd be surprised. He asked me to bury him there, on the old family estate. I gave him my word."

Gail pressed her forehead against his shoulder.

The realtor cleared her throat a few paces behind them. "Are there any questions I could answer for you?"

They turned around, then looked at each other. Gail said, "I like it."

Anthony said, "You're sure?"

She made a laugh of pure delight. "I think this is the one."

Surprise flashed over his face, then he smiled. "I think so, too."

Gail looked past him toward the gazebo and waved at Karen. "We like it!" A cheer came from across the yard.

As they walked back toward the house, Gail tugged Anthony around and pointed. "You know what we could plant in that corner? A *framboyán.*"

"Ah, yes." He smiled. "I can see that."

She could see it too: The tree would grow over the years, spreading to shelter them with its shade, and in springtime the flowers would flame bright orange-red.

Brendt

NE